Path of Power

BOOK TWO OF
THE DIVINE GAMBIT TRILOGY

CHAD CORRIE

An Aspirations Media Publication

Copyright © 2006 by Chad Corrie
Interior Illustrations by Ed Waysek
Map Illustrations Copyright © 2004 Jeremy Simmons
Tralodren™ World Map © 2000-2006 Chad Corrie
Cover Illustration by Carrie Hall
Layout by Nancy Kurzweg and Jennifer Rowell
Design: Nancy Kurzweg, Jennifer Rowell and Chad Corrie

LIBRARY OF CONGRESS CONTROL NUMBER: 2006923911

ISBN-10: 0-9776043-2-2
ISBN-13: 9780977604326

MANUFACTURED IN THE UNITED STATES

First Printing September 2006

Other books in The Divine Gambit Trilogy

The Seer's Quest
Path of Power
Gambits End (2007)

Forthcoming Works:

Tales of Tralodren: The Beginning*
The Adventures of Corwyn

*Graphic Novel

Thanks to:

Jesus, the true path.

Mom, Dad, and friends for helping to keep me on the right path.

Ponder the lives of men who have set no boundaries to their passions, the men who have reached the very summits of glory, disaster, odium, or any other of the peaks of chance; and then consider, "Where are they now?" Vapor, ashes, a tale; perhaps even not a tale. Contemplate the numerous examples...any instance at all of what pride can set its heart upon. How ignoble are their strivings! How much more befitting a philosopher it were to aim at justice, temperance and fealty to the gods- yet always with simplicity, for the pride that swells beneath a garb of humility is of all things the most intolerable.

Marcus Aurelius
"Mediations" Book 8 Paragraph 27

What follows is ever closely linked to what proceeds; it is not a procession of isolated events, merely obeying the laws of sequence, but a rational continuity. Moreover, just as the things already in existence are all harmoniously coordinated, things in the act of coming into existence exhibit the same marvel of concatenation, rather than simply the bare fact of succession.

Marcus Aurelius
"Mediations" Book 4 Paragraph 45

There is a way which seems right to a man and appears straight before him, but at the end of it is the way of death.

Proverbs 14:12 Amplified Bible

Chapter 1

There is a place outside time, outside space, that none know exists. Far from Tralodren, far from the cosmos itself in which that world resides, there is a realm where only two entities dwell. Each the opposite of the other, they draw their strength and substantive nature by these polarized distinctions. It is here where only a faint shimmer of white illumination swims about like uncollected waves in the vast sea of darkness around it. It is here where these two beings ponder the fate of an insignificant dot in a stellar array of an ever expanding cosmos.

These two entities are old. And it is an old game they play too. The rules set down before matter came to be before the cosmos itself was known and formed. These rules held all things together — keeping the balance in all things. Without these rules, there would be nothing again, with nothing to follow. So it is by these rules the two entities, and all the cosmos are bound.

"So we have returned to this world once more," the one who could be compared to light asked.

"We have," The Darkness shifted. "It is our nature and our pact if you recall."

"So it is the same rules then, the same pattern as before?" The Light shimmered like the sheen of the sun on a wave.

"The very same," The Darkness replied. "I have a feeling this time I may succeed."

"You might, but don't forget the resourcefulness of the inhabitants. Its defenders have defeated you before, and might do so again." The Light chuckled.

"Ah, but you forget the clause of the pact we made: degeneration, entropy. It has whittled them away to a weaker form than what they were before." The Darkness churned in glee. "They are not what they once were when they first opposed my will. I, however, am eternal and unchanging."

"I must admit, your plan has worked so far," The Light continued to shimmer in The Darkness' glee.

"Yours does not seem to be going so well," The Darkness stated. "Already those you have gathered have scattered away. Your opposition is severely lacking at best. You must be foolishly optimistic if you think you still have a chance at beating my best."

"Wait and see. Patience is a virtue," The Light remained calm amid the taunting. "Your puppet has yet to secure what you'd have him wrought as well."

"I have faith in absolute victory," The Darkness sounded as if it was speaking through a rather large grin.

"So it is still the same plan then it would seem," The Light repeated the age-old rules to The Darkness. "Though with a different champion. Even though when last you worked this plan on their location of the cosmos your previous champion was defeated."

"Recall when last that champion was used, it nearly defeated all it set out to destroy." The Darkness grated against the luminous waves. "The plan was nearly flawless in execution".

"But not quite," The Light pertly stated.

"I have corrected that flaw." The Darkness let loose a bit of its wounded pride.

"Have you?" The Light swirled about The Darkness with its sardonic words. "We shall see then."

"I believe it is now your move." The Darkness shifted once more amidst the perpetual illumination of The Light.

"So it would appear," said The Light.

"You put too much trust in your champions, and your sentimentality for this meaningless world is pathetic!" The Darkness' displeased tone rolled through the expansive hidden realm. "What are they to you, but an afterthought; a breath?"

"It is my nature, and the defining quality of who I am — what I am," said The Light. "Knowing you still don't understand my reasoning on these matters further encourages me that we are secure in our existence.

"For what has oblivion to do with creation?"

"Opposition," The Darkness answered as it rolled around the edges of The Light, skirting its borders.

"Opposition," The Light agreed. "Now, I must be about my work."

"You should hurry then," The Darkness spoke. "My plans have been well laid. To stop them now would be a challenge indeed."

"Perhaps," The Light reasoned aloud. "We shall have to wait and see. It is still far from over…the game has just begun."

Chapter 2

Thousands of miles from the Midlands, in the temperate waters of the Sea of Bithal, rested the Republic of Rexatious, home of the Patrious elves; founded because of an argument between two elven princes; Aero and Cleseth, the Republic had long been governed by a collective form of representative rule. This was in opposition to their Elyelmic kin, who tended to be more autocratic and despotic. They eventually developed into an imperial cult of order centered upon Aero and his political descendants.

The Patrician Republic, however, had begun to change in later years. The chief representative, called the Elucidator, was named ruler of Rexatious and her people and over the House of the Voice and its various speakers. The change was organic, and kept in check by various political counterweights, but in the end, the Speakers of the Voice were losing these checks by a plethora of means — both minor and major. The voice of the people was still present. However, with each new Elucidator, the hold of the people slowly ebbed away in favor of a single enlightened ruler — and thus embracing more autocratic traits and tendencies in their government.

Many commentators found it sadly ironic those of the race who had once left because of just such a government, were now returning to it — and all things going full circle. Still though, with the general longevity of the elven race, this regression would be slow in coming. Compared to the shorter lived humans, and their own nations, which fluctuated as often as the wind changes direction, the elven nations seemed nearly eternally unchanging.

Regardless of its changing nature, the Republic stood with grace, honor and wisdom. It was one of the true jewels of the West, filled with ancient mysteries and riches no other race could boast. Even the continent where it resided was a breath of inspiration for bards — and the stuff of dreams for yet many more.

The idyllic land was awash with sun, greenery, and elegance of architectural wonders and breath-taking landscapes even beyond dreams to illustrate properly. Rexatious' rocky coastline gave way to soft rolling hills, thick forests and crystal clear lakes, rivers and streams. A few snow-capped mountain chains even ran their brief race across the land until they collapsed deep underground, to slumber from their journey on a bed of lush, green canopy.

Legends even were told that the first followers of Dradin, the god of learning and magic, came from this land. Along with them were the first bards — springing from the wilds and infused with the divine gifts of Causilla, the goddess of bards. Causilla herself was said to have a love for Rexatious' fragrant, flowering hills. Indeed, it was here the fabled Great Library could be found.

It was deemed even by those who hadn't and never would see it in their lifetimes as a Tralodroen wonder, rumored and built into a collection of legends claiming it held all the knowledge of the world. To those who spun tales — and those who believed them — this was the cornerstone of the ancient mystical West whose secrets could change the world if one sought them out to master their profound insights.

Often, even the Patrious who lived there were made into fable and myth by outsiders. Not that many folk in the Midlands, Northlands, or even the Southern Lands knew much about them, let alone that they existed. The same could be said for folk in the Western lands knowing about the Elyellium, and other Eastern races. Only a few well-traveled folks and the Patrious knew the whole truth of the matter. To the rest of mortal kind, the world was confined to the context of their understanding of local affairs and boundaries.

Delightful cities mingled amid small towns and villages scattered about Rexatious like grain hefted into the air to land in random localities. Though seemingly disconnected from each other, each town, village, and city was within access of wide, wheel rut-worn, cobblestone roads packed so tightly together not a single blade of grass dared show itself. These roads, the arteries of the Republic as some called them, crisscrossed the land on route to Cleithious, the capital of Rexatious, the heart of the Patrician Republic itself.

It was to Rexatious Gilban traveled after he completed his mission for Saredhel. A word of prayer took him from the steamy jungles of Takta Lu Lama back to the gentle nation of his birth. He took with him the fruit of his quest: lost knowledge of the Ancients on imperial might and its maintenance; preventing it from falling to the hands of the Elyellium.

He lost his assistant on the way back, but wasn't worried for her absence. She'd felt called to help another mercenary who had been taken captive by an unknown figure who appeared near the final moments of the quest's completion. In her place, Gilban had acquired the services of a goblin, named Hoodwink. They had recently liberated him from a tribe of hobgoblins that had made the ruins where they'd found the knowledge home.

The more he had gotten to know the short, green creature since their return, the more he felt there was something about the goblin he couldn't quite place. He sensed that destiny, the very hand of Saredhel herself, was powerfully upon the goblin in a very personal way. It was a way he didn't quite understand or interpret.

There was something else too…something even greater he couldn't yet fathom It was almost a visible weight Gilban could see in his mind's eye upon the slightly stoop shoulders of the short creature. It was a compelling mystery even he couldn't seem to unravel. He trusted Saredhel would reveal these things, as she had others, in due time. For the moment though, he had more important matters to attend to.

The two had appeared in the chief temple of Saredhel called The Temple of The Goddess of Mysteries, in the heart of Cleithious, when they first returned by Gilban's prayer. Hoodwink had been overcome with shock from the whole ordeal of his arrival. Though glad to be free from his almost certain death in the jungles, he found himself in a jungle of a different sort. The inner workings of the temple and the city at large dwarfed the small creature and caused his mind to lock up in confusion. He literally didn't know what to do.

Hoodwink, like others before him, had found the Patrious were a very artistic race. Gilt covered all things around him: rock, sculpture, and dress. The temple where he'd appeared with Gilban alone was pure splendor. Pools of mercury were used to see into the future as small bronze basins of the same liquid held aloof tiny ivory boats sat on top various marble pillars stuffed into random empty alcoves and spaces. Golden life-sized statues of great leaders of the faith stood in various niches around junctions and corridors, behind which hung rich, motley tapestries of silk depicting past deeds of the Republic and Saredhel's faithful.

Every corner, opening, and space spat out opulence. It was soaked in it. It swarmed, breathed, and seemed to draw life from the riches. Everywhere was the fragrance of the rich incense, which the priests and worshipers used in their services: a fragrant cinnamon and honey mixture tied to a few other spices, flowers and herbs the goblin couldn't quite place.

It was often said by bards and those who listened to them that to be in the Republic of Rexatious was to walk into the gates of Paradise itself. Hoodwink had to agree. After they'd arrived, he dared a look out a temple window to see the city around it only to be more amazed that such a wonder could be contained in just one place.

The city appears as if the gods or giants had built it. Towers and spires; fluted stone blending and twisting with marble and brick, wood, glass, and steel. It was more than he could take in with one glance, and so he pulled away to try to make sense of all he had seen in such a short glimmer of what might very well have been the most beautiful city on all of Tralodren.

The next morning, the former jester found himself covered in a rainbow of light flooding in from the stained glass windows of his modest room. The colored images showed the history of the faith and how the temple was built. In one of them, an image of a radiant woman was seen touching the head of a kneeling Patrician man, behind whom a collage of multicolored glass reigned supreme. Hoodwink stared at the windows — wishing he could understand them, but Gilban had been too busy to help explain them. It wasn't the goblin was slow of wit, it was just that the images — like the temple — were just that; images. The priests of Saredhel loved to study, speak in, and look for symbols, riddles, and their meanings. Theirs was the language of figurative texts, and revelatory concepts. In the eyes of the untrained their meaning was lost — or worse still — incorrectly translated.

Upon their sudden arrival the night before, Gilban informed the priests of his order of his desire for Hoodwink's safety. The priests agreed to his wishes, and put the goblin in a smaller section of the great temple where he would be 'safe from harm'. But Hoodwink really knew this meant 'to cause the least amount of harm to them, the temple, and its activities.' Though Patrious were known to be more accepting than other races of Tralodren, they still were weary of creatures that held certain destructive and evil tendencies, such as Hoodwink's kin.

Goblins, along with hobgoblins didn't have the best reputation on Tralodren. Hoodwink, if he left the confines of the temple, might come to harm or certainly be put into a far worse state than he currently resided. The priests made sure they'd given the goblin a simple chamber to rest from his journey, and allowed to roam a small scantly-used section of temple apart from the major areas, lest he also interfered too heavily with the day-to-day activities of the temple and the clergy who made it their home.

He didn't.

The goblin was far too tired to do much more than walk around the small, yet richly decorated hallways in the section where he was confined, and contemplate his decision to join Gilban and leave his former world behind.

Hoodwink was the exception to many goblins. Most of the races descended from Jarthals, the parent stock of hobgoblins, goblins, and ogres. None of the three descended races really like each other, let alone other races. Hoodwink, however, was curious about other races around him, and possessed a strangely odd and strong desire for self-improvement. In most other respects, though, he resembled his common kin. Goblins were shorter creatures that tended to be lanky and lime-green hued, bald, or possessing thin hair.

Though goblins really couldn't read and write that well, Hoodwink was actually fairly bright. He could read and write Goblin (the language of both goblins and hobgoblins), Telborous, and a splattering of Elonum. His interest in the past — and trying to learn from it — separated him from his kindred as well. While at his stay in the ruins of Groledron in Takta Lu Lama he had strived to gain as much insight as he could from the fallen city. He'd constantly retreat to ponder about its builders; trying to piece together a greater picture of the whole from the shatters surrounding him then.

The goblin thought about his choice to follow Gilban more and more as the hours in the temple lengthened. It was just about all he could do. Gilban left to report to his ecclesiastical superiors, and finally the Elucidator about the mission's success. The little goblin felt abandoned in the old priest's absence. Lost in an even stranger world, he sat down upon an old worn chair in his chamber. It was the only thing lacking rich gilt he'd seen so far, and he sulked deeply. His own tiny hands removed the jester hat from his bald head. The rest of his former garb still remained; the orange leggings and purple tunic had seen better days now that they had survived the great blaze the goblin had escaped, but the life he'd known had gone up in smoke with the rest of the ruins.

Hoodwink had in him the spark of something great, at least Gilban had told him that before he left the temple for his audience. It was said in hurried passing mixed amid the assurance the priest would return shortly — but it had a great weight to it. The saying hit something deep inside the goblin, which he couldn't readily identify. Gilban didn't seem to want to elaborate any further on it — not even after his meetings today, of that Hoodwink was certain.

So if the small word of encouragement said in passing by the blind elf was supposed to help him feel better, it didn't. He had no idea how he could have the spark of *anything* great in him at all. He was smarter than his kin, he knew that, but he wasn't much further along than the rest of them. In fact, in many cases he had been below them. So what did Gilban mean? More importantly perhaps, why was he here now? Sure, he got away from his old life to perhaps a safer location — but what now? These were some powerful thoughts he had to contend with if he wanted to move forward with his life and make sense of what had happened.

Hoodwink had sunk his head in deep contemplation as he waited for Gilban's return; heavy-lidded eyes closing in his thoughts. He found himself thinking back to his mistreatment by Relforaz. He was glad the priests here had been able to heal his most recent wounds, dealt him by his former chieftain, with some healing ointments. He rubbed his previously swollen lip in gratitude and remembrance.

What now though?

So many of his kin would never come to this point in their lives They would never even be in such a wonderful land as this — so now that Hoodwink was here, where did he go? What did he do? He used to tell himself one day he would be great, and he always knew such a proclamation was predicated on the notion he would have to first be free of Relforaz and his tribe…but he never planned beyond that. He realized now that he never really saw himself as being free from the ruins and his previous situation his former position in the first place and so never dared to dream beyond that past reality.

It was disheartening, to say the least. He now understood the nature of his inner most thoughts. He had only been hopefully wishing — spinning a fantasy instead of a solid plan. He'd attained a level of freedom, and he didn't know what to do with it. The goblin knew it was the oddest of fates that could ever have been dealt his kind.

He couldn't stay here forever, and doubted if he'd find a home in the city. If there were any goblins on Rexatious, he wasn't quite sure if he was so keen on joining them either. So he was placed in a rather difficult spot, which was becoming more uncomfortable by the moment. However, Hoodwink wouldn't remain with this train of thought much longer as fate had other plans for him...

"Rise, Hoodwink," a soft, inviting voice suddenly spoke to him — startling him from his ponderings.

"Who's there?" the goblin jumped up and hastily looked around.

The room appeared empty.

"I have a task for you," the voice continued in an almost feminine tone.

"Where are you?" Hoodwink circled the room with his gaze.

"Here," the voice seemed to pick up weight in front of the goblin's view, where it was joined by an ethereal shape becoming solid before his sight.

The figure appeared to be of a womanly build, though Hoodwink couldn't tell much more about her as she was wrapped from head to toe in a long, black, hooded cloak which, besides obscuring her frame, engulfed her face — shading it from view.

"Saredhel?" The goblin questioned nervously. After what he'd been through, he thought it was possible for the goddess of the temple to pay him a visit. It seemed no less bizarre than what he had experienced so far.

"No," the soft voice spoke again.

"Who are you then?" Hoodwink's face was troubled.

"Peace goblin. I am not your enemy but simply a messenger," the figure was a calm image before him.

"*Whose* messenger?" Hoodwink tilted his head to try to look up into the inky shadows of the figure's hood.

"Someone who has had their eye on you, Gilban and your previous allies for quite some time."

"I don't unders-" Hoodwink began to shake his head from side to side in confusion.

"Here," a pale hand darted out of the black cloak. At the end a medium-sized, red silk pouch dangled before the goblin's eyes. "Take this."

"What is it?" Hoodwink simply stared at the object.

"Something you will need for the next place you're about to go."

"What if I don't want to take it?" Hoodwink asked sheepishly. His eyes tried again to peer beyond the stranger's midnight hood. She wasn't a Sarellianite that was for sure. The dress was all wrong — and the way she carried herself — a regal bearing, spoke against a priestly nature as well. So not a goddess or a priest...

The goblin frowned. "Who said anything about *me* going *anywhere* for that matter?"

"You are free to make that choice, but understand all who have been chosen cannot deny their purpose for long." The figure answered. "Deny me now, and you will only come to see my offer is the only one you can take in the end.

"It is the way of things." The feminine form's words were authoritative but pleasant.

"I might be at peace if I knew who sent you or what you *really* want." The goblin continued. Again, there was the hint of a greater purpose for the goblin. Was he the only one to not now about this? Did everyone know he had some great calling to perform? Then why couldn't *he* see it?

"I don't have time for questions. Gilban will understand all the questions which shall arise from what I have spoken and will know what to do with this." She tossed the pouch at the goblin's foot where it hit with a solid thud.

Something was inside it.

Something hard and round.

"He will?" Hoodwink spoke to his feet as he looked at the red pouch before him, not even wanting to touch it with his orange-covered appendage.

Looking up, he noticed he was alone once more; the figure had vanished as quickly as she had appeared.

"Well," Hoodwink backed up to get as far from the object as possible, scrapping the chair's legs along with him on his path toward the wall behind him. "If Gilban is supposed to figure you out, you can just wait for him them. I don't want to even touch you if I don't have to." The goblin retreated to the far corner of the room where he sat down in a huff.

"If they can't even tell me who they are, or who they are speaking for then I don't want anything to do with them or their *gifts* either. I'm not dumb enough to start getting into any mess now — and in a temple of Saredhel no less.

"Yep...we'll just let Gilban take care of you when he gets back. I'm not about to be dragged around on some other crazy journey just 'cause some strange woman appears, tosses out some goodies, and then disappears again.

"Priests." Hoodwink muttered as he fought against the urge to turn his head back toward the pouch, to stare at it with a curious eye.

Was that pouch tied to his greater purpose in some way?

He settled down to his thoughts once more. Thoughts telling him he was mad; that he didn't really have a purpose here at. But perhaps, if what this woman had said was true then maybe...

Nah, that was even greater madness.

Why risk his life again to just find his way out of this land when he had just barely managed to keep little over a day ago? No, it was better to make his stay here, see if Gilban could help get him settled here on the continent somewhere and hew out a life as best he could after that.

But if he was fated to take part in this to some degree as she had said...

The goblin let out a frustrated sigh.

His brain hurt.

Chapter 3

"So your sagacity, the mission was a complete success. We not only retrieved the information, keeping it from the Elyellium, but burnt the ruins themselves, keeping them safe from the rest of the world as well," Gilban paced before the Elucidator with his chest full of pride. He and the Elucidator both spoke Pacoloes, the language of the Patrious.

The room he spoke in was lavish and empty save for the Elucidator, Gilban, and a few guards. The Speakers of the Voice, the elected representative branch of the government that ruled on a good many matters and who also brought some issues to the Elucidator to pass judgment on (which was becoming more and more with each passing election cycle) were absent for this debriefing.

The Elucidator requested it. The Elucidator had given Gilban leave to complete his task in the first place, and the elected ruler didn't see the need to invite them. He would tell them the news soon enough though, after he had time to better digest it.

Around the Elucidator's throne four guards stood watch over Gilban, the room, and the Elucidator. Garbed in polished steel scale mail armor, crowned with pointed, open-faced, turban-cushioned helms, and carrying tulwar, long spear, and shield, they were a fiercesome sight. The swords were strapped to their waists, the spears in their right hand; oblong medium shields rested against their legs at their side. Each was emblazed with the emblem of the Republic: a two-headed eagle looking in opposite directions.

Huge columns of black marble sprouted from the silver-veined, polished, slate-gray marble floor. The veins pulsated with life, split, rejoined and then shot forward once more to hold up a great dais of black stone shimmering like fresh crude oil. The great dais raised some six feet from the floor and was emblazed with thin grape vines creeping along the raised steps with silent caresses, intertwining along its base with black roses and thorns. The elegance was slightly downplayed and fit the regal chambers nicely where humility and splendor often mingled.

Statuary of every size and shape skirted the room as well. Made of white marble as well as precious metals — even glass; they deepened the profound richness of the room. The statues were of the past Elucidators since the founding of the institution many centuries ago. Like silent stewards of lore, they spied all the corners of the audience chamber not missing anything played out before their lifeless eyes.

The hard wood throne on top the dais dominated the room and made it seem that even amid this forest of columns and former Elucidators it was all that mattered. Its back was carved to look like great palm leaves fanned out, then interlaced; entirely covered in a shining gold overlay. The arms were crafted of thick cedar and shaped to resemble the majestic head of a griffin. Life itself seemed to just be a breath away from the carvings as if upon the slightest touch they would spring to open their beaks in a sharp, shrill cry. Between these arms rested a thick red velvet cushion, beneath which four golden talons upheld the whole seat of power.

"Praise the shade of Cleseth." The Elucidator, whose name was Diolices, smiled from his seat. Diolices was every bit the figure of the nearly perfect Patrious elf. He was built slightly smaller of frame than his kin, but still had the gleam of health about him. His hair was a cascade of churning onyx, his eyes were like violet crystals and his angular face was set tight in a regal expression that had deepened over the years. The slight gray pallor that was common to all Patrious' skin contrasted with his highly ornate, topaz studded, yellow robes of state.

He was a middle aged Patrician, and had seen many things change in the land of his ancestors while he sat on the throne of Rexatious. Newly crowned not more than forty years prior, the great Elucidator, was proud of his reign thus far. Rising to the position of Elucidator with the jubilation and appeal of his fellow kin and the Speakers of the Voice, now subjects, he was famed the best to hold the throne since the days of the first founder of the nation, Cleseth, the brother to the god and leader of the Elyellium, Aero, himself.

To remind him of that fact, a larger than life pure white marble statue of the great first leader stood behind the Elucidator's seat. The statue was strong and struck a pose of relaxed rule; the gentle subtle smile and clear clean gaze spoke of the power behind the figure. Dressed, in a simple flowing himation, the image spoke of the noble ideals of a royal prince who had given up his birthright to his fellow subjects and allowed them to control their own destinies instead.

Diolices watched the elder elf closely. He was always amazed with the way Gilban existed in life. He had given up his sight so that he might be blessed with the gift of prophetic insight from the goddess Saredhel. Gilban was old even when the Elucidator was young. He couldn't recall anyone his age or older who had ever seen the priest with normal vision. Though he was blind and to some, who didn't know him, seemed feeble, the Elucidator knew the truth. More than once the priest had proven his worth to the causes of the Republic.

His unique power of divine sight, more potent than that of his priestly equals, had saved the Patrious on many occasions. This time was no exception. Twice before, raids by wandering beasts had been halted and the priest had predicted a severe drought that allowed the Republic time to prepare and survive the potential disaster.

So, when Gilban came to him asking for means to get to the jungles of Takta Lu Lama, to stop the Elyellium from getting the secret knowledge of the Dranors, Diolices didn't hesitate. Upon seeing his successful return, the Elucidator knew he had made the right choice and that the Republic would be safe for many more years, as would all of Tralodren now that such knowledge was safely in their hands.

"The nation is pleased with the results Gilban. Truly we trust your consul on this and other matters, as your goddess has once again seen fit to bless us and make our nation safe from those that would seek its downfall. Where though is your chosen aid, Clara Airdes? Did she not travel with you as well?"

Gilban bowed his head. "Yes, Clara did travel with me, but she has decided to stay behind in favor of helping out a less fortunate Telborian mage of whom I spoke to you about already in my report. She feels responsible for her capture."

"Ah yes; a very admirable thing for her to do." Dioceses nodded.

"She is a good woman, Elucidator." Gilban agreed.

"Very well Gilban, I release you from my presence. Go and rest from your travels. Take heart that you have done a great service to your nation this day."

"Yes Elucidator." Gilban bowed.

Dismissed from the ruler's presence, the priest left to return to his quarters in the greatest house of worship built for the Mistress of Fortune, as Saredhel was also known. He had his doubts about how Hoodwink was hailing and just what was going to happen to him now that the goblin had been taken to Rexatious. These questions would have their answers soon enough he was certain.

"Blessings upon you great lord." Gilban uttered as he made his way out of the court. As soon as he left the two great doors allowing access to the chamber he began to feel a strange pull on the back of his mind. It felt like a person was pulling out the stuffing of a pillow, and his mind was that pillow. It was a strange clawing sensation, but not an attack, more an attempt at allowing the priest to better understand what was occurring around him, but without wanting to reveal itself all the same.

The troubling thought about the source of the presence felt on the goblin returned to him as he made his way back to the temple. These combined feelings gave him great concern.

What was he suppose to know?
What was his goddess trying to tell him?

Gilban walked through the picturesque capital with silent strides. He recalled as he walked down familiar streets, what they had looked like when he still had sight to behold their splendor, the wonderful aroma of fresh exotic spices and cooking fish and lamb. That had been over two hundred years ago but those days seemed like yesterday. In his minds eye the elf could see the tall spires of marble and granite. They were sculpted to look like fluted columns and seemed to support the very vault of heaven.

He called to mind the outside of the Great Library as he thought about the last time he went there before his vision had faded. The gigantic domed room capped in shimmering gold held up by solid granite and marble was a sight to make anyone's eyes mist over. Gilban could see again the eight caryatids holding apart foundation from roof as one entered the massive gold leafed covered, cedar doors. The old priest recalled being quite smitten with the eight lovely ladies, paragons of Patrician beauty in every sense of the word. The real wonder though was inside and that was something the priest would never see again, for what use were books for a blind man?

Gilban turned his thoughts from the library and toward the city once more as he walked along his way back toward the temple. As he did he brought to mind the bronze domes that capped off mighty buildings like inverted turnips. Dotting the landscape like gems in a splendid setting, they fought for recognition among tall colorful statues of heroes and maidens of shapely delights, fabu-lously painted frieze covered arches built in homage to mighty wars or reigns of past Elucidators, and fountains crafted to look as though the spouts and pools were alive and shimmered with the sun's reflection upon their golden gilt.

Color exploded all around the blind elf, and in his mind's eye it was radiant. Lost in his world of thought and darkness, he trotted over to the temple he knew more intimately then his own body. Having counted the steps learned the sounds and recalled the familiar smells he could gage himself just about anywhere in the city.

He measured his footfalls up to the grand staircase of the temple itself, then up the gray marble ledges to the silver door which had the emblem sacred to his order, The Eye of Fate, carved deep in its surface. It was the all-seeing eye of Saredhel, the seer of all things that are and will come to pass — a holy symbol with great significance.

Gilban traced the pattern of the eye with his hand. The silver crafted ornament was smooth and warm to the touch almost like living flesh. With a small effort the elder priest opened the door. The temple was the largest in the world dedicated to the goddess, but wasn't highly trafficked. Only when in dire need or perilous times of personal or national crisis would the steps be crowded with petitioners desperate for some insight into the days to come. During times of peace and tranquility its marble steps were often empty or sparsely populated at best.

On this day though, he was greeted with the soft aroma of lilac and honey perfumed air as the expensive collection of incense, made just for the temples use, was burned day and night for the pleasure of the goddess who was thought to be present at all times inside the temple. She was the force behind the visions that the priests were granted, and held back the veil from the eyes of the worthy to let them get a glance of what lay beyond. Without her efforts, to steward the curtain which divided the seen from the unseen, madness would ensue as visions would propel themselves into the minds of those who where unable to both handle and interrupt them as well as stop them from coming to them.

Now that he had reported to his religious and secular superiors, he would have time to speak with Hoodwink, and figure out just what his connection was in all of this. He couldn't rush the matter though; he had learned that long ago. Impatience was a terrible ally.

Gilban had once been very impatient. His youth was filled with a nervous energy that was uncanny for a member of his race. He seemed more human in that regard than any other in his whole life. As he aged though, the elf took in the fruit of patience like the maturing of a fine wine. His training with the priesthood had also taught him the benefit of a calm outlook in things. That realization had helped him greatly over the years as well. Such an outlook had saved his life in times past as well.

The elder elf played at his simple hemp belt as he thought about Clara's welfare. He chuckled to himself at the image playing in his mind of the young maid dealing with love for the first time amid everything else that was now before her. Though he could see some of her future, he couldn't see it all - and hoped that the experience would be a positive one for her, something to give her strength and further her development. She had a lot more of her life to live.

He didn't fear for her safety either. Clara was a very capable warrior. It was one of the reasons he had chosen her in the first place. Besides, Rowan was there to protect her, and Gilban had a strange sensation he'd be meeting up with her again in a short matter of time too, so the specter of her harm didn't loom anywhere near the days ahead.

Gilban entered into the temple courtyard, bowed to his fellow priests when he sensed and heard them draw near, then entered further into the sanctum of the house of worship. Respected members of the order, also garbed in their simple brown woolen robes greeted him as their equal. Gilban, though he was not the highest of ranked priests, was certainly elevated and treated with much respect. In light of his recent victory for the goddess, he was raised even higher in their sight.

Like him, the priests were impaired and maimed in some way in order to gain the blessings of their goddess — the Maiden of Mysterious. Some were lame, others deaf or blind. Some held weakness of limbs, body, or a loss or reduction of other senses. All had paid the price for the blessing they now carried: the ability to part the veil and see deeper things than other mortals could. None of them would ever claim that exchange as unfair.

Like Gilban also, they had shaved heads — another sign of their allegiance to Saredhel. The men having only their crown revealed, the rest of their hair closely cropped to their head; the females being shaved completely bald. Like the sacrifice of one of their senses, none spoke poorly of this either. To gain what Saredhel offered them was more than worth the mere loss of hair and any vanity attached to it.

Gilban continued to make his way quietly through the long and smooth halls. They were covered in slick gray marble, and lit with small pools of light that trickled down from lofty ceilings amid brass and glass chandeliers and odd pockets of clear glass pane windows that honeycombed the wall every so often.

The hall grew silent and colder as Gilban trod into sections that were older and unkempt with the years like the other sections had been. It was like walking into a dying part of some being; a rotting piece of flesh or wound on the healthy body that slowly weakened the structure with each passing day and month — stealing it's health and life.

Gilban silently approached the door of Hoodwink's chamber. It was unadorned and plain, rather like a simple door of a common dwelling, and not a high room of holy worship of a temple. The handle was also a simple wrought iron knob his hand found quite easily.

"Hoodwink," Gilban opened the door. "I'm back."

"Gilban?" The goblin's voice was more calm than normal and there was something about his tone as well. Something that seemed off...

"Are you all right?" Gilban questioned as he entered.

"Fine, but someone stopped by to drop off something for you."

"Oh, who was that? Hector? I thought he was off on a vision quest today." Gilban shuffled further into the interior.

"No. Someone else." Hoodwink was hesitant.

"Who then?" Gilban entered further into the room.

"I don't know. She talked like a priest, but was dressed all in black. She won't tell me anything only that you'd understand when you got it."

"Got what?" Gilban stopped.

"She left it on the floor in front of you."

"Strange." The elf tapped the ground before him with his staff, "So this woman was all cloaked in black then you say? Yes, certainly not a priest then…or a visitor or worshiper for none go this deep into the temple…

"She must have had quite an affect on you since you seem so shaken."

Hoodwink watched the staff grow closer to the red pouch "She was different… I can't describe it, talked a little like you, but she didn't stay long. Just appeared and disappeared before I could do anything."

"Really?" Gilban's eyebrow raised in interest.

"Vanishing before your eyes I suppose, eh?" Gilban weighed the information in his head.

"Yes, she did." Hoodwink found himself nodding, and then stopped when he remembered that he was talking to a blind man.

"Ah, here we are." Gilban had found the red silk pouch with his staff and had proceeded to bend over to pick it up.

"Are you sure you want to touch it?" Hoodwink flinched as the priest's hand drew nearer the mysterious pouch. "I mean… who knows what it can be?"

"Who knows indeed?" Gilban echoed the question as he picked up the pouch and stood tall once more. "I doubt though that if it is harmful it would still be here. The temple is warded for objects of such nature and Saredhel would warn me and the others of its presence should it still manage to find its way inside. This temple too has seen its fair amount of apparitions and visions in the past as well. After all, this is place of visions and revelations, so there is little need to worry there.

"So instead of wondering about this figure for a moment I think we can look toward what she left behind. Perhaps it's an answer to a question we don't know yet." The priest wanted to say it could be an answer to the thoughts plaguing his mind since he'd left the Elucidator, but withheld the comment. Such disclosure, at this point in time, would serve no purpose.

Gilban gently opened the pouch, put his hand inside and felt the hard, round globe with his sensitive fingers "Seems to be a pouch with a hard round object inside." As soon as they had connected, the seer's eyes grew wide, his face slack as if in a trance.

"Gilban?" Hoodwink addressed the elf. "You okay?"

Hoodwink stood took a step away from the priest and kept his eye on the door. He wanted to be ready on his feet for anything that could happen next. And from what he had experienced already with the elf, it could be a whole array of possibilities.

"Gilban?" Hoodwink dared a step closer now, skirting around the perimeter of the elf on route to the door.

Suddenly Gilban came to himself causing the goblin to jump from the unexpected occurrence.

"What was that all about?" Hoodwinked tried to keep his tone even keeled.

"We have to go to Doom Maker's Island." Gilban closed the pouch and affixed it to his belt.

"Doom Maker's Island!" Hoodwink's greenish face turned ashen and his eyes became as wide as egg yolks. "That place is cursed! The name says it all: DOOM! I can't go. It's bad. Very bad."

"Calm yourself goblin. I also share your concerns. Doom Maker's Island is home to many horrors, lawless bands, corrupt kingdoms, and beings not of this world.

"However, I have been assured we will come to no harm on our mission there."

"What mission? What are you talking about?" A knot was growing in the goblin's stomach.

"We have to take this pouch to Gorallis," Gilban turned toward the door.

"Gorillas! Gorallis the Crimson Flame?" Hoodwink clutched Gilban's robes. "We have to?"

"Yes," the preist remained calm.

"He'll roast us alive or worse." Hoodwink insisted.

"No, he will not. We will take this gift to the linnorm in exchange for an item he possesses that will aid the others in their continuing task. He will be more than happy to grant us safe passage," said Gilban flatly.

"Continuing mission? Others? What are you talking about now?" Hoodwink's brow scrunched up into a furrow of flesh. Now he had a sore brain, stomach, and a panicked heart. This was not a good day at all. "Who told you all this?

"Saredhel?" The goblin tried to discern and answer from Gilban's face.

Gilban only smiled. "All will be revealed in time.

"Come. Gather up what you took with you from the ruins, and we'll get the rest of what we need after I get some funds and supplies from my superiors for this new journey."

"Wait a minute. Who said that I wanted to go with you?" The goblin crossed his arms.

"Would you rather stay here?" Gilban stopped in the doorway.

"You *are* coming right back after this is all over right?" Hoodwink found it hard to withhold the mild form of concern in this throat.

Gilban remained silent.

Hoodwink's heart sank.

"I mean, you're not just going to leave me here...right?" The goblin's concern had grown; knot in his stomach tightening even more.

"I cannot say for too much is in flux at the moment. You are certainly free to leave whenever you wish; however, you are no one's slave." Came the priest's dry and predictable response.

"Yeah," the goblin rubbed his chin, "that's what everyone here says, but where would I go?"

"That is indeed a mystery," Gilban smirked while his back remained to the tiny creature; face looking out the doorway and into the spaces beyond.

Hoodwink didn't see any other real alternative for himself to go or do anything without the aid of the priest — it was more than a difficult road it was a near impossibility. What could he do here in this temple while Gilban was away or worse yet, never came back? He supposed that he could find a way to some new local if he survived the whole encounter on Doom Maker's island, but that was a big if.

With but a little deeper internal inspection, Hoodwink realized he had no plans for his life — at the moment anyway. What was he going to do regardless of the elf's option? Sit in this cold dead room for weeks while he tried to figure out how to get out of the city without getting accosted too much by the local inhabitants? That didn't sound too appealing either. So what had he to lose really? His life; sure, but besides that?

He might even stand to make some gain as well — find a spot that might very well come into his own restful life. The priest would protect him for the most part and, truth be told, he kind of liked the old elf and he would need some help Hoodwink was sure for guiding his way… It was worth a chance if the priest gave his word on the matter of him keeping his life. After all, Gilban was supposed to see the future and if he didn't see his death, then it couldn't be, all bad then. It might even be fun.

Well that much he doubted, but it was worth a try. Better still it might help point him into the direction he might need to discover this great potential or calling or whatever it was he was suppose to have in his life and was giving him such a headache…

After a moment, Hoodwink sighed. "Fine, I'll go with you — but only to get out of here. Just promise me that I'm not going to die helping you out on this new mission of yours."

"Don't worry. On this task, you won't." Gilban turned to assure the goblin with a knowing grin.

Hoodwink could almost hear the mysterious woman's words mocking him in his ear. He really didn't have much of a choice in the matter after all it seemed. Common sense had shown him that much. Common sense and fate he supposed.

"You're sure?" Hoodwink pressed.

"If you come along to help me this one last time you will be free to go wherever you want on your way back from Doom Maker's Island. You have my word on that. I just need your eyes for one more mission and I have no time to try and get another, but we have to hurry." He motioned for Hoodwink to join him.

The goblin was satisfied.

Gilban started to leave the room.

"Just tell me though, linnorms don't like goblin meat do they?" Hoodwink grimaced at the thought.

"I wouldn't know," Gilban replied, "I've never asked a linnorm or seen one in all my life."

"We're mostly skin and bones you know…grizzle and grime. Bitter too I would imagine with all our rage and aggression…" Hoodwink chimed on beside the elf as the duo left the room and walked through the halls of the magnificent temple; the wheels of fate turning in their great and unknowable sequence once more.

Chapter 4

The storm had plagued the sky with its dark countenance and noise for the past two hours and continued to shake The Master's tower in a fit of wrath. During that time, Cadrissa had stared at the rotting collection of cloth and bone that hovered over two books of ancient make like some ravenous buzzard.

He had taken one of the books from Elandor via possession of the wizardress. Just what it was about she had no clue, but it seemed important enough to almost ignore Cadrissa for the time being. Time, which the wizardress used to look around the room where she was now a prisoner. She hoped to try and discover any materials she could make note of, or perhaps occupy herself with one of the hundreds of books, which wrapped the wall around her.

She didn't dare make an effort to touch them though. She didn't dare do anything really. The Master's presence carried an overpowering aura compelling her to do next to nothing as he read from his book. After a short while of staying still and silent, however, she managed to move to a simple plain wooden chair and collapse into it to await what would happen next.

Cadrissa was a youthful example of the Telborian race — a group of humans who mostly populate the Midlands of Tralodren. Her hair was silken locks of black lightning that flashed slightly in the firelight of nearby wall mounted torches; her skin was soft and pink, though with a deeper tint from her recent wilderness wanderings.

She wore a golden robe stained with mud and brackish water from her recent travels in the Marshes of Gondad, as well as leather boots which went up to her knee that were also caked with mud.

However, her form, though slender, was more shapely than most and still held the curve of young womanhood about her, much to the delight of the bookworms with whom she often associated. Her eyes though were the most beautiful and powerful part of her anatomy. They sparkled green in the torch light like emeralds and consumed all that were put before them like an unquenchable fire.

It was in sitting that she thought of that medallion she had recently acquired in the ruins before her capture. It rested in a pocket by her side, but she didn't dare take it out to examine it — not here, not now. No, she had to do something else to occupy her time and thoughts. For who knew how long her captor would be in study. So as she continued to sit, her mind swam with questions as she fully took in her situation.

What kind of being could hold such wisdom, to stop the hands of time and prolong his life for pursuit of still further knowledge? Could this mage in fact be *The Master* of all things magical as he professed? Could he be so strong as to defy the very will of the gods; to seek knowledge out for himself so that he could become the greatest mage of all time?

Cadrissa was mesmerized by the new thought.

She was in the presence of the most powerful mortal she had ever known and had the greatest opportunity to learn from him, yet she was powerless to act upon any of it. Seeing the situation of her capture as an opportunity to increase her own understanding, she found herself being less frightened of what would befall her and more concerned with how much time she could spend with her captor. The only question really was how to get him to share such insights?

During her schooling at the academy in Haven, Cadrissa had given up on the definition of good and evil in the realm of her studies. She now saw things as good for her cause, and bad for her cause. The parameters being based more on her personal development rather than adhering to an acceptance and reality defined by moral absolutes. It was the way of academia it seemed. She didn't think that a rigid definition of good and evil was possible in the field of magical study. Her recent abduction by The Master was proof enough for that.

He may have been and still was very evil, in the realm outside arcane insight, but he was a wizard nonetheless, and the way of wizards was not that of normal men and women. They walked one of two paths. One was the Path of Knowledge: seeking the way to enlightenment and understanding through the arcane arts.

The other was called The Path of Power: the pursuit of power and the accumulation of still more for the sake of ownership and exploitation of that power alone.

She knew that she herself pursued the Path of Knowledge, her very curiosity and personal choices on such matters answered that for her. Cadrissa also knew with the Path of Power came wisdom, though it was wisdom gathered for the wrong purpose. She only needed to think about how to get at the wisdom of her captor, to learn from it herself without the incompatible philosophy of his path spilling into her own. With such knowledge and power already he could very well be a former Wizard King. If that were true, then he would certainly be the last Wizard King in all of Tralodren. And that alone filled the mage with nervous excitement.

Not since the days of the Wizard Kings, which ended more than 750 years ago following the Divine Vindication, wherein the gods removed the ability of mortals to use arcane power, relying instead upon prayer and faith as the sole channel of power mystical activity did the world have such a proficient and skilled practitioner. When magic was returned to Tralodren, a little more than two hundred years ago, not even the mages that emerged had any inkling or control of the arcane workings that the Wizard Kings of old could unleash. The Master though seemed to shadow the ancient mages' insights; his abilities were more innate natural talents.

In the very least, she figured she could observe him and understand his craft in action. If that failed, she could read a tome or explore the tower and gain something of use…she hoped. She hated to let such a great chance at the accumulation of such lore escape her grasp, though she had to be mindful of her situation at hand as well. Getting killed would not be beneficial to any one of her goals.

Rescue wasn't even at the top of Cadrissa's thoughts. She doubted she'd even be rescued anyway. Those from whom she had been taken were nothing more than mercenaries. She didn't expect they'd feel the urge to seek her out unless someone paid for her safe return, but she knew no one would do that. No one knew she was here or would really miss her for some time. So, she supposed it was escape or comply with The Master's wishes — hoping he intended to let her live afterwards. And when it came down to just those two choices, there really wasn't much of a choice left to make.

Her thoughts were broken by a clash of thunder that shook her in her seat. She was the only thing that seemed upset by the noise. None of the other interior items or portions of the tower were disturbed by the disruptive clamor. Not even the air seemed to tremor in the crackling quake.

"Endarien is quite persistent." The Master turned another page. His flaming eyes never ceased their downward gaze upon the text.

"It sounds to me as if he'll crush this tower in a matter of moments." Cadrissa shivered from the resounding echo of the thunder.

"Hardly, my powers are far superior to his," The Master looked up from the book. Cadrissa wished he hadn't. She had tried to erase the horrid memory from her mind. She had to suppress the urge to scream in terror and disgust when she viewed it once again.

His face was nothing but a skull, the sockets blazed with hungry blue flame instead of eyes. He looked at the young wizard-ress for a moment, and though he had no flesh to do such a task, it seemed to Cadrissa as if the lich smiled at her. It was almost like he was savoring her fear.

"H-he is a god though." Cadrissa shook at the image of her captor.

"A god in name only," said the lich, "I can, once I've practiced what this book has taught me, level whole civilizations with the mere swipe of my hand. I crafted this tower in my last living days over almost a thousand years ago. It was made to endure until the end of time, withholding all who sought to enter it or attack it without my consent. No god, no matter his strength, can knock it down."

The tower shook violently once more, then silenced as if to prove his point. The howling winds seemed to slow, and even the thunder stopped. Then, an echoing scream, much more like the screech of a hawk combined with the yell of a man, erupted from the turbulent air around the tower. Cadrissa was filled with true horror as she understood in her inner self, that the noise had to be made be Endarien himself, the god of storms and birds, weather and sky, as he vented his frustration.

"You will never prevail, godling!" The Master shouted, and ran toward his shelf of books. "Your days are numbered. My hour is fast approaching!" He pulled out a dusty tome bound in deep magenta scales and thrust it into Cadrissa's chest, shoving her hard into the chair's back. "Read this!"

"Wha-" Cadrissa could barely keep track of what was going on.

"I'll have other matters to attend to soon. You will read all you can about Arid Land before my return. Then we shall leave. You will be one step closer to freedom, and I shall be one step closer to my goal!"

"You would instruct me then?" Cadrissa was both surprised and fearful. She had never hoped the undead mage would be so accommodating to her wishes to study, especially since she hadn't voiced them. How long he had to rest and where was also an issue. She could also escape in his absence…but how and where? She was uncertain, and so put such foolish thought from her mind at the moment. It seemed she had little option left but to do as her captor ordered. If she wanted to live she had to stick this out to the end and do her best to make the best of it…and manage to stay alive too.

"To some extent," The Master barked dryly; "You will have to know more than you do now to aid me in my search." The Master turned another page in his tome with a dry rustle and a brief spray of dust.

"And after you have finished with me? After, I have fulfilled my usefulness to you?" She put the book under her arm as she stood and smeared the already mud-stained garment with dust as thick and old as time itself.

"You shall yet live if you do as I say," The Master pointed his bony finger at the young woman. "Read. You will prove to me your worth by how productive you are in my absence."

The Master then left his hideously comprised podium with a flourish of his remaining rotten attire that followed him out of the room like a silent, stagnant wind.

Cadrissa said nothing as she watched her captor disappear into the hallway. She was tempted to follow him, to see where he was going, to learn more about this tower, and the knowledge it held… However, fear of what would befall her quickly stopped such thoughts. She had been spared once already from The Master's wrath by her compliance before she had entered the tower and she'd be unwise to bring his wrath upon her before she had time to at least get a glimmer of things beyond her ken.

So it was she gathered her thoughts, and turned her attention to the book The Master had thrown her. The few symbols carved on its cover were filled in with gold. They looked to be the ancient letters of some language she wasn't too familiar with; they seemed to denote historical accounts of some type. The magenta cover was crafted of some strange, scaled hide, the likes of which she had never seen before either. She wondered if such a beast still existed on Tralodren. A small pinch of energy then began to flow through her as she touched a piece of history. The book had to be as old, if not older, than The Master himself.

What wonders could it reveal to her?

The wizardress opened it where she stood and read the title, wonderfully scripted in letters that spoke of an age far before her own in an older dialect of Telborous. The title read: *The True and Accurate Account of Arid Land*. Below that was a subtitle: *Home to the Syvani Elves*.

Syvani elves?

Cadrissa had never heard of such a group of elves before. She'd only been aware of the Patrious who lived far to the west, and the Elyellium who dominated the Midlands. The thought of a third race of elves that had escaped her knowledge simply stirred her mind to no end with possibilities. She hurried toward The Master's podium and placed the book on top of the others there, discharging a plume of dust as she did so. Filled with a curious energy, she eagerly began to read the tome, totally forgetting her surroundings as she was fully taken a hold of by the book.

Chapter 5

The Master turned toward an old, worn door at the end of a lightless hallway, deep in the tower's heart. It was the only part of the tower showing its true age. Magic had helped to prevent most of time's effects upon the structure. The door was cut whole from the trunk of an age-honored tree even, as the tower was first being built. As thick as the stone wall it sat between, the door had grown gray over the years, but still held firm. The mystical energy coursing through it held it as fast and true as the day it was first set in place.

Speaking but a single word, long since forgotten in mortal memory, The Master waved his skeletal hand in front of the door, which seemed to open by its own means. It didn't creak or sputter in the least, but was as silent as the grave.

Behind the rectangular portal was darkness.

"Light," The Master hissed from a tongue-less jaw. His voice sounded like parchment being crumpled, and echoed back to him in a slightly, out of time murmur.

The room erupted in a dim glow, similar to torchlight, which grew from a dingy yellow, to a brilliant, day-like shimmering, which radiated from some unseen source as if the air itself was phosphorescent. The lich took in the old room in silence. It was here he'd worked to become the mightiest wizard the world had ever seen. It was like looking into his heart-the very roots of his power and dreams themselves.

The room itself was old and huge, at least fifty feet at its widest length and eighty feet from the ceiling to the floor — like a tower unto itself. Books lined the far wall of the room in giant shelves which were as wide as the wall and reached all the way to the ceiling, Crafted to be larger inside than out, the room could exist in the tower without affecting the towers makeup in the least. It was one more example of the lich's clever arcane inventions from which he took great pride.

The books and scrolls in the shelves were bound in a variety of covers and frames, which looked like a rainbow or a gem-encrusted walkway stretching forever skyward. However, they seemed so old they might have crumbled to dust with the slightest touch or breath. The Master wasn't concerned with the books, however; they had served their purpose, and he had learned from them all he could. His attention instead focused elsewhere — toward the opposite end of the room, where an old wooden table rested. On top of the table lay what looked to be a humanoid form covered by an old, dusty white cloth.

Years before his departure into the Abyss, he'd made a series of plans to keep himself safe and to secure his future in the land he so loved to rule. He'd taken his magical arts and a newborn baby, and cast a spell on the infant with the last remaining drop of his human blood. Once he'd cast the spell to become a lich, he simultaneously cast a spell to preserve the baby and enhance it with part of his own spirit.

As The Master fell into undeath, the baby was forcibly grown into an exact copy of The Master's once living frame. The child's spirit was ripped from its body and replaced with part of The Master's dark presence, and had remained so until his present return.

This had been a safe guard should things not go quite to plan. The Master took great pride in his safeguards, as they have served him well, and protected him more than once over the years.

His mind raced back to the time when he had first entered his chamber, and placed the mound of flesh beneath the cloth. He'd been younger and more powerful than he was now. He didn't want to tell Cadrissa he had less mystical might than she did at the moment, but slowly lost power with each passing year in the Abyss over those dark days when magic never graced Tralodren.

Each year there he felt weaker and his spells dimmed, then faded from his ability to perform them all together. In the end, all that remained of his power and influence over his servants were his staff and his scrying skull. All else faded from him and was lost to time. He knew he had to escape the ravages on his magic, or he would be undone as well. His spirit had been maintained in his rotting body solely by the very magic he was losing. In time, he would cease to exist as well.

He'd hoped Balon and the other beings in his service wouldn't see this, and he could act as he had once done before: intimidating them all into submission. It seemed to have worked up till the end, but he knew his days there, and his chances to break free dwindled with each passing moment he remained. It was that reason alone why he'd pushed so hard for Rowan, a young Nordic knight who had been part of Cadrissa's group, to be his means of escape. That was what had pushed him to near exhaustion, and worthless wasting of power to meet his goal.

He had to be free.

He'd used that stupid mage Kylor too. He had been The Master's first choice until he became aware of Cadrissa. Kylor was going to be the mage to set him free by means of the same portal in the ruins of Takta Lu Lama, which he had used to get there in the first place, again by The Master's guidance. It took him years to set everything where he needed it, manipulating events, conserving his energies, and keeping his wits about him in the infernal politics of his prison.

Instead, he found he could better be served by Cadrissa. She was much easier to control than Kylor, already in the company of Rowan, and could retrieve the book he needed as well — saving him a trip as she brought it to him in the ruins. Besides, the unstable nature of Kylor was a concern for the lich. The more absorbed Kylor became with the blue column, the more he was driven to madness.

The Master was more than happy to step in to settle matters via the final battle with the hobgoblin chieftain, Relforaz, who almost slew Kylor thanks to The Master's blocking of his protective amulet. The mercenaries finished the job Relforaz had started, and once Cadrissa had been secured, The Master was free to travel to his tower.

However, it seemed things had gone — and were going — almost too easily. Not that The Master was complaining. If he had a few fortunate opportunities, then so be it. For now he had to be quick for the task at hand.

Time was never on his side, but occasionally he could trick it into obeying him for a while. He needed a brief moment to collect his power, focus his abilities, and gather his knowledge in order to attain his final goal. He'd need Cadrissa for a backup measure as well — hedging all his options and their outcomes. She was expendable when the time came, but until then, he would have to be somewhat civil to her to command her continued cooperation in his matters.

What she did after he'd met his goals — if she survived — was no concern of his. What *did* concern him was the vast longing in those eyes when it came to begging knowledge from him. She had a hunger for the mystical arts that rivaled even his own. Yet she didn't crave it for power, but for the mere sake of knowing such things. That was what concerned and confused him. What would she do with such knowledge once she had attained it? If she continued, she'd be on the Path of Knowledge and far from the path that he had taken — possibly even a threat to the lich in time if she survived her usefulness to him.

Not that it mattered though. The paths only became more relevant as the mage grew in their understanding and abilities with the arcane arts. At the moment, he'd set her mind to race on a somewhat related errand to keep her thoughts from straying to more important issues — like exploration or escape from the tower, or examination of the book he'd had her retrieve in Elandor and left behind on the podium. While she might not be able to make sense of the text he'd left behind right away, over time she might and then become a threat and grow…but not right away. She wasn't that great a mage yet. Once he started his next spell he'd be weak, and unable to stop anything she might plot so he needed to start right away, while she was so distracted.

Using Cadrissa did save him some time though from retrieving the spell book he had placed in the holding of a member of the Tarsu. The enduring order of mages who had first brought magic to the world in the First Age of the Wizard Kings had kept it alive during the absence of magic which followed The Wars of Magic and Divine Vindication. The Master had taken the tome of Kurahi the Dark; a Wizard King he'd conquered in his ascendance in mystical might, and given it to his most trusted students and followers before his departure from Tralodren.

All the Wizard Kings had followers of some small number — acolytes who came to them to learn the ways of arcane mysteries, master spells and the knowledge of power. Those who had followed The Master had taken the book and returned to the Tarsu as they were ordered, held it in one family — passed it from generation to generation until his return; as per his last orders.

Knowing this, The Master simply had to seek out the family members to keep track of the book. It was an easy enough task to conduct from his previous location with his scrying skull. He didn't want to take the book with him, and have it lost in the Abyss. It was too valuable to him — and too deadly a weapon to hand to his enemies. Inside it told the secrets of the ultimate Path of Power, the path Kurahi never got to start, but The Master would finish.

Having Cadrissa pick it up for him rather than having to go after it himself later saved him much time. It was a good thing too, considering how he now felt. He might not have made it to that old shop in Elandor. The added benefit was he refreshed his mind to a potent spell he could invoke and it greatly enhanced his abilities for the next stage in his plan. Again, fortuitous in the nature of how this all coincided to his needs, The Master paid it little

Chad Corrie

mind at the moment. He had some more pressing business at the moment.

As he thought these things the lich could feel his strength ebb from his very bones like blood from a wound. His bones creaked and crumble into dusty chalk with each step. His clothing was in shambles — and worse still, the magical force holding it all together was fading like a frost-laden kettle placed over a fire. He never anticipated needing the replacement for his body in the manner he know found himself, but was glad he had the foresight to plan ahead none the less.

The Master doubted whether the spell placed on it to keep it preserved still held after all these millennia. He hadn't planned on being away for so long. A spell cast long ago often faded in power over the years, and had a way of destroying the very object it sought to protect. It cannibalized the enspelled object for energy in some occasions to continue its own existence. He just hoped that wasn't the case with the inanimate flesh now before him.

"Gorneal Orthel Feanborthin. Waqure To-rahl!" the crumbling wizard shouted. The last of his energy faded from his grasp and was channeled through his staff to shoot toward the body like an electric arrow. No more than a novice in strength then, he stood silently by and waited for the spell to finish.

He felt it first in his bones, a sort of warm wind — a sensation of an unraveling that first traveled up his legs, then pelvis. Like a kitten slowly pulling apart a ball of twine, The Master felt the energy binding him together falling away, and the warm wind of oblivion coming for him. It felt strange, almost like the pleasant sensation of deja vu'. He hadn't been so close to death and rebirth in ages, yet he knew he'd never get used to the feeling. No one ever could. One's very spirit hung in the balance between two great and eternal divides — paradise or damnation. No matter the frequency of such an event, it was still awe-inspiring and terrifying at the same time, to ponder that spacious division.

There was no means of comfort for the aged lich as he hung in that balance, as the untwining of his magic traveled up past his

40

chest and arms, then neck. He heard the cracking of ancient bone as it fell to the floor and then into the dust it should have become hundreds of years before. He felt, if he could still say he felt when he no longer had nerves or flesh, his head begin to unravel and his point of view sank as his legs, pelvis, and chest collapsed into gray, billowing dust. He knew his skull no longer burned its blue flames from their vacant sockets, turning to cold black, then slate-tinted sand. He heard his staff fall to the ground to join the debris with a thin clank, then darkness overcame him.

Chapter 6

Cadrissa found herself again looking about the room a second time. The book she'd been reading had long since moved off of the subjects she presently found interesting. She had enough insight into the culture and land of the Syvani to aid The Master in whatever he might desire though, and she supposed that was enough. They were a very interesting, if not a barbaric people, who lived like wild men in the great wilderness of Arid Land.

The only thing that struck her as strange was how they feared literacy and books. Oral traditions and their own memories were how they told the stories of their race. It seemed the Syvani feared if something were written down, it would be forgotten forever.

Cadrissa thought it an interesting theory, but found it lacking on many fronts. Chief among them was that if knowledge is not recorded and stored for later generations to use and understand, then the insights die with those who hold it, namely various sages — and even the race itself. Their method seemed to be a very quaint, if ineffective, system of retaining valuable information.

Following this information the topics presented in the book had then trailed into mundane measurements and meaningless reflections of a very fulsome and ill-educated sage of some sort. The tome had so far proven only as useful as a simple terrain primer, if even that.

It had been a while since The Master left her with the book and, fearing to touch any other tomes in the room; she had begun to occupy herself with the room's interior make-up once more. At first she tried to place the room in the tower's construction, trying to see where it would be placed on the tall shaft of brick and mortar. She'd surmised she was on one of the middle levels and more was yet above and below her she hadn't seen upon her forced arrival. However, she had an odd sensation the tower was larger inside than out, It was probally a sort of spatial trick, she supposed, if one knew the right spells to enact such a thing she believed The Master very well could. So placement of rooms in the tower could become speculative under such a hypothesis.

This game, too, quickly bored her, however, and the pungent aroma of dust, dry vellum and leather was beginning to dry her eyes, and cause her nose to itch. The added time have her more than one occasion to occupy her mind with the loss of the books and scrolls she had stored in Elandor to retrieve after she had returned from Takta Lu Lama. She hoped and prayed they would be there when she had a free moment to return to retrieve them. She hated to lose some of the most precious aids to her study she had yet retrieved.

Dwelling about their loss won't help her at the moment, and so she had tried to fill her mind with other things to hold her ponderings until the inevitable time came when The Master would return. So her thoughts raced over what could lie still above and below her. What rooms full of wondrous things had she yet to find in this relic of a building? Her eyes grew wide as she thought about the prospects. It filled her with a sensation that tingled throughout her entire body, making her shiver with excitement and longing.

How could such a wizard as The Master live in such a place, filled with such history, and yet not be tempted to run his bony hand over every single volume in his library, touch every object his tower held, to study and think upon it once more? She couldn't imagine living out her days without searching for the answers to such questions as the origin of all creation, or the reason things occurred, or why magic worked and priest's prayers sometimes failed. She couldn't settle for trite remarks or unproved specula-tions to still her curious mind as it answered everyone else's. She needed to find such answers herself and delve into it — to feel it in her spirit.

The book from which The Master had been reading was still under the one she placed on top of it…what had been so important about it that The Master had her retrieve it? It wouldn't hurt to take a small peek she supposed. She could always cover the tome up again with the magenta book she had been reading previously should he suddenly make an appearance again.

Nervously she made sure she was alone, and then gently lifted the right half of the magenta book off the one beneath it. The parchment was old and yellowed, the ink was spidery, and a brownish red — probably blood from the looks of it. The words though…she couldn't make them out at all. They were as nothing she had ever seen before.

She thought it was familiar at first — something about the shapes perhaps, but that was all — and even that faded when her eyes took a stronger focus on the text itself. It was then the mage felt a heat on her leg. The warmth came from where she had placed the medallion and seemed to intensify the longer she stared at the words. Unable to bear the curious nature of the event much longer, she returned the magenta book to the top of The Master's book and picked out the medallion from her pocket.

Denied time to look it over thoroughly before, maybe she could do so now, and even benefit from some of the new resources at her disposal since she'd lost all her own books, scrolls, and notes in her capture. She carefully studied the golden object.

It was small; about a hand's width in diameter and thinner than a finger in width. It felt light and soft in her touch, like a gentle flower or delicate glass carving. Around its edges were simple runic designs the mage knew held some key to its identity and abilities. She also knew though she couldn't read the script and so the medallions true function remained hidden from her… for now.

Suddenly, she thought she heard whispering coming from around her as she held the medallion tightly in her hand. It was soft and distant, but growing in volume as if those who were creating it were drawing near. Could there be other things in this tower stirring about? She supposed it was possible. What would be their disposition to her, though?

Cadrissa was startled by a soft clicking noise.

She turned toward it, and saw the door into the room — the door she could have sworn The Master had locked with his departure, was now slightly ajar. A thin stripe of darkness between the door and the jam tempted her.

She eyed it for a moment, and then drew away, trying to gather her thoughts. It could have very well been a misplaced shadow or some other such thing playing tricks with her mind. Such things were not uncommon to a wizard's tower after all. But no, the thin stripe of darkness, no more than an inch in width, taunted her as she looked back toward it. It seemed to call out to her for exploration, so that it might share its secrets with her. Stranger still, as she fought the internal battle within herself, she heard a faint whisper from the hallway outside.

"Cadrissa, mistress of the arts arcane." Its faint tone was coming from behind the darkness.

Had she accidentally summoned something, or called something to her?

Instantly, the mage hid the medallion on her person.

The whispers silenced.

"Yes?" She looked coyly at the opening as though it were breathing.

"Arise and follow me, for I am to take you to greater things," the voice was slightly louder this time, and the mage thought she saw a faint glow outside the opening as well.

Had The Master returned?

"Be not afraid. I am nothing that can harm you. Behold!" The door silently opened wider, Cadrissa nearly fainted from the excitement. Her heart had become a great drum threatening to explode from her chest with a mule-like kick. Behind the opening was an apparition of sorts — a man of great age with a translucent quality about him. Cadrissa oddly considered him for a moment, totally fascinated by the specter. He was, after all, the first ghost she had ever seen.

He stood motionless and looked quite peaceful. His face was old with years. He had a bluish white, misty beard trailing off like wisps of smoke as it reached the middle of his chest. His head was bald, and showed age spots, which had no more actual substance to them than his clear eyes. The ghostly image wore a gauzy garment of a robe that was simple enough, yet possessed a high collar that seemed to pass the back of the ghost's head then trail into tendrils of white smoke. The ghost's legs couldn't be seen beneath the robe but from what Cadrissa could surmise if sought for, they would turn up missing amid a vaporous cloud. The whole image seemed to have an odd, floating characteristic about it too telling Cadrissa the being in front of her could glide through the dark hallways better than her small feet ever could walk.

"Who are you?" Cadrissa moved closer to the door, nervously flinging some stray hairs on her temple behind her ear. She had no idea what horrors or tricks lurked in the tower — and if they had any disposition to her. Without The Master to keep them at bay, she was effectively helpless.

"I must show you something. Only you can help me and the others trapped within this tower," the ghost spoke to her in a louder voice.

"What if The Master returns and finds me gone or in your company?" She stepped a little closer, but not too close. The image intrigued her, but not so much as she wanted to reach out and grab it — trusting it fully.

"He will not. At this very moment he still slumbers as he tries to regain the power he has lost over the years. We will have ample time to complete the task I must ask you to participate in. Rest easy child, I cannot harm you, I am one of your order," the elder man's shade smiled faintly.

"My order?" Cadrissa was dumbfounded.

"Yes, you have all the markings of a daughter of my order," the specter seemed slightly comforted by this realization — if any comfort could truly be said to be given to a ghost. "Though you are under skilled in some areas, time will fill them out for you. The Path of Knowledge is a wise path for any wizard."

"The Path of Knowledge?" Cadrissa was a bit confused. "You mean you were once a wizard on the Path of Knowledge? What happened then? How did you get to such a state as this?"

"That is what I must show you. It is vital you know the truth of what is to come. For we know what The Master plots."

"We?" Cadrissa was cautious in her questioning. She didn't want to risk the ire of any other towers denizens.

"Please," The ghost's outstretched hand appeared to the young mage a gentle welcome, "I have much to tell you, but not much time."

Strange as it felt, Cadrissa suddenly trusted the long-forgotten shade. Why? She couldn't totally say. He had a soft look about him, almost like a fatherly aura making her feel at home and safe. What really got to her heart and told her this image from the grave meant no harm were his eyes. They spoke of a gentle will and a congenial heart that would never seek to do her harm. That was hardest to create should one's motive be false. There was that...and something else too. A sensation, which she couldn't place, though mundane in nature, compelled her to accompany the shade.

"Very well," Cadrissa swallowed hard, and then boldly took a brisk step forward.

She would not grab the ghost's hand though, that much was too far beyond her state of adventurous pursuit. She still had entertained the thought of gaining such knowledge from a first-hand experience though for a moment before she had refused the notion.

"Lead on," she took up a stance beside the specter.

Silently the shade floated onward; his robed flowing gently around him. Cadrissa shivered at the thought of such a cold, stale air that still followed the ghost around in death.

"Watch your steps carefully, for you travel through a treacherous hall filled with many a loose flagstone and devious trap planted by the one who now keeps this towers ownership."

The ghost lead her down a flight of stairs for what seemed like hours, though she knew they were just minutes passing. The dark interior was kept at bay only by pale and dying embers in wall-mounted sconces as she passed onward. Her companion's faint incandesce shimmered a milky sheen upon his area of occupation so that it mingled with the dim, red light of the braziers; giving all he passed a soft, pink glow.

She wondered where she was being taken.

The tower was old and certainly full of many dangers. She was sure the ghost had been right about that, but had he insinuated The Master would be returning in time? How much time had already passed on this journey? Suddenly, she felt cold sweat bead on her forehead, and her heart increased its pace as well. She quickened her stride and tried to get the ghost to move faster, but he stayed his path of steady fluttering. Too far from where she had been and now stuck in the middle of her destination and the library, she had just to stick it out and see it through. For good or for ill it was too late to change her mind.

"Are we almost there?" She asked in a nervous tone.

"Yes, we must go beyond this door," the ghost stopped in front of a simple wooden door they had just come to. It appeared to lack a lock or handle to open it.

"Then lead on, quickly," Cadrissa said with slight impatience.

"You must open the door," the ghost looked politely at the golden robed mage. "I am afraid I am unable to do so in my current state."

"Very well, if I must." She gently pushed the door inward.

A creaking protest was the only thing prohibiting her from peering into the darkness. Stale air and dry, dust saturated gusts flew into her face. After her eyes stopped tearing up from the assault and she could breathe again, she peered inside the room.

The darkness was there for only a moment when it was chased off by a sudden burst of green light.

The light emanated from a large orb about three feet in diameter resting on a pedestal made of three dwarven skeletons who looked to be straining their bony backs as they supported the pulsating globe above them. Positioned back to back, the skeletons glowed a sickly green as well, as the light from the orb spilled out onto them, adding an even more gruesome highlight to the macbre design. The shining glow further poured out of the middle of the room to cover it all with slime-tinted brilliance.

Tapestries and paintings congested the walls around the green sphere. They were varied in both size and color, and displayed pictures that had faded and gone the way of all material things; yet a few still held their stitches, and it was to these Cadrissa was drawn.

One, on the far wall, looked to be a scene of a peaceful valley with a deer and rabbit in the foreground as the glade slowly rose into hills and rolled off into the horizon. Trees and colorful foliage dominated the picture with a serene grace making Cadrissa's eyes mist over slightly with the beauty of the work.

"It is a picture of my homeland," the ghost spoke up as he followed the mage's gaze.

"It's beautiful. Where is this place?"

"In a distant time far away from you or me," the ghost said solemnly. "All these pictures are of a different time. Each face was a friend or closer still. It still fills me with joy to see them. I have such memories of them."

Cadrissa turned toward the ghost who sullenly enjoyed a picture on the wall to the left of the mage with a ravishing woman of Telborian heritage. She was a vision to behold. Her flesh was smooth and white, and her hair was like golden wheat. The dress spoke of days Cadrissa could not place on the timeline in her mind.

"She is very lovely," Cadrissa spoke softly.

"Yes, some called her the most radiant being in all creation." At this the ghost smiled ruefully, "but those days are past from time's glass and there are things to do at the moment. I called you here for a reason. When you first entered this tower, I felt the nature of your spirit, and it filled me with happiness to find a like person after nearly a thousand years of existing alone with the evil of this place.

"I had to call you here so you will be prepared for what lies ahead of you, for I never was and that was what brought me here. You shall have the benefit of foreknowledge. That, and another wishes to speak with you."

Cadrissa looked into the misty image with a stern and studious eye. She was indeed interested in what this ghost could teach her — but was now starting to have her doubts. She needed more information about the whole situation before she could comfortably commit herself. Though now why she had suddenly adopted a skeptical outlook was beyond her. She just felt something was a bit off with the entire situation. Things where happening far too quickly for her liking, and there was something else that was not being said as well — a fundamental piece behind all this interplay.

"Who are you...or were you then? I want to know before I commit myself to your trust. This place can hold some fiercesome devils I'm sure — and I want a better idea of what I'm dealing with."

"Very well," the sigh, which fluttered out of the ghost's mouth, unsettled Cadrissa. "I am the spirit of a Wizard King who followed the Path of Knowledge some twelve hundred years ago. My name is Embulack, and I served justly over my subjects and fellow mages who had joined me in the alliance. All was well and good until *he* came." For a moment a glint of malice reflected off Embulack's dead eyes. "It is because of him you must trust me, and peer into the orb. It will give you the answers and will not hurt you, for it was once mine upon a time, until he stole it along with my life."

"*Who* did this? The Master?" Cadrissa grew a bit more concerned.

"The very same monster that haunts this tower, the same one who at this very moment is regaining his strength in his secret chambers. He calls himself The Master now, but I knew him from days of old. He once was called Cadrith, and wasn't as he appears today, nor was his evil vision as far fixed and full grown. No, when I knew him, he was but another wizard who had not yet even become a Wizard King.

Embulack's eyes found Cadrissa's with a fatherly near-warmth that seemed out of place with the specter's unnatural presence. "He is evil though, child — and he has foul plans. He mustn't be allowed to complete them. I can say no more. There is so little time left. Look into the orb, and you will know the truth."

"So you are his enemy then?" The mage was trying to piece this all together— get a full understanding of what was going on.

"Yes. I am one of many," the ghost rapidly pushed the words from his mouth.

"You work against him even now — and want me to help?" Cadrissa continued her interrogation.

The figure of Embulack nodded silently.

"I just wish I had more proof here to help ease my concerns," said the wizardress.

"You'll get the proof you seek if you just look into the orb. Hurry!", An urgency had overcome Embulack now.

The mage sighed, "I supposed I'm trapped here as it is already. It can't get much worse."

Cadrissa looked at the pulsating green eye, and then at the ghost. She stepped up to the green orb and placed her hands upon its smooth, throbbing surface, then took a deep breath and closed her eyes, and a new world was open unto her.

Cadrissa's vision swarmed with emerald light as bright as day, and as painful as a dagger point to the heart. Her mind felt as though it was like a tightly stretched piece of cloth ready to be torn asunder at any moment.

She tried to scream, but found no voice.

The light lasted for a short while, slowly faded, and then fled into a murky scene, which unfolded before her. Thick smoke filled the horizon with dark, billowing clouds. Ash and flames filtered out of the smoke at irregular intervals like a serpent's flickering tongue. The aroma of burnt flesh and wood, along with the tell tale metallic stench of spilt blood came to her nose. The odor was heavy upon her and filled her with dread. It was then she suddenly had a terrible feeling she'd been tricked into entering the Abyss.

As she attempted to calm herself as best she could, Cadrissa got the feeling she was slowly descending through the greasy pitch clouds before her. She didn't understand how it was possible, but she felt some sort of ground approaching her feet as though she'd been aloft in the utmost heights of the atmosphere slowly falling toward land. This thought was further confirmed when the clouds turned from a deep, charcoal gray to a misty, greenish gray and finally a thin white. They parted to reveal flaming ramparts and smoldering dead bodies scattered about like incendiary debris. The mage observed the fallen figures and saw jet frames sizzle like bacon in a skillet upon a charred and blood drenched field.

The ruins of what looked like a large castle still stood, as parts of it continuously exploded in bombastic shards upon the desolate field around it like popcorn in a kettle. Cadrissa saw no survivors, but could smell the taint of magic on the air.

Powerful, destructive magic.

What had this battle been for, and who was fighting whom? Why was so much magic unleashed in such a deadly and obviously overpowering manner?

She studied and questioned the scene, yet couldn't attain any answers. All the while she was lowered toward the black and blood smeared soil beneath her. When her feet touched the muddy earth, for a moment she thought of the Marshes of Gondad and the dead bodies bobbing up from the mire to meet her. The mage closed her eyes and made herself forget the grim memory, confident such a thing wouldn't happen again.

She couldn't see much of anything save destruction and ruin all about her. The place appeared too had been a meadow at one time, but now its trees were up rooted and chopped down with axes, burned, and even served as posts for skeletons and mutilated bodies which hung from them in macabre disarray around the flaming and popping castle.

She knew this wasn't Arid Land. It couldn't be, the Syvani weren't that hostile, nor could they wield magic. It wasn't in Talatheal either, of that she was certain. She didn't have the experience yet to think of any other locations, but she somehow felt she knew its location — there was a faint scratching at the back of her mind.

Suddenly, the wind picked up.

The small puff of air grew into a medium breeze, and then escalated into a great gale in a matter of seconds sweeping all the putrid hazy fumes away as it filled Cadrissa's ears with a fierce roar. Her hair and robe were blown in wild chaos as dust and ash flew into her eyes; temporally blinded her to the surroundings. Then, just as wondrously as it had occurred, the same wind simply stopped in mid-force and all was silenced except for the buzzing of flies, the crackle of a few nearby small fires and the hiss of blood extinguishing flame. With the opaque canopy of clouds gone, the light of day shined upon the gore-drenched field in all its grizzly splendor.

Cadrissa wiped the gummy tears away from her eyes and tried to work on getting herself placed in the surrounding area, when she spied a lone figure moving toward her from the distance. The form looked human, that was all Cadrissa could discern. It seemed to be rather tall and of good build, perhaps even a warrior.

Panic instantly seized her.

She didn't want to be under the sword of anyone, especially in such a gods-forsaken war zone. She cursed herself for not thinking things through once again and chasing the advisement of her curious habits and urges, which had brought her here. Confident the figure had seen her, and was heading her way, she had no option left other than to just go with what was presented to her and hope for the best.

"Hello?" The young mage called out. Fear still crept into her voice no matter how hard she tried to mask it.

No response.

"Hello? Who are you? I'm unarmed and can't cause anyone any harm even if I wanted to." Cadrissa tried to stand still as she readied what she hoped would be an effective spell to halt the stranger should he prove to be dangerous. She may not have been armed, but she could still defend herself if cornered. The Master hadn't drained her strength that much using her to get to his tower. Still, her well of mystical energy inside was close to depletion — and she didn't want to risk more than she had to should she need it for a life or death emergency.

The figure loomed closer.

As he drew nearer, Cadrissa could discern he was a Telborian man with the manner and grace of a fellow mage, and carried no weapon, nor wore any armor. He had on a pure white gown tied with a golden rope, which shined with an odd tarnished glow, like bronze or gold, in daylight. His face was clean-shaven; his eyes were green and young. On his face a serene countenance played about his features. He looked like a young adult in years with brown, shoulder-length hair clustered in gray and white streaks like tiny waterfalls about his head.

"What is going on here? Where am I, and who are you?" Cadrissa tried to stand defiantly, but her legs shook with uncertainty. She thought she would break down and cry at any moment from the fear and stress she felt nearly overwhelming her. Though the man had a mild, fatherly manner, she wasn't taking any chances. In the arcane arts one learned very quickly that appearances meant nothing. Great power could be hidden in a small babe and the seemingly most deadly of foes could also do nothing but blow smoke.

"Peace, my good child and rest easy," the man spoke in a way that seemed more like a gentle breeze than a voice. "I am a friend; your guide. The ghostly mage has drawn you here so we may speak."

"Who are you?" Cadrissa dared a brave face.

"Endarien."

"Endarien? He's a god. Everybody knows you can't see a god and live. You'll have to do better than that." The wizardress readied a spell and prayed for protection from the madman who was in front of her — another hopeful mage bent on accumulation of greater power. How many were there who called this tower home?

"Gods can appear to anyone they wish that is what being a god is about: limitless possibilities. I have chosen this image so not to upset you too much. I have many faces and many duties to match those faces. Right now I speak to you as you are in a very interesting position. None have been so close to The Master as you are now over the past centuries.

"He's trying to regain his full power which he possessed when he once fled in the guise of a lich. He will fail on his final quest, but I want to teach him a lesson first. He has a spot in my heart reserved for only those most accursed. It waits for him, and I long to show him its confines." The Telborian claiming to be Endarien smiled to himself a wicked little grin that made Cadrissa truly fear for her life, despite the supposed 'god's' claims of his benign nature.

"You will simply place this amulet upon his person and I'll do the rest." He drew out of the air a small, gray stone disc no larger than an acorn in diameter, crafted with the image of a golden lightning bolt, which ran across the surface of the object in a zig-zag fashion. "That is all. My quarrel is not with you, and you will not be harmed in our dispute, but The Master…" The man chuckled to himself as thunder boomed in the background.

"Assuming you are a god — which I still find hard to believe — why do you need me to do this?" Cadrissa studied the mage with an intense eye. "Why not do it yourself and leave me out of it? Aren't gods supposed to be all-powerful? Can't you just send down one of your lightning bolts and be done with it? And if you are Endarien, then why couldn't you get into his tower before?"

"The Master has too many protections about him," he explained, "He will feel my presence before I can act. I want to surprise him as he surprised me so long ago. I have also tried to do this before as you have said, and he has proven a worthy opponent — more so than any other mortal foe I've yet faced. His tower cannot be opened by my hands, as you might recall. That is quite a feat indeed." His eyes grew distant for a moment, and then refocused. "You are below his notice and an easy pawn at this time."

"This *pawn*," Cadrissa spit out the word, as she hated the thought of being yet another's toy in a game she neither understood nor cared for, "wants proof of your good will and validation you are who you claim to be once this is proven, then I will take on the task, and as you ask. Only a god could protect me from such a monster. I'm not going to throw my life away on some foolish squabble between mages."

"You are very right in that assumption, and should fear The Master. Be at peace, however, I will protect you. If you want proof, then you shall have it."

With that, the figure before Cadrissa faded away, and a being composed of light, appeared to her and blinded her with its brilliance. From the light she could see other realities open before her. She could look into the worlds lying between her own and a new, more brilliant reality than she had ever thought possible.

It was a strange and alien place, yet it spoke of peace and power beyond her mindset; knowledge she'd never be able to completely absorb — even if she had till the end of time to do so. It was then she knew she was in the presence of a god, for the very nature of his being as it was displayed to her, was more powerful than any mage or lich she had yet encountered. Such sights couldn't be mimicked by magic, and her very spirit fluttered in the waves of illuminated power emitted from the being before her like a lone butterfly in the breeze.

"I believe you," Cadrissa half-whispered, half-croaked through her clenched and covered face. It was then the mage also noticed she'd fallen to her knee under the penetrating light of the god, a position she did not alter after this epiphany.

"Good," Endarien's voice echoed like a retreating thunder-clap as he returned to his previous form in a flash of lightning. "Arise. Here is the amulet. Take it and return to your time and place for The Master will awake from his slumber of rejuvenation very soon."

As soon as the amulet was in her hand, the whole scene before her vanished. She found herself in the old, green-lit room in The Master's tower once more. The familiar ghost stood beside her with a faint grin as if in relief. Somehow Cadrissa thought he seemed to look more frail and older than when last she viewed him.

"You must go back to the room where The Master left you. He will return very soon." Embulack's face was now slightly lined by panic.

"Who are you then, Embulack? You ally with a god, are you another god?" Cadrissa took in the ghost. Trickery and hidden agendas seemed to be the way of things in the tower and those who associated with The Master. She dreaded the outcome of being wrapped into so many twines of factions and fate. Sooner of later it would have to form some type of binding or noose and she didn't wish either upon herself.

The ghost laughed.

It was the sound of a wheezing man upon his deathbed, and made Cadrissa shiver.

"Truly you are on the Path of Knowledge, for you wish to know that which is even irrelevant. Part of my tale you already have heard. I was called Embulack the Great during what you now know as the Fourth Age of the Wizard Kings. A powerful Wizard King myself, I made my mark on the world and was already posed to take over my home on Belda-thal, when The Master came and slew me. What you saw in that orb was what remained of my forces once The Master had finished his fell work.

"He slaughtered my troops, razed the lands around my castle, and stole my enchanted possessions, my magic, and life. My spirit was trapped in this orb, where it has remained to this day. He has caused me never ending suffering and torment by both this bondage and the seeping pain his evil has brought to this tower and my own spirit from his own malignant being.

"When Endarien came to me, he told me he could free me if I would but bring you to him it was like a gentle rain from heaven. So I did, and when The Master is dead, then I will be free.

"Now you must do as Endarien says — and you must hurry!"

Cadrissa looked down at her palm and saw the small amulet once more. She couldn't help but wonder at what it did. What strange powers it possessed. She wanted to study it more closely, devote more time to unlocking its secrets. But she knew she couldn't — and something she hated to tell herself was when she couldn't study something. It took all her strength to make the amulet slide into a hidden pocket in her robes and away from her sight, but not away from her mind.

"Show me the fastest way back," her heart had started to pick up speed, "I don't want him to get any more thoughts about me than what he already has."

Leading the way, Embulack moved into the hallway once more, Cadrissa in tow.

Chapter 7

The Master felt himself return to consciousness.

Before him was a sable-colored sea until he recalled he had eyelids once again and drew them open. He noticed his vision had turned white and was impaired with the cloth above him. The Master flung the covering from him and sat up amid the explosion of dust the action unleashed. He felt muscles and tendons twisted, and moaned as they awoke after their long dormancy.

The Master looked down toward the room's entrance opposite him and saw a pile of dust. All that remained of his old body was in an ashen pile. Already he felt it was no longer part of him — a skin shed from an old form. He now had a new form, a form with a heartbeat and his rekindled arcane might. He could feel the deep well inside him hum with power. He looked down at his hands, feeling them move, and saw the flesh on them. Fingernails and peach colored skin covered the dry bones he was used to seeing. He put the hands to his skin and felt life pulse beneath his checks; warm and full of movement. Blood was in him once more! It was an odd feeling to have the sensation after becoming used to the cold emptiness of undeath emanate from inside him. He traced his fingers around his eyes and felt the supple flesh surrounding them. Flesh that now held in piercing blue orbs rather than empty, flaming sockets. He laughed as his hands ran through his black hair now cut short to his head. The mirthful sound wasn't hollow or dead sounding at all, but alive and full of warmth. He had forgotten what it was to live. He needed to see himself.

Saying nothing, only thinking of the object, a full-length mirror appeared in the room before him. He left the table and walked naked toward the viewing glass. The Master took in his reflection marking him as a man of thirty years with a body of health and vitality. He had a build that marked him as a mild man of arms should it come to fisticuffs, but no trained knight or warrior.

The former lich stretched and turned in the mirror, looking at himself with pleasure. He'd forgotten how handsome he looked, and why the women swooned over him so long ago. He'd also forgotten those feelings of the flesh. He found it amazing they were still very potent and clung to him still after all the years of his existence. More important than his supple new frame though, was the return of his power. He felt it course through his veins like lightning; energy and will to make all that he desired come to pass.

He laughed again.

The mage delighted in the fact his lips now added to his charming manner as he did so. He had forgotten the simple pleasures of the flesh, but he had to limit his indulgence in them. He would only be enjoying this form for a short time. He had tasks to complete — goals to meet.

First, he needed clothing and his staff, and then he would be ready. As soon as he'd thought of such matters, they appeared to him. His staff slithered into his grip and a deep purple gown covered his frame. The gown was embroidered on the hem with silver scrollwork and covered with ruby studs an inch in diameter, glowing with a light all their own. Black gloves of fine silk, and boots of strong leather, dyed black as well, climbing to his knees, also appeared on his frame; coming from nowhere to wrap around his naked skin. A pure white, golden rune-stitched hooded cloak pawed the ground slightly behind the mage and gathered thickly around his neck where the deep hood nestled itself. The eternal wizard looked at himself once more in the mirror…

He liked what he saw.

"This should do nicely," The Master pulled the hood up shadowing his blue eyes in dim, gray light, and walked out of the room with a strong stride.

Chapter 8

Cadrissa's chest heaved.

Cold sweat poured down her forehead. She took a position back by the book she had been reading. Fear chased her through the halls, back to the empty room. The thought of The Master catching her or even seeing her run through the halls as she fled the green-lit room, made Cadrissa not to even lift her head from the book she now pretended to read. She dreaded having him in the doorway looking in at her — probably even knowing just what she had been about, and what she was about to do to him by the decree of his own worst enemy himself.

Somehow she was certain The Master knew what she had done; what she planned to do and he would turn his wrath upon her and make her suffer. She tried to calm down, telling herself she was free from harm at the moment; that she was still needed by The Master — or so he said — and this ensured her safety for a while at least. Desperately she willed herself to slow her racing heart and galloping chest.

She needed to be calm.

It took a few short moments to do this, but then she was at peace. A peace arriving just as a figure appeared in the door.

"You found something then?" The figure spoke in a voice that sounded new, but was washed with a familiar trait the wizard-ress couldn't identify.

"Who's there?" The frightened mage stammered. The last thing she wanted was more of the tower's haunts and spectacles coming to seek her out. She had already worn herself out with the previous ghostly encounter.

"Who do you think, girl?" The image entered the light of the room.

Cadrissa was taken back.

The figure looked vaguely familiar, but it was a strange familiarity, like his voice. He was a wizard, that much Cadrissa could discern from his dress…he seemed to have an aura of malice about him as well…. He glared at her with his deep blue eyes and she saw a flicker of cold blue fire dance in their reflection. It was then she knew who stood before her. Such a trait could never be hidden in any form, as it was a person's spirit itself.

It was The Master.

Cadrissa's eyes went as large as Rexiums. "You're alive again but-"

"Yes. I've gained a new body to see me toward my journey. I am once again as I should be: The most powerful mortal alive." He glided over to his captive with a devilish glee.

Cadrissa took a step back when she saw the flesh move on his face for the first time. With the skin and muscle, she could see the cruel and selfish energies that had driven the mage in life, for they'd been etched deep into his visage.

"So what have you discovered while I was gone? Tell me about Arid Land." He had to test her best he could; keep her guessing as to what was going on until it was too late, and he had no further use for her.

Cadrissa sputtered a bit. She hated to think he was watching her with those newly formed eyes. To see him in undeath was one thing, but to see him now clothed — in living flesh — was a far more different discomfort all together.

"The land is a massive forest, filled with all manner of bird and beast, and the Syvani. They are said to be savages, or so they were said to be by the writer who claimed to be an Elyelmic sage. They dress in animal skins, have deep red hair, and even decorate their bodies with gold adornments, and body paint.

"They worship nature, and even revere the common animal as a god of sorts. They hold no true god up to worship, and it is said they do not even have the knowledge and skill for spell craft. They are a very lowly race, but they are plentiful and dangerous because of their wild nature."

"Good," The Master moved to place his hands over Cadrissa's shoulders. She shuddered with revulsion.

His touch had become warm with his new transformation, but she still felt its sinister drive seep into her flesh, and it chilled her to the bone.

"You have gained some new insight then. You have begun to fill that head with a greater understanding. This should help us both in the next stage of our journey then. You seem to like stories, so let me tell you also about a tale you will not find in that tome, nor many others." He closed his cobalt eyes for but a second. "You will have to hear it if you are going to be of any use to me on the journey, so listen well."

The room grew dark.

Silently, with bated breath, Cadrissa looked around herself as The Master released her. The room slowly became a different place. It sparkled like stars in the dim light, and seemed as if the night sky itself had descended to inhabit the room. The Master walked among the stars, then took his hands and made a simple gesture, and the room was finally gone. The stars had been replaced with large planets varied in color and shape. Cadrissa would later learn all their names, but at the moment, only a few came to her mind, chiefly Tralodren itself.

"It is not commonly known by the races the gods were not the first divine beings in the cosmos." The Master continued. "In truth, they are part of the creation as much as we are. They were created from the same things we were: energy."

He then began to float through the created universe, drifting to and fro, circling, descending and rising, — he was always in motion. Cadrissa seemed to follow him on her own linear course as if she trailed the former lich like another planetary body shadowing his orbiting lectures.

"This energy I have named negative and positive. All things have this energy in them, and it is by its regulated amount we are made to exist. Those with higher amounts of the negative energy die faster, and we call them mortal or finite substances. Those with higher amounts of positive energy are longer lived and are called by some elves, dwarves, or even gods.

"Long ago," His face drifted close to a large, blazing yellow star which flared outward, close to his eyes as he drew near, "after the gods were created, there were left over pockets of this energy combination that remained active. Some of this energy even gained sentience."

The Master's face disappeared once more, and then his skull reappeared over a large blue planet. "The Ancients knew of an energy collection in Arid Land, which they called Galba. It has rested there for many centuries. It is here we must go, for history speaks of this energy being able to grant godhood to those who could prove themselves worthy of such a prize. Handfuls of people seeking the divine have sought out this self-created being over the course of time, but none have succeeded in their goals."

"What makes *you* think you will?" Cadrissa spoke up. She had totally forgotten where she was, and to whom she was speaking.

The Master's skull turned to flesh once more as the whole universe around the two wizards faded away like mist at the coming light of dawn. All was darkness and night. Cold, like the very touch of death, fell upon her and burrowed into her head.

She shivered.

"I am the most powerful mage in the world." The Master's voice was like the lash of a whip. "I have killed hordes of demons, sent kingdoms to ruin, and even challenged gods and lived! I am the last Wizard King of Tralodren! My will was strong enough to live though the ages in a rotting body, and my magic is the mightiest weapon for any to suffer. I won't fail. I cannot."

The former lich then became a bit calmer. "There is so much for you to learn. Mayhap when I'm a god, I'll make you a prize pupil, and you will learn the *true* way of things."

"Mayhap…mayhap not," Cadrissa shivered at the idea from some deep-seated part of her being. Somehow the offer seemed more of a curse than blessing though she couldn't fully understand why. Later on in her life she would come to understand the wisdom of such rejection.

The room grew light and warm, allowing Cadrissa to notice she wasn't wearing the same clothes any more. Her soiled golden robes had been replaced with a white satin gown tied with a golden silk sash. The gown was cut in a "V" shape plunging from her neck to chest; it stopped its descent over her cleavage to show off a large ruby pendant on a silver chain that had appeared there. On her back was a hooded gold cloak composed of some lightweight, yet durable, fabric that glistened like stars. When she moved to touch the new cloak she noted she now wore golden fingerless gloves reaching up to her elbow. Even her footwear had changed. Now she donned fine tall black leather boots rising to her knees, encircled with silver and ruby studs at their lip. Though it frightened her with what had just happened, she also found the outfit flattering and quite beautiful as well.

She was amazed at the splendor of the garments and found herself loving their play across her frame. All the while, at the back of her mind, she knew these clothes were *gifts* from The Master, and it unsettled her to think of his intentions for such a generous and extravagant wardrobe. Yet she did like the way they felt on her, and the pendant was very fetching. She looked at herself in a mirror before her, appearing from nowhere, without realizing what she was doing. The same mirror The Master had viewed his new form now bore the image of the young wizardress, and the influence of the dark mage whose touch was corruption and death.

"It suits you," a cold levity walked amid former lich's words.

"Wha-" Cadrissa suddenly caught herself, and awoke as if from some delightful dream. She saw the mirror, realized what she had been doing, and grew angry with both herself and The Master.

"What is the meaning of this?" Cadrissa did her best to contain her seething emotions.

"You should look more like royalty if you are going to keep company with me," The Master flashed her a chilling smile. "I *am* a man of taste after all."

You aren't even a man at all, Cadrissa thought — and wanted to tell him, but held her tongue. She already walked on enough eggshells with her captor as it was.

"Besides, these garments reveal your true nature." His smile chilled Cadrissa's soul. "We must be off then. You are now dressed, and all that you need you have on your person. Come. We go to our transport." The Master flourished a snowy swipe sending his cape into a whirlwind as he exited. He was gone in seconds, his staff thumping out the rapid rhythm of his step.

Cadrissa made a quick move to feel inside her pocket. The same pocket on her old garment where she had hidden the disc Endarien had given her. She was surprised and relieved to find it still intact. She grasped it in her hand and felt its circular body dig into her flesh, then closed her eyes and sighed. Another search of a second secret pocket relived her concerns about the fate of the medallion as well: it was still safe in her possession.

She hoped she would have time to study that as well on this journey; something to help relive her mind of her situation. She longed for a simpler day than what she currently was going through. Such as a quiet day in the library or a mild trip to some ramshackle ruins. Even the Marshes of Gondad would have been welcome again — anything but to be used as a pawn between The Master and Endarien. Things had gotten much too complicated and deadly far too quickly.

"Come girl, to me," the wizard's voice echoed down the hall, dripping with irritation.

The pressure of the whole affair was beginning to wear on her. She prayed she'd be kept safe from anything looming on the horizon before her. She wasn't certain of anything any more. Following her silent self-reflection, she ran out the door, after The Master. Behind her, the room grew dark and instantly cold as if any previous life and light in it were mere illusion. As Cadrissa's cloak fluttered out the doorway, the heavy wooden door closed with a whispered click, and all was still as the grave once more.

Chapter 9

Like a great tree of ebony stone, The Master's keep rose up from the grass-covered island. The sky had grown lighter since the wrath of Endarien had fled, but thick clouds and a gray tint still lingered to taunt those who saw it; the god's moment of return uncertain as the next incoming breeze. The slick flagstones of the roof, welcomed Cadrissa and The Master as they sprung from the bowels of the tower in silence by means of a trap door. A somber mantle rested upon both of them. The Master's drawn white hood contrasted with the black stone around him; Cadrissa had left her golden hood down as she followed meekly behind her captor.

"Come girl. Time is fleeting." He walked to the end of the rampart, and then stopped. The air was fresh with the smell of rain, wet grass, and flowers. In front of the former lich a hideous gargoyle leered out toward the world — a reptilian horror screaming at those below. The gargoyle's black stone face reminded Cadrissa of the visage of the demon The Master had slain on his entrance into Tralodren through Rowan's sword. She drove such troubling thoughts from her mind.

"I'm coming. I'm coming." Cadrissa huffed as she lowered the thick, wooden trapdoor in place to cover the stairs behind her. She found it hard to keep up with the ancient wizard. It was even harder when the dark mage was constantly having her close doors and do small, last-minute tasks behind him as a means of securing the tower until his return. "How do you plan to get to Arid Land? The maps say it's far to the north, near the Northlands."

The Master turned to her with cold eyes and a cruel, gloating expression. "We shall ride the very remnants of Endarien's own wrath which he has so kindly provided."

Cadrissa walked closer to the mage, but still kept a slight distance between them. Now out of the tower, and the influence of its counter spells and magical resonance, she could feel the mystical presence of The Master better and clearer than before. His corruptive aura was like an ever-expanding ripple on a pond, pulsating from his very spirit into the air and then her being. Though she held a rather neutral stance on the matter of good and evil in academic and magical pursuits, that mindset was beginning to be challenged. In being so close to someone who was so clearly focused on evil — who even seemed to embody aspects of it, she began to see how perhaps the priests were right.

Perhaps absolutes in morality were real. She wondered if he knew she had spoken to one of his enemies in his very own tower. She dreaded to think what would happen if he knew about the amulet she had received from Endarien.

The wizardress was beginning to think this whole affair wasn't worth the effort or the knowledge she would gain. It had ceased to be a learning experience and was moving into more a form of slavery with varying masters claiming their ownership over the mage with each passing moment. As much as she hated it, all she could do was continue or suffer a worse fate.

Cadrissa's body felt as though it was a piece of granite. With getting little rest from her recent adventure in the ruin of Takta Lu Lama, she had become the worse for wear. She could scarcely move, and yet the wizardress had to. She had to continue. It was too late to stop. Cadrissa had to see it through to the end, and then take her leave of it, but not before then, not without her life and some increased insight. It was the least she could hope to receive — the silver lining to this dark horizon.

"You still fear me?" The Master cackled his cold brand of mirth. "Good, you are learning to be wise, girl. Now see the full abilities of this mage who will soon rule over this world, and to whom you and all of Tralodren will bow to as god."

He raised his hands in the air, and shouted so it echoed across the landscape. The hair on the back of Cadrissa's neck stood on end, and she felt a chill in the air around her, as if a freezing breeze was passing her way. Her arms and legs turned to gooseflesh, her teeth set on edge.

"Calroth salene! Calroth morta! Yorn uthlesa waquesh oplua denn rothe..." The Master continued to shout as his spell was spun.

In his words Cadrissa found a presence she had never known. It rocked her very being, and sent her mind aching to achieve the understanding of such a spell. Nothing like it had ever existed before — not in any book she'd ever read or instruction she'd ever received, and that revelation served only to further entice the curious wizardress. There was indeed much she could gain from this situation if she kept her wits about her.

A lone cloud the size of a jousting ring began to descend closer to the tower by its own accord. As it floated, it grew white and clean, and began to form itself into a boat-like shape. Continuing to grow closer, it took on more mass so Cadrissa noticed it transform to possess all the characteristics of a real boat — a caravel, save it was all made of white cloud. At the prow, a dragon figurehead presented a sinister snarl and seemed to move as if it was alive, seeking out some new victim to devour as it sailed closer to the tower.

Thin, white, membrane-like sails billowed in the breeze as the cloud-boat continued its descent toward the tower. A pennant waved on the foremast like a kite in the sky adding the final touch to the illusion the cloud was indeed a seaworthy vessel. As it became level with the tower's ramparts, Cadrissa spied the rigging and rope all around the ship, and felt if she touched them she'd find they would be solid and able to support her weight as any real rope would. She didn't know if she was so keen on testing out the theory, however.

The spell cast, the boat silently docked with the tower.

"Get in," The Master pointed toward the boat with his staff.

"I trust it will hold me," Cadrissa coolly looked at her captor as she gauged his response.

"We must be off before any other eyes cross my path. Get into the boat now. I want to waste no more time!" The former lich growled and forcefully jabbed toward the vessel with his staff.

Cadrissa lifted her foot from the rampart. She stepped on it to get a decent bearing on the ship as she boarded; double-checking the soundness. Stepping over the port bow of the vessel, her foot touched a hard surface that felt like wooden planks. She placed her other foot over the side and it felt like solid planking too.

The wizardress walked over to the upper deck and stood there for a moment, surveying the whole scene. It all seemed so strange and bizarre, yet the longer she stayed on the ship and looked around, the more natural it felt. She had no idea magic could do something so amazing as this. It seemed too new, too unreal for her to fathom almost and yet it existed. The burn to learn more from her captor grew inside her even more so than before.

She would have to do her best in observing all she could. There was still the matter of the amulet, however. The Master boarded the vessel with little effort, and walked to the wheel above the main deck. There, he motioned with his hands to the East, and the cloud-boat silently moved away from its moorings and began to sail through the air as though it were on the sea and manned by a full crew of trained sailors. It took a simple turn around the tower, and with great speed, left it behind; the wind flying with great force into Cadrissa's hair.

The mage fought her way through the torrent of wind until she got up to The Master's location. He stood defiant against the air, which ruffled his cloak, and made him appear as some kind of corsair.

"What manner of magic is this?" Cadrissa questioned the wizard at last, unable to hold back her inquisitive tongue any longer.

"It is but a fraction of which I am capable now that I'm totally regenerated," he shouted over the wind and looked behind himself. All he could see was the clear turquoise water beneath him, and the peaceful blue sky. The thick cloud cover parted like mist until it grew to a thin fog, then finally dissipated into the heavenly expanse.

"How long until we reach Arid Land?" Cadrissa asked as she placed her hand in the secret pocket in her new robe. Her fingers found Endarien's amulet, and fumbled with it nervously.

"I believe we'll be there in no more than a matter of days. This boat will take us there faster than its slower, water bound kin. Besides, up here there are few distractions and even fewer worries." The Master's response was distant. His mind was already elsewhere forming the next step in his plans.

"I wish to retire for the day then. I will need my strength too." Cadrissa looked dolefully at The Master, who squinted his blue orbs at her in a studious gaze, pawing over her with a dry and rough touch as he came back from his thoughts. Her heart fluttered in her chest as she did all she could to keep from shaking in revulsion. The hand that held the amulet in her pocket fumbled with the disc and icy sweat seeped from her appendage.

"I will need you rested as well. You can have the cabin under the stern. I made it especially for you," he smiled once more and Cadrissa felt her hand grip hard around the amulet as she pulled it from her pocket. She needed to use it. Somehow she felt an urgency she needed to use it very soon, almost like a window of time was being passed. She just had to think of a way.

"I'll retire then," Cadrissa nodded slightly trying her best to give some believability to her statement. "I've had a long day."

"That you have. Go and rest I will have need of your services soon enough." The former lich again was drifting deeper into his thoughts.

Cadrissa left The Master for her cabin. As she did, she used a small bit of her own mystical energies to make the amulet fly from her hand and land on the lower hem of The Master's robe, behind him. It was a desperate move, but she had little choice. It flew and landed there without any incident. Then with but a whisper it turned invisible to the naked eye. She hoped The Master wouldn't find it, and prayed she hadn't been noticed doing it, either.

She looked to The Master once more, and saw he had become fully distracted by the sea and his dark musings. He had totally forgotten she was there — or did he? She knew the dark mage was just as tricky as he was old. She knew she'd find out soon enough. Cadrissa swallowed hard and tried to keep her heart steady. Whatever happened though, she would be better suited after a full night's rest. There was little she could do now.

Cadrissa was awakened just a short while later with a loud boom, followed by the laughter of The Master. She rose quickly from her bed, of soft pearl satin sheets resting on the milky wood structure of the boat. The room was Spartan — just having the bed and a chest at its foot. At first she awoke with fright from the loud noise, then realized where she was and what she was doing and she felt as though she'd never awaken from the nightmare in which she was trapped.

A second blast was followed by the wicked laughter of the former lich, which inspired the wizardress to investigate. She'd no need to dress or ready herself — she slept in her clothes, not wanting any part of her to be more susceptible or in plain view to The Master's clutches. The last thing she wanted was to be the object of any newly found physical desires that might have accompanied his regeneration.

Cadrissa ran from her cabin and climbed the empty stairs toward the stern. It was there that The Master hung over the starboard bow, continuing to laugh.

He'd just finished a spell.

Cadrissa felt a sharp shift of air around her as though it had changed temperature, then a loud and body shaking *boom* enveloped her frame as the clash of thunder filled the sky.

"What is this all about?" Cadrissa shouted over the noise. She was half blinded with anger and forgot whom she addressed and where she was.

The Master ignored her and raised his hand again as a wide bolt of lightning fell from it and sharpened the air once more. The following thunder this time made her eyes ache and feel as though her head would burst. Again, her curiosity took over, though it was also covered with the thick syrup of rage, she managed to get a grip on the railing beside The Master as he let loose yet another bolt of electrical fire.

She peered over the side and looked through a clear opening in a patch of clouds beneath them. It seemed like a pond in the middle of a field, and actually looked more like a small rain puddle than a break in the cloud cover. Below, Cadrissa saw clear emerald water and a small collection of boats. She couldn't discern their type, but knew they numbered around six. One of them was on fire though, and tilted in the water like a diving duck. Tiny black ants clustered around it as men fell out of the sinking vessel. The whole scene then struck Cadrissa with a deep and profound awakening.

"Stop this! This is madness!" She flailed her limbs against The Master's body, and then shook with fear as he turned to her.

What had she done? She had *attacked* him. Well, *hit* him anyway, and that was bad enough. She had to do something to stop him from harming more innocent lives, but she might have sacrificed her own life in the process. Cadrissa swallowed hard as she tried to look as defiant as she could with a sick stomach and weary head and heart.

"I can show you madness my dear," he snarled. "What I do is none of your concern, unless I tell you otherwise."

"Those are innocent people down there," much of her rage had fallen away into a lukewarm rebuke.

"They're mere test subjects. Do not interfere!" The Master's eyes seemed to take on a more brilliant sheen of malice.

"Test subjects?" Cadrissa was shaken to the core when another dark facet of The Master's true self was revealed to her in full. She had no idea what she could do, though. The whole situation seemed to be so far removed from her, and she seemed so powerless and insignificant to affect anything. Even as she thought, The Master raised his hand once more then stopped.

His face had the look of deep concentration, not the sick mirth she had seen moments before. His eyes squinted against the sun, scanning the horizon. Cadrissa studied him for a moment, and his tense frame made her worry. She surmised that if The Master could get uptight over something, it was not to her benefit.

Before she could think further though, her eyes were drawn to the amulet she'd placed on The Master. It was no longer invisible. A small halo of golden light shimmered on the lower hem of The Master's purple gown. The former lich drew away from the railing as a monstrous screech made its way across the sky. Fear ran thick in her veins at the sudden realization. What was happening now?

"What was that?" Cadrissa started as she unconsciously drew closer to The Master.

The Master seemed annoyed at the recent discovery. "Nothing that I can't handle, though I have my theories as to what sent it."

"You mean that something out there was sent after us? For what purpose?' Clara fearfully mused aloud.

"Sent after *me*. I'm the one who needs to be killed, you forget. My list of enemies is as long as the ocean is deep. I think I have it narrowed down though." The dark mage sneered.

"Really? How is it-?" She stopped as a gigantic thud took over the boat. Cadrissa was knocked down toward the deck and shuttered as she felt the fear of the unknown seep into her pores and veins even more than before; chilled mud pulsating all over her body. The Master remained upright to look defiantly at the threat; staff clutched with a white knuckled hand under his black glove.

"Have you come then at last?" The Master shouted. "I thought it wouldn't be too wise to test your patience too much. The slaughter of innocents from such lofty heights by your own weapon of choice might give you a bad name." He laughed as the boat collided with the unknown force once more with the sound of rending seams and breaking wood echoed in the heavens.

"What is it?" Cadrissa screamed as she tried to grab onto anything that might help her keep her balance as the boat began to teeter and fall from the sky.

She received her answer when a large, brown wing fluttered beside the port side of the vessel. It was the size of the entire boat itself! The feathers were so massive and thick they reminded her of tall trees tied together, end-to-end.

It was as if Cadrissa had shrunk to minute proportions and everything else had become gargantuan in comparison. When the wing beat down, a great gust ran through the boat and nearly blew the helpless wizardress across the upper deck, as she fell very close to the stairs to the stern. A brown-feathered bird's head, not unlike that of a hawk, appeared next. The whole head was about twenty feet in diameter she estimated, with bright yellow eyes at least a foot across. The beak was golden yellow, and seemed to be sharp enough to chip a mountain away.

"Behold a Roc!" The Master shouted as the giant bird screeched a terrible noise like the grinding of two metallic mountains. Cadrissa felt as if her mind would explode from the bird's volume, then it was over.

The Roc's eyes first looked at her, then The Master. They flickered with a seeming intelligence beyond animal intellect, and were encircled with a golden light Cadrissa could now place as the same halo effect the amulet gave off on The Master's hem.

With bestial strength, the great bird rammed once more into the cloud-composed vessel, and the sound of rending wood, like torn flesh, cascaded down the heavens along with brown feathers, free from their fleshly bindings, fluttering into the air around them.

"It's trying to destroy the ship!" Cadrissa panicked.

"I can save it the trouble," The Master raised his head to join his hands arched with black, tinted energy. "Let this be ended then!"

The dark mage shouted. The vessel melted then like dew in the morning light. Thin vapors snaked around Cadrissa's legs and arms, as she felt the sky beneath her and nothing else.

Cadrissa screamed.

"Hesle caron. Waquesel aboria!" The Master shouted over the excited cries of the Roc and Cadrissa as both he and the wizardress stopped their descent to hover in mid-air.

Nothing save the huge Roc remained.

Cadrissa tried to calm herself for a spell in self-defense, but couldn't. She hadn't fully recovered from her adventures, and was still drained to a low point, and very afraid. She needed time to focus and replenish some of the mystical energies inside herself. For now she had to rely upon The Master's and Endarien's good graces. The uncertainty of such a reliance though gnawed away at the back of her skull.

Before she could think any further, the Roc swooped down beneath her and The Master rising up to meet them so suddenly that the mage found herself holding onto the bird's feathers as it flew off like a comet toward the horizon. The wind rushed around her ears and head like thousands of screams. She could barely withstand the sonic assault. She could also feel the giant bird rise higher and higher into the sky, even beginning to feel cold as the night sky appeared to her. She dared a look down and saw a great round ball of blue with white streaks beneath her.

She couldn't believe it! She was above her own world! She saw her planet as the gods did! It seemed so small and almost comical: a white-veined blue marble amid a sea of blackness, but she could stare at the sight forever. It was something that simply took her breath away. How they could be so high above the world was beyond her understanding. Just as she was filled with a new rigor for the whole scene, the bird plummeted and she felt her head and body go numb, then fell into unconsciousness.

The last words she heard over the roar of the wind were The Master's. They erupted out with such a forceful manner she was beginning to wonder if anything truly made the wizard cringe with fright. He sat in front of her, straddling the bird at its neck as if he rode a simple stallion, his own garments rattling in the gusty assaults.

"Take us to your master." Cadrith's tone was mocking. "I'm sure he will be pleased to see me at last."

Chapter 10

Rowan was asleep but his mind wandered in a dream. For the better part of three weeks he had traveled back from Takta Lu Lama toward Elandor, where he had started his journey for the Knighthood more than two months ago. He'd completed his mission, but had learned and experienced much more than he had expected during the journey. Traveling with Clara, a Patrician woman from a group of mercenaries who shared his quest, they managed to survive the long walk back toward civilization. Without horses, the going had been more of a challenge, but with the help of the Ghin, newfound allies of the knight, they had managed to get enough provisions to see them through.

Wagon traffic on the outskirts of the marshes from nearby villages, various caravans and other migrating groups, allowed them a faster pace by hitching a ride, but the trip still took time. No matter how they made their progress toward Elandor each night Rowan had the same dream.

In it, he was in his armor — without any weapon — in an open green meadow with nothing and no one around for miles. Then, from out of no where, an unseen force grabbed him and struggled with him; pulling him to the ground to jostle about until the knight could finally manage to maneuver himself to see his attacker's face. When he did so, he discovered it was his.

It was always at this point Rowan awakened. Sweaty and belabored of breath, he would sit up and clasp his knees to his chest in a defensive reflex.

In such a position he'd try to make some sense of the dream, but to no avail, it haunted him daily with it's shaded truths and meaning. Even looking to the superstition of divining, the fate of his day from his clothing along the trip did nothing to ease his mind — save give him fair favor in his continued travel. Even his prayers to Panthor on the matter seemed to go unanswered.

And so it was with each following night.

However, in this present dream, Rowan noticed a few things were different. This time he was not alone in the meadow, but a comely woman was with him. Though she kept her face from him, allowing only her cloaked back to be seen, the intuitive logic of dreams told the youth that this was Panthor herself. Her silky black hair fluttered in the gentle breeze, and splashed in its fall over the bunched brown wool hood gathering about her neck.

"It's been a long journey you both have shared," the goddess spoke to him in a way emphasizing both tenderness and authority. "How much longer will you allow yourself to suffer?"

"Panthor?" Rowan dared a step closer.

"These dreams are a reflection of what is happening in your spirit and mind. How much longer will you endure this conflict?" She remained still.

"I don't understand…are you saying that — that I'm in some sort of struggle with myself? That I'm willing — even allowing — a struggle with myself?" Rowan took one more step toward the woman, and then stopped. He didn't want to be too bold in his approach. .

"*Within* yourself," the goddess corrected.

"Ho-" Rowan started.

"What do you recall of the tests you took before your introduction into the Knighthood?" Panthor interrupted the knight.

"The panther attacking me, and the warrior who nearly killed me — or killed me… I wasn't quite sure about that, to be honest…" the knight's mind became clouded with the confusing experience of his initiation.

"Nothing else?" Panthor's voice encouraged him to look deeper.

"Nothing," the youth's face drew more concerned.

In truth, the whole ceremony had caused some unrest in the young knight's mind since he was told there were three tests to pass to be found worthy of the Knighthood. If Rowan counted correctly, he'd only faced two — maybe only one if the panther and warrior was just a two-part test. He thought it was odd, and had buried it in the back of his mind as the excitement of getting accepted — and he was accepted — into the Knighthood, overwhelmed all else.

But the knowledge behind the incident; the fact he didn't really know if he had passed the three tests wore on him now more and more as they journeyed home. Course, this too was shoved aside once and a while when the knight was forced to battle his own thoughts and feelings in regard to the elven company he kept...

"You were found worthy Rowan, have no doubt of that," Panthor seemingly read his mind. "I've chosen you for a purpose. You have a great calling to be worked out, and only you can bring it forth. This will not happen, though, if you continue to battle yourself."

"I don't wish to do anything to displease you, great goddess." Rowan hung his head as the words coming from his lips tore at his throat and tugged on his heart.

He knew now she was talking about his feelings and thoughts of Clara. She knew how he was doing battle in the day with his conscious mind, and in his slumber he was waging war with his subconscious. Again, this came from the eerie clarity of the dream-state; an insight and truth greater than what he could hope to have revealed to him in his waking hours.

"It's just your teachings, the teachings of the Knighthood, hold me to a higher ideal. I'm still weak in trying to stand in the light of your code. If there is any conflict, then it is this: I fight against my old nature to live up to the expectations of what you'd have me be as your knight." Rowan's head remained low as he spoke.

Path of Power

"This battle isn't natural," the woman turned her head slightly, though nothing more of her face was revealed. "You are my champion in light of your truest self, not what men would have you be. Understand this, Rowan; you have faced the tests of introduction and passed. It was not for any great work of your own, but for the potential I saw in you, and your own spirit itself. I have waited for someone like you for a great while. Someone who can come to know my heart on many a matter, and work out the purposes and plans I wish to manifest in the world and to my followers."

"But great goddess, I am unworthy of such a high honor, I have only just now completed my first mission, and am returning to the Knighthood-" again the knight's speech was cut short.

"Do you *think* I am bound in *one* keep?" Panthor's words were soft, but stern. The figure before him had now gone rigid.

"Forgive me, I didn't-" Rowan hung his head lower.

"Do you think I am bound in one keep?" The goddess repeated.

"No Panthor, you are a goddess who has called out humanity as your own, and your dominion is therefore all over Tralodren — and not in one place." Rowan raised his head a bit, and swallowed hard. He didn't understand where this conversation was going, and was a bit fearful he might have done something wrong — maybe even said something insulting to his goddess.

"Then listen to me when I speak to you of your purpose Rowan. For while I didn't create you, I have claimed you as my own. My purposes for you are larger than any knighthood. You delay and frustrate them, however, by this endless strife within yourself. Let go, and be free of it. Let go and embrace the destiny I hold for you." The goddess' words struck the knight hard in the chest.

"You didn't create me? What you say goes against all I've learned." Rowan now was bewildered from what he heard. All of the faithful who called Panthor their goddess knew and were taught she had created them along with all humans...

"Do not dwell upon this mystery, Rowan." A warning hand came from the goddess who still would not face the knight. "Focus on the task at hand."

The knight became drowsy for a moment, his eyes droopy to the point of near collapse before a quick shake of his head brought him around again. All thoughts upon the matter he had been dwelling upon just recently completely forgotten, and a new focusing taking its place.

"But the Knighthood has said you are the Queen of Valkoria, and the Knights of Valkoria are your champions in the world. What they teach and what they honor are you and your edicts. I am trying to let go of my old ways and embrace what you would have us embrace as your will and your code." Rowan dared to look up at the back of his goddess as he pleaded his case.

He still could not see her face.

"Understand this, Rowan. It was not I who rose up the keep in Valkoria, but the hands of mortal men. It was not I who started the Knighthood, but these same mortal men who called upon me. I answered them, for their intentions where pure and good…but now there is coming a change.

"The day is fast approaching when I will raise up my true knights, and they will bring my will to Tralodren for all humanity. None will say there is a knighthood in Valkoria that speaks for one race of humanity, but the coming order will be a grand sight to behold; a new age ushering in the change I have fought to bring about since the beginning of my ascension.

"And you will be the champion of this cause You will lead the first charge — for you are of the same mind and spirit as I, and it pleases me to see my will come to pass through you. None of this will happen though if you still cling to internal division." Panthor then turned around to face Rowan, whose eyes grew wide at what he saw. Before him was not the visage of a goddess, but that of Clara! The elven maid stood before him with a soft expression and gentle eyes. The black hair of the former womanly form was now silver; her alabaster skin tinted a light gray.

Rowan found himself smiling at the vision.

She was a beauty, but also an elf…

A knot in his stomach twisted over itself at her presence, a knot of emotions and dark thoughts; fears and hopes, dreads and hates. Then she smiled back, and in that instant Rowan felt all the feelings, all the thoughts, lift away. He felt himself being introduced to his true inner man for the very first time. It was a wonderful homecoming to a familiar spot with rest and peace as his two allies to comfort him.

"You have to let it go Rowan, and latch on to your true self." Clara lovingly spoke to the young knight, though he knew the words of his goddess were still behind the elf's voice.

Then Rowan awoke.

He didn't curl up into a tight ball this time, as he had when awaking previously from the dream, but lay still in his roughly made bed. His heart still raced, and his breathing was hard, but not as in his previous awakenings.

This was something different — a peaceful awakening that had eluded him for the past few weeks, and he was more than thankful for it.

He shuffled the collection of blankets shoved under his head and back; his own cloak covering him from the slightly chilled breeze blowing down the road where he and Clara had camped underneath a tall oak. They had camped here after they had been dropped off the wagon of some religious pilgrims seeking to worship near Elandor. Since then, they had managed to set up a simple and effective rough camp (some bedrolls and modest blankets) and fell fast to sleep from the long day's journey amid the tangle of vines and roots.

Rowan now turned his head to take in the slumbering elf who was curled a little ways from him; twisting her own frame around the fat oak tendrils and wide trunk of the tree. She looked so peaceful and it added to his own inner tranquility. He learned a lot more about her on their journey back toward Elandor. She even wanted to come back with him to Valkoria to help him on what he felt was his purpose in helping Cadrissa get free from her captor.

She didn't have to, yet she felt obligated to and that caused Rowan to wonder more about this elf. Turning to get comfortable again, he laid his head back and began to stroke the mummified panther paw necklace Panthor had given him. He kept it hidden beneath his undershirt, next to his flesh, throughout their journey since he received it in the ruins of Gondad. He never let it into plain sight if he could help it, for he didn't really know what it would or could mean to others — let alone do in general. He suspected it to be capable of much, wanted to gain greater insight into its functioning,

It was another mystery amid a whole cloud of topics he didn't seem to have the answers to. Not even his goddess seemed willing to help shed the light upon the nature of the amulet...but she had said much tonight though hadn't she? Something he knew he would be pondering for days to come...

He knew there was something in his heart for the elf that was certain enough. He recognized the feeling he'd had toward other maidens that had caught his eye in his younger days. Only this time it was a feeling hedged inside more feelings — anxieties and dark doubt. It was this inner torment he knew his goddess referred to and knew it had to be dealt with as well... in time. He didn't want to face it really, he didn't want to think too deeply about it, but now Panthor had told him to — and that was even more stressful...

He knew the dream had been prophetic; —it told him something of the truth he already knew but the words — the revelations were quite harsh and confusing. Was Panthor telling him the Knighthood was not where he needed to be? Nabu told him the Knighthood might have taught him some things that might not be true to the Panthorian way of faith. Now there was this vision with similar, but farther reaching words…

She'd said the Knighthood was built by mortals, not by her. She had honored it because it followed her and her teachings. But if she hadn't founded it, then who did and why? And if she didn't form the Knighthood, then what was still keeping it in her favor if she seemed to hint her growing displeasure with the Knighthood.

What was going on?

There were too many questions.

He'd had enough questions and struggles for one night, and decided to take advantage of his sudden find, and so closed his eyes.

They would be in Elandor by the following day, and then it was off to the Frost Giant, the vessel from the Northlands, and the journey back home. Big enough tasks to be done, and would in short order — but all of them needed a well-rested body and mind to complete them effectively. Rowan let out a sigh and relaxed his mind. Sleep claimed him once again, and took him till the coming of dawn.

And for the first night since leaving Takta Lu Lama, his rest wasn't troubled.

Chapter 11

A new dawn broke over a distant grassy hill as two priests readied themselves for battle. Their robes were of a parchment shade closely matching bleached bone in hue; tied with a red woolen sash around the waist. Around their necks each wore the silver medallion of their faith, the symbol of Asorlok, the god of the afterlife, death and journeys; two crossed sickles in simple relief. The rest of their garb was nothing more than common leather sandals, and a brown leather backpack each had flung over their shoulders.

Both were Telborians, but of differing countenance. One was shorter and more youthful, with a clean-shaven face. His red hair was cropped close to his head. Soft, youthful, white flesh marked him as not more than twenty years, but his dark brown eyes spoke of a dedication and understanding far beyond his young appearance. His name was Cracius Evans.

Beside Cracius was an older man with dark brown hair with graying temples. His face was covered in stubble, and his skin was tan and rugged, like a woodsman or farmer. He was called Tebow Narlsmith, and looked more like a common man than a priest. However, when he peered about himself, it was formal and aloof, like how those of nobility often viewed their subjects, his green eyes pondering and intelligent.

Both men had served with the order of Asorlok for a while, Cracius since he was ten and Tebow since he had been twenty-eight, some twelve years ago. They belonged to a sect of their faith dedicating itself to the eradication of the undead, and those who would cheat the god of death of his just prizes — namely the spirits of the dead.

The pair had left the confines of the temple to walk in a nearby grass-laden field. They'd brought the needed garb and gear, which Tebow carried in a large brown sack slung over his shoulder and backpack. After walking about three miles from the secret temple, they came to an even more remote location, and then stopped.

It was here Tebow carefully opened the sack. The objects inside were slightly dangerous — even to the priests. They were powerful items of faith, for they had a high cause — a great calling — and the Priests needed such implements to fulfill their duty. The temple hadn't spared any resources when it heeded the command of their god to slay The Master.

"We will have to prepare quickly. He already has a jump on us." Tebow pulled a soft black hooded cloak from the sack and another followed it. The cloaks were the ceremonial garb of the priesthood when it came to enacting a great calling, or performing high rituals of the order. The hunt and destruction of The Master were considered high ceremonies, so the garb was needed at all times while the task of tracking down and eliminating the lich was engaged. He handed one of these garments to Cracius.

"Are you ready for what will be expected of us?" Tebow asked his younger companion as he put on the dark cloak.

"I'm as ready as I can be. I've said the prayers of blessing and protection. Once we are properly dressed, and invite the invocation of Asorlok, we'll be as prepared as any mortal can be." Cracius' manner was matter of fact as he donned his own cloak.

"True," Tebow huffed.

The older priest then proceeded to take out a small, silver chalice sculpted to look like a skull turned upside down minus its lower jaw. It caught the suns rays in a scintillating shower. The chalice was part of a rite necessary should the two priests hope to be successful in their mission.

"I'll start the ceremony then." Cracius took the chalice and walked a short distance away into the empty field as a gentle breeze gathered the grass around him, swaying in its grip. When he'd arrived at the destination, he placed the chalice on the ground before him. The priest first whispered a soft incantation to his deity, which soon increased in volume. As he did so Tebow unpacked the rest of the sack. All that remained inside were a collection of fresh rations for their journey and two great silver hammers, the head of each was made up of an elongated skull. The hammerheads were half a forearm in length and as wide as two fists placed side by side. Each hammer also seemed to be somehow eerily sentient, like it might open its bony mouth in a scream or gaping yawn, at any moment.

Money had also been provided by the temple, as had a slight packing of provisions such as traveling clothes, maps, torches and similar fare that would help the adventuring clergy in their trek. All this was already carried on their own person tucked way in simple belt pouches and backpacks. They had prepared physically and mentally and now had only to ready themselves spiritually for the task.

"Oh Lord Asorlok, god of the outer world, and gate keeper to the realms beyond. Hear my prayer." Tebow spoke with stern lips and clenched eyes as he lifted his hands toward heaven.

Cracius quickly walked to the elder priest's side.

"Open the door between us oh Lord of Death. Make the path clear so that we can find the one who has trespassed upon your greatest command and sought to cheat you of your spoils, he who has cheated death." Cracius continued in prayer.

Tebow then bent down during the incantation and lifted up the chalice to the clear lapis sky above him.

"Come Asorlok. Fill your chalice with your favor so that we might be sustained and blessed with your will long enough to complete the task which you have called us to undertake." Tebow shouted as his head tilted skyward.

Together the priests waited for their god to act. The time dissipated quickly. Tebow felt a cold chill cover his hands like frost creeping up and over his flesh, and then knew that the chalice had been filled with the elixir of his god's will. "He has filled it with his will." The older priest lowered the chalice to his face and peered inside.

The silvery skin of the chalice held back a seething brew of red slime that clawed and clamored with protoplasmic tendrils for release from its prison. Upon the gaze of Tebow it grew more excited and seemed to actively press out to try and reach the priest, appearing to almost scream out in frustration when its efforts were thwarted — wishing to connect with the living flesh more than anything in the world.

"Thank you my god." Tebow turned to Cracius. "You know what to do then?"

"I do." The younger priest had opened his eyes to face Tebow.

"Then let it commence. Into your will and spirit I walk Asorlok." Tebow bowed his head before the chalice then took a drink from its churning contents. Red ichor stained his lips, dripping down the corners of his mouth for but a brief moment before the liquid scampered between the priests lips all of its own accord. Tebow handed the chalice to Cracius.

"Into your will and spirit I walk Asorlok." Cracius bowed also then supped.

Both then fell to the field in convulsions. The wracking of their bodies seemed to be endless. Bone and muscle fiber twitched and pulled against itself as nerves and even skin stretched and fluctuated in shape and color. In mere moments their skin was flooded with a jet-black hue and their images — their very faces were lost in a shimmering inky pool of darkness. Only the vague outline of a humanoid form survived to tell what the priests' frames had once resembled.

As rapidly as these effects had occurred, however, they left the two priests. Together both rose up from the field with a stiff burst. As soon as they did so, the ink-like gel drained away from their bodies and into their invisible spirits so that they appeared normal once more. Each looked at the other in silent affirmation. They knew then that they had the full blessing and power of their god and for the time being, as long as the quest was being waged, then they would have access to a brief taste of some of his powers as well. By the divine will of their god, they had become more than simple priests, they had become his champions on the mortal realm, Champions with a divine mission.

"Let it begin then." Tebow spoke in a dry and even tone.

He raised his hand before him and an old wooden door appeared before them. It had the look of antiquity upon it and stood defiantly amidst the short grasses around it — totally independent of any supporting structure, surreal, as it was old.

"Are you clear on what has to be done then?" The older priest turned to Cracius.

"Yes. We will walk through the doors of Asorlok and take the lich unaware. His death will finally be achieved." Cracius smiled.

"Take up the chalice. Asorlok has told me by his spirit that we are to use it in the final rites of the lich's death."

Tebow stooped to pick up the chalice and placed it into his own backpack, which he had swung over his black robe. "Here." Cracius handed Tebow his weapon. The hammer shined and glowed for a brief moment when the older priest took it up, then fell silent once more.

"Let's go." Cracius walked toward the door and then into nothing.

Tebow smiled with grim delight and did the same.

The door then closed and disappeared behind them.

Just as suddenly as the door had appeared in the grassy field, so too did it spring up on the island of The Master, just outside his tower. There it opened and out of it walked Tebow and Cracius. Both had their great hammers raised at the ready expecting to meet with opposition as soon as they crossed thorough the mystical gate.

They found none.

All about them was the silent green beauty of The Master's island lair. Both took in the fare in silence. Neither knew what to expect or how to act in light of the event. The place seemed a juxtaposition of images, which they hadn't been expecting. More importantly, something seemed off...something seemed to be missing... Where was The Master?

"So The Master is *here*?" Cracius searched the dark tower before them with studious eyes. The land smelled and felt as if it has just recently endured a great storm — flowers recently shaken by storm wafting their fragrance heavenward though now the bright sun was coming out and a warmer breeze was draining away the cool damp air.

"No. I don't sense him here anymore. He is elsewhere now; somewhere east of here, very far away. I'm not certain where though. He's using his magic to block any attempt at directly locating him." Tebow stared off into the east, the crow's feet on his cheeks digging deeper into his flesh.

"Maybe there is something in his tower that we can use. Some kind of enchanted trinket or map that would tell us where he went..." Cracius began to move toward the imposing spire of The Master's tower but was stopped by Tebow's strong hand.

"No. There's very little time and that tower holds more evil and deadly traps than what we could hope to deal with by ourselves, even with the anointing of our god's presence upon us. We have to be wise in this endeavor and seek him out before he seeks out the ultimate of blasphemies and tries to claim godhood."

"A very good idea indeed." A small, high pitched voiced came out of nowhere.

"Who's there?" Cracius spun around with his sliver hammer gleaming in protective fury.

"Don't harm me." The voice returned. "I'm but the messenger."

"Where is it coming from?" The younger priest spun his head in a myriad of directions.

"I don't know but it sounds like it's getting closer." Tebow joined the younger priest's efforts.

"You say you are a messenger then, huh? Then for whom do you speak?" Cracius stopped his searching when a small-multicolored bird suddenly landed on his shoulder. The bird was at least a foot tall and about half that in width, with a large rainbow plumed head, sharp beak, and more bright plumage which made it look more like an artist had spilled paint on the animal's feathers rather than arriving at them through natural means.

"A tropical bird? *Here*?" Tebow stared at the animal.

"I travel far for my lord." The bird ruffled its feathers.

"Who is your lord, I ask again?" Tebow took in the strange bird with wary eye.

"I speak for the Lord of the Four Winds, Endarien the Mighty."

"He lies. A trick of The Master." Cracius raised his hammer.

"No. He speaks the truth." Tebow raised his hand in defense of the exotic creature. "By Asorlok's presence I can sense the validity of his statements. Rest easy for a moment and you will too."

"What does Endarien want with us? We aren't his priests or followers." Tebow continued.

"He wishes to aid your quest. Anyone who shares his hatred of The Master is his ally in this matter. He wishes you well and blesses your efforts."

"Endarien wants to *bless* us?" Tebow ruffled his brow at the statement. He'd never heard of any god on Tralodren looking to bless another god's followers. Indeed, the thought would have been thought suspect if the spirit of his god, which now dwelled within him, hadn't urged him to accept it as truth.

"So what would Endarien have us do then?" Cracius looked at the motley bird, he felt the urging of Asorlok inside him now too.

"I am here to guide you to others that will help in your quest to defeat The Master. You're not powerful enough to do it alone," the bird answered.

"We are anointed by the great god Asorlok himself! We cannot fail!" Cracius curled his lips in a rough line. "How dare you accuse our god of being weak-"

"Not your god, his *vessels*." The bird chirped.

"Watch your words bird!" Cracius' hammer rose with his anger.

The brightly decorated avian flew off the younger priest's shoulder to land over on Tebow's instead. "We are all weak against The Master, even the limited form that my lord can create in order to confront the lich. He knows it, but is moving to do the best he can to stop him or even kill him if fortune smiles upon him.

"In the most realistic assessment though, he knows he will probably fail and that you will need help in defeating the lich and weakening him enough to take him to the lair of Asorlok. Thus I am here." The bird puffed his chest and spread his wings triumphantly. The action swiped bright feathers into Tebow's face, which he rebutted with a cough. "I will help you get the others who have returned him to the world and have fought him once before. With all of us allied to so common a cause, The Master's defeat would be assured."

"Others?" The older priest asked.

"Yes, there were others that brought The Master back to Tralodren."

"We know that already, but why do we need them?"

"I was told to get them all together, that's all. All of you gathered together in one group. Somehow it's important to stopping The Master." the bird continued to creak out its strangely Telborous speech.

"Didn't think we'd be enough huh?" Cracius' sardonic smile lined his face.

"I don't know" the bird squawked, "I'm just obeying my god's orders."

"More like helping to hedge a bet. So what's in it for Endarien?" Tebow raised his eyebrow.

"Revenge, and the joy of knowing that he has seen a hated foe fall into oblivion where he belongs." The bird chattered.

"Nothing more then?" asked Tebow.

"Nothing more." The bird echoed.

Tebow thought for a moment and then smiled. Asorlok certainly had opened up some doors to the priest. It would seem that The Master had made more enemies for himself than allies, and that was always a bad ratio with which to work out existence.

"We must confer with the spirit of our god first to see what seems right to him." Tebow returned.

"Fine by me." The bird looked him in the eye then turned toward Cracius as it changed its footing on Tebow's shoulder.

Both priests then closed their eyes. Each tapped into the spirit of Asorlok seeking guidance for this task, searching for his answer. After a brief pondering, each felt the will of Asorlok allow him and urge him to accept the bird's claims and join up with him. When each opened their eyes, a single glance at the other told them about their similar confirmation.

"Sounds like a fair wager bird, that is, if Tebow agrees to it." Cracius' smile deepened.

"I do. I feel it is a good omen and even better opportunity." Tebow peered deep into the bird's small eyes. "Though I can't say I understand the workings of this agreement."

"Gods are hard to figure out, that's for sure." The bird chirped.

"I'm curious though as to how you found us." Tebow asked.

"My lord is the king of the sky, there is little that he does not see from his lofty perch. He was aware of your plans and it gladdened his heart to send one of the Lords of Air to me to rely his concerns. So I came here." The bird explained his tale.

"I see." Tebow reposed.

"We should be going though if we wish to stop the lich." Said Cracius.

"I agree." the bird twisted its head in a sideways manner as it took in the older priest. "You ready?"

"I was ready before I came here." Tebow looked the bird in the beak and dark eyes.

"Then lets get this done and over with then." The colorful bird stated.

Chapter 12

Sunlight had ridden across the sky and with it came the outskirts of Elandor rising into view along the dusty, gravel strewn road leading into the port city. Both Rowan and Clara had reached the city walls by early morning with a ragtag assortment of others: religious pilgrims, traders and even a few shabbily garbed beggars. All made their progress toward the tall iron shod, wooden doors of the large entrance gate.

Rowan recalled when he had first seen Elandor. It hadn't been that long ago but now felt like years had passed since then. He had learned a lot since then. The young boy from the Northlands had indeed begun to grow up and learn about the ways of the lands south of his home. Now he was returning full circle, and he was looking forward to getting back home and seeing his family once more.

A hopeful prayer had seen him off at first light when he and Clara had risen to start their trek toward the outer walls. A prayer that the young knight believed would be answered in full: safe journey and a happy return. Having not been able to divine his future from his clothing—since he didn't disrobe in his wilderness slumber, he only had the faith in his prayer to undergird his hope.

At the outskirts of the doors stood two studious and stout guardsmen, the common rank and file protectorates and police of Elandor, which was also the capital of the kingdom that shared the same name. These dark haired Telborians took in the throng of folk, keeping a tight hand on their pole arms and looking stern in their banded mail armor. If anyone met their disfavor they'd end up barred from entering the city. So far none had been, but the day was still young.

Rowan and Clara passed their glare and moved inside. One of the older guards took a keen interest in the knight's dragon emblazed shield, which he had slung over his back, but let the interest go as the Nordican walked by. They also noticed the sheathed swords at Rowan's and Clara's side, but deemed them safe for they saw the emblem of the Knights of Valkoria on Rowan's armor and Elandor knew of the knights' nature. In principle they were no threat and so passed by unhindered. There were always exceptions to the given standard, they knew, but in truth they were a bit too lazy this morning to want to do much of anything regarding the two travelers.

Elandor was starting to come to life already. Most of that activity was on the docks where Clara and Rowan were going. A handful of alert guards on the other side of the doors paid them a moment's attention and then they two let them go so knight and elf were in the midst of the streets and corridors of the city. In a rather single minded pursuit the two travelers made a straight path toward their destination. Each had little money left to do much more than to take the free passage to Valkoria.

The wet air of the dock trailed over Rowan's skin as he spied the Frost Giant, the vessel that had carried him down from the Northlands almost two months ago and had rested in harbor while it emptied its hold with trade, repaired damage to its hull suffered from a linnorm encounter on route south, and waited for the Knight of Valkoria to join them on their journey back to Valkoria.

The air had the tang of autumn mixed in the salted scent and was cooler than when he'd seen the vessel last and knew that winter would be coming to the Midlands soon enough. He tossed back his head and let the cool waves of air flow through his auburn hair and across his neck. It felt good to be nearing the end of his journey. The youth's usually soft white skin had been tanned and burned by the sun on his recent journey from the jungles of Takta Lu Lama and his return trek to Elandor. Clara though was as radiant as ever.

Her face seemed to have developed more beauty with each passing day. She traveled with Rowan in a more dignified manner now than when the two had first met. Since Rowan's and Clara's awkward beginning on their journey, no other emotions had erupted between them on the surface. An uneasy tension played across their hearts and minds, only getting more taunt when further uncertain situations would develop such as their quiet wilderness camps in the past weeks as they made their way to Elandor.

With nothing but the wilderness, each other, and the fire, they fought off the inner feelings that grew within them with each passing day. Though each knew that Clara's simple kiss, given outside the ruins, spoke of their true feelings, they fought with their own inner demons to come to terms with the reality at hand.

Rowan was battling his old feelings again. The quiet evening rest had left him with the dawn. He told himself that it was the love of the exotic, the different tastes of the world that he now experienced that were calling to him, nothing more. He'd even believed his deduction for a while, but the more he spoke with Clara he found they shared some similar ideas and thoughts, and in fact, despite his inner voices concerns, had managed to form a budding friendship as well. These ponderings mixed with the memories of Panthor's words hung heavy over his head and heart.

As Clara grew more common to the youth, the exotic nature of her initial presence began to fade to familiarity. It was here that he then battled with the thoughts of her true intentions. What was she after? Her mission had been completed and now she left to follow him to his homeland and then off to look for Cadrissa who'd been taken captive by an unknown assailant. Something didn't seem right about that though to the knight. What was in it for her? Why would an elf care to save a human woman in distress?

As Rowan walked the razor's edge of such conflicts in his soul, Clara spoke to her own inward critics and warnings about the youth. She first hadn't noticed much of the youth, but as they journeyed in their previous adventure, she had taken a liking to him more like a mother to a naive son. In terms of years lived, Clara could be the young Nordican's grandmother. Elves lived often as much as three entire human life spans. Her maternal instincts though grew deeper and move confused as she took stock of the knight's finer traits. They were raw, but time would define them into a great work, making a superb vessel of manhood. He had great potential to do a good many things.

Clara, like many elves, looked to the long-term result of things rather than the immediate like most humans and other shorter lived races. She had to constantly keep captive her actions and thoughts to keep the Nordican as a friend and also to keep herself from leading him on in any way to a certain chain of thoughts that wouldn't distort her true feelings for Rowan. Clara drew much of her strength and comfort for this effort from an old elven proverb which said 'Men war with swords, woman with words; men with the head, woman the heart.' It was very true indeed and didn't seem like she would be getting any relief from this warfare anytime soon. Still though, it helped to give her focus for she knew that Rowan combated similar feelings of his own. She could see it in his eyes and hear the clash of feeling and ideas behind his words. If this wasn't dealt with soon she knew there would be some increased friction between them.

Regardless of this situation, Clara felt obligated to bring back Cadrissa. She didn't feel right about leaving someone behind in a mission like the one she had just completed, especially to be at the mercies of such a creature who took her.

Rowan too was compelled to join the hunt to retrieve her. He said he knew of a wizard in the Northlands that might be able to help them. With little other to go on for aid or information at the time, Clara agreed to accompany the youth to his homeland to look for the mage. If she was going to get anywhere on this mission she'd have to take up the role of leader again. Rowan was still too naive and young to do what needed to be done when it came to leadership. She'd have to step up to the task to get this mission completed and at least make a diligent, purposeful effort to find the abducted mage. For the moment though, she enjoyed the aging day.

Her thoughts brought her back to all the activity she had experienced here in Elandor not that long ago. Here is was that she and Gilban had fought off a group of pirates, and assembled a mercenary band to keep some lost information from getting into Elyelmic hands. Here it was too she had first met Rowan — saw him as this young knight who seemed a bit lost but who now had grown into such a promising young man she thought.

These memories also caused her to think on what Gilban had told her as well when they had started out on their journey with the others and what it meant now. He told her she had a road before her that she could not help to travel down though she had been forewarned of it. What did that mean anyway? Was this the road then, this helping free Cadrissa? She didn't recall being forewarned of it. She chewed this over in her mind as she also wondered about Gilban's fate.

She could see him back in Rexatious milling about the temple and informing his peers and the Elucidator about the results of the recent mission. She knew that was what he was doing too. She hoped she'd be able to join him soon. Clara had discovered over the past few weeks that she missed her homeland a great deal. The longer she was from it the more she realized this deeper truth.

There was nothing like Rexatious in all the world and being so far to the other end of Tralodren just further confirmed how alien this side of the planet was to her. It was the world of the eastern lands and primarily the domain of Telborians and Elyellium. The lands of the West were the domains of the gnomes and Patrious and Napowese. A very different reality altogether, but one she was eager to return to as soon as she was able.

"There it is." Clara pointed to the boat on the sparse dock. The Frost Giant was an older caravel with two masts that flew deep blue sails, striped vertically in a shade of brownish-red that resembled dried blood. Seeing the ship again brought back another good handful of strong memories, but they were no match for the ones he had recently made.

"Yeah. I'm kinda sad that we're already here." Rowan stretched a crooked smiled across his lips. "I was enjoying the companionship."

"Well, we're here now, so we best be on our way before the weather turns worse" Clara replied in a dry tone.

It was time to lead.

They walked toward the great wooden vessel with steady steps. It was moored to a stout worn wooden post and was joined by a few other spattering of ships that were stocking up with a few more supplies before they traveled down south to winter in warmer lands.

Looking toward the gangplank, Rowan sighed, and then proceeded up the wooden ramp. He had an uneasiness about him as he did so, but put it out of his mind as he climbed the plank. Clara was fast at his heels. As he neared the deck of the boat, he began to spy a few Nordic sailors — rough and ready men, looking behind him with shadowed, disapproving faces. He recognized some from his previous voyage, but a few other faces escaped him. He assumed the new sailors joined the crew on a trip back to the Northlands after the winter seas had run the worst of their course.

The familiar fat captain greeted him and escorted him on board as he neared the top of the plank. It actually seemed that the obese man had gained even more weight in Rowan's absence. His face turned sour and dry though when he spied Clara.

"Glad to have you back lad. We thought something awful had happened to you and were getting ready to head out after the repairs were finished up.

"What do you think you're doing though?" The captain switched his conversation to Telborous, presumably for the benefit of Clara, with this question.

"I don't understand." Rowan responded in the same tongue. "I'm coming back on board and we're all going back home,"

"With her?" The fat man grimaced and pointed toward the elven maiden, his eyes resting a little longer on her sheathed sword before he returned his gaze to Rowan.

"Yes, with her. This is Clara Airdes-" Rowan turned to introduce the elf.

"I don't care who it is. She can't ride on my vessel." The captain broke up the formal introduction.

"What are you talking about? I'm a Knight of Valkoria; I have need to return to my order to relay the information I was sent to collect. This woman is important to that mission. She will be needed to speak to the knights as well." Rowan's eyes grew cold and dark as his gaze penetrated into the rotund man in front of him. He had no idea why the captain would be rude to a lady, especially one who traveled with a knight. The harsh words had struck some truth with the young knight though. As rough and raw as they were, he had a small spark of his inner being that agree with the captain. She was an elf, a frail and malicious thing after all she…no, no, no what was he thinking?

"She's an elf, we don't like their kind in the lands of the Nordicans. You of all people should understand that. Gods, it was the very Knights of Valkoria themselves that stopped an elven invasion at the end of the Shadow Years and have kept us safe from their new planned invasions ever since."

"Invasions?" Rowan was confused.

It was not I who started the Knighthood but these same mortal men who called upon me… Panthor's words came back to the young knight.

Clara rested her hand upon the young knight. "Calm down Rowan. He's referring to a time with the Elyellium during the Imperial Wars, a long time ago. Naturally, many people who aren't elves think that I'm Elyelmic. Rowan… I don't want to cause any trouble here.

"I can just get other transport to meet up with you there." Her words were soft and deeply touched the knight.

"No. There's no time and meeting you once you arrived there would be harder still. We'll have to travel together." Rowan returned; a newfound resolve coming over him.

"If he won't allow us on board, and we have to stay together, then there must be another way to get to your homeland." Clara tried her best to ease herself a step or two away from the captain, trying to take the knight with her. This situation needed to be defused before it flared up into a worse encounter still.

"No there isn't." Rowan continued to glare at the captain; "No boat travels that far north during the winter months. This is our only way to Valkoria."

"There has got to be another way." Clara whispered to her young companion. "We'll find it." The calm she was urging didn't see to take on her young companion.

"We *have* found it. *It's* here. *We're* here." Rowan coldly addressed the captain in as much a civilized manner as he could muster, drawing upon his training for a guide though his Nordic blood called out in more brutal terms.

"Let us on or you will suffer the disfavor of the Knighthood."

"No. The elf stays here. You can come aboard. I have no quarrel with you or the Knighthood of Panthor, but no elf rides my boat. Never have and they never will." The captain crossed the two flabby logs that served as his arms above his copious stomach.

Rowan's Nordic blood howled in fury. The rage he felt came deep from his family, his kinsmen who are fierce warriors and maniacal in their battles to the point of beserkers. That was one of the traits of his tribe: The Panther Tribe, one of a handful who called Valkoria home.

He wanted to kill the captain where he stood. Every muscle ached to do so, but he'd learned, and had begun to master, temperance from the Knighthood and had gained a great deal of mastery over his emotions.

"You do me a great wrong captain." Rowan spoke through clenched teeth. "We have to board this vessel and return home. Please be so kind as to let us pass, and Panthor will favor you."

The captain didn't move. He stood like a tall, fleshly oak, rooted to the lip of the gangplank. "Panthor already favors me, I'm a human," the rotund man chuckled.

The discourse between the captain and Rowan had begun to draw the attention of more of the crew. Slowly, they stopped what they were doing or worked their way to the scene, not wanting to miss a single word.

Like their captain, they sneered when they caught sight of Rowan's companion. A fairer sex nonetheless, she wasn't of human blood, and so they didn't trust her. Her kind were greedy, warlike, and liars. Backstabbers; they would cut your throat as they smiled… Or so the tales were told and had been told since the first elves of Elyelmic stock landed on the Valkorian Islands many thousands of years ago to expand the empire of Colloni.

"You're a human…" Rowan growled beneath his breath.

"Rowan, let's go; there has to be another way home," Clara tugged at his sword arm. The appendage was tough and stiff, his hand locked around the pommel.

"It would seem we have no choice," Rowan's eyes never left the captain's. "Panthor will get us home another way."

Rowan backed down from the boat's moorings. Clara followed beside him. The youth hid his face from her eyes. It was clenched in anger and fear. He hadn't wanted this trouble, this turmoil. He wanted everything to be peaceful, fun and easy, full of life and joy-like, it had been on his trip from Takta Lu Lama. He didn't want to suffer defeat from such a trivial matter as boarding a boat — especially from his own people.

You are a man now Rowan. The voice of his father echoed in his head again. If this was what it meant to be a man, then he began to understand while few men smiled. Life must be tough indeed to throw such obstacles his way. He could have left Clara behind he supposed, meet up with her later when his report was done. However, there wasn't any guarantee he'd see her again and that thought was worse than anything he'd been feeling.

Damn emotions.

Damn duty.

Damn life.

"Rowan," Clara softly spoke beside him. "There will be another way. Don't give up hope."

His heart was happy to hear her say those words and the warm sensation they provided spread throughout his body. He didn't know why, but when she said them, even though he doubted to some degree their validity, they seemed to carry the weight of truth about them.

"It'll be worth the wait," he turned to smile at her, "I'll get to know you that much better." He found himself putting a more optimistic spin on the situation. A spin thickened with the warm sap of uncontrolled emotions.

Clara smiled.

Both sat at the docks for hours and watched the sun climb to its zenith, then slide down its slope of diminished gleam. The fading light made Clara's silver locks explode like molten metal. Beside her Rowan was silent. He had watched the Frost Giant moor off after they performed a minor offering to Perlosa, dropping a gold coin into the waves, then dwindle away from sight. The captain, confused by the knight's actions, saw now more reason to wait to return to Valkoria if Rowan wasn't boarding the vessel with his elven maid, and so set sail a few hours after the confrontation.

As he witnessed the boat fade away, Rowan felt the body of Clara beside him, where she had joined him on a rustic, sea-pitted wooden bench a fair distance from the docks, which overlooked the waves. The knight had unslung his circular shield so it rested beside his feet. It helped to release some of the weight on his shoulder, but not all of it.

"Well, I guess I'm stranded here now," Rowan was quiet.

"Don't worry. We'll find a way. It's just a matter of time," Clara assured him yet again with a soft smile, though she too didn't know how they'd know how they'd get to Valkoria.

"How? "Rowan sunk his head. "I've failed already on my first mission. What kind of knight am I."

"A very *human* knight," Clara rose from the bench.

"I suppose *elven* knights are better then?" The young Nordican raised his head toward the elven maid in a childish frustration.

"Not by much, if any. You're still young, you need time to grow into yourself — find your cause and true purpose in life, and then you'll be the best knight this world has ever seen."

Rowan smirked.

"What is it?" Clara mirrored the young knight's grin.

"Are all elves as optimistic as you?" Rowan's dark blue eyes found her purple orbs.

"Just the ones who can see your potential and have faith in its full development over time," Clara's smile widened.

"I don't think your faith is well placed, Clara." A crestfallen tone had crept into Rowan's throat.

The elf placed her hand gently on Rowan's shoulder. "I just think you have to find that faith in yourself others have about you. You should give yourself more credit."

Clara got up and left him then to think things over. She retreated to the docks to watch the waves lap, and the seagulls play and scatter across the sky. In truth, she needed time to think as well — to form a strategy of some kind. This leadership mantle was a heavy one at times, and she had yet to grow accustomed to its weight.

Rowan sat and pondered everything that had come to him in the past twenty-four hours. The dream, the revelation of his change of mindset when compared to his kinsmen and of course, the situation with Clara. He couldn't seem to escape it…as if he was fated to be tied down with it all.

Thinking of fate made him recall Gilban. The old elven priest was something hard to forget. A priest who had dedicated himself to fate itself. Maybe this was all fated — maybe none had any free will to declare their own destiny. Many Nordicans thought as Rowan. Many held to fate, generational fate and its obligations and curses and nature. The Knighthood, though, had shown him such thoughts were incorrect, and destiny was a free willed choice, but Rowan was finding this wasn't true in all cases…

He placed his hand over his chest so it rested over the amulet buried beneath his armor and clothing. Beside his heart he felt it's dried surface, and drew himself deeper into his thoughts, praying for a miracle to come his way. For he certainly needed a miracle if he was to get home at all.

A slight breeze ruffled his hair as he thought and silently prayed. As he continued to gape at Clara's beauty, he let the petty gale rustle over him on its way toward other parts of the world. Rowan shook his head to clear his thoughts at what had just happened, trying to make sense of it all when his thoughts ceased at the falling of a shadow over his person. The knight looked up once more and noticed a lone figure standing before him with a congenial grin; soft greenish-blue eyes dancing off the stark contrast of a three-day-old beard smothering his face like melted snow.

"And why are you so crestfallen on such a lovely day?" The man spoke Telborous in a gentle voice. He was no more than forty or so winters old, with a short cropped head of white hair wrapped in a blue cloth band the color of the sky. His garb was like that of a sailor, with billowing green pantaloons and a loose fitting parchment shaded shirt. On his right shoulder a single seagull rested. Its gray-white head cocked to observe Clara who was still oblivious to this whole encounter thus far and stood behind the man; still watching the shrinking sun dance on the water.

"You seem to be a far way from home," the Telborian continued. "Aren't you a Nordican?"

"Yes, and it seems like I might be here a little while longer than I wish to be," Rowan gloomily gave answer.

"So you are stranded here then, eh?" the sailor's eyes squinted a bit.

"So it would seem?" Rowan returned with mild interest.

"Are you a knight?" the sailor raised a white eyebrow.

Rowan looked him in his eye at this question. "I'm a Knight of Valkoria."

"A Knight of Valkoria…" The sailor mused as he rubbed his stubbled chin with his right hand. "No stranger to the seas then…" He continued to rub his chin for a little while longer, and then stopped but looked straight into the Knight's eyes.

"I'm going to Arid Land. I plan to get some business there straightened out and return to Talatheal before the winter really grabs the land by the throat," said the stranger.

"If you are able to hold your own on my vessel I would be willing to take you aboard."

"You're going to Arid Land?" Rowan's countenance flooded with hope. That would get him just a little under one month away from Valkoria if the weather held. He could at least find some small boat there; some raiders he could ride with to get him back to Valkoria.

"It's a small kindness I can afford you. You seem like a good enough man," the man's face exploded into a field of wrinkles as his countenance brightened. "And I like to try help out folks when I can. 'You tend to get back what you give out', so the saying goes."

"If you'd have me then, yes," Rowan bolted from his seat, "I'd be very welcome to the offer.

"But can you get to Arid Land in one month? I've never heard of a trip that short in this season."

"The Storm Lord has been good to me this year, and these shifting winds that come during this season seem to favor my vessel as well." The seagull on the Telborian's shoulder turned to peer at Rowan; cocking his head sideways as it did so.

"You're an answer to prayer," the knight smiled with a soft laughter. "When do you leave?" Rowan looked beyond the man toward Clara.

"Well, I can't speak for answers to prayers, but we should be off very shortly. I'm just going to the boat now to get a few last things in order and then I'm off." It was the man's turn to briefly look at the seagull. The two seemed to exchange some hidden type of understanding before he turned to the knight once more.

"What's your name sir?" Rowan stepped in close.

"I'm Brandon Dosone."

"Pleased to meet you Brandon, I'm Rowan Cortak, knight of the great goddess Panthor." He extended his hand for Brandon to shake. "My traveling companion is Clara, that elven maid over there. Does your offer allow room for one more?"

"Certainly," Brandon shook Rowan's hand with a tight grip.

"You don't have a problem with her being an elf do you?" Rowan peered into Brandon's face as their hands parted. He was looking for any echo of the attitude, which his fellow kinsman had recently displayed.

"Her?" Brandon jabbed a thumb over his shoulder. "None whatsoever. She's a beautiful woman, lad."

"I know." The knight was satisfied Brandon harbored none of the traits for which he had been searching.

"I gathered as much," Brandon grinned.

"Clara, I think we've found a way to Valkoria," Rowan shouted to the elf.

"So soon? That's a nice coincidence then," she walked back to the two men.

"It seems Panthor is very favorable to us today," Rowan's enthusiasm was hard to contain.

"So it would seem," Brandon chuckled.

"Where is your vessel, though. I thought all the boats had sailed for the day. I didn't see any more on the docks —" Rowan started.

"I'm docked a little ways further up, away from your line of sight." Brandon smiled. "If you're all ready, you can follow me to the boat, and then we'll be on route to Arid Land."

Clara joined the knight behind Brandon as they followed him to his craft. "Seems you might be better at this then you once thought, eh?" She poked her elbow into his rib.

"It's the will of Panthor, not me," Rowan smiled back at her playful attitude and actions. "I simply prayed for a miracle, and she answered."

"I doubt many folks could get such a quick response," Clara turned back to paying attention to the walkway before her.

Rowan did the same.

About an hour later Brandon, Clara, and Rowan were in a smaller boat, not unlike the caravel Clara had used to get the group together to Elandor, or the Frost Giant itself. The vessel was plain enough. No decoration adorned its sides; no evil eyes painted on the sea-soaked wood to ward off foul spirits the boat might come across. No insignia or marker of any manner showed claimed ownership of the vessel. It was as if it belonged to none, or so it seemed to the elf. The boat didn't even have a name. It was a silent form entirely; as quiet as the breeze blowing across the Yoan Ocean, over which they would soon travel.

Instead, it had a simple blue mast, the color of the sky above them and was manned by a skeleton crew, all of them Telborian males of around the late to early twenties. They didn't talk to the new passengers, themselves, or even their captain. It was a very quiet, and slightly surreal setting.

"So you're all set then?" Brandon played with a few ropes along the riggings as he looked over his new passengers.

"Yes. We have all we need," Rowan spirits had lifted considerly as both he and Clara looked off the bow. The knight's trunk, which he'd left in the inn for safekeeping when he first landed in Elandor, had been placed below with the other cargo. Clara traveled very light, having lost a good deal in the hurried flight from the Lizardmen in the marshes. What she carried now was on her person.

"So you must be in a great hurry then to get to Valkoria. It's almost impossible to get there now you know with the weather and all. You have pressing business on the islands then?" Brandon finished with the riggings and turned to look his two new crew-mates square in the eye. They merely nodded silently, and then moved on to another task on the vessel.

"It is very pressing," Rowan started, " We are to report to the Knights of Valkoria immediately. They have need of some information we have procured from our most recent journey."

"Ah, I see," Brandon lifted his head toward the top mast when he heard the cry of a seagull — the same bird that had stood on his shoulder, now perched as a lone vigil amid the riggings of the topmast above them. Brandon smiled faintly at it before he returned to the two travelers.

"So when are you leaving then?" Clara asked.

A soft wind began to tickle the sails.

"How does now strike you?" Brandon moved toward the wheel.

"Just fine," she returned with a grin.

"Heave lads! We best take this spurt and use it to our advantage!" Brandon bellowed toward his crew.

The silent hands respond rapidly. They were like a swarm of hornets as they spun about the boat, letting loose the sails that swallowed the winds with a ravenous gulp. Then, the boat was off at a great, almost supernatural, speed across the harbor. It glided into the open waters, seemingly alive as it churned the waves before its prow like a farmer and his plow in the field.

"We'll be to Valkoria before we know it," Rowan's chest had puffed up as he turned to look at Clara. In that moment he felt victorious over all that had so recently plagued him. It was as if he was a new man embracing a new world.

"And then Cadrissa," Clara added.

Chapter 13

It was a carnival of sorts…well a small gathering of entertainers at best. They were the only bards bold enough to enter into the Tempter's District of Haven to garner some coin after dark. They had set up and performed for more than an hour. Managing to gather a small crowd about them off Tempter's Way, which was the main street through the area, which snaked its path along the worn plaster, faced, wooden buildings, and aged brick structures, they seemed to be doing rather well in collecting some coin.

The street was so named for it was by far the worst area in the entire city of Haven. In the city of Haven, that was saying much. The great city, perhaps the largest multicultural population center on all of Tralodren, was famed as the most crime-ridden and corrupt in the entire world. Behind its walls and more pleasant avenues, lurked dim and deadly characters that looked to cause discomfort to whatever met their eye. Brothels and gambling halls lined whole blocks behind temples and government houses like sickly shadows. It was the other side of the coin of civilization. Like most cities, Haven was built outward, as an expanding puddle, having the oldest sections in the center, and the newest ones outside to lure in folk to their treasures, as a spider lures it's prey into it's web.

The oldest part was also called the Tempter's District, for all the temptations that could assail anyone who simply walked through it. Tempter's Way was the only main through street bisecting the run-down district. The rest of the offshoot tributaries were nothing more than alleyways, littered with refuse and other things best kept to the shadows. Those of more "civilized blood" (usually those with money or station — or both) who were forced to travel through the area, never did so at night, and if they were pressed at daylight, did so by rapid coach; never leaving themselves vulnerable to the dangerous foot travelers of the dismal domain.

These bards, though, had been bold — and that boldness was paying off. From what they could see from the tin cups at their feet, they would have enough coin to survive another day, if not a few more beyond that. The four bards each enacted some special feat for the enjoyment of the crowd of some twenty onlookers.

One of them performed with lit torches, eating the flames only to spit them out once more in fiery bursts. Another juggled four-colored balls about while moving back and forth. Still another conducted acrobatic maneuvers, such as currently standing on his head and walking about on his hands instead of his feet. The last of their company piped a merry tune; a drunken ballad often heard in many of the taverns and inns in the district and which the occasional handful of patrons would together to sing the refrain.

Though the gathering crowd was far from overly impressed, the variety of the entertainment and the lingering effects of copious amounts of alcohol seemed to allow them to part with a few of their coins. One of the crowd though didn't give out any money — in fact he didn't even seem to notice the show at all. Though there was a kaleidoscope of distracting entertainment before him, his mind was elsewhere.

His blue eyes were fixed ahead; unanchored to anything but his own musings. He was a Telborian with a square-cut golden mane and a battle-worn face speaking of a harsh life seeming to make him look more like some grizzled war veteran rather than an escaped gladiator.

Dugan shot his head up sharply when a nearby robust man bumped into him as he clapped his hands ecstatically to the bard's irrelevant tune; a drunken glaze fresh upon his eyes. The gladiator scowled, then returned to his thoughts. His eyes fixed on the fire-eater, recalling his own past and the fire that ate him, and continued to consume him to this very day. It was an unpleasant allegory to say the least.

What now, though?

He thought about his past the whole week he had spent wandering around the hellhole trying to get answers to his questions. His questions were few, but powerful.

He needed to be free from the curse placed upon him by Rheminas. The dark god wouldn't have his soul! The money he'd collected from the recent mission had earned him his freedom, but it was almost gone. He'd spent it like water; enjoying the free life he'd been denied for so many years. Now that he was free, he pondered what to do with his newfound experience. The money wouldn't last forever — living like a free man proved to be more expensive than he realized.

Dugan thought he might find a way to free himself from his last chain of slavery in Haven. He loathed only one thing in life, and it was the eventual placement of his person after his death. His soul was promised to Rheminas, god of fire, revenge, and the sun. Now that Dugan was physically free, he felt as though he was still dragging along a ball and chain. The promised eternity with The Lord of Flame hung around his neck as a lodestone. He needed to be free from this problem, less his short life of freedom come to an end in the fiery realm of the god for all eternity.

The Telborian departed the crowd. It had grown late, and the entertainment had ceased to take his mind of his troubles, only fueling them all the more. He would need to find somewhere to rest for the night. He still had some money, and that would afford him a roof and a room, then he'd probably have to start sleeping in the streets, or wandering on elsewhere outside the city in the wilds as he continued his quest for freedom. Until then he needed to try his best to move faster, then his thoughts and hope he could outrun them by morning light.

And so he left the drunken crowd.

Night had grown cold over the shops and alleys. Autumn was in the air more forcefully than before. Such colder winds in Haven meant winter was fast approaching, but the stench of urine, spoiled food and fertile mud was still strong. Barking dogs, groaning victims, and cries of death mixed for an odd and fitting song for the alleyways the Telborian now traveled. It was the song of the hopeless. Dugan's eyes adjusted to the dim illumination the stars and half moon provided, spying vagrants and miscreants behind all shadowy corners and nooks. They looked like rats as they eyed him with mischievous eyes.

Dugan kept his hand on his left hip, on top his sword, ready for anything. He had traded the two weapons he gained from the ruins, and the gladius he had stolen from the hunters for a more potent blade in Haven. The rare dealer who had done the transaction told him, how the broadsword he now carried was able to do incredible feats of wonder in the right wielders hand. Just what those feats were, the man had been unable to elaborate, but after testing it out, Dugan noticed it felt like something more than a common sword — and when held to the light of the full moon, it hummed with a soft purple glow. However, he too had been unable to coax any wonders from the blade.

While the two blades he had taken as part of his payment from the ruins of Takta Lu Lama would have served him well, he didn't feel totally right with them on his journey toward Haven. They made him uncomfortable — uneasy, and he didn't know why. When he sold off all three blades (even in the arena he didn't need three blades) he felt a little more at peace. It was like he had gotten rid of and moved beyond some darker chapter of his life and now was ready to forge a new destiny.

Whether or not this new blade was enchanted, as the weapon smith who sold it to him professed it to be, he didn't care. He felt better with the new weapon, and it was really all that mattered.

The citizens of Haven didn't mind armed men in their cities. They had a strong and able-bodied guard to handle any uprising — a virtual army in its own right. Besides that, most sane folk knew it wise to keep a dagger, mace, or even a simple club in their homes for protection as well. Truth be known, the largest army

117

in Haven, should they ever be given cause to arise and assemble, were the citizens themselves. Besides, policing the populous over such matters as weapons possession would be not only an arduous and tedious policy, but very dangerous indeed. Best to leave it alone and let the citizens have their weapons. And so the Mayor of Haven did.

Dugan had traded his armor in too after getting to Haven. The scale mail shirt chaffed his flesh; the weight was burdensome for him and his current tasks, so he'd exchanged it for something more able-bodied. It allowed him to move in relative comfort, if not decent protection. He now wore a simple breastplate of polished steel, and tight-fitting leather pants. His shoulders where covered by leather studded in steel which gleamed in the moonlight.

His long, blond hair flowed like course straw from his tan head. His leather-booted step was rapid, yet well balanced, as not to attract attention of his wish to be quick about his exit of the slums. He'd been in Haven for nine days already. Before that he had taken the long ride down south from the Marshes of Gondad. The walking had been terribly slow; both he and Vinder had tired of the exercise rather quickly, so when they happened upon a village with some horses for sale, they made the purchase quickly.

It took five weeks to travel to Haven, but it had been an experience nonetheless for the Telborian. Wanting to keep as much money as he could, he sold his horse when he got into Haven. Vinder, left to his own path about halfway through the trip so he could go back toward his homeland, which was somewhere to the north of Haven in the Diamant Mountains. In truth, Dugan would miss the dwarf. He truly was a great warrior and, as they traveled, he discovered that he was a great man as well underneath his rough, charcoal gray exterior.

As the Diamant Mountains called Vinder, Haven sought out the Telborian — for it seemed to offer him the best chance at hope. It was said to be the biggest and most diverse city as far as any on Tralodren went. It was also said the city itself was the reason why

Talatheal, the continent on which it rested, had earned its nickname as The Island of the Masses.

It was in Haven that all races, creeds, and faiths were allowed. They even had an academy of magic where supposedly Cadrissa had learned her craft. They also had all manner of temples and shrines dedicated to a multitude of gods. Many of which Dugan discovered were fake religions put up by bureaucrats and thieves.

It didn't seem to bother the inhabitants, though as a great deal of them saw such actions as akin to founding a new type of business. Only the truly religious and pious were offended by such blasphemies. These citizens were never able to totally defeat the fake faiths as the very open nature of the city protected the godless institutions for the most part.

It was only if they broke some law like murder or insulted/ swindled a person of power and influence that they were then dealt with in a swift and often harsh manner. Naturally, these false faiths didn't cross the line often, if at all, and stayed in the clear most of the time. Nevertheless, it was these orthodox and nontraditional temples that interested the Telborian.

Dugan searched high and low across Talatheal on his journey to Haven for answers to his theological problem. Many temples of other gods offered him little aid. Causilla, Endarien, Shiril, and Asora could only bless him and send him further on a journey — which he felt was going nowhere fast.

When he reached Haven, he sought out the major powers of the Tralodroen Pantheon. Ganatar, Gurthghol, and Dradin. All failed him. The day prior, Dugan had finished with the last of the gods Asorlok, Khuthon, Olthon, and Saredhel. All had left him sadly peering into a dim and murky future of grievous uncertainty.

Following the answers to his quest, Dugan had drifted into a deep melancholy. Alcohol and depression had been his mistress these past few days as hope faded from him like the embers of dying fire. He cared little now what befell him. If he were to be damned, then he would have it over with. He grew tired of trying to find a cure for his problems when nothing was around him but cruel mockery and distain for his situation.

The gods be damned!

The Telborian wandered through the rat-infested road — prowling like a lion, looking for any sign or person who might lead him to his desired end. Oddly, the further he traveled, the less he saw. Not even alley cats and their bulbous rat prey scurried through the rank puddles. He realized he had enough money, that he feared slightly for someone trying to attack him. It wasn't a lot, but it was enough for about a weeklong stay in a multicultural city, living very conservatively, before he had to really worry. He could milk it out longer if he became even more frugal with his needs. Still though, he was amazed he hadn't been attacked yet, then realized few thieves would wish to have a tangle with a powerful fighter from the coliseum of Colloni, for he still looked and carried himself like a dangerous man. It seemed he'd live another night after all.

The hours passed as he traveled onward, and as dawn's fingers caressed the stars, the old center of Haven had been passed through without so much of an incident as a passing drunk. The Telborian was tired and in need of rest, yet his heart still ached with a dull pang. He'd grown extremely cross and had become more foul tempered by the moment. Fueled by the remnants of his drinking, the mighty Telborian barely contained his wanton need to lash out at the next person who crossed his path when one happened to did so.

"You are Dugan are you not?" A cloaked figure, much shorter than the Telborian appeared; out of the shadows of early morning before him.

"Who are you?" The former gladiator drew his sword and eyed the figure shrewdly.

"Answers later, you must come this way if you still wish to find what you seek." The figured moved to the shadows of a lone alleyway.

"This is all too familiar," Dugan remarked with a rueful tone. He tentatively followed the figure, more so because it was something to do than anything else. He had given up on anything aiding him in his causes and from his assessment of the man, seemed to be in no real danger. Besides, he could use something to take his mind off his thoughts for a while "So what is it that I seek?"

"I've watched you for days. You've traveled from temple to temple, looking and pleading for hope and release from your dark pact with the god of fire. I have heard you ask the priests for release from your pact with that dark god, but you have asked the wrong people."

"So you watch me like a vulture," Dugan squinted with the eyes of a hunter. Perhaps this figure was more dangerous than he first thought.

"Oh yes, I have known about you since the time you first entered the Haven. The others have too. We are the eyes and ears of this city. Nothing happens here we don't know about." The figure melted further into the shadows.

Dugan followed.

He tightened his reflexes and prepared for the worst as he did so. His earlier estimation of the man was now definitely coming into question. "Others? You're saying then I'm to speak to you, and you are to give me better insight, where all the other priests and gods have failed?" He held his sword tighter as mistrust bubbled up inside him.

"There is much to tell you, but it cannot be spoken in the open, on the street. Too much can be overheard, and we are not the only eyes and ears in Haven. Come with me and you will be given the answer you so desperately seek, and maybe even find a purpose for your newfound freedom." The man's voice went softer still.

Dugan thought about the proposition, and had to admit it did sound good. It was the only positive result he'd received since he entered into Haven. Still, he didn't like the feeling in his gut. It spoke to him of falsehood and the unwillingness to face the facts of the situation before him. However, he felt as though this was his only option left. He wanted to deny it, because it felt so fake and insecure to him, yet he didn't really have any options left. He hated to admit it, but this was the last scrap of desirable hope to come into his path, and before he could deny it, he needed to investigate it. Even, if it would turn into ash in the end.

"Very well," he lowered his sword slightly, "tell me about your offer then."

"Follow me," the shadowy figure spoke as he totally disappeared into the shadows before the gladiator's eyes.

Together they traveled through near unfathomable darkness, though the rays of dawn scoured the dismal alleys and walkways of the Tempter's District. Dugan was quickly lost as they turned through a never-ending twisting arena of alleys, walls, and even secreted areas none seemed to know about, save the mysterious man who lead Dugan onward by his chaotic dance between darkness and light.

They then suddenly stopped.

"Why have we stopped?" Dugan looked about him, ready for treachery; his sword partially drawn from its stealth, muscles tensed.

"You would do yourself the best service if you would follow my every command and action, for where I am about to lead you is thickly clustered with traps and protective devices of every sort. One wrong step and you would be a faint memory," The figure pressed a small section of brick wall in an alleyway before them. One would never have known it was there at all, if the cloaked figure hadn't made it known to Dugan. Dugan began to wonder how many such secret areas and underground caverns dotted the city. How many had access to them?

He was beginning to see how this man, if not many others as well, could follow him or anyone else and learn their actions from anywhere in the city. It was an unnerving realization, to say the least. It seemed Haven did indeed have some very large rats. Intelligent and potentially dangerous rats scurrying between its walls.

Suddenly, the brick wall smoothly fell back into a pitch doorway smelling of moisture and rot. The man motioned for Dugan to step through the portal, and smiled with a slight baring of his teeth, which were yellow and cracked, like stale corn that had been dried from the stalk. "Enter Dugan, but step every other step, or you will be in for some trouble."

"How can I trust you? You go first." Dugan spied the other with a penetrating glare shooting into his core being like a dagger through the heart. The man, not one to be a fool, took this as a sign of being studied very closely. Silently, he bowed in submission and began the descent.

"Very well, but remember every other stair you must step upon. If you so much as brush the top of the wrong stair, you will know your time is over in this life." The man descended into the gloom-laden tunnel as the rays of sunlight finally fell upon the hidden alleyways as well.

Their trek down the stairs was very quiet and labored. Dugan didn't want to even come close to the steps he was to avoid. He had seen many manner of strange and dangerous devices in the arena in Colloni invented to slaughter and ensnare gladiators. Sometimes they were machines or very deadly traps built into gauntlets the gladiators were made to confront in order to please the masses. Many died by the gear wielded and counter weighted blades of such death machines, and he had grown to have a healthy respect of such contraptions.

He also dared not speak out of concern of his guide being distracted by a question, and worse yet, discovering he traveled this staircase by himself. He stopped for but a moment when the urge to see if the man who was supposed to be in front of him was still there, or if he had blended into the darkness itself, leaving him to fend for himself in this dank corridor. He had sheathed his sword, as he needed both hands to help him traverse the darkness and traps awaiting him. Dugan waited for but a moment, and then heard a soft rustle of fabric in front of him.

"Why have you stopped?" The man asked Dugan with a silken voice. The Telborian still couldn't see him or anything else in the gloom, though his eyes were adjusting to the darkness better than they had been before.

"I had to see if you were still up there," the Telborian didn't want to say he couldn't keep this up forever. "How much farther is it until we reach our destination?"

"Not much further," he fell silent once more.

"How can you navigate in such darkness?" Dugan grunted as silently as he could as his foot tried to get a hold of the next step which would prove to be safe footing.

"You will get used to it in time. All people do, if given enough patience to allow it to happen," the silken voice of the shadowy man floated back to Dugan from the darkness. "For now just trust your inner instinct and step after me. There is much too talk about, and much to do.

"When you enter the next room, you will meet my brothers and they will give you the information you seek, but you must let me do most of the talking. They are a very distrustful lot, and do not take too kindly to those they do not know entering their most sacred chambers."

"If they threaten me, I'll make short work of their hollow claims," Dugan boasted as his own iron nerves and practiced movements caused his hand to go for his sword, which he had sheathed to better maneuver in the darkness.

The guide stopped and turned to the gladiator, this much Dugan could make out of the darkness before him. "If they threaten you, your last breath will be in their presence." His guide spoke in a hushed tone. "Warriors are nothing compared to my order. We are the ardent defenders of our faith."

"Wh-" Dugan was cut short by the other.

"Beyond that door is the room I spoke of. Be careful and let me do most of the talking. Understood?" The man's words were sharp and forceful.

Dugan's stern eyes answered for him.

"Good," the figure returned.

Dugan watched in amazement as what seemed to be a solid wall; was pushed open by his guide with the slightest of effort. A dim light, fainter than normal torchlight, seemed to waft toward him from beyond the secret doorway.

The mysterious portal mystified Dugan. Suddenly, he had grown very apprehensive about the whole situation; it was beginning to seem very awkward and surreal. He knew he was doing so when he let the guide lead him, but now he was faced with the utter helplessness of the entire position. He was lost in some lightless underground maze, and was walking into what could be a trap. He had no idea if hundreds of other *guides* hovered about him, waiting for a signal to kill or subdue him for their own means.

Oddly reassuring to the Telborian was the thought sending him grinning his concerns away. What had he to worry anyway? Why would they kill him, a lone man — a worthless stranger in their eyes? If anything he'd just end up in Rheminas' domain that much sooner. They could do little worse to him than what his eternity had to offer.

"Please be so kind as to enter." Like a floating feather, the guide motioned Dugan to the opening with a silent hand. For the first time Dugan noticed his face as the small gathering of light highlighted it in a sinister and deathly fashion. It looked long and narrow now, much like a rat or fox's snout.

Dugan let out a sigh, and eyed the dark clothed man as he entered the doorway. Though the gladiator had seen his face under his hood, he instantly found it hard to recall, the image blurred in his mind's eye as he tried to focus upon it. The smell of food and exotic spices pushed this thought aside as the aroma found its way to his nostrils as he walked further. It also grew lighter so he could see things more clearly.

The first increase in the light hurt his eyes as he had began to grow accustom to the darkness, but in time he could make out a stone-hewn tunnel made of dry, gray bricks that had seen the years pass over them with great cruelty. They looked as though hundreds of picks had assaulted them with vicious strokes, and deep gouges glared back at him with sunken eyes. He doubted they'd hold up the ceiling for much longer. Even as he walked past a wall, he saw a large chunk of it fall to the floor with a heavy *thud* failing to bring an echo to the tunnel.

Dugan turned to see what had transpired. As if in answer to his question, he saw the black clothed figure slither silently behind him. His thin smile was all that Dugan needed to see. The Telborian turned and continued onward until, at last, he came to a large room, covered in candles, torches, braziers, and a fireplace roaring from the wall opposite him.

The room was large, created from the same decaying bricks as the hall, but painted a deep red making the room seem to shift and squirm in the flickering light all around the gladiator. No more than ten feet in front of him was a fifteen-foot-long wooden table covered with food.

Breads, meat, and various mounds of fruits and vegetables were spread over the well-worn oak table. To Dugan the smell was both intoxicating and inviting. He walked toward the table, intent upon looking over the contents, when he suddenly stopped. The pool of saliva grew cold in his mouth when he turned his head all about him, and saw hundreds of black robed figures emerging from the walls like ants or flies to a carcass. His hand went to his sword, but his guide's words stopped him from any further action.

"Hold Dugan, you are in no danger. These are my brothers, fellow followers of Shador. It is time for us to eat. There is no ill will bidden toward you, mighty warrior. You are our guest. Please, sit." The dark clad figure's words were like silk.

Dugan looked around as the silent forms shifted in their dark robes, and sat before the feast, quietly taking what victuals met their fancy. The Telborian also noticed they had neither plates, nor silverware. He found that odd for civilized folk, but his mind, which was raised in the arena, didn't put too much to the matter. No one else seemed to notice — or if they did, they didn't bring it to anyone's attention.

Together they feasted and devoured the meal before them in silence. All the while Dugan studied the room. It was large, and well lit, which eluded him in his previous passages to the chamber. He made a quick count of the priests and discovered they numbered about three hundred fifty. He thought he could see more though, sulking behind the shadows in the distance, outside the circle of torchlight, in the deep shadows. They reminded Dugan of lesser scavengers waiting for the first to take their fill of the kill, and then claim the scraps left behind.

The Telborian managed to take a leg of turkey and devour it, as the night of drowning his sorrows was over, and he felt as though he could do with breakfast, and so make a good meal of it, since he might not have enough money to eat this well ever again, and his stomach ached for the opulent display of foodstuffs before him.

After the meal was finished, and the multitude of priests had left to their other tasks, Dugan spied the rest with predatory eyes. His belly was full and satiated, but his mind was still alert. He began to see their faces slightly as the light and shadowy pool created by the priest's hoods clashed at odd moments. He saw the outline of elven features, those of humans, and even a few dwarves in the distance.

This form of communal interests and dedication to the same goal frightened the Telborian slightly. He'd never known a group of men and women (for he had seen women there as well) to be so formed to a cause that it set aside all barriers of race, age, and sex. Truly they must serve a higher purpose, and the purpose must be an ideal so strong it was greater than anything Dugan had ever known. Dugan surmised the god they worshiped, this Shador, must be a very powerful and wonderful god. Why they remained hidden and secretive with their faith was still a mystery though. Perhaps theirs was a new faith that was persecuted, or they held beliefs that made them live this way for esoteric theological reasons. Such deeper ponderings didn't really concern him if they could be of some help — it was the true measure of their worth to the Telborian.

Dugan continued to silently observe them as his guide whispered to a larger man whose racial heritage Dugan could not discern. This man was dressed in rich finery and dripped with gold, silver and jewels shining on his black cape and garb. His hooded face let the white sheen of a smile emerge and pearl-like semblance, appeared eerie and unnatural in the pitch pool of the hood. He seemed to be very cold and distant, but at the same time he radiated a warmth making Dugan seem to trust him like a father, though at the same time his mannerisms reminded him of a snake.

"Welcome Dugan," the larger priest spoke as he drew closer to Dugan and sat across from him at the table. "Please be at peace here, for you can come to no harm, and we are a peaceful people."

"I was told you would answer my questions," Dugan spoke with tight lips.

"That we will; that we will. First though, I must see if you are willing to truly be free of your past." The priest's tone was as warm as a loving father.

"What do you mean?" Dugan hid the excited and nervous shaking of his heart and hands as best he could. The hope of getting free was a powerful stimulant in his blood.

"I am the leader of this religious sect, and as such, have direct voice to our god Shador," the head priest motioned to those gathered around him.

"All hail Shador," the others gathered chanted in a monotone. They fell back into the shadows outside the chambers once more, but watched the conversation from their vantage point, like hungry wolves amid a dying animal.

"He has told me of your plight with your past problems, and your need to be rid of your curse. He has taken pity upon you and wishes to free you from your problems should you wish to partake in a quest for his cause." The head priest folded his hands before him.

"This god of yours, he speaks like many of the other gods I've encountered, but they did nothing to aid me. Why should your god be any better?" Dugan's face became hard and rocky. His eyes looked like beads of fire as they pierced the head priest's dark eyes. The Telborian thought he could make out some bushy eyebrows above those eyes — thick brown caterpillars crawling over pale flesh.

"A good question, Dugan. You are wise to question those who would give you something for nothing. We do not offer such a deal, though. If you will but take on the mission appointed by our god you would be free from your curse after its completion. I can offer this to you with a free heart and will." The priest smiled — a crescent moon of white in the pitch-black hood.

"Again, you make promises you cannot fulfill totally at the present. I want proof this is indeed possible," Dugan looked behind the priest and saw a collection of younger priests move aside, from the grouping they were once in, to form a wall of bodies. In front of the priests in the middle of the line, stood a wrought iron censure belching out thick, dark smoke. It seemed to move like an ebony tide which sought to grasp all it could; to try and get the things around it under its blacken grip.

"Remove the sacred knife of Shador, "the head priest chanted with a dark tone.

"All hail Shador," the others responded as two others drew forth a small, black hilt knife from inside the censure. It still dripped with the noxious fumes and wicked looking red-tinted gleam the censure produced. They then approached the head priest, and handed him the knife. Dugan drew restless in his seat. His muscles grew tighter, and his right hand descended to meet his sword.

"Behold the power of our god and his valid promises to those who follow him or do as he bids." The priest held the knife high over his head, and said a word that was ancient and forgotten.

As he said the word, a thin bolt of black energy struck Dugan's left shoulder where he felt a strange pinch on his flesh, then nothing.

"What did you do?" Dugan's hand was tight around his sword hilt.

"Be calm Dugan. Shador has just shown you his favor. He has removed the mark of your physical slavery, thereby making you free whilst you live. He will remove the final piece of your slavery — your spiritual slavery, when you complete his quest for him. Then you truly will be free." The priest then returned the knife to the censure-bearing clergy. They then placed the blade back inside the smoking censure and left the same way they had come.

"I don't believe you," Dugan growled.

"Naturally," The head priest pointed toward the gladiator's left shoulder. "Look at your shoulder."

Dugan uncovered the metal and cloth hiding the section of meaty muscle from prying eyes faster than a dangerous wind rips through a forest of young saplings. Within moments he had a clear view of his flesh. Once marred with the dark designs of an imperial branding, claiming him as property, the mark of the Elyelmic Republic was gone. All that remained was firm, tanned flesh — unmarked or touched, but for time and his own hand as he ran it over his shoulder.

"See this Dugan and know. Who among the other gods could have done this for you? Asora, the very goddess of healing herself, couldn't grant you this. Nor could the others you have petitioned. It is only with our god that your wishes shall be granted and you will be blessed with the life you deserve. All this has been made possible through Shador." The head priest's voice was now a mixture of theatrical charm.

"All praise Shador," the others again returned their chant.

"Will you listen now? " The cult-hooded leader leaned a bit closer to Dugan. "Will you trust now?"

"Will you ready yourself to undertake the will of Shador in order that you may forever be free?" The head priest then folded his hands in his robes.

The room fell silent.

Dugan needed but a moment to contemplate the matter. With his last glimmering of hope sparkling before him, he knew that he wanted to — had to — reach out and grab it. If it failed him then he would forever be doomed, but he would die knowing at least he had exhausted every last possible chance to try to reverse his position. Once more it seemed he would be another's mercenary to gain a chance at freedom. Though he recognized the pattern, he swore to himself it would be the last time he did so. It had to be.

"Yes," Dugan relaxed and turned his gaze to the head priest.

"Excellent. There is much to be done to prepare you and teach you. You have made a wise decision, Dugan." A faint sparkle of two grinning eyes shimmered from under the head of the priest's hood.

Chapter 14

The Diamant Mountains scraped the lofty blue dome above them. Hard stone stretched into the cool and cloudless sky like the very spines of a dragon. These jagged peaks made anything compared with them seem no more than a pebble, a mouse among giants. So too did they render the frame of Vinder minuscule. The timeworn dwarf rested on a rock on a small plateau near the upper reaches of the great mountain chain.

Like most dwarves, he was shorter than humans, but was well built and strong; more like a square column of stone than tightly bound structure of flesh. Vinder was one of the slightly shorter examples of his race; closer to his hill dwelling kin height, truth be told. Long ago, when the great dwarven nation broke up into various factions, some chose to live in the hills, the others on the mountains of Tralodren. As became the case, those who lived on the mountain tended to be slightly taller and bulkier than those who chose the hills, though each retained their dwarven nature and frame despite this, for it was tradition — and tradition was strong among all the clans of dwarves that called Tralodren home.

Vinder's skin was a gentle charcoal gray like the very rocks on which he stood. His face was weathered and rough from years of the wind playing across it and the hard life he'd led on the path of a mercenary. His lone steel gray eye stared out like a beam of light from his face. The left was covered in a black leather patch with a golden rune inscribed upon it matching similar runes carved upon his great axe resting at his side.

His beard was salt and peppered, and flowed from his chin, sideburns and nose to just above his collarbone. He had freshly bathed and trimmed all his hair and beard, letting it all now flow free. Once he would have placed his beard into three braids, dying the tips of it red, but not now. He was about to make petition to his clan, family and god. Tradition held that a dwarf wishing to do so should be humble, without adornment of any kind, that he should be as pure and natural as rock itself. When he had left his homeland he had worn his beard thus, and now he did so again with his return.

The old dwarf took in the view before him with a misty eye. The mountains — his homeland — were beautiful. He thought he'd never see the sight again. He thought he had tired of them and the whole vision of the rising rock, the snow-capped peaks, and gentle veins of pure water flowing from deep within the mountain's heart would make him sick to see. The clean, crisp air even caused his stomach to turn in homesickness at the familiar scent.

How wrong he had been?

One hundred years had come and gone since his feet had touched the safe and pure landscape he was enjoying. He'd been a fool, a hotheaded fool. What he had sought for he found, but it wasn't what he was expecting. That was just the way things were though, he supposed.

Youth and anger were both his greatest foes and allies in the past years of his wanderings. He had wanted nothing more than to see the world and what it held now that he had found it he knew he was lost. He had forgotten the beauty of his homeland. It was a part of him that was stronger than anything else in the world, a gem that was his heart, and very life force itself.

Tears fell from his eye as he took in the majesty he'd left behind. Near him was a great chest wrapped in chains and locked so securely that it looked to be more metal than wood. This too he spied once in a great while as though it were a child with a habit of wandering away from its parent. Always though, he turned back to the mountains, and what they represented.

In his hand he clasped the small carving of Drued, which Heinrick had given him in Elandor. It had given him much comfort as it filled him with hope of what could be. Vinder took it as an omen, and came to believe, with each passing day of his journey back home, it was a favorable one at that.

He was home and would be free from his past if his clan, family, and god forgave him of his past sins. Though he had reached the farthest he ever thought he'd get in his journey, he felt fear twinge in his stomach like a rodent digging in a burrow. Just the same, he didn't know how he would be accepted on his return. He hoped the clan would welcome him back, but he wasn't so sure.

The clan and his faith commanded a lot from him in the way of penance, he only hoped he had enough. Tradition called for a priest of Drued to meet with the penitent soul before he could be granted entrance into the clan for judgment. Then it would befall him to be forgiven by his family, then faith and clan publicly. If just one of those groups or persons failed to forgive the trespass, the dwarf was forever banned from the clan.

There was no hope of a second chance.

Tradition, honor, and family were the discipline that played out the lives of a dwarf. He drew his worth from them and was held captive by their edicts for good or ill.

When Vinder had first appeared near the mountains, he sent word through the first watchman he encountered to find a priest to perform the rites of remission to enter the nation. He had spoken in Druelandian, the common dwarven tongue to the watchman, but in his homeland, from here on out he would speak High Druelandian, the dialect of the mountain dwarves, his whole time present for this was tradition.

The watchman Vinder had spoken to was one of many dwarves who dedicated their lives to the protection and sanctity of the exterior mountain home of Clan Diamant. They were the only collection of dwarves allowed to interact with the outside world in a limited basis, being traders, scouts, and protectors of the Diamantic way of life. A few were even granted leave to have limited interaction in the means of trade with the communities around them from the few items the clan could not produce or get on their own. Such was the case in which Vinder had met Heinrick.

Mountain dwarves lived both on and under the mountains, building great cities high upon the tallest peaks, under their snowy domes, and larger cities on the base of the same peaks, where amid the rock and rough dirt patches they raised livestock and farmed. It was the way things have been since the very beginning of time, and it wasn't about to change. Tradition would see to that.

Once notified of Vinder's request, the watchman had left and allowed Vinder to climb up the mountain as he had sought his peace. That had been a while ago now. He wondered what had happened. Had the priest not even seen him as worthy? Had he been left alone to waste away on the mountain as a joke or punishment?

All he could do was hold tight to the small necklace of Drued and keep a silent prayer going about his head for some of the god's favor to fall upon the outcast making his way back home. There came a noise from behind him though and his myopic attention turned from the peaks to the even older figure that had suddenly came up beside him.

He too was a dwarf, but looked more regal and defined, even though old age wrinkled and covered his frame, but left alone his dark purple eyes shimmering in the daylight. His snowy white beard was braided into four braids with golden clasps crafted to resemble hammers and axes ending in the same length as Vinder's own newly trimmed beard. His skin was of a gray tone too, though lighter than Vinder's skin, which had been tanned from his journeys. His dress was a ceremonial outfit only allowed to be worn on special occasions like which the priest currently presided: a robe of simple white adorned with golden symbols of hammers and anvils.

Vinder wondered and wanted to ask the priest how he'd gotten to him so quickly without being seen or heard, but thought against it. Tradition declared he couldn't do such a thing during the rite. His place was silence until he was given leave to speak in the litany, which had now begun.

"Brother dwarf, prodigal son, you have returned. You have come looking for forgiveness, but are not yet pure." Such was the traditional greeting of the priest of Drued to the outcast.

Vinder turned to face the priest more squarely, but didn't look upon him, rather the ground beneath his feet. He had no right to look at him yet, not until he had been readmitted into the clan.

"I have come to regain my pride and honor. Forgiveness is what I seek, great priest of Drued, my example and my god. I have come on forlorn feet and seek to be forgiven. Cleanse me from my foolishness and selfishness," Vinder soberly spoke.

The priest then took out a pouch of sand and dumped it on the head of Vinder. "Like the sand, you have forsaken the path of your ancestors. You have broken from that path, and are great with fault. Like sand you have lost the strength of the knowledge you were formed from the toughest stones in all the world under Drued's hand. However, Drued is great in his mercy, and he will forgive you for all your foolishness and welcome you back into the fold of his clansman."

"Honorable priest, I seek now your forgiveness. I have been too long from the ways of my clan; my home. Will you show the joy of a father when his son has fallen lost?" Vinder continued the rite with downcast eyes.

The stone like face of the priest then turned to one of warmth and openness. A thin smile parted the dry lips of the old dwarf.

"Son, I forgive you," the older dwarf answered. "Your time of wandering is at an end."

Tears flowed from the wells of Vinder's eye as he rose and hugged the priest with a mighty grip. "Thank you father. I've been so stupid and selfish. You were right. You were right, and I couldn't see it. I've missed you and mother these long years."

"We all have." The priest, who was also Vinder's father, sobbed as he hugged his son back to his breast. "Your mother will want to see you as well as your sister. Come, they are eager for your presence."

Chapter 15

The hall inside Diam, the Clan Diamant's capital, was grand. Thick tapestries as old as the stones they covered dominated the walls. Their bright colors and images were undamaged by time's passage. They showcased the true wonder and pride of the dwarven nation, as well as the honor of Clan Diamant. Honor that had been sullied by Vinder's actions.

Vinder carried that grief and guilt a very long time. Even when he thought he was happy and free from the stifling laws of his clan even then, in his most joyous hour, he was saddened. It was at that moment when he realized he missed his homeland, his family and his people. The longer he strayed from his clan; the more sorrow permeated his being. The clan had been something that served to give him meaning — a foundation on which his world could be built.

The dwarves of the mountain clans were not like their kin who dwelled in the hills. The mountain was forbidding and strong. It welcomed no one in its solitude. So it was held every dwarf must be like the mountain living in the rugged heights. Vinder hadn't agreed with this tradition and cultural law. He'd been seen as siding with his 'lesser kin'; the hill dwarves, he welcomed the friendship of other races. It was this that caused him to be exiled from his home, and to have all his hair on his head and face shaved off to live in shame during his exile.

That had been a hundred years ago. A hundred years of looking for a way to get back into the home he'd left because he'd shared pleasantries with a local Telborian explorer and thought the life he lived in the world below was more interesting and meaningful than the life Vinder was living above.

His father though, once he had forgiven his son, and preformed the ritual of forgiveness, had taken him into the various tunnels, hidden passages and unknown trails winding their way up to the secluded mountain top dwellings of his clansmen.

As they traveled, Vinder allowed himself to relax a little. He'd met his father with success and forgiveness from his god, but he was still worried about the rest of his family and the Konig, the ruler of his clan. Would he be able to get forgiveness from them? Not to mention the Council of Elders. Would they forgive his errors?

When he and his father had finished the rite and reconciliation, they both traveled back to his home to get forgiveness from the rest of his family. His family and faith were easier since his father was a priest of Drued. Upon their travels into Diam, Vinder learned his father had been given a vision of his return, and had been waiting for him before the watchman could find a priest to perform the rite. Both men took it as a sign showing Drued's favor.

He didn't tell his father about the necklace given him by Heinrick, nor his hope of the favorable omen it could mean to him. He didn't feel right to share it at the moment. Instead, he had hidden it under his clothing around his neck where he could feel it against his skin, but didn't risk showing it off to any who might take offense at one who had been outcast from the clan proudly wearing such ornamentation when none was allowed for the traditional rite.

Vinder had taken much money to pay back the clan, for he was a valued member of society, as were all dwarves, and his contribution would have meant profit and abundance in certain areas. By his loss, the clan suffered financially. In order to procure the sum he had to take to being a thief over the last few years of his exile, and amassed an amount, which he hoped would help him pay off the debt he had incurred from his clansman. It was this large pool of money he had lugged up the mountainside to meet his father in the chain-wrapped chest.

He wasn't proud of the thieving — it wasn't the most honorable thing — but he consoled himself, most of it was done to opponents who had honorably fallen in battle. He also took heart some of the money was payment for services he had rendered as a mercenary on previous adventures.

Putting these thoughts away, Vinder realized how overwhelmed with the strong faith and religious power his father held. When he'd last seen him, he was no more than a fledging priest of the order. Now he had risen to be a high-ranking cleric of great distinction and honor.

Even with this change in his father's previous station, the more the old son looked around the lands and areas he had left, the more he realized how little everything had changed amid such scattered developments. It was like he'd walked into a strange world where it seemed like the sun hadn't moved in the sky since he left the mountains the previous century. It was an odd dichotomy to say the least...

Shortly after he went deeper into the mountains, he returned to his family home and found it very similar to when he had left it. It was the first of many solid structures dominating the landscape on the mountains before him. A sturdy box-like shape, that seemed to blend quite well into the surrounding rocky reaches and edifices. It even used the mountain for strength to keep its own walls upright. The building was a tall structure as well, with towering, narrow windows allowing just enough light in for practical sight and air to flow, but not enough to fully look out of, or allow other forces, like the persistent and harsh mountain wind, to gain easy access.

His family's home was just one of many buildings spread through the mountaintops and crevices. Some buildings he knew were underground, like the temple of Shiril, goddess of metals, crafts and industry. But some, like the grand palace of the Konig, were above ground and massive.

For beings that weren't known for their staggering size, the dwarven architects liked to build things big. Such was the manner of the palace. It dominated the landscape, being built in various terraces on top of the tallest mountain peak in the area; thin lakes of snow just dusting its peaked spires and roof.

All of the buildings had solid square bases leading up to slanted roofs. This helped keep the snow and rain from piling too high on top the structures, but the palace had rose another story above the tallest of these lesser buildings. None could build anything higher than the Konig's palace. The palace represented the mountain they lived on — the very symbolic source their government rooted in the strength of honorable tradition.

Besides being taller than all other structures, the palace was also decorated with the best of stones, hewed out of the sturdiest of rocks to make a home for the Konig eternal as the mountains themselves. To this end fat granite pillars, as smooth as a newborn's lips, lifted the overhanging rock, which was the upper level, from ground level below in a stoic colonnade at least three times the height of any dwarf. Iron doors, studded with blonde, white, and black diamonds were as giants to the common dwarven guards who stood watch before them.

The exterior walls were dressed in relief carvings rising from the floor and falling from the high roofline above. The whole history of the clan, from its founding to its current events could be found in the images they conveyed.

Besides this, the roof was shingled in onyx, the rising towers varying in size coordinating with the tall peak of stone, which the entire palace had been built into. The whole of the structure both dug into and encompassed the peak with hundreds of tunnels throughout it and were built within the ancient building. From what Vinder saw, it seemed that dwarven values still held true.

He looked at the lower level entrance to the palace a moment longer before he turned toward the less splendorous dwelling of his own family. More squat, plain, and entirely underground — but practical in a few geometrical and runic looking decorations. To

140

Vinder, though, the sight of his home seemed more splendid than the most glorious of palaces, and he sighed when he saw it.

He would be inside the palace soon enough, but his attention and heart were for this smaller building now, and the occupants therein. Though harsh feelings and dark memories might have plagued him through his journey back, when he reached the threshold of the door of his family home, Vinder's heart was lifted.

He gently pushed on the thick wooden door in front of him. It opened silently.

Behind it, Vinder's one-eyed visage cascaded in emotion. His mother, Gilda, stood attentive as ever with a warm smile and open arms serving to greet the mature man she had last seen as a reckless youth.

"Vinder, my son!" She ran to her child faster than a storm birthed gale, and took him up in her embrace. She was old by dwarven standards, and stood shorter than her son. Her hair was long and gray-streaked with patches of black and white managing to blend her entire head of hair into a shade of furnace-cast metal. She wore common garb; a modest dress and leather shoes, and had no adornments.

"I've missed you!" Her eyes were a clear gray beaming with light and love as they flooded with tears.

"It's good to be home," Vinder pulled away from his mother then, and looked deeply at her. "Mother, do you forgive me?" Tradition called from him to do it, and he had to follow its laws if he ever wanted to be back in his home and clan again.

Gilda stepped back from him a pace and looked him over with slick eyes, and a tear-washed face. She stared at her son — her child she hadn't seen for a hundred years — with maternal eyes. Emotions pulled at her heart and head, but she had to do her duty to both her family, and to herself. Years of training and discipline in this torn insight from the dwarven culture had trained her well.

"You have left your family, your home and your parents. Selfishness and shame followed you out into the corrupt and

failing world, and you want to bring it back with you now?" Gilda
fought back the maternal in favor of the tradition. It was hard, but
she managed, as all present knew and expected she would be able
to do so.

Vinder bowed his head with shame and humility as was
required of him, and as he truly felt as well. His father looked
onward as stern as he could be, just as custom decreed.

"I have come back," Vinder hung his head, "but humbled
and broken. I have seen the world, and it offers nothing. Its promises are vain and hollow. It is with my family and clan that I am
given truth and find my purpose and meaning."

Gilda's face then ripened into a smile so deep and emotion-
laden that it flourished across her face like a field of flowers in the
wild.

"Then welcome back Vinder. I've missed you so much."
She ran to collide against him in a powerful embrace.

"I've forgotten how much I missed this place. It's been too
long." Vinder's eye cried out tears of joy mingled in love as his
mother smoldered him in an embrace.

Gilda looked up at her son's face then, her own hair became
tangled in his beard as she did so, her eyes narrowed for a moment
as she looked once more upon her child. Then it was as if she saw
him as he was for the first time, the childlike image in her mind
gone — and she became concerned.

"The years have aged you, my child. You are much older
than you should be, and what has happened to your eye? By
Drued! What happened to it?" Gilda's eyes went wide in motherly
concern.

"I would like to know too Vinder," his father, Heimrick,
spoke up.

Vinder gently withdrew from his mother's embrace, stepping
back a few feet as Heimrick moved to stand next to his wife.

Vinder let out a deep sigh, and then looked his mother and
father in the eye. "I cannot lie. I lost it in a battle for my life with
a band of desperate brigands I first met at the beginning leg of my

banishment. I was hungry and alone. I looked to them for aid, but instead found cold steel — and it nearly claimed my life. Thank Drued it only took one of my eyes. I have become stronger though because I've lost it. Stronger in character and wisdom than I have ever been.

"You're right mother, I've gotten older than my years proclaim me to be, but it was for a good cause, for it showed me the error of my ways."

"You have come back to stay then? You're sure this time? Once you've atoned to the clan, then you cannot be taken back once more should you decide to leave again." Gilda observed her son closely, shrewd as a hawk looking for its prey.

"Mother, there will be no need,"Vinder's penitent timbre echoing the reality of his heart. "I'm home, and I can accept that. I long for that like no other time or place.

"Where's Gretta?" Vinder turned to Heimrick.

"Your sister is deep in the forges. She is a fine smith now, Vinder. A mighty talented craftsman and weapons-smith." Heimrick's chest rose slightly with pride. "She has found a suitor, too."

"Shouldn't we wait to see her first then. 'Tradition is a fool for no one', the saying goes. If she hasn't forgiven me, then it would be pointless to move on to the clan."

"Vinder," Heimrick let a small smile caress his lips, "your sister was the first to forgive you the moment you left. She told both your mother and I when you were exiled. We told her to be quiet about it, she was just a young maid then, and didn't understand, but each year after that she hasn't wavered in what she first spoke to us. She loves and has forgiven you, Vinder."

Vinder's lip and eye quivered for a moment before his stoic visage regained control once more. "Well then," he coughed away the remainder of any tearful emotion, "I suppose we should notify the clan to the ceremony."

"That has already been done," said Heimrick.

That had been hours earlier. Vinder dwelled upon the thoughts for a few more moments as he looked at the tall marble walls glimmering in the flickering flames of torches, candles and braziers. The multitude of dwarves assembled looked like a field of statues in the rocky cavern. This was the clan — Vinder's clan, his brothers and sisters, their fathers and mothers from Clan Diamant. They had all been called together when the news of Vinder's return had been announced. He'd been forgiven of his lack of faith, his betrayal of family, and now he would ask forgiveness of his clan and Konig.

All of the dwarves were dressed in finery and wealth. Tunics and trousers of heavy twill made their appearances in a myriad of earthen hues, browns and greens, beiges and creams…even black. Leather boots, rough and polished stones, gems covered the rest of them in the form of rings, necklaces, earrings, and bracers. The men also took care to groom their beards — combing them, and tightly braiding them into one strand for each fifty years lived, then dying them in shades of blue, red, green, orange, and even yellow.

It was a solemn and high occasion. The priesthood of Drued was present as well in a sacred band, Heimrick among them that rested behind the throne of the great Konig Stephen, a middle-aged dwarf with a more regal character than his peers. His medium-length hair and beard were a deep black; four blue braids decorating his beard as it fell to the top of his collarbone exactly. He stood just under five feet, wearing a golden gown of state, and silver crown.

The priests were like silent sarcophagi. Stephen was the same. Neither looked Vinder in the face or eyes. Vinder lacked honor and they wouldn't give him the benefit of dignified recognition. Nine elder men of the clan, all of the Council of Elders, stood even more stoic in a semicircle before the Konig. Vinder knew they would be the toughest to convince, following the Konig.

In each clan, the foundational seat of authority started with the family. The intermediate and extended family was all one unit and could be very large at times. The oldest male members or patriarchs were the ones who set the precedence of the family moral and ethical values inherited by their descendants. This was one of the many roles of Heimrick.

The next form of authority was the Council of Elders — an elected body with nine seats whose members were elected by all the dwarves of the clan. The most respected or favored elder of a family was elected to serve a term of twenty years on the council. The council addressed the matters of their electorates, and the needs of the people so that the Konig could make a wise decision upon matters.

The final form of rule was that of Konig. Held by the ranking royal official of Clan Diamant, the Konig could trace his lineage back to the first founding dwarf of the Clan's. The Konig ruled all other aspects of life the council and patriarchs didn't govern.

As was the custom, Vinder remained silent, and held his head down. Beside him was the large chest of money. The silence in which he waited was deadly. The dwarf felt as though he would die on the spot of fear, dishonor, and great embarrassment. Finally though, when he could bear it no more, and when his silent and desperate pleas for Drued's aid were all but exhausted, Stephen spoke.

"Shame upon you worthless pile of sand," the Konig's voice vibrated through the chamber. "Disgrace and disobedience to our clan, your family, and god. These things you bring with you and they scream out in howls of unworthy declaration. You have no place here, yet you return and wish for us to acknowledge you. Why would you dare come before our presence?"

Vinder kept his head held low; his mind and heart true to the cause at hand. He needed his full concentration as the priests were reading his intention as the clansman were judging his character and duty to tradition every second he was in the chamber.

"I have come, oh great and honorable Konig, to beg forgiveness from both you and my clansmen who I have dishonored and shamed long ago. My selfishness and pride took me from the land of my birth, my people and heritage to the lands of those who do not hold up such high virtues as we are commanded by law and divine creed. I ask for only the chance to offer up a compensation for my great transgression."

The gathering was then washed in silence once more, as the ritual of the mountain dwarves played out its drama in full force. To be accepted back into the clan, Vinder would have to offer up the treasure he had collected solely for this purpose. He'd been forgiven by his father, his family, and Drued had seen him safely here. Stephen now would seal his fate.

"Has your family taken you back, and forgiven your shame?" The Konig's comment was dry and formal as Stephen looked out toward the opposite end of the hall not wanting to see the figure of Vinder.

"His family has forgiven all that has been done to them by his foolishness and his pleas are sincere." Heimrick answered from behind the Konig, though he too looked beyond his son into the far end of the chamber.

"Has the great Lord of the Dwarves forgiven him, according to his priests?" Stephen continued the traditional dialogue.

"That too has been forgiven and vindication of past faults has been undertaken." Again Vinder's father responded in kind to Stephen.

"Then it is by sacred custom we should allow him to speak his mind at least once to see if he has proven worthy to be granted forgiveness and accepted back into his clan."

There was silence once more.

The silence lasted for only a moment when it was overcome by the song of Drued coming forth on the lips of the faithful priests of the clan. The melody was deep and strong, like the everlasting nature of rock.

The mix of baritone and tenor dwarven voices echoed in the chambers like a soft waterfall of sound. Drued was praised, and it felt as though the very air around those assembled pulsated with an energy and strength all their own.

It was the forge and anvil of Drued that seemed to push Vinder down with an energy that seemed to crush him as though the very weight of the mountain itself was upon him.

Drued had forgiven him that much was certain.

He couldn't be driven from that fact.

He had to prove true.

He knew this was the final test before his clan. He had to be judged by all of them to be free and allowed to enter into Clan Diamant once more.

Vinder took a deep breath, though his chest was heavy with the eyes and thoughts of those around him. He felt waves of sadness, grief, and anxiety crush him with a full weight of what he hoped would never be or do should he prove false in his statements. He wanted to heave the weight off of himself. It somehow felt untrue to him now. More than when he had first scaled the mountain peaks of his home. He knew he was worthy; he just had to hold out through the supernatural pressure on him.

As he stood, he clasped his hands into fists as the sweat began to pour out of his forehead and snake into his thick eyebrows. His single eye twitched with the rhythm of his heart, which had become fast and almost uncontrolled beneath the strain. He just needed to hold out for a few moments more then he would be free to offer up his plea and gift to buy his redemption.

It was at the final breaking point of the prodigal dwarf, that the song stopped and silence returned to the chamber once more.

"What then do you think you can do to gain back your honor? You have been allowed to speak for this answer, and this alone." Stephen was combative in his speech.

Vinder took a deep breath then spoke; "My brothers and sisters, I offer up to you this amount of riches. It has taken me a great time to amass them, but as each coin and trinket was placed in the pile, it was done with a deep, thorough understanding of my shame."

Vinder than walked over to the great chest and opened it. The locks and chains fell as he picked up the great lid, and let the sheen of the gold, silver and other treasures light up the eyes of those present.

"I offer up what possessions I have," Vinder's voice was as soft as talcum powder. "I beg, in the name of Drued, that it pleases you and can allow you to wash my sins from the past in which I have so greatly sullied my clan."

Vinder didn't dare look up to see what was transpiring. The lack of sound was all he needed to know. He didn't dare raise his head or the very tradition of the clan would be sacrificed by his eagerness and lack of following the divine conduct of this society, faith and personal conviction.

Vinder heard the footfalls of the Konig fall from his throne and travel toward him. They stopped by the great chest and from his limited vision; Vinder could see the great leader began to paw through the treasure like a rodent digging a burrow. The rustling of coins lasted only for a moment, and then Stephen spoke.

"This is hardly enough to make us forget your failings."

Vinder felt a great block crush his back and neck as his heart was torn from his chest. What had he left to desire or hope or plead for? He felt like an empty husk, of a dwarf; meaningless and without direction.

"What then is left for me to do, oh great Konig? How can I — what do I have to do to have your favor once more?" Vinder fought back his emotions.

Stephen turned from the chest and walked back to his throne in measured steps. "Your trespass was great. To compensate you must do something equally great for the clan."

"What is it?" Vinder spoke with a desperate conviction. "Name it and I will do it."

Stephen returned to his throne and looked at Vinder hard. The penitent dwarf hadn't raised his head at all from his submissive pose.

Stephen spoke in a clear tone that all could hear. "You must rid the world of the Troll, Cael."

Vinder's eye grew wide, and his heart began to beat with a rapid pace. He felt as though the rock on his back had grown to a mountain. A Troll? How was he to fight a Troll? He was only one man.

"If that is what must be done, then so let it be," Vinder bowed in deep respect at the Konig

"It is the clan's wish, Vinder. Slay Cael, and you will have proven your worth to the tribe by doing an action that is as beneficial to the clan as your original action was destructive.

"In one hour I will send you the information you need to seek out Cael and understand him as best as we do now. With this knowledge you will take to the giant's lair and prove your worth. Even if death should take you, then honor would be satisfied, and you will be given a hero's burial," Stephen's statement was final.

"I understand," Vinder softly complied, leaving the chamber and the chest behind him, only to pick up another filled with a great weight of questions, fears, and self-doubt.

Chapter 16

The stench of the Cael's lair overwhelmed Vinder. Shortly after his plea to be accepted to the clan, he'd been ushered to a back chamber where he was told what he had to do: kill the Troll, Cael. The same Troll that not even the bravest of hero's would dispatch since the prodigal dwarf had been a child. Nevertheless, if this is what needed to be done to reclaim his honor and place back in his clan; then so be it. He would do as his Konig decreed. So he had set out on his mission shortly after his audience with Stephen.

Cael's threats and actions had become more violent as of late, and so the Council of Elders, in accord with the Konig, decided to look for matters that would suit them in getting rid of the beast before too much time had passed, and his demands grew harsher and dwarven lives were lost or severely wounded in the outcome. How this would be done, though was being decided when news of Vinder's return reached the Konig's ears. It seemed perfect to have the prodigal dwarf take over the task of ridding the clan of their problem. Praise Drued for small favors.

Stephen was more conservative than some of his predecessors, and took the line on dwarven tradition to an unshakable and inflexible bedrock base. Stephen didn't really want to welcome Vinder back. To him all dwarves who fled the clan should never return. They should be considered dead, and treated as such for all time, for they had wounded their own honor, and sullied their family's standing as well as marred the clan itself by their actions. There should be no repentance for such an act.

Indeed, the Konig thought the very concept of giving them a chance for redemption was a terrible idea. It just showed him the laxity of the ways of the clan that had been eroding since the foundation of the clan by Diamant himself. If he could get Vinder killed rather than accept him back into the clan, then so much the better. And Stephen was sure he would die, for he was just one warrior, a dwarven warrior, true enough, but a lone warrior nonetheless, and was no match against a Troll. He'd die sure enough and, because he had to be mindful of the elders, he would welcome Vinder into the fold in death — for he was already dead by departing in the first place, wasn't he? There would be no harm in such an action, and all would return to normal once more. Stephen would be rid of this troublesome issue and if Drued was truly smiling on his twelve clans, then perhaps Cael might be wounded as well — perhaps even mortally. Vinder probably could get in at least one good strike before the giant struck him down…Yes indeed, praise Drued for small favors.

For Vinder though it was another matter. Fear overtook him like nothing he'd ever experienced before. As he walked down the mountain to where the Troll resided, Vinder tried to recall all the past tales of the giant he could recall from his childhood as well as what he'd been told by the elder dwarves who informed him about the lair of the creature.

Cael was an old Troll, a race of giants that, like linnorms, had survived from the old world (the days preceding the Shadow Years). While they were not as deadly as linnorms, they were tenacious and frenzy prone, they could rend a small company of warriors limb from limb before more than a handful could attempt to attack. Even when not frenzied, Trolls were deadly killers.

Trolls, like linnorms, had hounded the dwarven race since it first emerged. The two races had been at war from the very beginning, and would be for all time legends claimed. Though Trolls dwindled, and the dwarves excelled in numbers, they still met with bloody and disastrous consequences from time to time. The conflicts were usually over land and territory. Both dwarves and

Trolls preferred hilly and mountainous regions, making sure the lineage of warfare would pass on for more generations to come.

Cael was old when Vinder was young — Vinder's father telling him tales of the creature's age when he had been but a lad on his father's knee. Though no one had ever heard of a Troll dying of old age, no one thought they were immortal, just no one was sure as to how long they lived. While Cael might have been old, he would be far from infirmed or weakened by age. Rather the opposite was true of his race — they grew stronger with age, not weaker, as did the mortal races. This knowledge only added to Vinder's growing apprehension.

He didn't know what he was going to do when he got to the Troll's lair. He'd been told only a little more information than what he already knew from childhood, namely how Cael had warred with Clan Diamant since the longest living dwarf could recall, and then about two generations beyond that, so they claimed.

From time to time the Troll had proven to be a menace to them, but hadn't been much of a rampage of destruction, as some Trolls had the reputation as being. However, his status was well ingrained in Diamantic memory, and was what mattered most to Vinder and the clan.

Vinder continued to mull dismal thoughts over in his head as he neared the giant's lair. The entrance was a cave hung with threatening stalactites and littered with carrion, charred rock and earth. The stench became overwhelming as sulfur and rotting matter, both vegetable and meat, mixed into Vinder's nostrils.

He squinted his teary eye as the foul odor hit him, the acidic nature of the breeze stinging the orb like a thousand needles. He stopped just short of the deep darkness ebbing from the jagged portal, gripped his great axe in his hands — a reassurance of reality and his place in it. The only thing driving him forward was his dedication to the task to allow himself access back into the clan.

No lone warrior had ever faced off with a Troll and lived.

Thoughts, words, and deeds flooded over him. His whole life traveled through his mind like a rising wave cresting and then fell into the present with a violent energy reminding him he was mortal. He had fought for honor in his youth, and then to regain that honor — and later for survival. He never had to face such a foe as the one before him now. When Vinder stared into the dimness of the cave he saw the face of Asorlok return the gaze.

Was honor worth his own death?

Was he sure this is what he wanted, and there was no other way? As these thoughts screamed through his mind, he could not help to make a weakened smile. His time with the humans certainly made him something different than what he once was. He seemed to question and reason more, to look at things from different angles. It was time now to think in the dwarven black and white frame of mind, and leave the gray realities of the other worlds behind him. He had to, if he wanted to come back home and embrace his clan once more.

Vinder shook his bearded head. He was sure he wanted this. Sure he needed it to prove his worth and redeem his mind and spirit that had been at torment with themselves since his exile. He'd been deluded in his selfish pursuits. He had gained the world, but lost himself, his soul and spirit. He wasn't the whole dwarf that he once was.

He'd change that, though.

Honor. Family. Tradition.

These echoed throughout the cave of his mind as a wind, then took hold of his face and eyes. It was gentle and soft, like the touch of a young child; a parting feeling of love in the den of hate he was about to enter.

He took a deep breath, and set his foot into the cave.

The dwarf could get no further than one step before a violent tremor bloomed all around him. The aftershock sent the warrior on his back with a violent force. Small, loosened rocks and boulders flowed down around him, as dust and smoke flooded his sight. The following noise was deafening, like thunder at the heart of the storm.

When it subsided, the silence was more deafening than the first explosion.

Vinder sat up and brushed the dust from his chest, beard, and face.

"Shiril's Pick, what now?" He scraped the debris from his eye and mouth, spitting out a gray, chalky paste in frustration.

"By Drued, I'm getting sick of this. It's always something in my way."

Vinder bolted up and ran toward the cave, a war cry on his lips. If he was going to die he wanted to do so in honor and glory.

His time had come.

He had waited long enough, and nothing was going to stand in his way.

He ran into the lair and vanished from sight.

Chapter 17

Time flew beyond The Master and Cadrissa as they rode on the back of the Roc. Day had turned into a cool evening, but the sun still shined above them. Below, the world was covered in darkness. The two of them — The Master wide awake and Cadrissa slumbering behind him — flew with the great sphere of Tralodren beneath their heels; the stars and planets above and about them. Had Cadrissa been awake, she would have marveled at the whole scene before her — how the whole of the solar system itself was displayed out wide before her, beckoning her to study it as in-depth as she could. However, the mage could do little more than slumber.

The Master had been silent as to his present state, thinking as the wind blew through his dark hair. The reborn wizard knew he would have enough arcane might to at least survive an attack of the foe he was readying himself to face, but he wasn't so sure he had enough power to defeat him, and still accomplish his goals. In dealing with such matters of uncertainty in the past he'd always held fast to his unwavering belief in his own supremacy of the arcane arts. Now though, things were different. He'd have very little time to work his craft upon Tralodren; very little time for the delays he currently faced.

If this enemy had found him so soon after his arrival, then other enemies could as well. And he'd made many enemies in his long, unnatural life. Too many to dispatch at once or in succession should they plan to organize their retribution. He would have to have more aid, more power.

His living eyes settled upon the skull on top his staff. This distraction he was facing would have to end, and he would have to be free to pursue his goals before anyone else tried to stop him or he became too ragged, lost too much of his focus and magic before his goal was insight and accomplished.

His staff had been taken from another mage like so much of his other items and understandings. He'd built his knowledge upon the magical arts so fast because he stole most of it from others. His lust for such gain called him to do so. He wanted all the power he could gather, and wasn't often enamored with the idea of working hard when so much was ripe for the picking for those who knew how around him.

He had taken much — devoured it like a devilish raven. In a short matter of time he had risen to be one of the most powerful Wizard Kings in the fourth and final — Age of the Wizard Kings.

That was many years in the past, and spawned the dark days of war and mistrust of magic following it for many centuries. The Fourth Age also turned many magical insights and discoveries over to oblivion, further limiting the potential revival of powerful magic, which The Master still knew, but none other could ever hope to perform on their own. Following the ages to come after the Fourth Age, magic would never be the same and those who practiced it never again would rise into such heights of power as the previous eras once allowed. For practitioners in this current span of years were mere shadows of the great mages who once straddled the world as colossal towers of mystical might.

It had been in those ancient days The Master had taken the staff from a wicked wizard who made his magic focus in the darkest of spells. The former lich had learned much from that long dead wizard, most importantly, how to make himself into a lich.

The staff had been created from the skull of a child who was the offspring of a god and mortal woman who had long sense been forgotten in the waves of time. Such offspring were typically called godspawn, and were very rare in the times of The Master's mortality — even rarer in the present day. They had the potential to be great forces of good or evil should they grow up, but they were still mortal in the end, despite their divine pedigree and died of old age or more common maladies as did any mortal. Such was the case with the donor of the skull for The Master's staff.

He had been born to a woman who didn't want the child of the forced sexual union (The Master never did figure out what god had sired the child), as the dark wizard who formed the staff promptly killed her after she gave birth. The same dark mage had taken the child's skull and bound it to the powerful magic already at work in the staff. The result was a special power no other enchanted item possessed at that time, or has since. The staff could unleash the full fury of a dying god upon any person the owner so chose. The Master had never dared use it since he took it as a trophy. He knew such a release would be near impossible to control, and even harder to survive, taking the staff and most probably himself with it.

The loss of his staff would cause him a temporary reduction in power, but more so, it would cause him to rely upon himself more since he didn't have any other crutches to rest upon and conserve his energy. It was a serious choice, since he would be left open to a wider array of attacks should his enemies chose to make them. Still though, he kept this thought in the back of his mind as an option birthed by desperation. He no longer dreaded losing his own existence in the unleashed blast of deific fury. He had become more skilled and stronger since he had first acquired the staff, and he was at the pinnacle of his powers as well...

The Roc flew lower after some time, and daylight again returned to the wizards. It was like being the sun itself, emanating the rays of light to those who lived beneath them, so tiny and distant, so insignificant...

Even as the great bird of prey flew toward a large cloud, The Master laughed out loud at the scene unfolding before him. The chilling effect of his mirth woke the slumbering Cadrissa, who had regained some of her strength, but not enough to wield any mystical energy. Dazed at what she'd seen, she had to regain her senses and get herself refreshed for the current situation...if she could, that was.

The ability to wield magic was an inherited trait; some believed it was passed on from the purity of lineage from the Dranors — whom many claim were the forefathers of mortal kind. The handful of mortals who had such an ability were able to wield influence, and control over the sixteen Cosmic Elements: fire, water, air, earth, life, death, good, evil, light, darkness, time, space, ice, magma, chaos, and order.

This ability was made possible by their strength of will, spirit and inherited cistern of ability, often called a Mystical Well, residing in each mage. It was this three-fold force that made it possible to cast spells. However, the vessel that still cast them, namely the mage herself, was still given to the limitations of mortal kind and couldn't do so forever. They needed rest to recover from the pressures placed upon them by focusing their will and spirit to draw forth from their inner 'well' to manifest a desired effect.

Mages were able to increase their abilities by various methods. Studying the forgotten tongue of the Dranors aided them in better being able to tap into their inherited nature. This created the need for many spells to have incantations to help align the three-fold force mages were focusing into a more effective manifestation.

Studying from previous mages who had long since entered Mortis was also helpful. Many a mage could learn from them and gain new ways to cast spells that they might have never been able to come to perform on their own efforts. Adding gestures to some spells, and some components to spells helped the potency of the mage's will by giving them something to focus their will and spirit. The components were also helpful, as they became conduits of the mystical energy they were commanding. This helped ease the strain a bit on their inner well, thus making the spell not as overwhelming as it could be, and allowing more magic to be worked by a wizard who might have been the case without such items.

Practice in the art of casting spells allowed the mage to grow in strength and ability. Their inner well of energy was like a muscle in many ways, and the more it was stretched, the more it was worked, the stronger it became, and the longer it could hold out and supply energy to the spells a mage wanted to cast as long as his will and spirit held out. These too, though, could be increased in their level of endurance by continued effort. This was why the nature of the arcane arts was so disciplined and regimentally focused in nature.

If one let their craft slip in practice long enough, they would find their grasp of the intricacies of magic slipping from what they once had been. Cadrissa had learned this at the academy in Haven where she'd studied from learned masters. She'd see many students take time off from their studies, and then return weaker than they had been before they left. It was because of this revelation the wizardress resolved to always be a student. And this experience was certainly going to teach her much, if she was able to survive it.

She looked at the hem of The Master's cloak where she had placed the amulet Endarien had given her, and saw it still blazed with the golden halo of light radiating from the eyes of the Roc upon which she now traveled. Fear swam in her stomach as she dreaded what might happen next. She'd played a role in all this, and she prayed Endarien was true to his world and protected her regardless of what transpired in the moments ahead.

She directed her view ahead of the Roc, and watched as the very cloud before them turned into something more tangible — various collections of shapes and designs starting to form a structure of sorts. Like the boat made of cloud, this too seemed to be formed from something weak and fleeting, to a strong, solid substance.

First, a tall spire resting on a square foundation appeared, then a wall around the tower about a mile in length. As they neared, she could make out details in the tower; small bricks began to form in the walls of cloud making up the form. Then, smaller rooms of stone shaped clouds appeared around the larger tower. As Cadrissa grew closer, she surmised the tower's full height at about eighty feet. Its base was large too, and as they landed on the cloud, before it faded from view behind the tall wall before them, she judged it to be about fifty feet in width. The whole cloud crafted community simply amazed her at both its size and construction. It was like a small village or abbey.

The Roc landed gracefully, making no sound, as it stood almost motionless before the great wall surrounding the newly created buildings. The barrier floated along the bare outskirts of the cloud itself, having just about twenty or so odd feet before the cloud lost its structural integrity, and fell into churning mists.

"This is our destiny my dear," The Master dismounted in a fluid motion from the back of the giant bird.

"Wha-Where are we?" Cadrissa looked about her with a wonderful expression, much like that of a young child. She'd given up trying to make sense of everything — her every increasing role in things. It was just too hard.

She dismounted cautiously. Not wanting to trust the cloud at holding her up, but knowing in the back of her mind if it supported The Master, it could support her too.

"We are here to settle some unfinished business," He ran his fingers through his wind tussled hair, then looked at the wall and began to march toward it in a stiff manner.

"How does this involve *both* of us? I certainly don't have any business on a giant cloud with monstrous birds and flying vessels made of cloud." Cadrissa kept her distance from the dark mage. This wasn't her fight; wasn't even her place. Let The Master and Endarien have their confrontation. She had done her part, and now wanted no more involvement in it at all.

The Master stopped and then turned toward her. "How do you expect to gain power, to gain knowledge if you don't begin to raise your expectations? A wizard is a being who wields more power than any mortal should. He is limited only by his will and ambition to succeed and ability to achieve more; to be stopped only by things of his own imaginings."

His vengeful eyes reflected hot blue flames of hate, motioning to Cadrissa with his hand as he clenched it into a fist. "To me," he commanded.

"I've gone along with this so far, but you forget I'm a mortal, and not fit for most of this journey you have forced me through." Cadrissa braved to speak aloud her thoughts. "Just leave me here, and I'll ride the Roc back to some other land and be out of your life, then I can begin mine once more." She feared just what might happen next, and felt the stakes were already increasing to staggering heights that made her wish to be somewhere else.

Perhaps it was time to go if she could. Mayhap, even Endarien was allowing her to depart now by aid of the Roc and so it certainly was an opportunity she might avail herself. It had been a real experience to learn alongside the mage, but now it was getting a bit too challenging and she truly began to fear for her life. She had to take the opportunity to try and get out from his clutches, no matter how feeble the action might be.

"I wish it could be that simple. I grow tired of your company as well. However, I still have a use for you. You will come with me and witness this confrontation and then witness my ascent into godhood. Come, the hour already grows long." He turned and began to walk once more toward the seemingly solid cloud wall.

"I can certainly just wait for you by the Roc..." Cadrissa turned and saw nothing was behind her.

It was just an empty cloud.

Not even a hint of the giant bird remained.

Cadrissa was dumbfounded, and began to feel her head spin with amazement, then excitement at having been witnessed to such an exciting thing. Where had it gone to without any sound?

"Satisfied?" The former lich mused darkly, "You have no choice. For better or for worse you are now bound," The Master's tone was solid, "to me."

Cadrissa looked once more at the spot the Roc had been, then turned toward The Master. It seemed she indeed did have little choice but to follow The Master if she wanted to get off of the cloud, and ever get a chance of having her life back. Hoping for the best, she followed the dark mage. She prayed Endarien wouldn't let her be harmed and the whole affair of his with The Master would be over and not involve her at all. For if it was the god himself whom they were about to meet — or was it re-meet? She had already met the deity...even though that had been a meeting of just one aspect of the god. Cadrissa didn't want to be anywhere near the two foes as they eyed each other once more after their centuries long absence.

Behind her a soft wind had begun to blow.

The Master approached the wall.

His hands touched the rough-hewed surface that should have felt very soft and fluffy — almost insubstantial. The wall instead conveyed the very essence of stone. It was the same magic that The Master had used to work his spell with the boat. Cadrissa was sure of it.

The clouds were a weird reality all in themselves. She found herself having dizzy spells, and her legs seemed to float out from under her and quivered like jelly as she navigated the cumulus domain. More than once she thought she would lose her balance and fall through the 'ground' beneath her to plummet to her death below. So far she had been spared such a fate.

Above her, thicker clouds billowed outward across the blue expanse of sky. Birds circled above, and the sun poured down upon them. It was as if she had ventured onto an island in the sea. Except this island was in the sky and crafted by the will of a being she could never hope to understand. When not fearful of falling, Cadrissa felt like a spirit upon them; so peaceful and free, yet the image of The Master in front of the wizardress made her suddenly lose any giddiness that had bubbled up inside her.

The stern form before her held no emotion, nor made any movement at all. Even his cloak and robe didn't blow in the wind picking up around them, making him seem like a statue instead of flesh. The uneasiness of the silence made her rush to fill it.

"So…what have you discovered?" Cadrissa approached the mage.

"Your boldness is beginning to grate on me. We are in a portion of the past, revived into the present. That is all you need know for now." He didn't turn to address her, but continued to touch the stone with his hand, then withdrew it.

"I don't understand. What do you mean? What is this all about?" She spoke in haste, and again, wished she hadn't, as she again remembered to whom she was speaking.

A cold serpent slithered up her spine, and she began to break out in an arctic sweat all over her body. The Master turned around, with blue flames leaping into the centers of his pupils and a snarl upon his face.

"Silence, or you will be silenced!" The words were just below a shout. "You will do what I say! Your life hangs in the balance, or have you forgotten? You were promised lessons if you behaved — and up until now you have — so watch and learn! Pester me with your prattling questions once more, and I will not be so kind!"

With an explosive burst The Master turned back to the wall and let loose a handful of black energy shooting out from his hands in thick bolts. These bolts flew into the cloud-constructed wall and ate away a large hole in it. The area around the hole widened and crumbled to the ground with a large, jagged opening remaining in the middle of the once solid barrier.

"You will follow," The Master said flatly, then strode over the debris and entered the inner area behind the wall.

The wizardress stepped through the opening, and into a courtyard of sorts. The squat, square buildings she had seen earlier were stationed around the tall tower. They looked like barracks or simple lodge rooms for travelers or the like. It was eerily silent on the other side of the wall, as it had been on the outskirts, near the cloud's end. What struck her as odd though was there was a stronger breeze in the courtyard than what should be expected. It puzzled her how there was no way for such a thing to have occurred in terms of logic and nature.

"Stay close," The Master said as he walked toward a building on his immediate left. This part of the cloud had been made to mimic some kind of storage room or living quarters. Short trees and bushes, all shades of white dotted the cobblestone walkway before them, and wound around the tower. The whole scene became surreal to Cadrissa. She looked and saw a well in the distance. Even the minutest details had been sculpted into reality. As she viewed the landscape she was amazed at the entire experience. It seemed so real — so filled with a purpose, though none was presented to her.

The wizardress thought about her surroundings further as a breeze swept her face. She felt dizzy for a moment, and then a thousand voices called out to her all at once. She felt sick, and warm and could smell fire, burning flesh, and wood. In the distance she heard the sound of screaming people, crying out like they were in their death throes. Explosions rocked her head, and she felt singes of flames near her mouth and nose.

And then the world around her grew hazy and dark…

Cadrissa blinked and found herself in a mountainous area filled with smoke, ash, and a heavy, hard wind. She could hear the cries of lament from countless people around her, though she couldn't see them. She could smell the stench of death, burnt bodies and other foul things. Her eyes became red with pain, and she felt as though they would burn themselves from her sockets as hot, ashy debris flooded her vision.

Tiny embers landed on her face and body, singing small portions of her skin like miniature fallen stars. Her lungs began to burn up inside from the heated, sooty air scraping around inside her chest.

Just when she could no longer endure the experience, and felt as though she would scream, a strong wind blew across her face. She coughed as the smoke and ash choked and blinded her, but the air also smelled sweet too…

Cadrissa blinked again, and found herself behind The Master on the cloud, and supposedly safe. The young Telborian was more taken back by the fact she had just visited a different place. She entered into a location that didn't exist in the same reality she did. She'd felt the difference. It was stranger than the experience she had in The Master's tower with Endarien. She wondered if it was the same scene, and then thought against it. It seemed too different, yet she felt she knew part of it.

What was its purpose though? What had it to do with her and maybe The Master as well? She closed off her mind to all other distractions, and tried to focus on this new interesting fact as she kept her foot and eye trained on The Master ahead of her. She watched as he tried to open a door on one of the shorter buildings. Returning as she did from the visit to the other reality, the wizardress had no idea what was going on anymore, and felt very afraid and frustrated.

Cadrissa noticed though the golden disc on the hem of The Master's garments still glowed. She wondered why the former lich hadn't discovered this yet, and just counted it a small blessing he didn't.

"What was I thinking?" Of course he wouldn't have gone to such lengths," The Master spoke to himself as he tried once more to pull the handle of the door which wouldn't open.

Cadrissa studied The Master. She thought it was safe for her to get some answers — minor ones if nothing else. She had to sense at least one of her mental dilemmas had been answered so some sanity remained with her.

"The doors are locked?" Her voice was small and unassuming.

"No. They're not fully formed. The walls are all a front, as was the wall, and this tower. This is just a prop for a much larger play. I should have realized that even he wouldn't go to such extremes to deal with me." The Master walked away from the door with disgust, apparently in a good enough mood to humor Cadrissa with an answer. "This is all just illusion."

"Very good," a voice echoed across the sky. "I knew it wouldn't take you too long to discover that fact."

"What's happening?" Cadrissa dashed her gaze around as fear lined her face, and made her hands quake. "Who is that?"

"Welcome to my domain," a thin, old man appeared before them. He was balding on his wrinkled, pale head and possessed the frame of a bent twig. He was clean-shaven, looked to be of Telborian descent, and wore a simple albinistic garment shimmering with silver streaks of light whenever the wind caressed its folds. His eyes were like ponds of pure blue crystal, and his very manner spoke of higher breeding than his state of dress conveyed.

"Who are you?" Cadrissa asked, as her mind had not yet caught up to her mouth.

"What your companion has been avoiding to tell you my dear is that he and I have a long history together. I am Endarien."

"*You're* Endarien?" She cowered on her knees instantly and felt as though she would grow sick with fear, recalling the way the god revealed himself to her before in The Master's tower.

The Master laughed, throwing his cloak recklessly to the ground.

"The gods are not meant to be worshipped by the likes of us, child, they are beings equal to ourselves," The Master took a closer step to the old man, but kept a fair amount of distance between them.

"You could learn much from her humility Cadrith," the old man motioned for Cadrissa to rise up from her knees.

"Rise, Cadrissa, and be at peace, my battle is not with you. I have to finish what this fool started so long ago. As was spoken, my promise to your safety shall remain."

"I thought as much," The Master spat. "I knew you'd try to use the girl against me, I just didn't know how or when. Now that you've shown your hand, I can be done with this and finish using her for my own purposes free from your taint," The former lich's blue eyes flashed azure, "After she has been punished for her actions."

Cadrissa arose slowly in confusion. The Master's threat didn't faze her as it might have earlier. Things were too surreal to her now as if she had wandered into a play a bit late and now was trying to make sense of what was being acted out before her as well as trying to make sense of what had gone on before she had arrived.

She wondered if this form was the true shape of Endarien. He looked different then how she'd seen him in The Master's tower. She knew from her studies gods could take any form they wished. Endarien had told her as much when they had last met, but why did he feel the need to take on such a form as the one he now presented? What was the purpose of a form that seemed rather weak and unimpressive to even her?

Why was Endarien after The Master anyway? What was the reason a god would fight a mortal? More importantly, why did the Master seem so sure he'd win such a conflict? She was quite intrigued by the mystery.

"Now is the time for retribution," the god spoke. "You'll pay for the innocent blood you shed; the destruction you have wrought."

When he again returned his full attention to The Master Endarien felt like something overshadowed the dark mage, further darkening his cruel visage. Something he hadn't seen until just then. Yes…something was certainly there, something he doubted even The Master knew was present. The god still couldn't be certain, but he figured an outside force was behind The Master — an external entity infused with him, empowering him more than the former lich realized. Worse still was the Storm Lord had an inkling of who that entity just might be…

He would have to test his theory out some more, try him in battle before he was sure, but for now it was a very possible theory. The arrogant fool probably thought the boon it gave him of his own making. Little did he know what was going on about him, but the Endarien figured Cadrith's eyes would be opened soon enough. That was, if he survived this encounter…

"Really?" The Master smirked. "You really can't let that temple go, can you? What are those people to a god anyway? They were mortals — long since turned to dust. What are they to you?"

Suddenly, a brilliance overwhelmed the mind of Cadrissa and she knew what the smoldering image she'd seen earlier had been. It was the ruins of the very place where she now stood! The clouds had been crafted to appear like the real structure, which had fallen away into ruin.

The Master laughed, and drew his staff close to him. "I thought this place looked familiar when we first landed. It wasn't until I got behind the wall that I recognized it fully. You thought to fight me in the very copy of the temple I destroyed.

"I must admit though, the image you have chosen to represent yourself leaves much to be desired for a god. The high priest of the temple died begging me to have mercy on him. Not a good omen for you at all, old one."

The Master tapped his staff with his hand. Instantly he was covered in a bright red nimbus shining for but a moment all around him before fading away.

Cadrissa could do little but stand dumbfounded on the sidelines as the great battle began. She didn't even see the cloud seat form beneath her, nor feel her body crumble into it with a sigh. All she could think and concentrate on was the conflict that would soon be in front of her.

"Let this be over with then. You will not detain me from my goal," The Master brought forth a bolt of black energy from the skull head of his staff, which struck the god full in the chest.

The Lord of the Winds was knocked back onto the ground by the blow.

Endarien leapt up from the ground to throw a silvery white bolt of his own making at the dark mage. The crackling javelin of death bored toward the lich with deadly accuracy. However, as it neared, The Master simply held up his staff, and the white lightning blended into the air before it touched him.

"You have grown very weak, Endarien. You should have learned I can't be beaten. Not now, and not ever."

"The dog can bark, but his bite is not even evident," Endarien brushed off the charred spot on his robe where the bolt had struck him. Small chunks of ash and blackened flesh fell away from the wound as he did so. The god paid it no heed; as though it had been a bug that had annoyed him. "You forget I'm a god, and my time is eternal. My power is divine and unending. "Now, let me show you how a *real* master works his craft."

The Storm Lord then faced his palms out toward the dark mage, and unleashed two large bolts of golden lightning. This time when they struck The Master's magical barrier, summoned by means of the red nimbus he enacted earlier, it didn't hold. Instead, The Master flew into the air as both strikes hit him close to his heart. An explosive thunder followed, shaking the very bones of the nearby god himself. Ozone hovered all around the cloudy domain, and a thick mist swirled where The Master had once stood.

Cadrissa was terrified, and at the same time couldn't move. Was the battle over already? Had The Master lost? Unable to answer any of these questions, her eyes simply grew wider.

"It seems you are much more mortal than you would have yourself believe," Endarien laughed.

"Dalor yonire calobin! Ambrea esol esol! Cambioa!" The Master's voice came from behind the god.

Endarien turned just in time to see The Master's hand, now a charred ruin of bone and burnt flesh, pulse with a magenta glow, which the former lich released in a beam toward the god. He'd lost most of his robe, and flesh on his body. Parts of him still smol-

dered, and a flame blazed on his head, which was now just bone
— his face a patchwork of flesh, bone and charcoal remnants of his
former visage. He appeared to be a hybrid of his former, skeletal
self, and the one of flesh he had recently adopted. Only his will
kept him still holding to life — his spirit within the body of ruined
flesh. Will and the immense well, of mystical energy within him.

The beam struck Endarien's right shoulder where it quickly
overcame him, enveloping his entire body in an opaque magenta
globe whose outer surface took on a mirror-like sheen as it swelled
to envelope the god.

Endarien screamed, and all Tralodren drew silent at the
horrid noise.

Like some hideous demon, the lich gloated over the success
of his spell; the charnel fumes of his singed and searing flesh
surrounding him like a stinking, shadowy mantle.

"I've learned much from my time as a Wizard King. I've
even learned to use the darker side of the very binding energy of
the cosmos itself while I bided my time away from this world," The
Master's ruinous eyes narrowed. "I can do things no other wizard
ever could."

"Even gods die, Endarien," The Master laughed once more,
as dry, coal-like chunks and flaming substance cascaded from this
face and body.

For a moment there was silence.

The Master too was still in his observation. He had unleashed
one of his most powerful spells — an enactment of mystical energy
dealing death to even the more stalwart of foes. However, he was
a god, and though The Master knew this was only a representation
of Endarien, it was still a god-like being nonetheless. His spells
might not be as potent as they were upon non-divine foes. Still it
should wound him deeply, maybe even mortally, he hoped.

Cadrissa still watched from the sidelines. Safety from the
attack had slipped her mind as she mentally scurried to take in
just what The Master had cast, and how it was done. She tried to
learn of, and from, the spell and the nature of Endarien's magic

even as the battle waged on. Cadrissa had become drawn into it not so much from the sheer violence of the conflict nor for how she would be treated by either party after the outcome, but by the amazing insight into the realm of the arcane arts which she had yet to see presented in any other place save this.

The Master took a step back and readied his staff when the globe around Endarien splintered, then shattered in an explosion of white light.

Endarien then looked up at The Master from a crouched position where he had been inside the globe. The god appeared to be a gaunt skeleton; like a poor wretch who hadn't had a meal in months. It was a wonder his feet and emaciated legs could support his meager frame at all as he rose and seemed to be barely able to hold him together, let alone upright. Yet his spirit and voice were still true and they sneered at his challenger.

"Had your fun, young man?" The extremely elderly Endarien then raised his bony, liver spot-covered hand in the air where it greeted a crash of lightning as it fell upon him, swallowing his image wholly from sight.

"Now stay dead this time!" A blinding flashed caused both The Master and Cadrissa to momentarily shield their eyes from the spectacle. "The Abyss has kept a place for you for a long time, and Asorlok has gotten very impatient to host your arrival."

A new form of Endarien followed the display. He looked as he did before the battle started, healed and whole, and no longer aged beyond all time. His face was resolute, the trace of a thin smile upon his chiseled lips.

Endarien also surmised his theory had indeed been correct. There was a force behind The Master, silent and transparent, but there none-the-less. He grew more concerned when he began to gain an understanding of just what the force was exactly. He'd faced off with it before…the past memory did little to lighten his concerns instead they deepened. Perhaps though he would be able to win out still, the darkness over the lich was a shadow at that, a thin flickering of the real essence it conveyed…perhaps…

The Master took a step back, clutching his staff closer to him, trying to use it to shield him from any more attacks from the god. "Impressive," his lipless mouth stated.

"Yet another ability you will never have, Cadrith," he raised his hands into the air, and began to rotate his wrists.

Instantly, this action summoned a large whirlwind, twisting it out of the very air itself around The Master, snatching him up in its claws. Inside he was flung around like a rag doll drug behind a raging bull. The sensation was maddening.

The Master couldn't stop the whirlwind, and he couldn't focus enough to bring any spells to mind. He was adrift in the center of the wind, tumbling and turning about wherever the funnel cloud so cared to move him. There was not much he could do to end this ordeal, not at the moment at least. He had little choice but to ride it out as best he could. Even as more of his crisp figure was shifted from him like chaff and wheat, he began to muster his will into a tight beam, focusing it as best he could on the one last thing he could think of to end this battle, and allow him to escape Endarien.

This sidetrack had taken far too much out of him already. If he continued this battle, he knew he would lose. He just couldn't beat Endarien — not now, he wasn't prepared for such a fight. It needed to stop — and stop now.

"You'll be happy to know, Cadrith," Endarien crossed his arms over his chest, gloating over the success of his work, "I've been told your old allies wish to offer you a special greeting as well. Namely a creature by the name of Balon, who wishes to personally greet you upon your arrival."

The Master's cooked and fleeting face turned to the staff in his hand, while a still good eye was slowly being pulled from its socket to join his other melted gooey globe as he looked at the object of power.

It had come to that moment of desperation. He had no other recourse now, and time was already short. His will was strong, but it wasn't strong enough to keep him alive in this body. He could cast a spell to revert back to a lich, but he needed somewhere private and safe. He had to be able to do so quickly too, for he wouldn't be able to live much longer in his current state. No such place or time was afforded him at the moment, however.

It was a gamble, but so too was trying to win out against Endarien. That was a gamble with worse odds still. No, he had to follow through and be done with it, whatever might befall him.

His condensed eye peered into the skull on top of his staff, the skull of that tiny godling slain so long ago.

He felt the energy that was buried there long ago.

It was a wild, chaotic energy — the very heart of a god itself. What better way to kill a god than with a god? Though it wasn't Endarien's true form itself, the satisfaction would be just the same upon his death; even if the former lich should go with him, at least he'd have that satisfaction in the end.

The Master concentrated all the willpower he could muster into protecting himself from the blast that was sure to come from the staff's destruction. He then used his mystical understanding of the staff to shift most of it to the form of the god— ensuring his destruction. Pulling against the strong gales of the whirlwind to extend the staff before him then leveling it in front of himself toward Endarien with muscles that were being torn away from ligament and bone.

In his mind The Master spoke the final word to unleash the staff's long enshrined potential. He felt the eldritch forces begin to build in an expansive explosion deep within the bone and wood shaft as he witnessed the skull's eyes glow a brilliant white. The binding spells held back from the death throes of the slain godling now being unfettered after millennia, were not diminished in the slightest.

"Endarien. You have failed," The Master shouted from the wind even as he felt his joints being racked apart from the great stresses of the wind.

"Ever the braggart. Enjoy the afterlife in torment Cadrith!" Endarien's face was as stern as a cliff. He watched with delight as more and larger chunks of the former lich's body were torn away, his clothes now almost ripped to shreds, splintered into mere trailing threads.

"We shall see!" The Master fought against the wind as though they were rapids in a river, and managed to aim the staff as best he could so the skull faced the god, lining up his sights as he timed the rotation of his being just right so as to face the god when he let go the godling's final cry.

Steady.

Steady.

Now!

"Taste the fury of one of your own!" The Master let loose the confined spirit in his staff. A thick blast of gray light, laced with pink veins, flew out of the melting skull on top the staff and toward Endarien.

The impact was powerful, knocking the god backwards as he staggered in a brief dance to stay balanced and upright. The Master was flung from inside the whirlwind, destroying it as he was expelled, and was just able to throw the worn wooden shaft from him his bony grasp before it exploded into millions of white, hot splinters. He lay on his back, propped up by his elbows as he tried to recover from the ordeal, watching the effect the attack had upon the god.

Cadrissa joined him in that stare, a dumbfounded, open mouthed stare causing what she witnessed to stay emblazed in her mind till the end of her days.

Endarien's frame shattered in a brilliant display of light and darkness, color and nothingness. Millions of minute demons clawed his skin, ripping out tiny pieces of bloodied muscle as the very cloud-formed substance on which he stood grew thinner, and then disappeared altogether. The small spirits pecked and pulled, tugged, and dug into the semblance of the old priest with a ravenous frenzy. Endarien tumbled to his knees, bursting into an avian screech as gray flames erupted from his pores. He'd been beaten, but this wasn't over, not yet.

There would yet be a reckoning.

He would have his revenge.

"This isn't over," Endarien screamed as he, and his creation, simmered into the morning sky like fog being banished by the sun. The god's former frame now was falling into dull, lifeless ash.

Endarien had his answer then. The shadow, which hung over Cadrith was indeed stronger still than what he had first thought possible. This was not a good omen, and he knew the others would discover it too in short order…they had to prepare for the worse then.

The Master was silent.

He was weak too.

Too weak.

The battle had taken more out of him than he had known. His bony elbows slipped and he fell back to the ground, passing into unconsciousness as the very world the vanquished god had created began to dissolve back into formless mist.

Cadrissa screamed as she felt the ground give way beneath her, quickly coming to her senses once more.

"We're doomed! The very ground is being taken from us!" As soon as she had spoken, the tower, walls, floors, and buildings around them melted into normal, amorphous clouds once more, then began to float away. Everything that had once been was now lost in the moist vapor.

The two wizards, unable to be held aloft anymore by such cumulus material, sunk into the thinning mists as if they stood on top melting marshmallows. However, this sensation, too, faded as quickly as the sponginess of the ground gave way to a soupy marsh…

And then there was nothing under them at all.

Cadrissa could feel her feet slipping through the cloud, and touching nothing but air underneath. Then she felt herself slide down to her knee, then thigh… It was then the clouds parted and there was nothing all around her flailing frame.

She was able to see through the fleeting mists as she sunk through. She screamed as she beheld Tralodren now racing up to smother her with its crushing embrace as the last of the opaline tendrils of mist let go their retreating grip.

Chapter 18

The hard blunt stick hit Dugan again.

The great force of the blow forced him toward the ground with an irritated growl. He lifted himself up with his bruised and bloody arms and looked up at his attacker. The cloaked figure was silent and still. He didn't gloat over his victim or jibe him, merely watched him with an intense gaze. Dugan could see the look of calculated thought and lightning fast reflexes underneath his hood, he was finding more than his match in this challenger.

"You are strong and quick, but you must learn to use deception and stealth if you are to complete the task at hand," the robed figure said as Dugan stood once more, frustration sweeping across his brow.

"Let me rest for a moment now. We've been at this since dawn, or as near to it as I can figure in this dungeon you call home," Dugan growled.

"Fine," the figure bowed, "you may rest for a moment."

Dugan went over to a wooden chair near the far wall of the small, dimly lit, spartan room, and collapsed into it. He let out a heavy sigh as he felt every sore muscle and bruised bone in his body. The Telborian shook his head, and let fly a great shower of sweat from his scratched and bruised head. He'd been training for the past week under the tutelage of the cult of Shador. They fed him and kept him full of health, but drilled him from dawn to dusk. They had taught him how to be silent and unseen at times, and how to feel out a situation before one enters into it.

He was being taught intuitive and roguish styles of combat while at the same time lessening his dependence upon brute force in every situation. Encouraged to learn this new way of fighting to aid him in his quest, Dugan seemed to be grasping the insight into the style very rapidly, but it seemed that he wasn't grasping it fast enough.

"You have learned much more than I could have hoped, Dugan," the robed figured glided over to the blond warrior. The Telborian still knew none of their names, or hardly any of their faces — only vague shadows and limited glimpses. He grew to learn they preferred secrecy; it made him feel at a disadvantage and think back to the days when he was a gladiator under a different instructor, but similar circumstances. In some ways he felt powerless in this situation as well — almost as if it was a reflection of his former life in a way.

"Have I? I feel like I've wasted the past week with getting bruises and sore muscles, and made to be the fool." Dugan looked up with a wary head toward his instructor. He was already tired and the day was just beginning. He wished he could just roll back into the soft, goose featherbed the cult had provided for him. Roll back and forget.

The Telborian rubbed his bare chest and arms, using the profuse sweat as an ointment. He was barefoot and wore nothing else save his tight leather pants with signs of scuffmarks and other abrasions from repetitive blows and scrapes gained during his active training.

"No, far from it," the cultist confessed. "You have progressed beyond what most members here could only hope to learn before they die. You must learn to contain your rage though, and wait with patience. This is your biggest enemy. The task at hand is one of stealth, cunning, and accuracy. You will not be able to complete it if you charge into it like a raging bull, goring all in your path."

"I've killed many a man that way in the arena, and lived to tell the tale," Dugan stated plainly, feeling at least some energy retuning to him as he recounted all his past victories over death's grip in the coliseum.

"This won't be the arena Dugan. The stage is too large, and the danger too great to act as you once did. To kill the Mayor in his very bedroom you must do things our way, or you won't survive to be freed from your curse." The robed figure fell silent once more, and floated over to the middle of the room.

Dugan still cringed slightly at the mention of the task he'd agreed to perform for these cultists. He hated to think he'd improved his lot in life from gladiator to mercenary to assassin, but it appeared this was what had to be done to be totally free. His only reassurance the past week of his arduous training, and the matter of his current task, was his healed shoulder. The bare flesh was nothing short of a holy relic; a sign to his freedom was just beyond his grasp. Freedom he wanted so badly he was willing to do just about anything for it.

He kept telling himself each day, as he checked it when he rose from slumber to do more training, the slaughter of the Mayor was nothing to him when compared with his freedom. He had to keep his own perspective in this matter, or else suffer the pains of too much thought, and a moral argument. He wasn't ready for such a thing, but was waiting to deal with it after the deed was done, and he was truly a freeman.

Why he should have such an ill time about the matter when he had killed men and beast on a regular basis before now, made little sense to him. It was as if being freed in his physical life, his own conscience was unleashed a bit as well. The sensation was far from natural to him.

Again though, why it would chose now to arise from its former depths he didn't know. Pushing the thought aside, he focused on the task at hand, breaking it down into the bare requirements and steps, mastering those as best he could in order to end this new task as soon as possible.

"Let us begin again," the robed figure spun his stick in a great circle, then stood like a statue as the gladiator shook his golden mane once more and approached.

"You must avoid the blows and anticipate their arrival, before they come to you," the figure dryly instructed. "In this battle it is not the strongest who wins, nor he who charges into the fight, it is the swift and agile; the thoughtful warrior who is successful. You must learn to take heed of that inner sense of self. It will save your life more often than you think."

The figure swung the stick toward Dugan.

It was low on the ground, and struck his feet, which knocked them out from under him, causing him to fall to the floor. Dugan shouted violent curses as he hit hard upon the flagstone surface beneath him.

"*Concentrate*, you big ox! Stop looking outward for how you react to a situation first presented to you, but respond before the first blow can land, see the path it will take." The figure waited for Dugan to stand, who snarled a few protests under his breath, but managed to right himself once more, and eye his trainer with a contemplative glare.

The cultist stood without any kind of motion or look of action. Instead, he simply hovered with the ash wood staff in his hand. Dugan was furious as he looked on this as a mocking gesture. Still though, he tried to hold his ground, and make his body feel outward with a stronger sense of perception. He had done so for days.

Long days.

Long, painful, days that could have been weeks — and he hadn't found any improvement in this method of training he was aware of. Still though, he tried once more. He had to master it if he would be deemed worthy to aid the cultists in their mission, and get his own reward. It was then, he felt the first twinge of air around him, and knew the cultist had moved his staff. Where though, he couldn't yet discern, but he knew it was close to him. The gladiator stared at the cloaked man for a moment as he came toward him.

He thought it odd how he looked to be moving very slowly all the while the Telborian observed him. Dugan could see his every move, and now could see where the staff was falling. He stepped to his right and felt the air twinge around his left shoulder, as the staff struck empty space beside him. Dugan then smiled at his own accomplishment as the world returned to its normal speed once more.

"Well done Dugan. Now you learn," the figure gloated at the Telborian. He had straightened himself from beside the gladiator, and was once more in the familiar, stationary pose. "You have taken a better grip of the lessons, and now as we improve those skills, then we will make you unstoppable."

Dugan had other plans though.

Confident with his own abilities now upon seeing his recent success, and fed up the time spent training for his mission, he didn't want to take any more time or suffer any more blows for this task. He had already wasted enough days as it was preparing for the cultists' mission. He didn't need to be trained to do what he was being called to do. Killing was killing, and he'd been trained to do that for years now. He'd had enough. The time had come for his task, or to simply leave it behind him. The wait and agony of it all was over.

"I think I'm unstoppable enough. The lessons are over now," Dugan shook his head once more, and shed his sweat like a wet dog. "Take me to the head priest, and let's get this thing over with."

"You don't understand Dugan, you've made some progress yes, but you aren't yet ready to undertake the mission. You will need a few more months to get this training learned correctly, and then we must fine-tune it. It needs to be refined if the mission is to be successful," the figure hovered closer to Dugan.

"You'll take me to the head priest now, or I won't go at all. Do you understand that?" Dugan growled as he flexed his arms and jaw in a menacing fashion. A fire had risen inside the Telborian. He had trained long enough. What Dugan craved more and more was freedom, and he wasn't going to get that locked away beneath the world as he was training for a mission in the distant future.

The cultist then stooped and relaxed his hold on his staff. "Fine. It shall be as you request, but don't expect the high priest to let you still go on this quest if he thinks you're not committed enough to undertake it."

"I am committed, because my freedom depends on my success as well, and I have confidence I can get this task done as soon as you allow me to go to it," Dugan stretched.

"Very well. I will go speak with him — but expect nothing. I will speak the truth in what I see in your performance." The figure hovered toward the door as Dugan sank into the chair once more.

As the cultist left the room, a smile slithered across his mouth and the devilish gleam of his white teeth in his gloom filled hood seemed unnatural. To even add to the terror a slight chuckle escaped his mouth as he left toward the cult leader's chambers.

"Finally," the hooded form muttered beneath his breath.

Chapter 19

ugan found himself in a massive room that was very unnerving. It was covered in upside down, jawless skulls of all races and sexes. These skulls jutted out of the walls like exotic bricks, making the poor quality of the structure look rich — as though they were draped in fine pearls. Inside the skulls burned a reddish liquid by means of a single tongue of flame blazing with the hot glare of the forge. The unnatural manner of the flame filled Dugan with dread. He was used to seeing such sights, for death was a daily occurrence in the arena, but to see it in the presence of a thing with no meaning was senseless.

He'd never felt such a horror flutter over him as he stood before the high priest of Shador. Why would they decorate with skulls? Who were they from and why were they gathered? Such thoughts he would later ask himself, as well as wonder how he could have been so blind to the truth. Until then, he wanted to believe he could be healed and freed from his curse.

He wanted to release Rheminas' hold over him.

That was all that mattered.

"Approach, Dugan." A voice Dugan recognized as belonging to the cult's leader, spoke to him from the red-tinted shadows in front of him. The Telborian squinted his eyes and looked ahead as best he could. Nothing was there but absence of light and the red-tinted glare. He knew from what he'd been told though, somewhere ahead of him resided a large throne crafted from silk and bones. On that throne rested the mysterious cult's leader, who he had met only once before when he had healed his shoulder.

"They told you my mind then?" Dugan advanced slowly toward the end of the room, not wanting to see what lay beyond the red shadows around him, but driving himself ever onward.

"Indeed they have. They have told me of your progress, of your willingness to learn and understand most anything they throw at you. You say you want to begin the journey for our order? I say you first must prove yourself to yourself." The high priest's words were like satin.

"Now you're sounding like a priest. You've started the flowery, empty speech they all speak," Dugan pressed onward toward the voice, and felt his journey ended as the red light seemed to increase in thickness and the outline of the high priest was made known to the Telborian's trained eye. "What are you talking about in real words?"

He saw the indiscernible figure upon his throne, his hands resting in his sleeves; a pose the other followers of the order seemed to adopt. He still couldn't see the true image of the high priest's face, however. Only in shadows and small glimpses behind strawberry light could Dugan even come close to understanding the cult's leader was at least a human of some kind.

"Look toward your soul and spirit, try to discover what and how you think you'll fare in this endeavor. Are you ready to face the challenge we will place before you?" Again came the even toned voice.

"Yes." Dugan stopped before the image of the cult leader as the cloaked figure glided toward him on a cushion of silent air. To Dugan it appeared as though he never moved from his seat, though he now stood before the warrior, as eerily silent as the others of the faith of Shador moved about.

"If you are confident in this task, then take hold of this chalice, and drink deep from its contents." The high priest drew forth a peridox studded golden chalice, from seemingly empty mid air then handed it to the Telborian, who stepped back for a moment, but then quickly recovered from the episode.

He was learning to be more comfortable with the magical nature of the world around him and of gods and their priests. However, it was a growing comfort, and many things still astonished and unsettled him — such as the recent action by the high priest. "You will be given your answer if you do not fall faint. This is the sacred blood of the god Shador. It will prove as the final judge in this matter. Drink and be made clear of mind," the high priest gently insisted.

Dugan was puzzled by the gesture.

It seemed too showy in a way, like a stage actor in a bard's tavern might undertake for a grand gesture. Then again, most of the experience Dugan had with religion was of a showy nature. At first he thought it was poison, but then denied the thought. He wondered why the cult would want to have him take part in their quest, and then kill him right before he even began it.

He sighed, took the cup and drank a deep draft.

The blood was cool to the touch of his throat; it tasted and felt like water. He wiped his mouth with the back of his hand, and then returned the chalice to the high priest's grasp. Dugan paused to look at his hand and found no mark from the blood only wetness like water would leave behind.

"That was *blood*?" Dugan questioned with a deep, thoughtful voice. "It tasted like water; even looked like it."

"But has it helped you?" The leader asked with a serpent's grace. "You haven't grown faint, so it must have given you insight."

This was getting ridiculous. High rituals and grandstanding he could have gotten from the nobles in the coliseum. He needed to be about action, and getting out of this group of cloaked fanatics as soon as he could. He needed to claim his prize and be off again — a freeman.

"If that was blood, then I think I would have known," Dugan protested.

"Yes, but when have you ever had the blood of a god to sup from? Who can say what it would taste like; to swallow a piece of time, and the stuff of dreams." The cult leader silently circled Dugan as he spoke, his hands making small, but odd motions as he did so. Dugan was unaware of it all and in fact, felt as though he was making more sense of the whole situation. It was almost like a voice was telling him what to do, what to think, and believe.

"You know this to be true, Dugan. Shador has favored your quest and your mission has been answered with great success. Take this as the sign it was meant to be — and fulfill the mission. Go with Shador, and you will succeed." The high priest then motioned toward the door with his hand.

Dugan walked out in silence under a trance-like demeanor making him seem like a sleepwalker. As he left a nearby cult member, the same cultist who had been training Dugan, spoke with the high priest.

"You think he is ready then?" The cult leader's voice was low.

"He will serve our needs, and that of Shador," The leader responded. "It didn't take you too long to raise him to a level of annoyance great enough to risk all on this task. It seems you were right about how desperate he was to be released from this curse of his."

"Indeed," the other spoke in a hushed tone as he watched the great door to the chamber hall close behind the Telborian. "The gesture on your part with the blade, and now this spell of compliance were very well done, my master."

"A simple task," the cult leader waved the compliment away with a dismissive hand. "I am more concerned with the real matter at hand. Dugan is no longer a concern of ours. We wasted enough time humoring him. It's time for action to be taken. Then we can be rid of him."

"I agree master. All has been readied," the lesser figure floated toward his master's throne, where the leader had taken up residence once more.

"Do you know for sure the object is now safely in the possession of that idiot Mayor?" The cult leader snarled to the other.

"Yes, our reports have made this very clear, and we have no doubt this is the case. With Dugan and three others, the task should easily be completed. The dumb ox will distract the Mayor and take the blame as we take the amulet."

"My spell will keep him from assuming too much until then. Make sure that you do as you speak. I don't take kindly to failure. Neither does Shador." The cult leader's words were chilled daggers.

"Yes my lord. All will come to pass as I have declared it to be." The cultist bowed.

"Take three others with you to ensure your success. I want that amulet. We have waited long enough," the high priest snarled with a demonic gleam to his eyes, which the shadows of his hood could not hide.

"Yes my master, it shall be done," the other then departed the chamber.

Chapter 20

The next day Dugan awoke in his room. The sparse look and feel of the whole area gave him slight comfort. His bed was soft and covered with silk sheets. The touch of elegance in an otherwise simple room intrigued him.

The cult appeared to Dugan as being very well to do, and were ardent lovers of silk, among other luxuries. Though Dugan often wondered why if they lived for such pleasures, they existed hidden in the decaying tunnels and warrens like rodents.

He wasn't thinking such thoughts now though, but instead smiled as he rolled over on the bed once again. The plush service was a welcome feeling for him after the hard labor and suffering he had endured previously under the hands of his trainers. He'd quickly grown to like the lifestyle they afforded him. If this was freedom, then he could learn to enjoy it — even come to be addicted to it over time.

A soft light radiated from a single brazier glowing in the far corner of his room. It never seemed to deplete itself of fuel for such light as long as the Telborian had been staying in the room. Dugan surmised it was enchanted to some degree or was the byproduct of the secrets of this hidden cult, and the mysterious deity they served. At any rate, it didn't really matter to him either. He stared at it as he tried to make sense of recent events.

The last few hours seems a bit cloudy. He recalled the cult leader giving him the chalice to sup from, and then a strange tingling sensation overtook him. Perhaps the chalice was indeed the blood of a god. After he drank, he recalled the words of the cult leader telling him he had proven himself, and something else too…

An eagerness like he'd never known for any task overcame him, and he felt like a caged animal being set free to kill and feast. The time to do the deed was now, and he had a burning need — a fire inside him, to complete the mission. Stranger still was the fact his mind grew even dimmer on the recollection of the details involving the whole mission itself. They never seemed to be training him for anything other than attacking the Mayor; breaking in and killing the Mayor, but never how to get away when it was done.

Before his mind could secure a harder grip on that thought, it was ripped away from him, and faded into a mist of forgotten images and concerns. Suddenly he became drowsy. He needed to sleep, he would need the extra energy for the mission, and his sore body cried out for rest.

Later, the Telborian awoke again. The light from the brazier was the same, perpetual soft glow, and Dugan still felt a relative peace, but he knew it was close to the time of the mission — he didn't know how long he had slumbered, but he had a feeling it was a good many hours.

He had to prepare, and so he got up and began to ready his gear.

The cult had given the group leader the time and the locations. Getting there would be easy. Completing his purpose on the mission would be the more challenging task. It still didn't feel right to him at some moments as he thought about it. Trading taskmasters both ordering him to kill to be free made the simple hope of gaining his freedom sour in his mind and heart.

It seemed to him he wasn't really free at all, and he had begun to harbor thoughts he never would be. Though the cult had promised him freedom, and he'd tasted it briefly with his mind's eye, it seemed somewhat hollow... How many would he have to kill for his freedom? Was it worth having the guilt of this and possibly other murders over his head? The thought now intrigued him, for he'd never seen killing another man as murder. His whole life had told him kill or be killed — it was a matter of survival. Yet with a limited view of freedom, his outlook had changed when reflected against the mirror of the outside world he'd be allowed to explore at will. He didn't know what to do with such an ethical issue.

The questions were too deep and painful.

The mighty Telborian fell down upon his bed consumed with emotion and thought. He tried to find serenity and relaxation from the chaos inside him as he looked toward the flickering flames of the brazier. It was a simple enough exercise, but the focus wasn't so much on the flames themselves to ease his mind, but what they signified to him. He couldn't help but think back to another time when he had been racked with indecision and hatred of taking on the duties prescribed to him by another taskmaster.

The arena cell where he was held before his escape, then flooded, his mind. He hated to think of it, but he could see himself there once more. He remembered the night when he'd met Rheminas, and sold his soul for revenge. The thought wasn't a welcome one, but his current experience showed him the mirroring of the two events. He dwelled more upon this strange coincidence as he stared into the illumination more closely.

The metal object was cast in an orange light quivering in its own dirty hue. Dugan watched the flickering shadows it produced on the wall. They seemed to form the outlines of people and beasts as they paraded across the stone surface. It was the only source of dim light Dugan had yet encountered in much of the secret lair of the cult besides the room of the high priest and where he was being trained or led. It seemed the cultists thrived on darkness like cockroaches and other vermin. They seemed more like murders and thieves in the light of Dugan's thinking than an order of priests and devoted workers. But how was he to judge them if they gave him what he desired? They could do whatever they wanted as long as they helped secure his freedom.

Including ordering him to kill a Mayor…

He continued to stare at the dancing images as his mind wandered from him. He wasn't aware of his total surroundings that much. Though he could still jump toward any threat that approached him with catlike grace — even when his mind was elsewhere. However, he wasn't able to detect the supernatural as easily.

As Dugan's mind wrestled with his ethical and emotional thoughts, tiny sparks fell from the brazier. They hit the floor with silent whispers. They first fell like light snow, and then became like a minor flurry of flakes. Finally the sparks poured down the wall, and on to the floor like sand from a broken hourglass. These glowing pieces of spent flame pooled at the bottom of the wall to form a stout image beneath the braizer no more than two feet in height, and a foot in width at the shoulders.

Dugan jumped with sudden awareness as he realized what had come to stand in front of him; shaken from his mental battles. The ash-born creature smiled at the Telborian with carbon-covered teeth as jagged and uneven as ruins in a jungle. Its eyes glowed a faint reddish glare reminding Dugan of a dying fire's ember. The form looked like a very ugly goblin with elven ears, a pile of soot, and claws ending the unnaturally long arms sticking out of a dirty and worn hooded cloak.

"Greetings," the creature spoke perfect Telborous in a dry, raspy voice — like sandpaper on bone, as dust and soot flew from his cracked lips.

"What are you?" Dugan's sword was in his hand, and he was off the bed in an instant — alert with his warlust rising. "What do you want?"

"At ease human. I mean you no harm. I bring a message from my lord, Rheminas." The squat creature bowed in a strange parody at prostration. As he did so a thin, wispy cloud of ash floated up from him like the last gasps of a fire.

"Rheminas?" Instantly, Dugan was filled with anger and loathing. "Leave, before I kill you." Dugan gripped his sword tighter as he spoke. His arm muscles tensed with the anticipation of slaying a representation of the god.

"I wish no harm to you, but must relay the message which was spoken to me. I will then leave and trouble you no more." Came the flat reply.

"You'll die and return to your master!" Dugan swung his sword in a deadly arch, slicing the creature in half. A monstrous cloud of dust and embers immediately filled the room, flying into the Telborian's face. Hot, tiny claws dug into his throat, eyes, and nose causing the Telborian to fall to his knees, coughing in searing pain.

As quickly as it was released, the gray cloud of ash reformed itself into the creature once more. Its eyes glowed with gentle amber in amusement, then nothing.

"That was unwise Dugan. You will now listen to the words of Rheminas." The creature's words grated the Telborian's flesh.

Dugan looked at the creature through red, searing eyes. Blood leaked from his mouth, and thick, black tears streamed from his face. A slight layer of ash covered his whole body with a deep gray and black. He looked like some sort of half-cremated corpse.

"Leave me alone. He has my soul, what else does he want?" The Telborian spat at the creature in his disgust. The reddish-black projectile struck the creature on the chest, and rolled down his rough, grimy, cloak toward the ground in an oily black ball.

Rheminas' messenger didn't seem to care."What you seek here is in vain, for none can free you from our pact. What you find here is false hope — false security," the god's messenger conveyed to the gladiator.

"If all Rheminas can do is boast about his might, and try to frighten me, then I don't need to hear anymore," Dugan's rage grew deep within his gut. "The very fact he is trying to frighten me now, is proof I'm on the right path toward my redemption. You can tell him I'm not backing down from the last ray of hope I have. I know that is the one, true salvation of my soul from his fiery grip."

"My lord continues," the small creature straightened its stature, "His advice is you would be much better off in slaying all these cultists now, and forsaking this foolish quest they have obligated you to undertake."

Dugan snorted. "Throw away the one place I've found hope — trample it underfoot?"

"Tis as false hope, and a vain thing that is hoped for. 'You are forever mine', says Rheminas," the somber creature continued. "Slaying them now will spare you a great heartache that is yet to come."

"Since when did Rheminas know things of the future?" Dugan was deeply sarcastic. "It sounds to me that your master is scared of losing what rights he might have on me given that there might be someone more powerful than him who can release me from our pact."

The messenger was unmoved by the Telborian's sarcasm and growing rage which had begun to waft off his warm flesh like pulses of fiery heat. "In this matter Rheminas has a clear assurance of what he speaks. The future events, should you continue on this path, will end most sorrowfully for you."

"Since when did any god, especially Rheminas, care for my plight? You speak lies, and I grow tired of them." Dugan clenched his jaw. He hated to be played like a fool, or even a puppet. He wanted very desperately to be free of the whole experience before him. He wanted to be free from it all. The more he fought for his total freedom, the less free he felt, and the more anxious and angry he became.

He found himself thinking things through very carefully. Rheminas was either playing with him again, or…or the small creature could be speaking the truth. Doubt began to wrestle with his once iron-hard commitment to his need to be freed at any cost. Had he compromised too much with these cultists? Did he really know their true intentions? Worse still, were the words of Rheminas true?

But what if he didn't obey either side's wishes? What was Rheminas playing at? Could these cultists really help lead him to freedom and the Vengeful One was now trying to hold him back from achieving it? That would indeed be rich: getting the Telborian to slaughter his own chance at hope by his own hand. Rheminas would certainly take a great delight with such an action.

He took in his shoulder once more. His left shoulder that once had been marred by the mark of Colloni was still free from indication of his former slavery. That was real…wasn't it?

Of course it was real.

It was solid and tangible.

None had been able to do such a thing for him till now. No priest, no faith, no one… He'd have his answers from this messenger, and then be done with it. The Telborian was free enough to make up his own mind, and it would take a lot more convincing than what the dark god's messenger was sharing to win Dugan over to his side. He had nothing as tangible as what the cultists gave. His words were nothing more than flickering seeds of doubt looking for a home in his head and heart.

He turned his attention once more to the dark figure in front of him. The amber orbs of the smutty being seemed to tear into his soul. Before he decided though, he must have some answers. He would hear what the figure claimed to known about the cultists, and their *true* agenda.

"So Rheminas wants me to stay from joining the others in the mission tonight? Why? What's his angle? I've learned from my searching and experience he doesn't do anything without a reason favoring him in some way." Dugan's eyes narrowed.

"This cult has long raised the ire of the Pantheon, and it has fallen unto Rheminas to now enact the judgment decreed upon them." The dark being's eyes found the narrowed center of the Telborian's. "My lord has chosen you as the means of enacting this judgment. It is both an honor and a blessing, for he is sparing you from future disappointment and harm should you aid these gods-cursed folk."

"Assuming what you say is *true*," Dugan tensed his muscles in a rage covered expression, "how is aiding Rheminas a *boon* to me? You say many things, like all priests and sages, but where is the favor? Where's the aid in killing off the only people who have come to offer to get me free from this bondage I've been unfairly tethered to — with proof?"

"I'm not in the business of debating that which was spoken," the messenger of the Flame Lord was curt, "but of relaying what has been said. That is all that my lord has spoken."

"Then you have no more business here. I trust the words of your master as much as a glutton guarding the larder. He's lied to me from the start, and still does so today.

I'm not going to retreat from the mission tonight or kill the cultists for Rheminas' dark pleasure," Dugan scowled. His mind has been made up once and for all upon the matter.

"Then what should I tell me master?" The creature glared at the gladiator.

"Tell him to go to the Abyss with his false promises!" Dugan almost shouted.

"As you wish," his frame then rapidly disintegrated, turning to a small pile of inert dust.

Dugan looked at the debris for a moment, then stomped his foot down upon the ashen pile, scattering it further under heel until it wasn't more than a memory. When he was satisfied he returned to his preparations. He had to be ready for the night's mission.

Chapter 21

Silent white vapors pulsated over each other with a seeming life all there own. Quiet in their movements, the mists slithered over the formless, brilliant, alabaster void for what appeared to be endless miles.

And in that silent space, a lone door suddenly appeared.

Like a simple wooden door that would grace a common room of some mediocre dining hall, the portal stood still. It seemed similar to a lone monolith — a solid, vertical shape in the mutable mass around it.

As suddenly as it appeared, the door opened to spill a drabber of daylight into the white mists. No light could compare with the illumination around the door. Even the purest daylight seemed off color to the purity of the illumination around it — as if the daylight on the other side of the door was a weaker reflection of a truer light or reality. Out of this open door came Cracius and Tebow, the multicolored avian flying behind them. With their exit the door closed and was soundlessly swallowed by the mists.

"Where are we?" Tebow scanned the indiscernible landscape around them.

"I don't know," Cracius answered as he did the same.

"What do you mean you don't know?" the bird chimed in. "Didn't you conjure up that door?" He fluttered about their heads as he spoke, taking in his own survey of the area.

"The door didn't bring us to where it was supposed to," Tebow finished his own searching.

"And where was that, then?" The bird fluttered to land on the older priest's shoulder.

"Mortis," Tebow turned his head to answer the bird.

"Mortis? You mean—" the bird's feathers fluttered as he came to land on Tebow's shoulder (which the death priest seemed to tolerate, though not thoroughly enjoy).

"The realm of Asorlok, yes," Tebow moved his attention to the misty terrain around him once more. "I thought it would be best to go there to think things out and to see just how we are to make our next move…but this is not Mortis."

"Then how did we get here?" Cracius wondered aloud.

"Good question," Tebow returned.

"A repetitive question if you ask me," the bird twisted its head between the two priests.

"How can a little bird be so sarcastic?" Tebow asked his shoulder. This wasn't getting them anywhere, and time wasn't slowing down for them either.

"The gods do mysterious things," the animal whistled back.

"You don't know anything about this do you?" Tebow's eyes narrowed as he stared into its avian eyes. He was trying to discern the matter from his god's spirit, but was unable to locate it inside him. It was as if the whole presence had been stripped away from him. Before he could grow too alarmed over the matter, it returned for the briefest of moments, allowing the priest to receive confirmation of the bird's innocence. However, It simply flickered into his head and heart, told him the bird was innocent, and then faded away again just as quickly to leave him disconnected from it as he had been before.

"No, you are innocent of this," the older priest muttered, pondering what was transpiring between the spirit of his god — what was troubling the connection he had so recently experienced.

"Then what do we do next?" Cracius looked to the older priest and Tebow could see from his own eyes how Cracius was having difficulty hearing from Asorlok as well. Tebow didn't like this one bit.

"Try to call forth another door, and go to where we wanted to in the first place. We can't afford any more distractions — time is short," stated Tebow.

"I agree," a soft, inviting voice replied. It sounded like the mixture of both a masculine and feminine voice they found a bit unsettling to hear.

"Whose there?" Cracius went for his hammer.

Before either could react further, an aged, gray granite doorway made of fifteen feet tall posts and a sturdy lintel lounging on top, materialized before them. It simply appeared and stood defiantly before them in the blink of an eye, daring them to make sense of its presence. Between the two posts was an empty five feet opening taunting them by a shimmering similar to a heat wave in the desert. Beyond that shimmering opening though, neither could see anything.

"Try this door and you will see who speaks to you and why," the voice seemed to be all around them, as if the two priests and bird where in the midst of the sound. Turning about to try and discern its source met with failure.

"Asorlok is silent here for some reason," Tebow turned to Cracius.

"Yes, he is," the other concurred.

"It might be worth it," Cracius was stoic as he looked to Tebow.

"Agreed," Tebow nodded.

Each nodded to the other when they realized they would get no answers standing in this cloudy realm, so they proceeded through the stone portal.

What awaited them on the other side though was another matter entirely…

Cracius had entered the portal first, and came out into something he never knew existed. He saw the stone doorway was one of twelve forming a wide circle around a peaceful green glade. Looking to the other stone doorways, he beheld various other images contained inside them, which spoke of different lands, under the waves and even various areas of the sky itself. All the images changed over time and flickered back and forth between them.

What was this place?

Tebow followed Cracius in similar wonder at what he saw. The bird only whistled in amazement from his perch on the older priest's shoulder.

"So where are we now?" Tebow moved up to be even with Cracius.

"Not Mortis or anywhere else I can think of. This place feels odd." Cracius didn't turn to address the priest, merely started across the glade to another scene of some galactic scope framed between the stone lined portal. Inside a star drenched ebony spill flowing, toward infinity. "And I still can't hear Asorlok."

"Me either," Tebow lowered his tone.

"Welcome to my realm," the same voice that had spoke to them before, though now more localized in the figure of a woman, came toward them.

"Who are you?" The bird chirped.

"Galba," the woman drew closer. She was cloaked in a heavy white gown, with pale white skin peeking out. Her hands and pieces of her face darted out from under a deep, alabaster cowl.

"Why have you called us here?" Cracius tightened the grip on his hammer, as more of the woman's graceful figure drew near. "We have an urgent mission for our god to complete."

"Peace. I know of your quest, and what I am about to say will help you complete it with great success." Galba's voice was soft, yet authoritative. It had the quality of both a mother and loving wife — nurturer and lover.

"What do you want then?" Tebow stepped a bit closer to the woman, who called herself Galba, trying to figure out more of her person along with her motives.

His hands twitched a bit on his hammer's shaft.

"The same as you: the frustration of what The Master seeks, as well as his destruction if need be." She stopped her advance a few feet from the two priests.

"Again why..." The older priest's eyes grew narrow as he started to speak.

"You won't be able to do this on your own," Galba calmly replied.

Now that she was closer, Tebow was awestruck by what he could see of the woman's face. Smooth, ageless skin, the color of cream, flowed over gentle cheekbones, with a slightly rounded chin. Only a small ruby canoe broke up the serene, white sea. He could also see small emerald flashes beneath the hood — the most of alluring sparkle of eyes he had ever known.

"We know — the bird already told us — and we're on our way to recruit mercenaries to help us," Cracius spoke up briskly. He wasn't ready to lower his hammer just yet. Without Asorlok's spirit to help him confirm anything, he was ill at ease about everything placed before him. Even the woman's beauty didn't faze him. Not even her crimson silken locks spilling out from the hood could move his mind and heart to her side; not yet anyway.

"I know this too, but you will only be needing to gather two. I will be gathering the rest. It is crucial that you gather them at the right time and place, and then bring them here," Galba continued.

Cracius was about to open his mouth again to ask why, but stopped himself when he realized it might be wiser to hear all of what this Galba had to say first before he passed judgment. Though he didn't have any clear confirmation by his god, the day had already proved strange enough with the alliance of two gods, it could well grow stranger still.

"I will gather the others by my own means and methods. You alone will have the needed influence on the remaining two to bring them to this location at the time I will designate to you." Galba lowered her hood then and both men were amazed at her radiant beauty.

She appeared to be a young Telborian woman, though her serpentine curls of red hair and shimmering emerald eyes could have marked her as a Syvani too, should her ears have been uncovered for viewing and had been pointed. The white gown she wore, while form fitting, wasn't too oppressive to her frame as to draw out too much of her feminine nature to the point of lewdness. Instead she appeared as innocent as and pure as a virgin maid in a forest following a spring rain.

"The Master will be coming here soon enough — and when he does, he will be at his weakest, and ready for an assault. Only then would you be able to make your best attack. However, you must make the choice as to what you want to do. I will not and cannot force you do anything. The choice must be yours, and yours alone. I merely am here to provide an option for the solution to your task."

"*Cannot?*" Tebow was still a bit shaken by the celestial visage and frame of the woman before him.

"There are rules that must be obeyed, and I am bound by them." Galba looked over into the older priest's eyes, and he knew the most splendid of peaceful moments — as if his whole body was being reborn in an instant.

"Rules?" Tebow shook himself free from the feeling and gaze before he was completely submerged by it, and made a half circle around the cloaked woman as he spoke. "You make it sound as if this is all some sort of game."

Galba remained silent.

"What if we refuse your aid?" Cracius lowered his hammer now, content the woman possessed no real threat to him…at least for the moment.

"Then you would be free to pass on to Mortis, as was your plan before." She extended her hand toward one of the stone portals, though what the image was between the stone posts was indiscernible to all gathered.

"If she has a plan, Tebow—" Cracius looked over toward his companion.

"How do you know all this?" Tebow cut off the younger priest. "You're not a god, or mage of any type. Are you some lord or divinity?"

"I am Galba. That is how I know." Ruby lips parted to let a thin sliver of pearls come forth.

"I see," was all Tebow could say. "Might you excuse us for a moment?"

Galba gently nodded.

The priests then turned to each other, their eyes taking in each other, the tiny eyes of the bird dashed back and forth between the two in frantic swings like some wild pendulum.

"I still can't hear from Asorlok," Tebow started the conversation in a whisper.

"Me either," Cracius also whispered, though he was sure Galba could hear them anyway. "She might even be the one blocking us from our god."

"I'm sure of it," said Tebow.

"So what should we do?" Cracius eyes widened a bit.

"For now, what can we do but two things: either accept this woman's offer, or reject it," Tebow stated flatly. "Though I'm a bit concerned why others have been seeking us out to help put an end to The Master. If we can't gain access to our god, then we have little option left than to make up our own minds upon the matter, and hope it was the wisest decision."

"Did we really have a plan anyway?" Cracius said after a few moments of silence. "After all, how were we going to convince all of the mercenaries to join us?"

"Appeal to their baser nature?" Tebow put forth the idea.

"Money?" The bird chirped brightly, not bothering with whispers.

202

The older priest's face grew more furrowed at the bird's rather loud statement, but continued the conversation. "It might work."

"For *all* of them?" Cracius wondered aloud.

"Not to mention you Asorlins don't have the best reputation with folks." The bird added, then pecked at a small area in his shoulder feathers for a moment before continuing. "You're about as popular as tax collectors."

The bird took to the air after his statement, then fluttered about the air for a short jaunt before landing in the grass below, pecking the ground, looking for any stray seeds or other tasty victuals to fill its stomach.

"Hmm. He does have a point," Tebow watched the bird hunt.

"If we did just need to convince two mercenaries and bring them here — assuming you are true to your word and bring the others as well, how would we get these two here then?" Cracius turned back to Galba, who had not moved the whole time — a figure of peace and eternal health.

"You would be made aware of where they are, and at what time would be most ideal for their arrival," she stated with a simple, pleasant air.

"So if we bring these two here, then we would still be able to work out our cause? We'd be able to destroy The Master, and you wouldn't intervene?" Tebow watched the reactions of the heavenly woman. He wanted to make sure he was right. He was walking blind into this situation — with only his own consul to fall back upon. He didn't see any sign of unease at all, only peaceful content.

"I would not stop you from what you decided to do," Galba nodded politely as she took a step backwards.

"Would you help?" the bird looked up from his hunting.

"No," she shook her head.

The matter was totally up to them.

"Do you have any other ideas?" Tebow returned to his younger companion.

"Not really," Cracius confided.

"Don't look at me," the bird turned its head up toward the older priest, a blade of grass between its beak.

"Consult your god if it will help bring you clarity." There came a small hand gesture from Galba, which was quickly lost on the priests and bird. However, both Cracius and Tebow found they were in spiritual communion with their god once more.

"You held back Asorlok from us?" Tebow looked over at Galba shocked that she would so openly reveal such a thing and she must have been able to perceive their thoughts as well to some degree, "Why?"

Galba gave no answer.

Tebow supposed she wouldn't either. If this were the true spirit of Asorlok, then he'd get all the answers he needed. She won't have to tell him anything more than what had already been spoken.

"You feel that?" Cracius asked the priest, and interrupted him from his thoughts.

Tebow did feel it. Asorlok was already speaking to them, confirming what he wanted to do — what the next step was in this quest.

"Yes. Confirmation," Tebow nodded. "But is it a manipulation by her or the true reality from our god?"

"If you don't know your god's voice by now, priest," came Galba's reply, "then you have no business serving him on this task."

Tebow's face turned stony at the comment. After a moment, he gave answer. "Asorlok has no fault against your plan," Tebow's words were dry. "We'll retrieve these mercenaries and bring them back here." The older priest stood before the woman with a resolute face. "Then we will bring Asorlok's justice to pass on The Master."

"Very well then, priest," Galba's breath-taking face was unreadable— a statuesque image of heavenly splendor. "You will take the doorway I direct you to, and it will take you to the two mercenaries you must gather. It will be at the time and place that is right for them.

"When you bring them back here it will also be in the future, to the day that The Master will arrive to complete his mission. You will be in time to face him then, and ready as well with those who will be gathered to face him with you."

"Okay, so when do we leave?" The bird chirped as it flew up now to land on Cracius shoulder. The younger priest was not amused by the action, but kept focused on the greater task at hand.

"Now," Galba motioned to a stone doorway a little ahead of them, outlined in white light. Between the posts, however, no one could see through the darkness within.

"I will be waiting when you return," she said.

The priests then moved toward the portal in a silent procession. Upon reaching it they looked back once more at the white figure, as if to make sure she had been real — her unearthly glamour had reality. To leave such perfection behind was suddenly a saddening affair presenting a stronger internal conflict, had it not been for the presence of their god — stirring them to his purposes. Renewed by this stirring, each then stepped into the blackness between the stones to disappear from sight.

Chapter 22

Cadrissa screamed as she looked above herself and saw the thin wisps of smoky haze that once had been the cloud built island melting into the periwinkle sky. Her eyes filled with dread as she gazed below, and the dark blue globe of Tralodren rushed forward to meet her. She wasn't alone in her descend. The Master fell silently beside her.

His flesh was seared and gone in some spots, his hair was gone, as well as most of his face. His robes and clothes were almost non-existent tethers and tatters, fluttering wildly in the wind. A charcoal visage, which looked like wrinkled cloth housing the gleaming white teeth of the former lich, and his white, liquid eyes. Tendrils of oily smoke streamed from his body as he plummeted toward the planet, and small patches of dying flame traced their way around his feet and arms, desperately trying hold onto their fuel and existence amid the fearsome winds.

The Master obviously was unable to help himself — let alone Cadrissa.

The only one left conscious, Cadrissa began to feel the powerlessness of the situation. She felt her throat become clogged with her heart and stomach as the wind cut through her hair and stabbed at her ears and face. Its roar deafened her to the sounds of her own beating heart and heavy breathing.

She plummeted through a few more, low lying stray clouds, even passing frightened birds in her meteoric plummet toward the growing globe beneath her. Silently, she cursed Endarien. He had promised no harm would come to her if she did what he asked of her. It would seem his words weren't true, since it now seemed certain she was falling to her death.

The globe started to widen — the land spread out, as well as the sea, like a dark stain on fabric beneath her. She screamed louder and tried to get a feeling of control over the situation, and discovered as she fell further, she wouldn't fall anywhere near land, but would be dropped into the deep waves of the uncaring Yoan Ocean instead.

This only heightened her panic, but she tried to calm herself as best she could in spite of it. She needed a clear head to think and focus her thoughts on will and what could be done. She wasn't going to die, not yet. She wouldn't let herself. Instead, she had to summon up all her strength to try and make the best of what was happening to her, or she would never get a chance at learning the mysteries and seeing the wonders the world had yet to offer. By sheer force of will, Cadrissa stopped screaming and listened to the growl of the wind instead.

She paid no heed to the matter how the churning ocean was hungrily opening its arms to greet her, nor to the insanity inducing pressure she began to feel on her head and chest as she entered into more of Tralodren's atmosphere. She simply listened to her heart and her mind as they merged. Through the fear, the torment of the wind, and the salty blast of the surf, she spoke the words of a spell. She had to focus upon them harder than ever or lose all hope for a chance to survive her present fate.

"Nexsa Nexsa Compra lou. Grolua Ortch Nevogh!" The words were torn from her lips by the wind's claws as soon as they were spoken. The mage didn't have a lot of strength to cast it, but she made do with what she could muster.

She prayed that it worked, and prayed to Endarien one last time, hopeful he'd at least respond in honor to his bargain with the mage to keep her safe. Perhaps somewhere he still looked over her, and was making ready to oblige that oath…

Cadrissa clenched her jaw tight and waited for the warm energy of the spell she'd unleash to overtake her body. She didn't have to wait long, as the spell began to envelop her. Warm wafts of air folded around her frame and she felt as if soft large wings began to slow her descent toward the waves below. Turning to The Master — whom she expected to see plummet past her — as she didn't cast the spell on both of them, was shocked to see his descent slowed as well.

She wondered why.

Suddenly, she found the reason.

A small spark of azure flame chased across the charred mage's eyes for a moment, his blacken and melted claws weaved a fragile, yet drunken mosaic of power. Then in an instant, the blue flame that danced in his sockets faded once more joined by the parting words of the former lich from a lipless mouth.

"You won't be rid of me so easily girl!" Even against the howl of the wind, The Master's faint words seemed deafening.

Suppressing a shudder, Cadrissa looked down again as the surging tide of the ocean churned away, even closer than she cared to imagine. The various land masses which had still been so close to her now melted away and fled into the distance as the waves took over her view; dominant in its struggle to reach out toward its nearing prey with lapping grasps of surf.

Cadrissa's spell continued to slowly lower both her and The Master, but she couldn't direct where the descent would occur. Like the lone feather adrift in the air, the duo hovered ever downward, and closer to the waves, teetering back and forth on the breath of fate. Cadrissa could see it was midday now, with a deep, billowing darkness festering toward the far horizon, meaning a storm was on its way.

How could she get out of this?

Where was Endarien?

The water clawed up toward them with icy cold talons, but failed to grasp them totally, and would continue to do so for a while longer. Cadrissa guessed she and her captor were about a mile from the water's surface, but falling ever faster toward it. As her spell was weakening, their speed was increasing little by little.

She could feel the salty air now cake her skin with brine, along with strange humid fingers groping her body.

As the waves came closer to greeting her, however, Cadrissa felt an odd calmness overcome her mind and body. For some unknown reason, she became at peace with the whole situation as it was presented to her. The young Telborian took it as a sign of coming to terms with her approaching death, as some of the books she'd read had talked about such an occurrence before the final hour of one's passing.

She had no fear of drowning…at least right away. Cadrissa knew how to swim, but doubted she could do so for more than a few hours at best before her muscles cramped and she was left to fend for herself. Away from any sign of land and a storm at her heels she didn't think her chances for survival was that great. She had to ask one final question before all logical process left her, and she was reduced to base animal instinct to fend for her life in the turbulent water.

One more plea for aid, and then she would surrender the idea entirely and fend for herself.

"Endarien, you promised me protection. I aided you in lure of this promise. Where is your protection now?" The tired young woman competed with the wave's growls, and hisses, only to receive no answer — no sign of the god's acknowledgement of such an oath or his even being bound to it.

Oh well, she tried.

She watched as the water increased, so no more than five hundred yards remained between her and the ocean. It was then she thought she felt a severe chill, like the very hand of the grave rose up to meet her, tracing the outline of her spine with a cold finger.

Looking with keen eyes she observed the approaching ocean more studiously. Something was happening. A small section of it, not more than fifteen feet, began to swirl into a whirlpool. As she was lowered toward it, the whirlpool began to increase in speed, but instead of forming a downward funnel, typical of a whirlpool, it formed a convex dome of clear liquid. Her present descent toward the water left her no more than a hundred yards from the surface of this odd bulge.

Cadrissa was struck with a fearful wonder as the bump of water rapidly formed into a sharp-toothed maw, behind which a deep purple abyss swirled. Revelation then caught up to her senses and eyes, which opened wide with terror as Cadrissa realized she and The Master were falling right into this mouth. There was nothing she could do. They were going to be swallowed whole by the strange liquid entity!

In this added dark twist to her assumed upcoming demise, Cadrissa felt the coldness increase, and the mage found the world around her growing dim, as if all the color; indeed the light itself was being seeped away like a leech taking its fill of blood from an open artery.

Cadrissa averted her gaze from such a thing.

It was all she could do as she felt herself being sucked down into it.

She felt the distance between her and the mouth dwindle to twenty feet, then ten, and then five. At last she felt the arctic breeze overtake her; ice crystals formed on her fingertips and eyebrows. The body of The Master followed her into the weird mouth of cold darkness. In moments she had lost consciousness, and then her world was an icy pit of gloom

Cadrissa awoke cold and wet.

The wizardress shivered in the dark as she sat up. Her body and mind felt as though they had been frozen in ice, and then left to thaw. A slight breeze glided over her soaked frame as she lay on what appeared to be a slick flagstone floor.

There was a strong odor of the sea and fish.

Only a single torch, crackling away on a far wall, glimmered with enough light to discern herself and a limited perimeter around her person. Turning her head, the wizardress was able to discern that the area, which she could see was wet as well. She couldn't see The Master anywhere, and began to wonder if he'd survived the descent into the dark mouth. She expected the dark mage to be right behind her. After his final efforts to tap into her spell, making it serve him as well. The thought played on emotions of fear, loneliness, confusion, and sadness all at once, making her sick in mind and body. She fought back a need to vomit, and tried to look around as best she could.

She had to get out of the mess she was in, and fast. With the cold around her, drenched clothing and body, she could plummet into further distress with illness added to her current plight. At least she was alive, that was something.

Maybe Endarien had heard her plea after all, and honored his oath to her.

Though why come to her aid by the means she had just experienced, then leave her here alone?

Cadrissa tried to scan the area as best as she was able.

Nothing but silence greeted her stares.

It appeared to be nothing more than a large, open room, though what was in it, and how large it was, she couldn't conceive. She pushed her black hair back against her head and wrung it out like a rag, twisting out all the water as she rose to stand.

This done, she flung the sopping locks behind her and checked her belongings. All were accounted for, even the medallion she had hidden away on her person. She still would have liked some time to really study the object — it seemed to call to her... And there was a strange heat about it flaring for a moment...but she supposed getting out of there and figuring out where she was and why were top priorities at the moment.

The mage took up a bunch of her robe, and rung it out as well.

Chilled salt water fell onto the flagstone in a tiny waterfall.

"Hello? Endarien?" The wizardress braved a few words into the darkness.

"Is there anybody out there?" Cadrissa walked with small steps toward the outskirts of the circle of light where she resided not daring to go beyond into the blackness and seek out what was in the dim orchid of the unknown just yet.

The Darkness was like a sea of sorts flowing toward her and then away as she moved into and out of the light. If the mage didn't know better, she'd swear the darkness was almost sentient. Following this thought, the gloom smothered her, covering her with cold, damp air. She shivered once more as frozen breath crawled over her neck and shoulders and down her back. It felt like knife blades slicing her flesh. Knife blades or sharpened finger nails...

"Hello? If this is you, Endarien, then thank you. I thought you had forgotten about me." Cadrissa looks out into the swimming pitch around her once more, hopeful of a reply. "I'm thankful for you saving me, but I don't know where I am now, or what's going on. If you could please return me to Haven, I-"

"Stay where you are." A deep and bellowing voice resounded all around, the startled mage. It didn't sound congenial, but wasn't outright hostile either.

"Who's there?" Cadrissa held her position.

Nothing.

In the silence that followed, Cadrissa tried to make sense of what she had just heard — what she thought was happening. The voice hadn't sounded like Endarien, but she hadn't really anything to verify the true voice of the god in the first place. She had only heard him speak twice before, each by a different aspect with different voices, and so how could the mage be certain what his real voice sounded like?

"Hello? Endarien?" Cadrissa dared to ask the darkness again.

Again, she was greeted with no response.

"Okay..." Cadrissa's mind raced for some type of answer. "So, what do you wish of me? Is there something else I still have to do before I can be taken back?" Cadrissa pleaded with the darkness. "I already placed your amulet on The Master." Fear, colder than the atmosphere around her seeped up from inside her stomach and was starting to slide up to her throat and head like chilled bile.

"*What* more do you want of me?" The wizardress' voice shrank in proportion to her confidence as she turned to look beyond the darkness, peering deeply into it, but could still see nothing.

She didn't like this one bit and hated it more and more each silent moment. She could feel something about the darkness though. It was definitely alive. The wizardress was sure of that now. She didn't know how or why, but she could feel some sort of sentient presence — a hungry force, which would like nothing more than to swallow her whole. How she knew this was unclear to her, but it was a deep-rooted reality in her mind and was more true and solid than the basic facts she had learn to accept and expect in life.

"Nothing," the response was flat and pert. The same deep tone she'd heard before.

"Then why am I here?" She braved a question to this unknown entity.

She was beginning to taste the cold bile of fear in her throat as that same frigid, gut born fright was starting to chill her mind; slowing it from rational thought, and moving it into panic. The sea of pitch all around her seemed to seethe and turn at her persistent questioning; turning as it did to and fro as if it were pacing the immeasurable chamber.

Cadrissa then heard a low moan issue out of The Darkness. It was weak and tired, yet close at hand. Venturing a step further, she found The Darkness retreated from her step, and the shape of a slumped man melted out from its confines.

The form was a familiar one.

It was The Master.

His body was still burnt and ruined; a cinder of a man rather than flesh and blood. Under him a charcoal puddle, the remnant of his sooty substance mingling with the soupy remains of the recent aquatic escapade, encircled and seeped outward like pooling blood. Amazed he still lived…to some extent; she knew he wouldn't be long in traveling to Mortis.

"Take him and return to your task," the formless voice again addressed the mage. It seemed to lack definition in some way; the wizardress wasn't able to assign a sex to the speaker, as one could with just about all voices.

Take The Master? Take him where? Why? Do what with him? He was obviously about ready to die, why not let it happen here, and put and end to this whole venture? What was Endarien playing at? He wouldn't have retained The Master, but let him die. He hated him — he had just finished participating in a battle against him. *What* was going on here? Cadrissa's slithering internal fear grew stronger as it gripped a hold of her heart for she realized…

"You're not Endarien."

There was silence again, and by this time the mage received her answer in it.

"W-who are you?" The fear took a tighter hold of her throat now, making it hard to breath, let alone speaks. "To what task do you refer? I don't understand."

"Obey and you shall live," came the response in stoic tones as dry and lifeless as a tombstone.

"But, he's dying, probably dead. How can he do anything anymore?" She tried to take a step back from the lich, but was hindered by her own fright. Her limbs were too petrified to obey her commands to move, the icy chill of her own fright having seeped into her muscles now making them stone like and immobile to her mental commands.

"Wh-why not just let him die and be over with it?" The wizardress stammered over her pounding heart.

"He shall not die, not yet…" the voice trailed off into the pulsating gloom. Thin tendrils of living pitch sought their way out of the dark and toward The Master's frame, where they attached themselves all over him, wrapping each limb — and then, finally, his entire body in their rope-like coils.

For a moment they held him bound fast, then released their grip to slither away from whence they came. Cadrissa was unable to pull herself away from the spectacle, and now peered closer at The Master's slumped outline. She was amazed to see him whole, restored, and looking up at her!

His face was a cruel etching of lines, though he was still unconscious.

Who was this being, and why was it helping The Master?

"Take him, and follow him. Help him attain his goal. The time and place have been prepared," The Darkness vibrated all around the wizardress.

"But-" Cadrissa started.

"Go!" The voice interrupted with a growing tone of irritation at the mage's prattling.

Instantly Cadrissa's vision and consciousness were stripped from her and the whole experience faded into a horrid memory that would be with her until the day she died.

Chapter 23

The past two weeks of Rowan and Clara's voyage flew by with no real events of note. The weather had been — and still was — unbelievable, a good gust always pushing them along. It never seemed to vary in intensity as it guided the nameless vessel through the calm waters, helping them make great time on their journey.

The crew, however, was silent.

The only ones who spoke at all were Rowan and Clara, both during and after the few small tasks they performed as directed by Brandon, to earn their keep. Occasionally they would be able to talk with Brandon when he wasn't in his quarters or working his men hard at their tasks, but other than that a hushed, almost reverential silence clung to the vessel.

Trying to strike up a conversation with the sailors was also fruitless as they refused all forms of communication offered them. Both Clara and Rowan thought it very odd, but tried not to let it bother them too much. Maybe they didn't take well to new people…whatever the matter, both he and Clara had transport, and the crew wasn't hostile — just perhaps a bit rude.

Rowan could deal with that, and so could Clara.

The middle-aged captain seemed simple enough. He was definitely a naval man, and loved the openness of the sea around him. He was strangely philosophical at times as well. Each night they got to dine with him — he'd even given them simple foodstuffs to keep them fed during the day. Neither Clara nor Rowan ever saw the crew eat, oddly enough…but they were an odd lot in the first place. From these dinners, and other times of private conversation. Rowan discovered that he carried a lot of knowledge from his brief life, and he was fascinated Brandon seemed to be oblivious to the vast insight he possessed as though it didn't matter and was really just a simple man when it came down to things in the end.

From these short conversations snatched here and there he'd built up a little bit of rapport with the sailor. It soon became a fun time of learning as Rowan gleaned from an older human knowledge that would probably help him in the long run as Rowan made his way toward manhood. Besides this, the youth felt a great peace when they spoke. It was like a gentle breath or reassurance was blown over him. It made him smile, and was slightly addictive to the point that the knight at times found himself anxious when he was outside Brandon's company for a any great amount of time. It was as if he had a second father, and Rowan didn't know how much he missed his own until they had started these talks. He hoped that he'd be able to see his father and mother again soon.

During his private time on the vessel, Rowan would return to his persistent thoughts: the words of Panthor, the necklace, and even his shield. The dreams had at least stopped and he was able to get some sleep again, but the questions racing through his mind during the day gave him little rest. He was beginning to think his questions didn't have answers…or maybe he didn't want to know the answers.

The closer he came to his homeland the more the pit of sickness in his gut grew. The closer he drew home, the more he realized how homesick he really was. It seemed much longer than the time he'd been gone and each day away only added to that growing sense of loss.

It wasn't just a loss of his family or tribe — but of his homeland, and a part of himself as well. He had left all he had known — all who he thought he was, behind for the Knighthood to journey father south than most Nordicans dared. And where was the Knighthood now? Far before him in the Northlands. He was the only piece of that institution, the only piece of his tribe and family in this strange land. All these things were inside him and he was their only representative — a lonely representative.

If this was the future of his life he didn't know if he'd be that enthused to keep going onward. After all, it was all self-willed out here away from everything he'd ever known. He had to fuel his own exploits, get support and purpose from inside himself rather than from outside. There was no Journey Knight here to crack the whip. If it wasn't for his faith in Panthor he'd be totally alone — even the dreams and other representations of her he'd experience since his departure from Valkoria were a welcome comfort.

Though these things and his prayers brought him comfort, Panthor hadn't answered him in the way she had before outside Elandor. Instead she remained silent, leaving only questions — a myriad of questions to ponder.

Would his fellow knights help him find the answers to his questions? Would they see his inner introspection as a sign of weakness? Perhaps unworthiness to the order? What if news spread from his action with the Frost Giant when it made port in Valkoria? These were just some of the questions but he at least had some relief from a few.

Panthor had told him he was worthy, and he had a higher calling. So why did returning home to the Knighthood fill him with so much unease?

Again, the words of his goddess haunted him. She hadn't founded the Knighthood; someone else had. A mortal. A mortal with his own ideas…what if those ideas were not totally in keeping with the intent of the goddess? What if…

Rowan stopped himself from thinking any more. He didn't want to entertain that thought, not now. But he would have to deal with the thought soon enough he knew, and when he did…

He thought of asking Brandon for some advice on the matter, but then decided against it. When the knight tried to bring it up an uneasiness flooded over his body, and pooled in his stomach. Rowan didn't take such a thing as a good sign, and so dropped the idea from his mind, and found other questions and conversations to occupy his time with the older sailor.

"Brandon, how far off are we now?" Rowan motioned to the man as he looked to be free from his daily toils for the moment.

"We're making good time," the older Telborian met up with the knight. "Endarien has chosen to bless us with favorable winds. We'll make it there in a little under two weeks now, I am certain."

"Those winds are really helping then," the Nordican moved closer to the older man.

"Yep. Seems like we've really been blessed by Endarien," Brandon drew closer to Rowan as well.

"Speaking of that, I've noticed your men don't pay homage to the sea and its mistress like men from my land do," Rowan stopped at a safe conversational distance from the tanned captain.

"No we don't, nor will we ever. We pay homage only to Endarien, and it looks as though he has shown us the rewards of our labors and honoring. No Rowan, you would be best mannered if you keep your tongue and mind from the goddess who rules the sea. That name offends me and maddens my crew," Brandon spoke to the youth as if he were a close friend — almost a son.

"I'm sorry Brandon. I meant no harm," Rowan bowed his head. He wondered why the captain and his crew didn't honor Perlosa as all other naval races and sailors did. After all, didn't she control the waves and the things traversing it? He wasn't going to press the matter and risk offense of his gracious host.

"None taken. Just see that you keep this lesson learned." Brandon smiled wide and all the seriousness that was there before faded away.

"Men of my land don't worship Endarien that much," said Rowan. "He is seen as a lesser worker of the world. How then do you and your crew pay homage to him? What means do you invoke? I haven't see it so far on this voyage."

"We pay homage to him by thanking him for his gales and breezes," Brandon gestured to the clouds above, "by offering incense into the air so that he might smell it, be pleased with us, and show us favor."

"When do they do this then?" Rowan looked puzzled, " I haven't seen your crew do this once during the voyage."

"Well, that was done before the voyage. As you can see, it has been most beneficial. If you will excuse me now, Rowan, I have matters calling me." Brandon walked off to his cabin where he often hid from sight throughout the day.

Rowan periodically wondered what he did in there. It shouldn't take all day to plot a course, and make sure that the boat was still on it. As he questioned their savior, a voice in his head urged him to stop the process. It told him he should be thankful they even had a way to Arid Land, which was a lot closer to their destination than Haven. Perhaps the man just liked to be alone and think or write. After all, he did seem a bit of a philosopher in nature. Maybe he was a budding poet, or chronicler of some tales. Was that any business of the young knight if he kept his end of the bargain, and proved to be a very accommodating man by taking them to Arid Land as promised?

The young knight thought not.

"Brandon says we're be to Arid Land under two weeks." Rowan trotted over to where the sliver hair Clara looked over the bow once more, peering into the silent waves.

"That's good." She turned to him. Her face was emotionless and strangely distant as she spied the expansive waves.

"What's wrong?" His own soft face became furrowed with worry at her dissatisfied remark.

"I've just been thinking a lot these least few weeks," her expression remained the same.

"So you found something that you didn't like then? What is it?" Rowan was growing concerned. "I thought things couldn't have gotten and better. This has been a true blessing from Panthor."

"It certainly did seem awfully convenient, but the more I think about what has happened both around and to us, the more it's seeming to form a certain pattern. I just can't help but feel we are being used here in some way. It just seems so…

"The more I think about the whole incident in Takta Lu Lama, and the monster we released…" The elf trailed off as she took in Rowan's concerned visage. A face, that seemed to look even adorable to Rowan in worry as when it smiled.

She had also been thinking of Gilban's words to her again — about the road she was going to travel, even though she had been forewarned of it. A path that it seemed like she would be forced to travel… and was she on the path now? Was this whole convenient captain, and strange, nameless vessel talking them on that path?

"It wasn't your fault. Nobody knew what was happening in the end, but we survived." The knight did his best consoling her fears, placing his hand upon her shoulder. "Because we live, we can go save Cadrissa now."

"Don't you get it, though? We were used," Clara turned her gaze out toward the water. "Used by that skeletal creature, and who knows what else, to set it free."

Was she sure of this? She had been until Rowan came beside her; he always caused a little emotional flutter around her — especially lately — but yes, she was quite certain of this now as she thought about it more.

"What are you talking about?" Rowan raised an eyebrow. "Nobody used anyone here. You and Gilban had a mission, as did I. The two just happened to intertwine. It's that simple."

"Is it?" Clara turned back to Rowan. He was still adorable in that naive sort of way. "You don't see the coincidences and similarities all adding up here?"

"Ah, come on Clara," Rowan removed his hand from her shoulder, shaking his head with a gentle smile. "Gilban got a vision from his goddess. He didn't have some secret plan we don't know about."

Clara shot him a queer look at this last statement. Didn't he? Roads they were being almost forced to travel even though forewarned and trying to avoid. What did that priest know he didn't choose to share? Had he been on a path he didn't have any choice but to follow as well?

"Divine favor indeed. I think it is just too fortunate we almost stumbled into Brandon, and this opportunity for a ride to Arid Land…"

"I don't think it was all smiles and laughs with the Frost Giant," Rowan countered. "No divine favor there."

"Perhaps not, but men can work in rhythm to fate if set to the right course, and left to their own devices," Clara held her gaze.

"Clara," Rowan chuckled, "you sound ridiculous. So what are you proposing now? Some god is behind this all then — this whole mission from day one?"

"Perhaps," Clara softly mused.

"Does Patrious think the same way you do?" Rowan smirked.

His half-hearted jest quickly faded away with his smirk when he saw the seriousness of Clara's convictions.

"You're saying Saredhel is at work here plotting things behind the scenes or something?" The youth mimicked a puppeteer controlling a puppet with a whimsical breath.

"Maybe," she replied softly as she returned to looking over the waters. It was plausible and Gilban was her priest…

"Clara, she's a *goddess* — one tied to divinations. I don't think she'd be used or use others," Rowan shook his head in disbelief.

"Are you sure?" Clara asked. "I don't know much about Saredhel, she's not my goddess, but it certainly does seem odd all these recent events transpired in part because of that quest we undertook."

"As much as you like to think they are, not everything in life is connected. Even I know that," Rowan looked back into the face of the elf, and felt uneasiness flutter amid the butterflies in his stomach. Even when she was making nonsense stories and conjuring up baseless fears she was stunning to his eyes. "And I came from a people who often swear by fate," he thought he'd add the thought for extra strength to his argument.

"We all have consequences of our actions, and sometimes they are tied together in large and subtle ways…especially if they are choreographed by another with still a larger goal." Clara raised a warning finger as if she was some teacher; Rowan her student.

"We both have a shared action with the ruins in the jungle, and now we are sharing a similar circumstances from those actions." Rowan countered, "Simple as that."

"All I'm saying is that for the past few weeks I've been thinking about the way this whole quest has turned out from start to finish — what brought us to this point now and I feel I'm a part of a play acting out a plot I don't understand," Clara ran a hand through her silver locks, catching glimmers of sunlight upon various strands as brilliant as lightning. How could she get Rowan to see what was becoming, and had become, rather obvious to her?

"For *what* and *whose* purpose?" Rowan protested. "Next you'll be saying *Gilban* is in on this *secreted plot* as well," the youth snorted.

"Yes. He might be too," Clara lowered her head.

"*What?*" The young Nordican pulled back from her. "That's insane. Gilban called you to join him on the mission in the first place. He was given a vision by his goddess, which we completed. Where's the secret agenda there?"

"I don't think Gilban is part of this *intentionally…*" she took pains to make the distinction. "He might be unaware of it all, then again I'm not sure. The ways of the priesthood of Saredhel are very mysterious. Maybe it's the whole faith of Saredhel that has a secret plan."

"Clara. Listen to yourself. You're making about as much sense as a toothless lunatic. I admit we may have been taken advantage of before by that undead fiend, it is possible in some way I'm sure — however, he used us in the context of getting another goal — The Republic of Rexatious' goal met.

That's all. It was just a convenience he took advantage of, simple as that," Rowan tried to dismiss the topic with a sideways chop of his hand.

"I'm not being used as a pawn to go back to my superiors and report my mission, nor are you being used by accompanying me. If anything, Gilban would have insisted you return with him to Rexatious so that his plans might have been continued.

"Instead, he seemed to be uncaring in whatever choice you made, including the idea to travel with me. He didn't even care what the others did really. Dugan and Vinder were just as free to travel, and do as they wished just like the rest of us."

Clara protested as she grabbed the youth's shoulder. "But what about the creature that was loosed? It wanted to be brought to this world. It wanted Cadrissa."

"Why?"

"Maybe he was lonely. Cadrissa is fairly attractive, after all," Rowan's smirk quickly faded from his face under Clara's angry glare.

"Sorry," he humbly apologized.

"Think about it though, Rowan, if we were used to free him, he must have wanted Cadrissa for something. Is it too difficult to imagine a larger plan at work here? One maybe orchestrated by this creature itself?"

"Clara, there's no secret plotting here. You've had just a little too much time to over think some things, and this is the result. Whatever Cadrissa's captor wants, and why he took her will be known soon enough when we face him — and make him pay for his actions. I doubt though it is as in depth and intertwined as you make it seem." Even as he spoke, Rowan's own experiences and thoughts began to interconnect to that emerging framework…

What if she was onto something here?

"Until then, let's just enjoy the journey. It will be getting much colder soon as we enter the waters of the Northlands." The knight tried to change the subject of his thoughts. Clara's newly found interest in this topic was distressing to the youth, and he would be free of it as soon as he could. Best to dwell on topics at hand — more tangible, real, topics like getting to Arid Land.

Clara looked up at Rowan with eyes rimmed in sadness. Her silver mane hung over her face, and partly shaded her visage from the youth, but her voice was calm and restrained. "Your head must have winter in it because your thinking is frozen. Gilban knew much more than he was letting on, that much I'm certain. I respect and care for him very deeply, but he never really totally confided in me.

Cadrissa, when we first approached her, was chosen by Gilban because he felt she had 'a greater calling still'. He never said what he meant by it, but he did tell me later on he chose all of us because we were linked together in a powerful web of fate. He alluded to me what ever happens to one is destined to happen to the others in some form or another," Clara looked deep into the eyes of the youth.

"So you see, we're all interconnected," her voice was small.

"He told you this?" Rowan returned the gentle stare with some concern.

"Yes," she nodded.

Rowan was speechless for a moment as he too then began to trace the lines linking events together, and began to think in terms of a larger, interlocking canvass of which he might indeed be a part...in ways he never imagined. Suddenly Clara's conspiratorial musing now seemed to be making a bit more sense after all...

"Okay...so what does it mean then?" Rowan watched Clara raise her head once more to answer.

"It means we are still bound to Cadrissa, and the monster who took her," Clara moved to lean against the side of the boat; her two thin, yet strong arms propping her up against the weight of revealing this revelation.

"True enough... I mean we are planning on trying to save her. That's how we are connected, right?" Rowan joined her with tentative steps, following her lead in viewing the passing waves.

He was beginning to doubt himself. He cursed Clara for jumbling his thoughts even more than they had been.

"Okay, you may have a few points here, Clara — points but nothing to back them up with yet. Let's not go jumping to some wild theories right away." The knight cautioned with measured words and voice.

"So you still plan to go to this wizard then after your report?" Clara stood up to her full height, as she spun around to face the young knight, changing the subject with a slightly arrogant tone. "Do you think he'll be able to help or even want to?" She crossed her arms.

Rowan thought these actions reminded him of some young girl, not the woman he had come to understand and grow to like these past few weeks.

"People say he's a very powerful Ice King. I believe if we could get him to help us, he could lead us to Cadrissa, and aid us in destroying her captor. I am more than sure he will be willing to help." Rowan kept one hand on the side, using the other to punctuate his growing excitement at the prospect of finding this fabled wizard.

"How?" Clara raised an eyebrow.

"I-I just know how to handle him from the stories and what history has said of him," the knight's hand dropped along with his slumping enthusiasm. He didn't like where this conversation was leading, as it began to reveal some issues the knight hadn't pondered yet, really failed to ponder, in all his excitement.

"But you never really have meet him or got any first-hand information about him or where his tower is or how he could help — if he even would help, have you?" She continued.

This was another blow to Rowan's fragile illusion.

"No. I thought I'd do that once we got there." More of his excitement faded.

Clara sighed. "Do you know where this wizard is exactly?" Clara dealt the final blow, and the glass supports Rowan knew now to be a fantasy more than a hopeful opportunity crumbled underneath him with a tinkling crash.

"No." Rowan sighed out the last bits of hope he had for the venture.

"Do you know if he is a benevolent or evil wizard?" The elf wouldn't relent her onslaught.

"The legends say that—" the knight tried to regain some ground, but it was hopeless, he had ceded it all to Clara. She made him see the massive holes in his plan — holes his naive optimism filled, and now revealed again as the plugs melted like wax in the oven.

Rowan sighed again.

He knew Clara had a valid point on the wizard. He didn't really have more than legends and hear-say to work from, and the idea to save Cadrissa had been done in the heat of the moment without much more then a simple knee-jerk reaction to the event.

They *didn't* really have much of a plan...

"Rowan, don't you see, we have no real plan, and even if you did, we still are being led around to another set of rings to leap through like trained dogs." The slight sarcasm was gone now from Clara to be replaced with some maternal love and concern.

"Well, we have about two weeks to think up something better," said the knight, though without any optimism as he once had.

The elven maid returned a soft, rueful smile. "I hope we can figure out what is going on here before then — who or what is leading us, who is taking advantage of that connection, and why." She lowered her arms; relaxing her pose, "Maybe figuring out just how we are all interconnected..."

"I just hope you don't rub off any of your paranoia on me cause you're starting to make a little bit of sense now," the youth placed his hand on his chest and felt the familiar, comforting panther claw medallion under his clothing and stroked it absent-mindedly.

"Well you have two weeks to think on it as well," stated Clara.

"Just don't go getting any more paranoid to where you start doubting me now," Rowan smiled. It was the soft smile of jest shared between two close friends. "I've grown too used to your company to have to part ways, or get into some kind of fight."

"Don't worry," Clara returned the appreciative grin, "I won't."

Though the conversation was over for now, each knew the matter was far from resolved, but they still had two weeks…for what it was worth.

Chapter 24

Dugan, dressed in black wool pants and tunic, stood before a stonewall. His hands were wrapped in dark gloves and his face was covered in a silk mask resting over the bridge of his nose and encircled his eyes with darkness. The rest of his face was smeared with an inky grease paint around his eyes where the mask didn't cover as well as his chin and lower jowls. The black substance was placed on in stripes of varying lengths and thickness, breaking up the contours of Dugan's face. The job had been so well done that if he didn't move at all, he almost blended right into the gloom about him — the perfect living shade.

His golden hair was tied back into a ponytail with a black ribbon, and he wore his sword strapped to his back along with a belt holstering three daggers, which were also smeared with pitch gel to prevent the sheen from any light source from revealing them.

Next to him were three similarly dressed persons. They weren't a massive structure of muscle like their companion, but rather thin, sinewy beings that looked to be more nimble and acrobatic by nature. Unlike Dugan's mask, they wore black facemasks covering their whole heads. Only a small opening around the eyes allowed them to see out. Each carried an onyx hilt dagger smeared with black gel at their side, and wore thin, ebony shoes crafted of leather and cloth.

Dugan looked at his comrades, who would serve as his guides and fellow practitioners in his mission for the cult. He was informed they would be there to protect him and secure the area while Dugan lay in wait to kill the Mayor. He ignored the gnawing pang in his gut and the anxious excretions of energy into his muscles as he pondered why three others were needed to protect him, but tried to focus around it as best he could.

He thought back to the words of the messenger of Rheminas instead. It was a fluttering thought amid many in his mind. He felt sure his faith in himself was not misplaced. There was just this one last task of service, and then he'd be free.

One more task…

"Are you ready, Dugan?" One of his companions asked, his voice a quiet whisper.

"Sure," the Telborian responded with an emotionless voice.

"Then I think we are ready to go. Are you ready as well?" He directed his attention to the two others. They nodded in silent agreement.

"Okay. Remember, Dugan. You have to kill the Mayor quickly. We have trained you to move without thinking, and to be a stealth-relying killer. Use these skills to kill the Mayor as quietly as possible. We don't want the guards to rush in and overwhelm us.

"We'll protect you like we said…however, we have been informed we are to secure the room more tightly now than before. We might be occupied in certain areas as we determine the safety of the room, so don't be alarmed by that. We need your strength and experience to kill the Mayor, and you need our talents to protect and guide you to him."

"That was the deal," Dugan grunted, totally uncaring words. He barely registered the conversation in his thoughts. His mind was elsewhere, to fanciful flights of freedom, to a joyful life and afterlife far away from here. Away from Rheminas, the suffering and killing for the whim of another man or god.

The others looked at themselves, and only nodded silently after the first had spoken to the Telborian. They then drew more quiet still as the first one of their number pressed a hidden stone on the wall in front of them. Silently, a three-foot section of the wall separated itself from the structure and sunk deep into a cool deep plum opening behind it.

"We should be off then," the lead cultist said.

They waded through the gloom silently.

Dugan had no wish to alert other beings or his guides in front of him of his position, though he was sure he could still be seen by the shadowy figures. The dark collection of cultists and assassin sped through the twisting, totally lightless corridors and hallways. Sometimes Dugan had to struggle though an opening no more than a foot across. On other occasions he charged through halls that could have had a chariot gallop through. In all instances he moved like a jungle cat cast of an onyx. The under streets of Haven were more vast and confusing than their surface counterparts. Hordes of folk could live all their lives beneath the noses of those above and never be known to exist at all, he thought.

The cultists had been eerily correct in determining the layout of the Mayor's mansion. The cult of Shador truly deserved the fearful respect they generated, for it was clear to Dugan's mind they could indeed be anywhere at any time, spying, or holding the life of their victim in the palm of their hand.

Dugan was living proof of the latter statement.

As he ran through the tunnels, he thought about the hidden pathways and secret openings the cult had provided him access to, and wondered why they needed him at all. They could do such an action very easily themselves, with minimal risk to any save their victim. An odd sensation had been rising up in his gut since they started this mission, and it troubled the Telborian. He couldn't place the feeling totally, but it had been growing in strength with each passing hour.

He had to concentrate harder as he came to the area designated by a cultist; he still didn't know their names. His silent footfalls slowed to a gentle trot, then a small step when he saw the faint glow of a dagger painted onto the wall to his left. It possessed a soft luminescence that seemed like moonlight to the gladiator's eyes. The sign had been placed by the cultists to mark where the Mayor's room was or so Dugan had been told. All he had to do now was slip into the room, kill the Mayor, and leave the same way he came.

Easy enough.

As he neared the wall, he wanted to be assured everything would be as it was said to be. He wanted no mistakes or any loopholes to be found in the task at hand. It had to be simple and fast, or he risked greater danger than what he had faced before he was freed.

The Telborian took a deep breath and waited to exhale through his clenched jaw. The time seemed to claw away at eons as he did so. His heart raced, though he thought he had it under control. He even began to doubt his abilities and wonder if he could even pull it off — if he was really ready.

Dugan passed the thoughts off as hollow doubts and shadows of the mind.

"Are you ready, Dugan?" a shadowy figure asked him, though where he was at the moment Dugan couldn't say.

"Yes," he finally said after he felt the last of his breath eased through his teeth.

"Then enter. We will be watching your back, and making sure your escape is assured, as we secure the room," the disembodied voice spoke once more.

Dugan took another deep breath, and then pushed the section of wall in front of him slowly. It crawled forward, then stopped short of one inch of a gap between it and the wall. Using what knowledge the cult had taught him, he pushed it slowly to the right.

It glided effortless without a sound. Just as it was described to him, he found a tapestry blocked the secret entrance into the Mayor's chambers from being seen. It was a perfect hiding spot.

Like a prowling lion, Dugan slid from the opening behind the tapestry; sword in hand, feet and body using the skills in stealth his cultist trainers had taught him. He was posed to deal out the full extent of what was expected of him as he neared the end of the wall hanging, and dared a covert look around its fringed edges.

Behind the covering was a thinly decorated room. It was framed in deep, rich brown wooden planks. Torches and candles lined the rest of the walls. It was about fifteen feet in width and twelve feet in length. A long painting hung on the wall opposite Dugan, being more than four feet in length and two feet in width depicting the view of Haven from outside the city itself. Dugan surmised it must have been how it appeared some time ago. The city was smaller and some of the buildings that were now old and run down appeared new in the picture. Dugan surmised that since the time of the painting, it seemed Haven had more than doubled in size.

Haven had become what many could realistically call a kingdom in its own right, but instead kept the name of independent city. And Haven was not alone in this claim, many similar independent cities were large enough to enforce their will upon others like a kingdom, but instead chose to remain free and independent, out of the hands of the other kingdoms around it or adopting much of their own was as well. Though the leader of the city was called the Mayor, he was more like a minor prince or lesser king than anything else.

And tonight he was going to find his way into Mortis before his killer.

Dugan had emerged on the far wall, opposite the door into the hallway. To his left was the unoccupied bed of the mayor. To his right was a wooden chest and simple closet containing some personal effects of the elected ruler, but nothing Dugan concerned himself about. A large glass window resided to his left, but shed only starlight into the room. After he looked around and was sure there was no real danger in the room, he darted back to the covered darkness of the hidden passageway.

"He isn't there!" Dugan whispered to the others.

"Our reports said he frequents his room at this hour," one whispered back.

"Could our reports be wrong?" Another replied.

"No, we are just early, or he is a little late. He will come, and we must be ready. Dugan — set yourself in behind the door while we search the room for any other dangers or hidden ways a guard could get into the room we do not known about."

Dugan didn't hesitate, but slithered inside the room. His feet tread softly upon the hard wood floor, covered with patches of bearskin rugs and knitted wonders of dyed fabrics. Taking his sword, he stood next to the door, crouched with anticipation for the Mayor's arrival. The other cult members ushered in then. Like silent, sinister, shadows, they wafted toward various corners of the room, searching with their trained eyes and hands.

"Over here! Quickly!" One of them whispered as he approached the portrait of the ancient city. The others were beside him in a blink of an eye. "I have found the strong box. It is behind this portrait."

Together as silently as death they lifted the picture from the wall. Behind it was a wooden plank wall with a one-foot-square metal door, latched and locked with a hard iron lock. Swift as predators set on their prey, the cultists pulled out a lock pick and began to work on the device with the skill and grace of a fine artisan.

Dugan noticed this from his position, but paid it little mind. He passed it off to securing the room. Since he had never seen a secured room before he wasn't sure what it involved or what more traps or secret doors the room might hide.

The lock sprung open with a click.

More rapid than the wind, the cultists' hands were inside the opening behind the metal door pawing the interior like scavengers looting a carcass hoping for some scraps. The activity intensified as they pulled out a small steel box, about a foot in length and six inches high.

Dugan was drawn to the object. He wondered what the box could be, and why it was so important. Could it be a weapon? Not likely, he thought. It seemed they were interested more in thievery than his safety.

"What are you doing? You didn't say anything about theft," the uneasiness increased inside the Telborian.

One of their number turned to the Telborian, "You watch the door, and we'll worry about our actions. This was stolen by the Mayor from one of our members. We are taking back what is ours. Tell us the moment you hear anything. The Mayor can't be too far away."

Dugan's brow furrowed at the comment.

He watched as the cultists took out a three-inch silver jeweled brochette from the hidden box. In the center was a lapis lazuli, cut in a brilliant circle setting which seemed to sparkle with an internal life of its own.

"We have it finally," the leader spoke in an awful reverence.

"Is it the real one?" Another questioned, his black clothed fingers reached for the gem.

"Yes. It has the markings. He will be pleased," another replied.

They looked toward Dugan, who now had taken to stare at them with an icy glare through his mask.

They knew their time was short.

"He suspects now," one whispered

"It is best we should go, our mission is complete," another replied.

"Make sure the distraction is taken care of," the third responded in a frigid tone.

The shadowy group then split up. Two of their number made their way back to the tapestry as a single form moved to Dugan who had the look of a panther about to pounce.

"What's going on here?" Dugan began to rise; malice and mistrust heavy upon his breath.

"The room is secure. You only need me here to help you make your escape," the cultist whispered back, as the two others vanished behind the tapestry.

"You didn't tell me about the jewelry. What else have you left out or forgotten to tell me?" Dugan's attention faded from the door and rested strongly upon the dark-wrapped figure in front of him.

"Just trust me, Dugan. We have no reason for bickering now. What our order does in the realm of the spirit is in no way connected to you or your goals. You will be freed from your suffering, believe me," the figure slowly walked toward the window next to the large tapestry by means of backwards steps.

Dugan didn't trust him.

He'd felt the acidic twinge of betrayal, and lies in his mind and heart. He knew this wasn't right, and somehow he was being used – and he would see it end in his favor if he could.

"What are you doing now?" Dugan began to rise up from his position.

"No. Stay down," one of the cultists harshly ordered, "I am just looking out the window to see what is going on outside. The Mayor is late, and I don't like that. Rest easy, but stay vigil, he could appear at anytime."

"Do you see him?" Dugan's eyes darted back to the dark opening behind the tapestry. Though, it was hidden by the falling cloth, he felt he could see the eyes of the other two cultists look back at him with slight amusement.

The gnawing in his gut intensified.

He had to act quickly or he might be worse off yet. He tried to think, but found it hard whenever the cultist got near to him, his thoughts would swim about the great dark lake of his head like a cauldron being stirred over the flame.

"No—" the words were drowned out by a crash of glass, and fleeting footsteps. "Farewell fool may the arms of Rheminas welcome you."

Dugan was lost in a moment in time. He had trouble processing all that had transpired. The cultist threw the metal box though the window, which shattered with a deafening crash in the still night.

The noise had brought commotion and shouts from the hallway. In the confusion, the cultist fled behind the tapestry. Dugan heard a faint click above the rising clamor.

Anger seized him as he rain toward the tapestry. "I'll kill you! You will be the first to greet him."

With a great movement, the Telborian tore down the cloth covering to reveal a solid wall behind it. He couldn't tell where the passage opening started, and the wall ended. He pounded the wall like an ogre shouting his rage through the mansion wall but to no avail. The very next moment the door crashed in and ten armed and armored men ran into the small room to greet the frustrated Telborian.

Before he knew what was happening Dugan was surrounded by five Telborian's who were barking orders and questions all at once. Dugan didn't care to answer the questions, or obey the commands. He would be free of the whole situation at least long enough to get his final revenge upon the cult, and then face the dire consequences of his actions.

Like a whirlwind, Dugan confronted his prey. The five men who stood before him suddenly fell into a pool of red ichor that sprayed and spread across the floor in a swelling tide. Their bodies had been slashed across the stomach in one powerful movement. It appeared their chainmail shirts hadn't been enough for Dugan's supposedly enchanted blade and his full-fledged fury when it was unleashed upon them. They tried to stem the flow of blood and innards spilling out of them, but were futile, as each knew their death was moments away.

Not stopping for a second swing, the gladiator stepped over his fallen foes on his way to the window. As he did so, five more men came into the room, drew crossbows, and fired at him.

Dugan's new training and his old skills saved him from four of the bolts, but one sliced his left shoulder as he turned to avoid it.

Dugan cursed as he made the leap, head first from the window.

The drop wasn't that great, but he managed to land into a roll unharmed. Even as he stood up, he heard the alarm being called, and the whole complex rising to oppose him.

His time was severely limited, with not many options open to him.

Trapped in a strange location he knew nothing about, being hunted like a dog, and wounded, the odds didn't seem to favor his escape let alone survival.

Why did this seem all too familiar to him?

Dugan looked above himself and toward the broken window of the Mayor's room where he'd just come from. He could see now it rested on the third floor of what seemed to be a very richly decorated stone mansion in an enclosed complex. He didn't let his attention linger that long on the structure.

The guards shouted curses at him as they lobbed arrows and crossbow bolts down upon him from the Mayor's bedroom. From what few could crowd and shoot out of the opening they did so with a fierce hatred. The Telborian managed to harmlessly dance around these projectiles with trained steps, while he cursed himself beneath his breath.

How could he have been so stupid?

The night air was filled with bobbing torchlights and activity. All around him he could see pinpricks of light growing larger by the moment. He knew he'd be surrounded with little hope of escape soon enough. This mattered little to him. All he could think about was revenge at the people who brought him here — brought him to this. He couldn't escape its grip and he found himself becoming its slave once more.

He'd been betrayed!

Vile and dark emotions consumed him like the fiercest blaze. He felt every muscle tighten, and every nerve in his body, every cell of his being, locked in rage. He tore the cut black sleeve from his left arm, and looked at his wounded shoulder. With a grunt he pulled the bolt out of his flesh; the red of his blood washing away any and all lingering doubts on the matter. As surely as it had been there before, the mark of his servitude — the branding of Colloni — had returned. Its disappearance had just been an illusion!

So *stupid*.

Furious, Dugan let out a boisterous and bestial howl of rage. His last hope had been nothing but a lie, and Rheminas had actually forewarned him of it all… The fury was hot in him now, boiling away what was left of his reason.

He'd played right into the cultists' hands; been their puppet and pet so they could get what they wanted, and he could get his reward: death. He wouldn't give them that satisfaction though. If he was to be condemned into the flames of Rheminas, he would send all those who played him for a fool to meet Asorlok before him. If the gods wanted these cultists dead, then he would oblige them.

He had to act fast though, or he would not have the opportunity to reap his revenge. The torches had come much closer since last he observed them. He saw them drifting out in the sea of night from behind the manicured garden that surrounded the Mayor's estate. The soft green bushes and artistically pruned trees peacefully growing behind the tall stone walls of the enclosure would only hold back his pursuers' eyes for so long before the torchbearers made his discovery.

He needed to get away very quickly. Dugan retreated further into the darkness of some bushes and trees, thinking rapidly for an escape plan. None seemed to be coming to him, and then a formless voice spoke to the gladiator.

This way Dugan.

The Telborian looked around and found nothing but the growing light of the pursuing guards setting the night ablaze. It seemed though, that Dugan could now also make out another light growing closer to him with each passing breath.

"Dugan. Turn toward me and claim your revenge," the voice seemed to come from this new light.

The nearer it came, the more Dugan noticed it resembled a ball of swirling flame hovering about three feet from the ground and was no more than the size of a man's fist in diameter. As it drew closer to the gladiator it seemed to grow at a rapid rate, taking on the width of a man within a few wild heartbeats. Dugan was awestruck, and at the same time frightened, for he knew what the fiery globe represented.

Rheminas returned to his favorite prize.

"You want me to kill these cultists?" A fearsome grin birthed of bloodlust and retribution covered Dugan's face as he greeted the fiery form. "For once we are in agreement."

"Good," the flaming semblance of a man continued. "Rheminas will give you revenge against your enemies once more, if you just step into the flames. You will be given all the power you need — and then some — to kill and make suffer those who would deceive you and bring you to utter ruin and despair." The flames before Dugan spoke a maddening music to the Telborian's ears.

Dugan then surrendered to his fate — accepting his final destination to death with a fatalistic resolution. There was nothing left to do, he was Rheminas'.

"You will be acting with the blessing of the gods as well — being a herald of divine retribution and judgment. This is being offered to you as a gift from my lord, for he greatly favors you. You but have to accept and this and your revenge will be granted to you."

Dugan looked at the flaming man the ball had grown into, then turned his attention from him to the approaching guards. He could even see some movement now getting closer to his position.

He could also feel the warlust rising even higher.

He was ready.

"Step into the flame and be free to commit your revenge, Dugan, or you can stay here and be killed. The choice is yours." Rheminas' messenger approached the gladiator, holding out his hand for the Telborian to take. Dugan closed his eyes and looked up toward heaven. The irony of his life filled him with sorrow and rage he couldn't take it anymore. It was time to stop fighting his ultimate fate. It was time to accept into whose hands he had sold his soul…

"It seems then fate has damned me to walk this path. Now I must complete it." His voice was calm and resolute like the condemned man walking to the gallows.

All his fighting had gotten him nothing.

His whole life he had been the slave of someone else. Nothing of freedom was ever known to him. Even as he was free from Colloni, he wasn't free from his past. It shook him to the bone. His demons wouldn't let him go, and he had grown tired of fighting them.

Like the tired general who knows that he is outnumbered, and the battle is over — his forces barely holding on from being overrun, Dugan made his choice to die on his terms at least and then be done with it all. If he could send these cultists, these liars who had given him false hopes to believe in to the Abyss in his final act in life, then so be it. Fighting and bloodletting had been all he had known and it was fitting he would end his days in the midst of it. At least it wasn't a cross — he could choose his death to be better than that.

The Telborian grabbed the flaming hand of the figure. It didn't burn, just as he knew it wouldn't. The figure then moved forward, and the two became as one. Flesh and fire mingling over each other in a wondrous display before both vanished from the spot.

All that remained was a puff of curling, greasy, black smoke, befuddling guards who neared Dugan's previous location. Only a singed, silken mask remained where he'd once stood.

Chapter 25

ᘯᖂᕼᖇᘯ

Gilban and Hoodwink sat quietly on a dark walnut bench outside the main doors to the inner sanctuary inside the massive temple of Saredhel. The doors to the holy place were a strong, deeply stained oak polished to a high shine. The doors were unadorned save for the Eye of Fate, the symbol of Saredhel resting upon the two halves of the closed portal — each part of the eye coming together in the center to stare down at the two before it.

The two of them had been sitting there for almost an hour. Silent and empty, the hallway outside the chamber contained them as they waited for an audience with Gilban's fellow priests. Gilban hadn't been much more open with his comments about what he was planning, or what they were going to do since they had left the small room where Hoodwink was staying.

Gilban had only instructed the goblin to change his outfit, and he had— donned a simple wool tunic dyed a bright blue, short boots of black leather, and plain brown pants. The clothing had come from a pile of donated goods the temple had received from what Hoodwink assumed to be a halfling, or perhaps a gnome, given the size of the garments. After this they both packed some meager rations, enough for a few days travel — Gilban said they wouldn't need much more than that.

When pressed as to why, the old elf remained silent. He simply led him to the bench, put his staff against the wooden seat, and sat down to await an audience he had requested with the highest ranked priests of the temple. This was in order to get the last threads of the blind priest's plan weaved together so they could move on to Doom Maker's Island.

Hoodwink didn't like the silence one bit, but figured he'd be filled in with more details of just what was going on in a little while. Both he and Gilban were to meet up with some other priests who were going to help on their journey. Just how they were going to do this the goblin had no clue, but he knew it would come to him soon enough as they were now outside the very center of the temple itself, the worship area of the priests dedicated to Saredhel.

Hoodwink let out a small sigh. They had been sitting here for far too long by the goblin's estimation and with Gilban not talking, and no one else about in the empty, elaborate halls, he was becoming bored. Bored enough to scream. The lone goblin peered up at the sightless seer with a quiet look of uncertainty playing across his green face and yellow eyes.

Maybe he could get some more answers out of the old elf. Then again maybe not. Gilban was proving to be a pretty stubborn old priest. At least though he could have some conversation to help pass the time. Who knew how long the two of them would be sitting there and he wasn't about to go wandering off in the halls now either…

"How much longer is this going to take?" He finally asked.

"Patience, Hoodwink," the blind seer continued to peer ahead at the doors.

"Why do you have to talk to them again?" The goblin persisted in his questioning.

"All will be revealed in time my small friend," the priest slouched a bit lower in the hard, wooden bench, adjusting his thin frame as he did so.

"You still don't want to tell me what this whole mission is about, huh? Why we have to go to Gorallis?" The goblin continued. He didn't have much hope of an answer but it was certainly helping him pass the time.

The priest said nothing.

Discouraged by the silence, Hoodwink scraped his boots across the stone floor for a moment. He was shorter than most races that would sit on the bench, but still managed to have the toes of his boots just touch the stone if he leaned over far enough in his seat. He did this for a little while longer, till he had an idea for a new line of questioning. Something, that might actually get the old priest to say something more than he had and share with him a least a few of secrets.

"You think it will be very dangerous, don't you? That's why we're here." Hoodwink kept his eyes on his boots. Perhaps keeping his eyes focused elsewhere might help. Maybe the blind priest could see him staring at him somehow, and didn't like it.

"One can never tell these things my friend," The old elf slumped down still a little lower on the bench. "You know that. Fate is not a game, and the future can never be totally accurate in one's own assessment."

"Aha! Then we *will* die?" Hoodwink turned to the priest, previous tactic forgotten.

"You will die just as I, and everyone else will die. There is no question in need of answering regarding that," Gilban kept his head focused on the doors before them. "The better question to ask would be when. However, as I have told you already, we will not die on *this* mission."

"But if you did know the fate of someone's life, would you tell them if they asked you?" Hoodwink cocked his head with an inquisitive face.

A grim humor then played across the priest's face. "Many have asked me that question, and yet I never grow accustomed to it.

"Let us just say then, Hoodwink, for the sake of argument, I would answer such a question. How would it benefit the person who asked such a thing? Would that person still die?"

"Yes, but then he knows when," Hoodwink stated in a matter of fact tone. Of course, such knowledge would be beneficial.

"True. Again though, how would it help that person?" Gilban raised some self-doubt into the goblin with his philosophical timbre.

"It would just help him in life… he'd be better able to live his life," Hoodwink straightened his head, but kept his eyes on

the priest. He was losing his train of thought, and certainty with the confusion brought forth by Gilban's statements.

"Help him *how?*" Gilban looked over at the goblin, though his eyes were blind, Hoodwink thought he was looking right at him, right *through* him.

"Like I said, you could get ready...prepare..." Hoodwink scratched his head, and wrinkled his brow. "It would help to know, so you could avoid it... I guess." He was losing the clear certainly on the matter now.

"Hoodwink. Do mortals live forever?" Gilban kept his sightless eyes on the goblin.

"No," the goblin replied sheepishly.

"How then could one avoid an event all mortals share? You wouldn't be able to avoid your own death. That's the point. You would spend countless hours, days, weeks, months or even years trying to stop the event from happening or doing works and services to pass the time, and work up a good name for yourself, pandering to your weaker and more selfish emotions. Life is about living, not fearing death, not trying to be something you are not in hopes of a greater reward in the afterlife or lines in some history book. Live life, and die in peace." At this Gilban returned his gaze to the closed doors.

"Oh, so you're *not* gonna tell me when I'm going to die, then?" Hoodwink looked down at the floor again — swinging his feet back and forth above the stone.

"No," Gilban smiled once more as he adjusted himself on the wooden bench. "Everything will be fulfilled as it should be. Don't worry about things you cannot control. Rest your mind. You will need it soon enough."

"You're still not going to tell me what this is all about are you?" The goblin tried one last time at getting some answers. "What's that thing inside the pouch said to you?"

Gilban returned to his silence. The goblin had his answer.

"So I guess we just wait then…" Hoodwink sighed again, and raised his tired, sore head to ponder the strange, almost frightful Eye of Fate.

"Yes. Patience Hoodwink." Gilban sighed.

"You don't want to tell me what you meant about me having a great purpose do you?" The goblin played his last card in hopes of getting at least one of the main questions in his head answered.

Gilban drew more still, a moment longer, not even taking a breath as he seemed to think over in his mind — at least the goblin thought he did. Finally he spoke. "I can't answer that yet, as it has not come clearly to me even. Still your mind and rest your spirit. All things will be revealed soon."

In truth the priest hadn't been thinking too hard upon it. His mind was elsewhere directed to the matter that had brought him here.

"Right," the goblin withdrew into himself once more. "Patience…"

While Hoodwink had grown more restless from his wait, Gilban had used the time to think. There seemed to be a lot of these events taking place of recently. First, there was the threat of the hidden knowledge falling into the hands of the Elyellium and now this. If time was progressive and not circular, as some philosophers claimed, then the challenges and threats would get deadlier and farther reaching as indeed this recent threat, as far as he had perceived it as the orb inside the pouch had revealed to him, seemed to be evidence.

His hand went to the side of his belt where the sack containing the orb rested. It was safe beside him, but it caused his mind to still wonder about the object and the fate it now tied him into — calling him to complete for it… Not more than the size of an apple, the small globe inside the pouch was smooth and hard, like marble. It was heavy too, like a lead weight; stranger still was the near bone-chilling cold pulsating from the orb when in hand.

The old priest recalled it felt colder than a cadaver's flesh when he had first touched it. Maybe not the wisest of actions to do, but he couldn't get any other answers from it without at least some contact — and the temple did have it's precautions, as he had pointed out to Hoodwink earlier. The orb though, was something of a puzzle that needed to be solved. So he had took it up, and welcomed anything it might chose to enlighten him with in his search for answers.

Being unable to see it with his physical eyes, he wasn't clear on how it appeared. He tried petitioning his goddess to aid him in discerning its image in his mind, but met limited success. All Hoodwink had been able to explain was the object was a deep, red globe — smooth and shimmering, with a golden red light which emanated from it when held. Unhappy with his ability to crack the enigma presented him, he'd tied it on his belt to keep it near him as they prepared for their journey.

Now, as he sat quietly in the bench, he tried to think on the orb. Tried to call it to mind, but was unable. This exercise he repeated off and on while they sat waiting for an audience. He wanted to better understand what was going on around him, what this whole event tied to the orb was about. Something blocked him from his searches, though. Something he couldn't understand — but felt its presence nonetheless.

He wouldn't give up though, and kept on trying.

Gilban continued his pursuit of the orb not just because it was a mystery, but because of what it first revealed to him when he took it up. The swirling sensations of light and sound it unleashed in his head made him think he had received his actual, physical, sight once again. It was in that vision he'd seen a cloud of shimmering mist, whose radiance was as if it was a bank of clouds at daybreak. Silver and gold bouts of dust mixed among the mist, which further served to enrich the gleam, and simple pleasure already present from the image.

It was from that light a voice told him to go and seek out Gorallis, to give him the orb in exchange for a relic from the Age of the Wizard Kings and then to take it to Arid Land; to a place called Galba. When Gilban asked why, he was told he had to help stop an advancing threat that was coming to pass. He was also told he would be joined by the others from his previous mission to help stop the threat.

Gilban almost didn't believe what he was told though; he didn't see why the orb was so important. He had asked the voice, actually questioned quite diligently for the reason of its importance and was rewarded with an answer. The answer he received filled him with wonder. Gorallis would agree to exchange anything for the orb because it was his own eye that had been plucked out centuries before.

Fascinating to say the least, Gilban had since tried to figure out just what significance the eye must have been to have survived all those years, and passed through who knows how many hands till it reached his own. To think he held in his grasp the very eye of a beast of legend, one who might indeed have seen the birth of creation itself as some legends spoke…

The priest wanted to ask more of the voice, but was unable to; something held his tongue, and stilled his mind — as it still did when he tried to probe for more insight and understanding. Instead, he was compelled with a sense of urgency to carry out the task as he has been instructed, the missing pieces being revealed along the way. Indeed, the vision was quite standard in that regard — a mystery in an answer. A question within a question.

Gilban had seen enough visions to know this one should be obeyed, even if he didn't understand who told him to take on this task. His goddess had been faithful to him and his comprehension of true and false visions as well as making him familiar with magical compulsions that could mimic visions. This vision he received was genuine. He may not have been able to figure out who had given it to him, though it was allowed by his goddess, of that much he was certain. It gave him all the foundation he needed to round up Hoodwink, some supplies, and be on his way.

Whatever this threat was, he felt it was close at hand. As to just what it was…well, that would be filled in along the way, he supposed. He did feel though, he should hide the orb itself, as something was going to happen in the future — he would need to safeguard it.

He supposed now was as good a time as any to do this since he had little else to do but wait for an audience. Gilban took the pouch around his belt and held it in his hand, mumbling a soft prayer to Saredhel. As he prayed, he rolled the pouch and orb together in his hands, working it into a tighter ball until it seemingly reduce itself in size. Slowly, but surly, the orb grew smaller and smaller until it was no more the size of a walnut; the pouch around it shrank to match such dimensions.

Following this, Gilban pushed the smaller pouch and orb into one of his secret pockets on his robes which swallowed the object whole. When it was done, there was not even a bulge in his robes to show where the object had gone.

Gilban felt better now about the matter as he opened his eyes from prayer. When he had need of it, the orb would be his once more.

Just then the doors opened and a younger, bald Patrician woman, a priestess of Saredhel, ushered out.

"We will see you now.

Inside the sanctuary, Hoodwink couldn't believe his eyes. Had he thought the temple and the city in which it resided were richly attired, then the inner chamber must have been its center. Beyond the sturdy oak doors a whole new world was presented him.

All of the circular room was covered with gilt. Gold and silver overlay covered stylized reliefs of vines made their way across the room, bisecting it in a foot wide stripe. On the bottom portion of the wall, under this stripe, ivory crafted into wooden planks provided a smooth and delicate touch in the already opulent decor.

Hoodwink craned his head high above to take in the ceiling, probably spanning the entire height of the temple itself, to see the vague outlines of minutely detailed painted figures on the concave surface of a concrete dome looking down at him below. He couldn't make them out from their great distance and the dimness swimming around the upper reaches of the sanctuary despite an enormous brass candelabra ablaze with a hundred silver candles descending from its center, covering all in of the spacious room in a shimmering metallic sheen of illumination.

The young priestess who led them into the sanctuary seemed to limp a bit with her right leg as if she had trouble moving it. Hoodwink noticed this as he took in the colorful polished stone mosaic on the floor. It was a sea of red and blue with a green circular outline around five silver basins arrayed in the chamber: four at each cardinal point of the compass and one larger one in the center of them and the room. These basins were filled with mercury and rested on top of some ornately designed silver bases. Though the goblin wasn't quite sure what to make of these, he was convinced they might be used in some sort of divination process.

The fifth polished stone circle, the one outlining the largest of the five basins with a wide swath was in the center of the three-hundred-foot-wide room. In this circle the Eye of Fate was painstakingly created with colored tiles to make it appear as if the unblinking orb was ever watchful of those who trod upon it. It was around this larger circle that five other priests had been gathered and where the younger priestess was leading Hoodwink and Gilban.

The rest of the room was awash with rich murals of priests and visions, symbols and tales older than the temple itself perhaps. Amid these aged frescoes a few statues stood silently, watching the two enter. Molded from pure white marble, they stood the full height of a man in each of the cardinal points of the circular room. Two men and two women each are opposing the other. They appeared to be of elven stock, dressed in flowing robes, which even to the goblin's eye seemed a bit antiquated. Hoodwink wanted to take a closer look at them, but didn't have the time as he saw the other five priests waiting for them.

All of the priests were of Patrician stock, and dressed in the same simple course brown robe, leather sandals and hemp belt as Gilban wore, but were of various ages and genders. Two were females of what seemed to be middle age and unimpaired in the least Hoodwink could tell (he thought it harder to judge the age of the women without their hair). Beside them were three men, one young, and two middle-aged. The youngest of the three had a shriveled left arm hanging limply by his side as if it was a dead strap of leather. Another of the middle-aged man, this one balder than the other, was blind, like Gilban. His companion didn't seem too impaired, but the goblin noticed favored his left leg over his right when he stood and moved about.

The younger priestess who invited them inside moved toward the gathering of the five, who stood outside the large circle surrounding the greatest of the five basins.

"Welcome, Gilban," the blind priest addressed the duo in Pacoloes.

"Thank you for your audience," Gilban returned in the same tongue.

"So these are the leaders of your order?" Hoodwink whispered up to Gilban in Telborous.

"Yes," came Gilban's reply in Telborous as both stopped just outside the larger circle, near the rim of its mosaic outline.

"No offense, but they seem...all the priests here seem..."

"Crippled?" Gilban finished Hoodwink's sentence for him in Telborous.

"Well — yeah," the goblin whispered back in the same language.

"What one gives up for the gift of second sight, the sight that parts the veil, is worth the sacrifice. To judge any of the priests on what we lack, or how we are deformed or crippled in some way is to ignore what we have inside us, and what we have to offer. That is the power of our faith, and our goddess," said Gilban, still speaking in the tongue of the Telborians, though not in a whisper now.

Hoodwink was silent and wide-eyed for a moment as he took in what he had just been told. He hadn't thought of it like that. Maybe things weren't always what they seemed. At least, it was the case he was coming to understand, here. In a world of symbols, allegories, and riddles why should he take everything he saw at face value...

"Gilban speaks the truth," the balding blind priest spoke in Telborous. "I may lack sight but my hearing is still good, and the boon of my goddess is worth the diminishing of my own eyesight as I'm sure Gilban would testify to as well."

"I'm sorry to-" Hoodwink started.

"No need to apologize, goblin," one of the middle-aged women addressed him in Telborous also. Hoodwink wondered if they had heard, and understood what he had just recently said, and assumed they probably had. "For all are judged by some standard but it is to our own in which we must find merit."

"Now Gilban," the younger male priest with the withered arm spoke in Telborous, as they all did from that point on, for the goblin's benefit. "We have prayed and mediated on the recent request you have made and we find ourselves in agreement to grant your request.

"While this latest revelation is not from our goddess directly, we sense her favor in seeking it out. Therefore, we shall do as you request."

"What are they taking about?" Hoodwink looked over to Gilban.

"They will aid us in getting to Doom Maker's Island." Gilban never let his attention leave the leaders of his order as he answered Hoodwink.

"So they have a ship then?" Hoodwink looked over to Gilban.

"Something better," Gilban's lips rose in a subtle smile.

"Indeed," the other blind priest spoke again. "Enter the circle."

Hoodwink and Gilban were helped by the goblin as they did so.

"As it has already been said," the blind priest continued, "We have come to the conclusion of our mediation. The time and place of your arrival have been set — and now you must go. For what you have proposed is linked with the nature of time as well, in a very intimate fashion."

"Because of this, you both will have to travel some distance into the stream itself and emerge further down river than where we now currently tarry." The middle-aged priest with the bad leg addressed them. "Do not be distracted by what you see. You will lose your focus by these images. Should you lose your focus, your pathway to your destination will alter — and you will end up in some other place, and some other time."

"I don't plan on messing anything up here. I'll just close my eyes or something then," Hoodwink spoke to the priest.

"Your natural vision will not be of any concern in this journey for you will be seeing with the eyes of your mind and spirit which can see though the natural eyes of the flesh though they may have been dimmed."

"Oh," came the goblins's reply. This wasn't sounding that safe after all. Too late to back out now, he supposed, but he wouldn't leave anyway — even it he could. He knew that the matter had been settled in his heart hours ago. No, he was in this to the end — might even be destined to be if he was inclined to believe that black-cloaked woman with the orb.

"So be mindful of where your mind drifts," the middle-aged priest with the bad leg concluded.

"So prepare as best you can," the other middle-aged woman now spoke.

"I have, as I know the goblin has as well," Gilban's words were dry and regal, resigned to the matter at hand.

"Then let us begin." The younger priest with the withered arm lead the others in raising their own right arms and extending them toward the center of the circle. "Stand in the midst of us brother and ally."

Gilban moved into the center of their hands as did Hoodwink, though more cautiously than the fellow he helped lead. Together they walked deep into the circle so they were a few feet away from the larger basin, which rose higher off the ground than Hoodwink was tall, and was about as wide and twice his height. Around them, outside the tiled line of the circle, the six priests surrounded them. The goblin could sense a shift in their mannerisms as they prepared for the ritual they were about to release.

The younger female priestess led the other in the invocation. Her peaceful voice gained a surreal, almost dream-like quality about it as the prayer was spoken in Pacoloes.

"Here is the beginning. Here is the end. Spawn of Dreams we ask your favor. We ask your presence. Send your favor upon this priest and goblin we beseech you, oh great Saredhel. They seek to complete a quest, which was birthed in mystery, tied to time.

"Show yourself in your great majesty through our petition and send these two creatures to their destined location across time and across distance. For what is time to you who has mastered it long ago, and what is distance that you should be hindered by it when you sit above the world looking down upon all?

"Come now and take these two into the river of time, and cast them off into the path they are to walk." She fell silent then, as did the others. Each now had their eyes clamped shut and was swaying rhythmically as if to music only they could hear. After a moment of this strange silence, Hoodwink began to feel strange.

The whole chamber seemed to swim before his vision as if he was about to faint and then everything was swallowed up in a silvery-gray light.

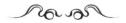

It was a swimming sensation at first, like Hoodwink was caught up in a tide he couldn't fight against; only do his best to stay afloat in as it surged forward. Yet it wasn't water, but a force like it, an invisible yet powerful force that compelled him beyond the silvery-gray light around him and into a panorama of images.

"What's happening?" Hoodwink shouted, though he didn't have to for unbeknownst to the goblin, Gilban was right next to him.

"Keep your mind focused on the task at hand," came the priest's reply.

Hoodwink tried to keep his eyes closed tight, but it didn't do any good. As he'd been told, the images rushed through his head, blurring past his mind. Images of forests and glades, caves and seas, and still more flew past his inner sight before he could bring them into focus.

"I can't keep them out!" The goblin grew panicked. He didn't want to end up in some other time or place… *Gods*, what was he doing here?

"Don't focus on them, just relax, and let the tide of time carry you," Gilban's gentle words helped to calm Hoodwink down.

Hoodwink tried to relax his mind, but instead found the pictures only slowed down instead. He couldn't seem to keep them from entering — from preventing him from focusing on one image alone. He saw himself now as he had been in the past, back in the ruins before he'd been freed.

Then the image was gone and new one came to mind. This one was of him just prior to where he found himself now. A small green creature amid the shaved headed priests of Saredhel. This image moved slower than the first, however, and he found himself drawn to it more as well. It felt familiar and normal and his mind tugged at him to join it there, to place himself back in that situation…

No! This wasn't where he was supposed to go.

Restlessly he shook his head to clear his mind only to have another image come into his head. This was the strangest yet. In it, he saw some gray expanse stretching on for miles upon miles. This expanse was littered with the debris of stone mostly from broken columns and statues — endless ruins of buildings spanning the same for as far as the eye could see. What was this place? The longer he let his mind dwell upon the location he found, the longer he began to see a lone figure in the gray gloom. This was the Telborian he'd meet briefly in the jungles of Takta Lu Lama — a real fire-branded warrior.

What was his name again? He didn't know, but he marveled at the strange outfit he wore, and the flaming sword he carried and his...

"Withdraw from the thought!" Gilban put a hand on Hoodwink's shoulder. The small goblin then realized the old priest had been by his side the whole time. This touch and revelation drew him back to his senses for a moment, disrupting the image he'd been viewing like a rock in a pond.

"You see the future but you see it too far. This is not where we are going to go, where we need to go. Focus on Doom Maker's Island, and let yourself feel the current the others have laid out for us to follow with their invocation." The blind priest's words had begun to sound hypnotic to the goblin.

The goblin tried to do as Gilban said but it was hard. The image of Dugan wanted to stay in his mind's eye, swimming back and forth amid his thoughts getting blurry to clear, blurry to clear. It was a very strange and compelling image, but Hoodwink knew that if he were to keep focusing on it that was where he'd most surely go...and he didn't want to be there. He scrunched his eyes tighter in concentration.

"Doom Maker's Island. Doom Maker's Island," He repeated to himself in a low whisper.

"Focus on that and you should be safe," he heard Gilban say to him from a far off place.

A few moments more and the image of Dugan amid that gray, gloomy desert of ruins was gone and another thought came into his brain to materialize into the picture of the wild and untamed land called Doom Maker's Island. He found the image pulling his mind to it, willing his body to follow along as he thought more on the picture — on the landmass. He could almost smell the waves he say in his mind's eye hitting a beach, almost feel the warm air on his skin…

Doom Maker's Island was really a continent, but like a few of the lands on Tralodren, was called an island because that was what the first discoverers thought it was, the name had stuck down through the generations. The land rested close to the southern most reaches of the world, near the Boiling Sea which was another fearful barrier and birth place of a few myths and legends all its own.

Because of its position Doom Maker's Island was first sought out for possible use in the spice trade dominating the southern nations, and so it was little wonder that it became a well-known home to pirates and other lawless folk.

It was a wild land with an evil dominion of influence brought about by the ancient linnorm Gorallis, only the truly insane or blackguard sought out the land. Nothing of any value ever came from it, and those who sought it very rarely returned, those who did return often with blood chilling tales.

It was also said Doom Maker's Island was host to strange creatures birthed of elemental substances. Beasts of fire, mud, earth and air; water that traveled and spoke and even ate as though it was alive. If such accounts could be believed, then it would be little wonder how the land got its name in the first place. Still though, legend and myth only went so far. If there was any danger it was in the form of Gorallis himself and the two of them were going right into his waiting talons…

Chapter 26

Cael had been slumbering in his cave when he was awakened by the smell of dwarven flesh. His ten feet tall meaty frame reclined on a stone slab he had made his bed. Only his clawed fingers and toes twitched when he had first smelt the dwarf and awaked him from his slumber, but soon the rest of him became active as well.

Thick ram like horns spiraled from his head and curled into fat dollops of beige bone. His hairy shoulders reclined on the stone, shaggy chest rising and falling in a slow rhythm. Cael sniffed the air lightly with his wide nostrils to take the smell into his pallet. Yes, it was dwarven flesh and only one at that. One dwarf stood in front of its lair. The Troll's bright yellow eyes widened in anticipation, his sharp, jagged teeth darted from his mouth covered in saliva.

It was laughable. Totally laughable to think such a fool would throw away his life so heedlessly. Very foolish. Very foolish indeed.

Cael, like most Trolls, hated dwarves. However, he hated them like no other of his kind on Tralodren. They represented the foolishness of the gods. They were shorter than practicality would have a race be, bent on tradition to the point of stagnation, and pesky as cockroaches, who could burrow out of their homes for defense in endless lines for what seemed like forever. More still, they could fight indefinitely — even to the death — having to war against them during times of armed combat when wounded.

Even then, one had to be sure they were truly dead and not lapsing for a recovery. He'd seen more than one dwarf awaken after a battle, healed and recovered slightly from the wounds he had received, to slither off and come back again like the vermin they truly were. One day he would be free of them and the mountains would be his once and for all. Until then, he'd have to put up with their occasional encounters and continued existence.

Trolls descended from giants. Legends told they were created by Khuthon, god of strength and warfare, when Tralodren was first formed. Not as tall as their other gigantic kin, Trolls were seen as more or less a brutal and savage expression of the giant race. Most giants thought them nothing more than wild beasts who had once been giants but had degraded over time. Others saw them as the impurities of the entire race being pooled into one line to keep the rest pure.

In either case, they were almost as disliked and distrusted by other giants as much as the scattered groups which called the Pearl Islands home. But those were misshapen and mutated from generations of inbreeding. Trolls were a pure strain in their own manner, albeit a strain that most of the giants didn't want to see in that light. No, for most Trolls they couldn't care what others thought of them — they were too busy concerning themselves with how to inflict pain on creatures…and Cael was not an exception there.

Cael hunched forward as he rose from his slab. He was now drawn away from the opening of his lair by a tingling sensation to his left. It had the feel of magic about it — no priestly power was coming toward him.

A flanking attack?

Perhaps the dwarves weren't as stupid as they first seemed. He didn't know what to expect, only preparing himself for the potential onslaught that would await him.

It really didn't matter; they would all die in moments, but it would allow Cael to eat again at least. He'd grown hungry in the past weeks, and a handful of dwarves made his stomach leap with joy. More so he could collect their gear and riches, and add it to his own for later use. One could never have enough possessions after all.

The sensation on his left had grown much stronger and he could now see a vortex of swirling gray mist in the same vicinity. What were they playing at? It wasn't like a dwarf to get too clever. They often just charged right into battle head on.

As he watched, a simple door appeared out of the mists. A double hinged, wooden, metal-reinforced door. That was something he'd never seen before. Stranger still was that it opened toward him and appeared to hold something behind it though the Troll knew that nothing could be behind it but more of his lair. From out of the door, came an even stranger sight: two priests, Telborian from their looks and smell, they were followed by a multicolored bird.

Very strange.

The Troll decided to play with them a bit and see what they had in mind. He simply kept to the shadows and watched what they were doing all the while, keeping his mind focused at the entrance to his lair as well, waiting for the best opportunity to act against them all.

The two priests were dressed in dark garb and had the look of being Asorlins. He smirked at such a thought, his rough, cracked lips curling up and over his yellowed teeth. A lone dwarf was at the door and two death priests in his lair. It was certainly working out to be a very interesting day, and quite a festive platter for his upcoming feast.

He continued to hide as they drew closer into his grasp.

"Where are we?" Cracius looked about himself.

"Where we need to be," the colored bird chirped.

"That's obvious," the younger priest snipped. "But who are we looking for?"

"I'm sure we'll make that introduction soon enough if Galba has indeed sent us to the right place and the right time." Tebow slowed his pace to look around the cavern as the door closed and vanished behind him.

"What's that smell?" Cracius wrinkled his nose at the pungent animal tang of the Troll's lair.

"I don't know, but its coming from that direction," Tebow motioned toward where Cael hunched hidden in the back of his cave, shadows caressing his hairy figure.

"Troll!" The bird suddenly squawked a warning, which brought alarm to their senses.

"Wha-" Tebow started to say, but was stopped short by the movement of corded muscles in the poorly illuminated cavern. Cael was upon them all before they knew what was truly happening. The troll jumped into their midst and rose up before them — unveiling his massive body — an engine of death.

"Hammers!" Tebow shouted.

Both priests raised their weapons in unison.

"Asorlok save us!" Cracius gripped his silver medallion from around his neck with his left hand and prayed to his god. The bird flew off into the darkness of the cave looking for some nook or cranny to hide from such a deadly creature.

Cael drooled in the excitement. This was going to be fun. The priests would make a good first course, the dwarf a nice second, and the bright bird would be desert. A massive claw flung itself back, ready to eviscerate the two priests before it, but a swift blow from Cracius' hammer landed hard upon the creature's beefy chest with a solid thud.

Cael bellowed.

The priests might actually cause him to work up a sweat.

A ripple of darkness ushered out of the impact site and rapidly pulsated over the entire Troll's body like some bitumen tide flooding all of the Troll's flesh. It was a sickly thing to see, and moved with the intent of an intelligent being looking to cause harm to all it crossed. The priests made ready for another assault, as did Cael. The Troll scarcely looked down at the place of impact from the blow, his mind was focused on clawing the younger priest's eyes out for the annoying attack...

Immediately the Cael's face drew slack.

Something didn't feel right.

Another blow, this one from Tebow, hit Cael's stomach and sent black ripples over his body once more. They were fast for priests…and their attacks were strange…well, no matter, he'd lived though many things and would live through this as well. They would still pay for this intrusion, however, and the Troll would still have his fun and meal…

"The hammers have started their work! Keep away from his claws and we'll be fine!" Tebow hollered.

Cael slashed at the two priests who scattered from his attack and nearly missed the deadly claws, save Tebow's cloak, which was shred to tatters as it billowed out in his escape. Each looked toward the Troll, who fought on defiantly against the unfolding ailment he couldn't quite understand. Had he stopped his aggression, he might have had time to better analyze the situation, and save himself from potentially more pain and suffering to come, but he was too focused on the death of the two priests — aided by his rising hunger — to give it much contemplation.

"Asorlok has him now," Cracius readied himself in a defensive pose, set for the Troll's next attack.

Cael laughed.

"Your god has no one, but will welcome each of you to him soon enough," he spoke Telborous in a guttural, booming voice rumbling throughout his lair. They had their fun now; got in their shots. Now it was time to end this and eat. He would enjoy ripping them apart limb by limb, and eating their appendages raw as his screaming victims watched in a growing pool of their own blood.

The Troll took another step forward, ready to lunge at his prey when he felt something burst inside. He didn't know what it was or where, but he was quite certain something within had broken open — and was now leaking all about. Cael halted his advance with a jerk, stumbling about as he found himself suddenly short of breath.

"What have you done?" The Troll leaned up against a nearby wall to steady himself as he had suddenly become lightheaded. His voice was still guttural, but quite as booming as before.

The priests said nothing, only watched as the Troll's skin was overshadowed by smoky tendrils bubbling up from underneath like fat pitch tentacles bursting forth in mockery of bulging veins revolting from their body. . Cael looked down at his hand and growled. It was swelling up and turning a putrid plum. His skin was now a deep black and he could feel a burning sensation all about himself.

"I'm going to eat you raw for this!" Cael scraped his shoulder against the rock wall, drunkenly stumbling closer to the two priests who simply remained on the defensive, backing up from his advance and watching what happened next.

Cael continued to struggle to move forward, to force himself onward but things seemed to slow down even more, his body reacting hours after a thought. He could feel the dark tendrils eating into his skin, pulling apart his muscle fibers, and even soaking into his very bones where they burned like acid upon his nerves and even spirit and soul. In frustrated waves of agony the giant moaned and cursed in his ancient tongue.

Oh they would pay for this.

None had ever come so close to wounding him and these priests would pay with a slow, agonizing death.

"Be patient!" Tebow dared a glance over to Cracius as both priests bumped against the cavern's wall. "Asorlok's work is nearly done."

Cael couldn't stand it anymore. He was in too much pain to do anything. It was then that the most basic and savage of his urges: animal survival took the reigns of his mind and he wailed in spastic movements. Frenzied clawing of the ceiling and the very walls around him sent chunks of debris around and on him in the process but did little to alleviate the pain.

The commotion reached the outside of lair and threw out choking bursts of dusty clouds, which fluttered quickly away into the outside air. A few more moments of the struggle and Cael fell silent. A massive boom echoed from the cavern followed by a ground shaking-rumble as his body fell, followed by silence.

Cracius and Tebow waited for the remaining dust to settle wiped it from their eyes then looked at the scene before them. Only a few black serpentine coils remained to wrap their way around the odd bone or two of the complete skeletal remains of the Troll, which had fallen to the ground like a crumbled marionette. His bones had been belched and still clung to each other as they sprawled out about the cavern floor even the Troll's malicious jaw was still frozen in a scream of silent agony. It seemed the will of Asorlok had had its way. The battle was over. Cael was dead.

"Remind me not to get on your bad side," the bird danced on its perched legs on top Cracius shoulder.

Together the priests gingerly stepped nearer the fallen form. The air had grown silent and cold. So silent that when the battle scream of a dwarven warrior ran into the cavern with him, all present turned their attention to it with amazed fright.

Vinder ran into Cael's lair at full speed. His body pounded with adrenaline and fear. He knew he was going to die, but he was going to do it valiantly, on *his* terms. He had run into the cave heedless of any surrounding scenery. When his brain finally registered what his eye was seeing, however, he felt they couldn't be believed.

His charged was stopped in mid-stride, a scream dying in his throat.

Before him was the skeletal remains of the very Troll he was looking to kill before *he* had killed *him*. The sight was amazing to behold, and held him spellbound for many a moment until his eyes detected other forms in the caves murky depths, then his defenses were rapidly raised.

"Who are *you*? What are you doing here?" Vinder addressed the two priests in Telborous as they all would use as their language of choice for the rest of their association.

The trio took in the dwarf before them with a puzzled gaze, as they further emerged from the shadows, their silver hammers glimmering with a soft light for a split second.

"We've found him," Tebow motioned to Vinder.

"Death priests?" Vinder planted his legs in the rock. "What in the name of Shiril and Drued is going on here?"

Cracius took in the dwarf with an intense gaze that dug itself deep into his soul. "Peace dwarf. We are here to help you."

"Help me do what?" Vinder huffed. "Get back. I said get back!

"You just keep yourself where I can see you. Now what is going on here? What happened to Cael?"

"Cael?" The bird tilted its head to the side to take in the short warrior. Vinder was taken aback for a moment by having the bird answer him. No bird he knew could do that. The surprise only lasted for a moment until the dwarf shook his head to clear it, then proceeded onward with this thoughts.

"The Troll," Vinder motioned with his axe to the giant's remains.

"Well, if that is Cael, then he has been slain. Killed by the great god Asorlok," Tebow answered with gentle demeanor.

"So you *killed* him?" Vinder wasn't making any sense of this at all. What was going on here? This was absolute madness. Death priests in a Troll's lair killing the very Troll he was sent to kill?

"We were the vessels for Asorlok's power." Cracius corrected the dwarf on this finer point.

"You killed him," Vinder took a step forward. "Asorlins came to the Diamant Mountains to kill a Troll I just happened to be after? Why?"

"He attacked us," Tebow lowered his hammer, motioning for Cracius to do the same.

"I gathered that much," Vinder spat back. "You still haven't told me why two humans came all the way up to these mountains to attack Cael."

"We came here for you," Cracius nodded toward the dwarf.

"*You* came *here* to find *me*?" Vinder tightened his grip on his axe.

"Yes," said Cracius.

"What do a couple of death priests want with me while I'm still alive? You want to kill me too? Rip off my skin, and make me like him?" The dwarf jabbed to Cael's skeleton with his weapon.

"Hardly." Cracius looked deeper into Vinder and used the spirit of his god to discern the leverage they needed to bring him to their side, since he had a feeling, money would not work with *this* mercenary. Both priests had instantly gleamed this was one of the mercenaries they sought after, now that they'd had a moment to see his face and Cracius had gained his name from his god.

"Let the wisdom of Asorlok lead us." Cracius whispered to Tebow then turned his attention back to the dwarf.

"Vinder, you were sent here to find this Troll, and destroy it for honor of your clan. The Troll is dead and you can claim you did it if you can help us in this one task that only you can perform." Cracius spoke in a causal conversational manner, trying both to calm the dwarf down, and invite him into the discussion of why he and Tebow had come.

"How do you know my name, and why I'm here?" Vinder's eye narrowed.

"We have come to find you, so we know much about you," Tebow took up the discourse now.

"Then you'll know I can't *lie* about what you've done. It'd be a hollow victory — a cheap claim giving me no honor at all. So you have come here then to insult me? To squelch my one chance at regaining my honor and then tell me you need my help for some damn foolish quest or some such thing?" Vinder's anger was growing. These Asorlins had stolen his honor. It would have been better to been killed by the Troll than have this.

"Hear us out," Tebow spoke, "let us explain everything. Your presence is vital to completing a certain miss-"

"What great cause is this now?" The anger and sarcasm flowed out Vinder's mouth in thick turrets now. "Seems like everywhere I go there is always some *great cause* that needs remedy. Some *great tragedy* that is going to destroy the world or some such thing... well the world is still here as am I, and I'm not too keen on being *your* version of hero right now. The world will survive without my aid... I'm sure of that.

I just want to retire to my clan now, and you took the honor out of the one chance I had to do that." Vinder ended his speech by turning his attention to ponder Cael's skeletal mass. To the Abyss with quests and foolish missions! He had his honor to regain and the remedy had been taken from him.

"We've come here so you can own up to your responsibilities," Tebow rebutted. He was working from a limited, intuitive knowledge he had received from his spiritual connection to his god — something that should get the dwarf's attention.

"What are you talking about?" Vinder's steel gray eye grew even more laced with rage at the suggestion that he was in some way irresponsible, in this act of redemption.

"You and the other mercenaries with you on your last mission freed something that should never have been set loose." The priest continued.

"That whole rotten corpse thing?" Vinder's face went slack. "The others said they would take care of it. It isn't my concern — not now. I'm back with my clan and I couldn't be happier."

"Well, that will soon change if the lich gets his way," Tebow started.

"He calls himself The Master, and if he has his goals met, he will become closer attuned to his name than he is now." The priest made a concerted effort to look the one-eyed dwarf in the face and hammer his message home. "He wishes to become a god. Without your help and those who unleashed him in the ruins, he will achieve that goal."

"That may be, but I'm still going to be safe in my clan. One more god is not going to change the world that much, at least for me," Vinder glared at them intently, face hard as granite.

What where these two really about? He'd been hired before by many men of varying merit and honor and didn't quite know what to make of this declaration. It didn't seem right or totally real. Why come here? Why kill Cael? Why do all this just to get to him? They were holding something back. He was sure of it.

"You and the rest of Tralodren won't be safe at all. Once The Master has attained godhood he will try to enslave the world to his whims. More so he will try to take out all those that would stand in his way, starting with mortals, then the gods themselves," said Cracius.

"Okay, now you're joking," Vinder laughed. "No godling, no matter how powerful, could take out the gods. Not all of them at least. Let the fool try it, and he will be destroyed.

"End of story."

"That need not be the case Vinder," Cracius replied with a dreadfully serious face.

"Go on." Vinder tried to contain himself, but he had begun to develop an eerie sensation that made his neck hairs stand tall. All ready the sudden burst of mirth had been swallowed up by this sensation. It was drowning out the rage he had felt as well, filling him with some sense of obligation.

What magic or spell were these two priests about now?

"Together, you, your companions and us, can take care of The Master before he begins his rise to godhood. We can stop him and keep hundreds of thousands of innocents from dying." Tebow took a small step closer to the dwarf.

"Death priests wanting to *save* lives? Now that's amusing." Vinder chuckled.

The sensation he felt before increased despite his attempt at reviving his sarcastic mirth. He didn't like this. Vinder didn't owe anyone anything. He always paid his debts. Even in his exile he was debtor to none — completing each duty to completion; keeping his word. No, this was some kind of power from the priests, a dark prayer of some type. They were trying to ensnare him to their whims for sure.

He had to get away from their presence as soon as he could. This wasn't doing him any good, and he couldn't get his honor back today, at least by slaying Cael as he had hoped. The uneasy sensation would not let him be though and troubled his heart and grieved his spirit.

"It's true short stuff," the servant of Endarien sang out in protest.

Cracius looked at the bird on his shoulder for a moment with mild displeasure then continued the conversation. "If you're serious about making your way back into this clan than you better help or else there might not be much of clan, if any to return to."

"So you want me to come with you to fight The Master? If I don't, then the world will suffer?" Vinder's head shook with tired familiarity. "Where have I heard this before?

"How many times can the world suffer the same fate over, and over again? You think it would get fed up, and just kill itself from all these false declarations of apocalypse." The grip on his axe grew a bit more slack. These priests weren't going to do him any harm — at least right now. They were trying to win him with words rather than weapons and the dwarf would still have none of it.

"You have it all laid out to you in truth. You are needed to help put an end to this evil because you helped release it. Come with us and we will bring you here after the task is done so that you can return home to your clan." Tebow extended his hand toward the dwarf.

"You want to take me away from my clan just as I got here and am ready to be taken back?" Vinder kicked the rocky earth beneath him. "I might be killed if I go with you and fight this insane lich. And then where's my chance at regained honor then?"

Tebow gently pulled his hand back to his side. "Something tells me you were looking to get killed anyway when you ran into this cave. You couldn't have survived the Troll's attack, and you knew it, as did your clan. You have just been given your life back. Use it to pay us back for the gift of your life by helping us finish off The Master." The older priest looked deep into the eye of the dwarf. He could sense something move inside his spirit. They were getting through to him — getting him to see his obligation.

"You cheated me of my desires!" Vinder threw his axe into the pile of Cael's bones. They cracked and fell into smaller pieces of debris with the action, making a sound like brittle twigs snapping underfoot. "You took away my *honor*, now you say it was a *gift*?"

"Peace." Cracius raised his hand toward the dwarf.

"Your peace is the grave." Vinder spat near Cracius' foot.

"It need not be today. Come with us and join the others who wish to make amends for what they have done," the younger priest's words dug deep into Vinder's rocky disposition.

The sensation wasn't leaving, instead growing more intense by the minute, welling up in his gut like some sick bile. A sense of his failed duty — a lack of following through on responsibility. *His* responsibility. And then he knew what the uneasiness was from: his conscience was condemning him for his own actions and championing the words of the Asorlins. And it was then, the dwarven warrior knew this too, knew they were using his conscience against him to get him to their side.

Damn them.

They were playing on his stronger traits, the traits all dwarves held true to if they would be called worthy of their clan. Traits he had come back home to idealize and embrace once again. Vinder had lived way from his clan for a long while, indeed it seemed to have lost sight of such a basic dwarven ethic: personal responsibility. He had been true to this ideal, but not as true as he could have been, especially on the matter the priests were bringing to his remembrance. Even though he could walk away from this all now, be free of the past as he embraced the future, he knew the deed would haunt him.

Even though he didn't directly cause the release of this Master character, he was still guilty by taking part in the venture that freed the lich, as went the dwarven law. He was with the others when it happened, part of their band, and so what happened to the group was also a reflection on what happened to him. He had been too eager to gain his coin and return home to see that then...but now, now it was very clear to him. Thought he might not have let the being out by himself — he was still responsible for his freedom. Other races may have simply pushed such thoughts aside and gone on with their lives, but not Vinder. Not now. Not if he was to reconcile himself to his race and clan.

How could he hope to embrace his clan once more— his family and racial heritage— if he failed to start living up to what he said he believed, and wanted to enter into practice with again once more? He knew he couldn't. It wasn't right. If he wanted restoration of what he'd lost, he'd have to be true to his newly professed ideals today, even before he won his honor back.

"You're right, damn you," Vinder lowered his head with a sigh. "You're right.

I've got to live up to my responsibilities. I was party to those who let that bony thing free even if by accident, and I have the responsibility to at least do what I can to own up to that responsibility...

Vinder raised his head. "...and go after that human mage too, now that I think of it..."

"There's no need for that," Cracius spoke. "The issue will work itself out very shortly."

"Really, now?" Vinder cocked his head in confused surprise. This was too much of a growing conspiracy to wrap his mind around.

"Listen, we don't have any more time to discuss this matter," Tebow took a step toward the dwarf. "Are you with us then or not?"

"I suppose I must, but when I return, how will I deal with Cael?" The dwarf took in the dead Troll, then the priests. "You can't bring him back from the dead, so I can slay him — can you?"

"Come with us and stop this lich, then we will take you back here to redeem yourself," Cracius sidestepped the question.

"I don't see ho-" Vinder started.

"Are you in or out?" Tebow hurried the conversation along.

"So be it," Vinder lowered his head.

If he weren't able to follow through on his basic responsibility than any honor he'd regain would be worthless anyway. "Let Drued guide me now, and take my soul if I'm slain before I can return to my homeland again. He at least has forgiven me, and if I go to his realm, then I do so with honor."

Chapter 27

The followers of Shador sat in a silent semicircle around their leader in the secret chamber deep beneath the city. The room was still draped in scarlet light from the skull sconces grinning down in gruesome approval of the scene below. A thick silence was hung from them and descended to all those below like an invisible sheet. From behind the gathered semicircle three forms walked toward the cult leader's dais.

Hooded and cloaked once more in regalia of their cult, they held aloft a claret silken cushion cupping the stolen medallion of the Mayor enriched by the red light of the room. As they walked closer, the crescent outline of dark-clad bodies quietly parted and allowed them full access to the throne of the cult's leader, who smiled at the three's approach.

"You have done well then," The leader addressed the three. "You have the medallion, but what of that oaf, Dugan?"

"He's been left as a scapegoat and a sacrifice for the great Shador." One of the three responded. All of them then bowed before their leader as they reached the foot of the dais.

"Excellent, then Shador will be pleased. Praise Shador." The leader raised up one hand in a petty ritualistic gesture.

"Praise Shador," the room echoed.

"Give me the medallion," the cult leader beckoned.

The three did as they were ordered. The one who held the cushion stepped up to his leader where he knelt in a supplicant presentation of his gift.

The medallion, once it was in the hands of their leader, glowed with a soft green illumination. "At last, the desire of

Shador's heart has been heard. We, his chief servants, have done as he has asked and look to serve him still more. Great is our god, and great is his benevolence!"

"Hail Shador, the great god!" The group chanted in response.

"Now, with this gift, we must summon our god to use it. Begin the ceremony!" The leader slapped his hands together, and the others fell into a trance. The chamber soon became filled with dry, low chanting in a language that none truly understood in their present age mindset. It pulsed with an eldritch power, flooding the stonewalls and floor, seeping into the inky cloaks of the cultists, causing the very air to tingle with electrical energy.

"Shador, Hail to you dark lord! Hail the Lord of Shadows, the Patron of Things Hidden!" The group chanted.

"Shador, I, your priest, your leader of your servants, call you forth great lord. Appear to us, and make known your will." The leader raised his hands above his head, the glowing green medallion grasped in his left hand as he remained on the throne now surrounded by prostrate cultists.

In time, the room skittered between the realm of the spirit and that of matter. Between this divide ushered forth a great inky coil, which shot out like a bolt of lightning to hit the ground between the prostrate followers and their leader. And in a moment, their god stood before them.

The image was unclear and shaken, ethereal and transient as it blurred then cleared slightly to dress itself with a type of watery clarity. Never more than a moment in a sharp, true image, the vision stood seven feet tall and swam with a shadowy form of a man with two purple eyes gleaming out at the cult leader and his fellows.

"I have come." The voice of Shador was deep and booming. Dust from all the corners and walls of the room around him fell like tiny showers of rain at his echoing thunder.

"Praise Shador!" The cultists sang.

"Great god of shadow, I am humbled to present this token to you," The cult leader fell prostrate before his god, kneeling on the top step of his dais where his own chair rested. "As you have requested, we have the mystical medallion of the Mayor of this city which will greatly increase your power over this land."

Shador glanced at the leader. A slit of white crossed his face, the only expression on the gloomy surface other than his amazingly bright eyes. "You have done well. I am pleased."

"Thank you lord," the cult leader let his head fall to his chest.

"Give it to me," Shador held out his dark, out of phase, hand.

The cult's leader held up the medallion and averted his eyes as to not fully look upon the shifting image of his god. Such a thing would surely invite his wrath — for he was a simple mortal, and not worthy to see his god face to face.

As Shador began to move toward the medallion, there was a change in the air. An incredible increase in heat — to such a degree the air around in the chamber exploded in a violent fireball. Flame shot out from the center of the room, burning many of the cultists whole where they kneeled while illuminating the room with brilliant light. Screams and commotion took over the fervent worship as flaming structures that had once been mortal flesh ran like scattered grain in the wind; expelling their pain-soaked screams as their garments blazed, and skin melted away. The explosion had sparked smaller fires, which now pooled and slithered around the room near objects to devour; tapestries, and like material bursting into flame.

At the same moment, a shape came into view from the center of the explosion. Unaffected by the fire, or even the heat, the figure rose from its crouched position with an even motion. By his hand a long sword appeared as it moved toward the flickering image of Shador and his trembling priests who now had risen upright upon the great invasion presented them. All of them were fearful and uncertain as to what to do next.

"Who dares defile my temple?" Shador snarled toward the approaching man.

"Retribution." Dugan stopped his forward progression. Still dressed in the dark garb he had worn to kill the Mayor — a murder he'd never committed, he had now changed into a vessel for extracting retribution, a reflection of the god that burned in his heart.

His face had become a frightening thing — twisting and pulling against his flesh with unchallenged rage and lust for revenge. His hair, like his face, also pulsated with life. It sparked with odd tongues of flame here and there that didn't burn him as they danced around his dark blonde locks like serpents amid tall grass. These same tongues of flames also flared out from his body in little bursts of self-contained combustion. Others wrapped around his muscular frame as veins of rage, a remaining sign of the gift given from Rheminas, who had transported him to the cultists to extract his revenge for both their pleasures.

"You have the mantle of the Flame Lord upon you," Shador cringed. "Fly you fools or face your own fate, I will not challenge Rheminas this day." Shador's swarthy shape dissipated as a breath, fleeing into simple mist to leave his priests fight this battle on their own.

"Great lord!" The cult leader reached out to the mist like an infant grasping for his mother only to grab a hold of nothing.

"Hah!" Dugan mocked. "Your god seems to be as good as your promises."

The Telborian grit his teeth and ran right for the center of the priests. Tiny gouts of flame trailed behind him as he raised his flaming sword high to attack. As he neared, the helpless followers scattered like sheep before him. They had lost their arrogance; secrecy falling away, like a simple puff of smoke with fear and animal survival taking its place. Dugan pulled out a dagger and threw it into the back of one of the fleeing cultists. It burst into flame when it hit the air like an arrow set alit before it dug into the flesh of its victim.

Dugan threw another, and took grim delight at how it lodged in the pale-skinned throat. Dugan's victim turned around so violently his hood had fallen down to reveal the face of a middle-aged, balding Telborian. For a moment his eyes grew wide, then closed as the flaming dagger sliced into his neck, spilling and spraying hot, tangy blood in an explosive fountain. The pale man stood for a moment more, swaying on his heels, then crumbled to the floor to be trampled by the other fleeing cultists.

"Who will be the first to taste my blade-the tongue of Rheminas?" Dugan's visage glistened with a demonic sheen.

Speechless and unable to act, the priests of Shador knew the horror and fear, of the deepest and most gripping kind. Dugan watched with delight as the weapon in his hands did its work. Flames still flickered off his body, and he still felt the heated breath of his master upon him. Rheminas had not left him, nor would he until the Telborian had drunk deep of the Vengeful One's cup. He was the judgment of the Pantheon and the indulgence of the dark god all rolled into one…and Dugan enjoyed it.

Like stalks of corn amid the farmer's blade, the priests of Shador fell. Amid blood and black cloth, crunching bone, bursts of flame, and flesh-rending screams, death came upon them all. How many were to fall by his blade he would never know. It was all just a macabre dance in which Dugan decapitated, disemboweled, and maimed his victims with a malevolent lust and skilled hand. His weapon shattered their frames within moments of contact and sent them on their way to Asorlok's Gate howling all their long journey to Mortis.

In a very short span of time the room was littered with priests who had either fallen by the gladiator's fiery blade or been overcome by the smoke or heat of the swelling fire. The smatterings of others had or were fleeing into the various hallways like the rats they were. The fallen bodies had started to burn as tendrils of fire crept their way hungry for more fuel to devour whole.

All during this time, the fire, which had been left unchecked when it was first spawned by Dugan's entrance, had grown so much of the room was alight. Smoke curled around the corners of the ceiling and slithered out of open portals, hovering at head level, trying to claw its way out, away from the growing inferno.

The cult leader, who alone still lived through the Telborian's viscous onslaught, could do nothing as he watched the advancing Telborian sprint up his dais with a red inferno burning in his eyes. His god had left him, his priests were dead or had fled, and he was certain his own life was now forfeit. At least he would face it bravely.

The cult leader reached for a dagger he kept in his belt, but the action was in vain. Dugan's searing blade plunged into the cult leader's flesh the same moment he pulled the dagger free. Burgundy blood seeped out like wine from his gut. It pumped out of him with a sporadic rhythm, spilling and splashing the fluid all around. Dugan himself was covered in a fine mist of the living liquid as he continued his deadly assault, maddened by the slaughter and satisfaction of retribution.

In reaction to the attack, the cult leader stuck Dugan in the chest with his dagger. The wounded priest was unable to pull it back out, his body already too weak to stand, let alone retaliate. The blade dug deep into Dugan's left breast, near his heart, but Dugan didn't cry out in pain. Even as the rivers and lakes of crimson fell from the grievous injury, his mind was set on one resolution.

"I'm tired of being lied to, cheated, and forced to choose between two damnations. If I'm going to die, I want to make sure at least you come with me." Dugan's face was the image of near insanity as he peered into the dying cult leader's dimming countenance.

With a deadly and powerful motion, Dugan pulled free his sword, then with a mighty downward thrust, he lopped off the priest's left arm in one swing. Raw sinew dangled from the cleaving as more blood erupted and spilled over everything like some sick fountain.

The priest could do nothing, not even give voice to his own agony. His arm fell helpless to the bloodied floor where it still twitched in spastic throes. Dugan watched with heaving chest, coughing bloody phlegm, amid the growing smoke from the inferno around him. The priest's life force faded away, dwindling to a faint trickle, then left him as cold and empty as the flagstone floor to which he fell. Satisfied with what he had accomplished, it was time to welcome his own end.

Dugan threw down his sword at the base of the dais, and ripped out the dagger in his chest. The wound flared to new life, drooling out greater streams of blood, which soon grew into raging rivers.

Dugan didn't care.

He had done what he had come to do, and now it was over.

The Telborian lifted his gory face and arms above him. "I'm ready now Rheminas." Dugan shouted amid syrupy coughs spitting out his own blood over his lips. "I've nothing left. No where to go. No one to help.

"Take me if I'm yours then!" The Telborian stumbled down the dais fell to the floor beside it to land hard on his butt. To his right he noticed his blood-painted sword. The fire had left it. Now it seemed just as it was when he had first acquired it upon entering Haven.

Dugan felt light headed, his vision blurred.

No matter.

He'd be dead soon enough.

All around him the fire raged; smoke drawing a tight stranglehold over his throat. The heat had managed to crack and shatter many of the bricks of the room causing the roof above to creak and groan in protest. It seemed his doom was fast approaching, and the Telborian welcomed it with open arms. Either flattened by a roof, burned alive, or bleeding to death: either way he would join Rheminas soon enough.

What the Telborian failed to notice in his dark nihilism was a black door that had appeared in the corner of the room. The door seemed to be of fine wrought iron, crafted into a solid image of a hingeless door, which opened to spill pure daylight into the hellish chamber.

Out of this door came Cracius and Tebow along with the colorful bird. This time the door remained open upon their exit.

Dugan barely noticed the two figures approaching him nor did he hear what they said. His sight was fading, and his mind found it hard to concentrate.

"You are the one we seek. Can you walk?" Cracius looked down at the battered and confused warrior.

Dugan didn't respond.

"Can you walk?" Cracius tried again, this time covering his nose and mouth with his cloak to keep back the smoke, which was already causing his eyes to stream with tears.

"I don't think that he can hear you Cracius. He seems to be too far-gone. He already goes to meet Asorlok and the hand of Rheminas is heavy upon him, blocking much of our insight. He might not be right for our needs after all." Tebow confided in the younger priest, and also covered his face from the smoke.

"We better get out of here soon, lest we perish in this inferno too." Cracius coughed as he drew closer to the Telborian.

His steps were even and silent. Gently he placed his hand upon Dugan's gore splattered shoulder. Instantly, the warrior reacted. Dugan took hold of the priest's hand with a vise-like grip, his face turned to him with a smoldering visage.

"No more priests," Dugan's voice was rough and gravelly amid the wet gurgle in the back of his throat.

"Please, we come in peace," Cracius pleaded over the roar of the fire.

"Liars," Dugan snarled. "Liars! You're all just liars. You have nothing I want, and none of you can help me. You just want to use me as your gods use you." The Telborian started into a fit of coughing rocking him to the point of collapse, blood flailing all about his person from his mouth and injuries.

"He's mad, Cracius. Leave him. He can only be a danger to himself and others. Let him die in peace and with some dignity." Tebow shouted back to his companion. "Just leave him before this whole place comes down upon us."

"You need him, though," the colorful bird chimed in once more. It had taken to roost on a crumbled body of a slain priest of

Shador, though a quick glance at the groaning roof above brought an unnerving appearance of fear upon the avian's face that seemed unnatural. "Remember what Galba said: We will need all of the former party members."

"He is certainly more than capable of dealing with foes greater than himself," Tebow spoke to the older priest while he took in the menacing Telborian. "Just look around us here."

A burnt wooden beam suddenly toppled between them from above, scattering embers, broken half-burnt bricks and other fiery debris in a blazing splash. Both had jumped away using their cloaks to shield them from the incident, but they wouldn't be able to shield themselves from the whole ceiling collapsing down on them.

As if to echo that thought, the entire chamber began to moan and scream.

"We have no more time," the bird squawked and fluttered to the air once more, heading toward the still present open door.

"By the will of Asorlok, sleep," Cracius held up his hand before the Telborian. For a moment nothing happened, then the works of the Sovereign Lord of the Silent Slumber overtook the gladiator. He fell to the floor in a blood-covered, muscular heap.

"We will have to sort this all out away from here," Cracius moved closer to Dugan. "The wound is a hard one, but not too grave to remedy if we can get him out of here. He will live…for now.

"We will have to carry him through the portal as well," Cracius motioned with his head toward the wrought iron door.

"Are you sure we can manage?" Tebow raised an eyebrow as he looked at the fallen man. "He must weigh a good deal, and any excess movement we take might cause greater harm to him still."

"Nevertheless we will have to manage — and quickly, this room won't hold for much longer." Cracius said. "And don't forget to get his sword — he'll need that."

Within moments, fueled by the spirit of their god and adrenaline, they reached the portal once more, and were walking inside, dragging the Telborian with them.

As soon as the dark door closed behind them, the rest of the ceiling fell, cascading the room in a pile of cinders, flames, timbers, and ash. All that had been the cult was consumed — lost to the vengeful flames. Nothing would remain but ash and crumbled bricks.

The cult of Shador was no more.

Chapter 28

Volcanoes bloomed a fair distance from the coastline of the dangerous land of Doom Maker's Island. Though they didn't erupted ash and lava, they were still very much alive. Five of these burning mountains were nestled together in a sulfur tinted and sordid clime of the land. These volcanoes were a chain of mountains called The Fingers of Rheminas by those who came to them. Named after the great god of volcanoes, they seemed to look like a cyclopean burning hand trying to claw its way up from the earth; struggling to break free from the terrestrial weight of Doom Maker's Island resting heavy upon it.

It was in this mountain chain where Gorallis dwelled.

Gorallis, the Crimson Flame.

All of Tralodren knew of dragons and linnorms. Few had ever seen one in their lifetime nor even generation, since the beasts were so deadly and rare they accounted for few witnesses. It was said the original two linnorms were the creation of Gurthghol. Made when the world was first formed, they walked Tralodren unopposed. Each, was also said to be attached to an elemental force. The debate as to how many elements comprised the world usually averaged out around four, but most scholars, priests, wizards and Patrious, claimed there were six: ice, magma, fire, water, earth, and air.

Regardless, these creatures were tied to the elementals forces quite strongly, making their lairs in and around the element and also seeming to draw some supernatural power from it as well. It was even said that in time, a dragon and linnorm could alter the very terrain where it dwelt as the creature bonded with

284

the elemental substance of their nature at an incredibly intimate level.

Over time, the numbers of linnorm dwindled, caused by personal wars among themselves, the coming of mortal-kind — which weakened them by more conflict and depletion of their habitats, as well as old age, which caused them to breed less often.

These factors all contributed to their decline. By the dawning of the Imperial Wars, they'd already begun their slow extinction. As they declined in numbers and strength, the dragons; who had made their appearance very near the beginning of the Shadow Years, started their ascendancy.

Legends also claimed, Gurthghol created the dragons who mortals called, New World Dragons, or just dragons. These were the dragons of the world stretching into the present day. Like the linnorms however, the dragons started to decline and soon, many sages surmised, Gurthghol would reveal still newer reptilian creatures to replace these dwindling beasts.

Dragons were territorial, and were tied to certain terrains rather than elements as with the linnorms. They lived in deep forests, tall mountains and even under the waves. Tundras, grasslands and marshes all housed a dragon or did at one point in time or could in times to come, so most sages said. The dragons though were smaller and weaker than linnorms. To see a linnorm and survive was something myths were made of, and of all the linnorms, Gorallis was the oldest and largest.

Born when the world was yet young, and mortal-kind hadn't even begun to establish its firm hold over Tralodren, he was an unstoppable force. Legends, stories and myths had been reported of him over the centuries. They often said that he'd lived on every part of the world moving as he grew more powerful, larger, and wealthier…and that might indeed be true.

Like most tales, it was hard to say what was true. What was known for certain was for the last two thousand years he had made

Rheminas' Fingers his home. Over those years he'd also gathered a great army.

Through the centuries he had enlisted a band of cutthroats, and petty thugs, turning them into the Red Guard — a feared and loathed agency of mayhem and evil. They would scour the lands of Tralodren looking for treasure their master coveted or what he had lost over the years and previous migrations to thieves and opportunists. They were relentless fanatics who could hope for nothing more than to die in the service of their master whom they saw as god.

The guards wore red scale mail, and horned helmets, carried deadly long swords, and wore thick red capes. On their breasts and banners was the emblem of their reptilian god: a crimson flame on a black background. Whole villages would empty upon first sight of such a banner. Towns would surrender before the first shot or attack was made. Fear traveled with the Red Guard on all occasions. It was a thick garment they wrapped around their crimson frames with reverential delight.

Over the years the number of the guard swelled so much that reports would have the hearer imagining a plague of locusts, rather than an invading group of zealots. Even the Minotaurs and their growing empire in the south held their breath when word of the Red Guard's passing in their lands reached their bovine ears.

The Red Guard prided itself on this word of mouth. They relished the horror they caused, for they saw it as justification of the respect and fear Gorallis was due. They took it as a sign of success and slight evangelism to all they met of their mighty god they represented.

The devout army lived in the volcanic valleys, around the lair of their great leader, god, and master. They formed small villages that were more like camps, and lived as simply as they could while always practicing their martial skills. They had no excuse to not be ready when their master called upon them.

As time passed into the more recent centuries, women began to fill the ranks of the Red Guard as well, and soon whole generations of children were born knowing no differing reality than being a servant to the great Crimson Flame. It was with the influx of children the camps slowly started to become more like home-steads and into the present era, more like small towns or villages.

As the Red Guard changed, however, so too did their master. Gorallis was thought to be immortal. Stories claimed Gurthghol created him with the other first stock of beings that populated the world in the beginning of time. If he was immortal, then he was showing some strange signs of age.

Often he would slumber for years at a time before waking and sending out his minions for more wealth and information about the world that had changed while he had dreamed. He often would then go out and gorge for months upon the local wildlife and population until his hunger was satiated. The aftermath of such feedings took decades for the land to recover.

As the years passed, his naps became longer. These stretched into long slumbers, becoming so expansive the current genera-tion serving Gorallis hadn't seen their master in their lifetimes nor had their parents seen him for some fifteen years before the birth of their children. It proved to be one of the longest slumbers the linnorm had even taken. However, none of the Red Guard was worried. They knew he would awaken at the right time, and when he did, he would call upon them, and they would be happy to serve the glorious beast in whatever he called them to do.

This awe and worship of the linnorm had sired a small sect of Red Guard who set aside combative means and began to form the workings of a priesthood of sorts. At first they were more akin to scribes; keeping the records of the commands and life of Gorallis along with the workings of the growing community of the Red Guard. Soon though it developed rituals and an air of rever-ence that turned it into a functioning religion. This was the birth of the faith of its priests.

Such a priest was the devout and wise Hilin; a slender, middle-aged Celetor. Unlike the Celetors of the jungles of Takta Lu Lama, Hilin belonged to a group of people who developed into an offshoot more attuned to the desert-dwelling Celetors living around the southern lands as well as in patches a bit further north from his present location. He still had dark skin like all Celetors, but his was a lighter coffee color, instead of a darker, ebony cast. His hair was straight too, not the curly short style common among Nabu's tribesmen. His eyes were a soft brown and his face was young and fresh, just given over to life as a new adult.

Hilin had been with the priesthood shortly after his birth. Joining it felt like the answer to a calling. He felt an urge to be part of the Order of the Flame as they were called. It just seemed like it completed him in some manner greater than anything else could. In the past thirty years he'd been working with the priests, he'd learned much of Gorallis and his nature. Hilin gained more devotion for Gorallis with each passing day. His god had lived through the Shadow Years, the Wizard Kings with their four ages, and even into modern times. Such a thing was unheard of for any mortal being, even a linnorm. Gorallis had lived longer than any creature Hilin had ever known real and mythical. This fact alone to Hilin's mind was proof enough Gorallis was equal with the gods, if not one of them himself.

Hilin continued to work on his scrolls in his tent (they had yet to finish the temple to honor Gorallis, so their places of worship and study were makeshift dwellings). He had comprised them in part from older sources and from his own observations about the last few years of his life. They were not so much religious texts as documentation of the whereabouts of his god. Gorallis hadn't awakened for some time, more than forty years and there was still no stirring of his form. He slept beneath the great magma lake in the heart of the largest volcano of the chain. Being a linnorm who was crafted from fiery magma, stories said, he was unharmed by the lava's heat and flame. It was just like he was inside the primeval egg which had bore him once more, waiting to be reborn into the world that changed around his unchanging form.

Hilin had many speculations upon when his master would awake and used them to work out formulas and mathematical equations to try and find this truth. So far though, they had yet to prove true. Every day he would try to seek out the moment when his awakened master would call him to go out and complete tasks for Gorallis' glory and honor. The young Celetor lived for such a day and prayed it came quickly, that he would see it before his death.

Today, as with days previous, he went over his calculations and prayed to what forces he could think of that his master controlled, the fire of the mountain, and the might of his name, to rouse him from his sleep. As he prayed though he felt a strange presence in his mind, unlike anything he had ever known. He felt as though he could see into things of the future…he didn't know how or why this was, since never had such an experience befallen him before. He took it with a glad heart — hoping it was a sign his god was indeed rousing himself from the deep slumber, his divine majesty, spilling out onto his priests. In his mind's eye he beheld an older figure in simple robes shimmering like silver with a red light in his hand.

Somehow that light made Hilin feel as though it would help his master; that the cause of his prayers would be answered. He knew all would be well. But when? The experience was so powerful he fell enraptured into it and couldn't leave…he wanted to stay, wanted to never leave this place of revelation but just as much as he wanted to stay a silent inner urging told him he had to leave and get ready for something to happen.

He knew it was important, he just didn't know what it was or when it would happen.

Suddenly Gilban and Hoodwink found themselves upon a soft brown sand beach, emerging out of the silvery-gray light as if they appeared out of nowhere themselves. The air was heavy with humidity and hot, almost stifling to the duo who began to look around the shoreline of Doom Maker's Island.

"Where are we now?" The goblin wasn't too thrilled at what he was seeing.

"Doom Maker's Island," the priest took a step forward, his staff striking the beach like a finger poking exposed flesh. The very ground felt alive, as if it was breathing.

Hoodwink looked around himself with short, uneasy glances. He didn't like the feel of the land either. There was something off about it he couldn't place. It felt like the rocks, the sand of the beach, even the heavy air about them was looking at them, watching them with heavy and dedicated eyes as they made their travel inland. It caused the goblin to shiver for a moment.

A little ways ahead of them, the goblin spied a tall spine of mountains after a seemingly endless expanse of dry, flat plains, These were the Fingers of Rheminas he supposed — the very lair of the Crimson Flame as claimed by hundreds of stories. He squinted and could then see the mountains all smoked like great candles, releasing grayish-black plumes like chimneys.

He didn't like that either.

He was beginning to see he really didn't like many things here at all — and now knew why they called it Doom Maker's Island.

"Where are we to go now?" Hoodwink looked toward the priest, who silently held his head in the soft, warm breeze. He would have nothing to do with this journey now. He would follow Gilban's lead entirely. He didn't want to leave anything to chance. Chance could get him killed.

"Tell me, are there any mountains around?" Gilban never changed his posture.

"Yes, they're very far away though," Hoodwink turned back toward the smoking peaks.

Gilban's jaw clenched tightly. "How far."

"Many miles, best not to go there, it could take all day and night and still we'd not be there," Hoodwink kicked some sand.

He really didn't want to hear what Gilban was about to say, that they would have to walk into those very lava-churning mountains to get to the point where they were destined to be: the meeting up of Gorallis.

"Hoodwink. It is very important you give me your answer as best you can. How far do the mountains appear to be?" The priest was fingering his staff rhythmically now.

"They look like five...no seven miles." Came the goblin's reply.

"Are you certain?" Gilban asked.

"Yes."

"Then take my hand," Gilban held out his free hand to the goblin while the other held his staff. His lips whispered a prayer to his goddess, the great Spawn of Dreams. As soon as the small goblin took the hand of the priest he felt a tingling sensation all over his body, like a furry caterpillar was crawling all over his flesh — both inside and out. He didn't really mind though as a certain form of peace overwhelmed him with the sensation as well.

The whispered petition continued until the goblin felt light-headed, then he saw nothing.

Everything went black.

No light, no sound, and no real understanding of his own body's existence.

"Where are we? What's happening?" The goblin tightly clutched his traveling companion's hand...or he thought he did, he couldn't feel anything. "Gilban?"

"We travel on the wings of fate," Gilban spoke dryly.

Hoodwink recognized part of the feeling but this time though, the experience was different. It felt less overpowering than the prayer that brought both of them to Doom Maker's Island. He suspected it might be because it was just Gilban's faith, and not the collected priests as who had formed the previous prayer. Maybe it was because the journey wasn't as far as Rexatious to Doom Maker's Island. Whatever the case, he knew at least he wasn't troubled by strange visions, and that suited him just fine.

Before he had any time to think upon the matter further, he was at their destination: The base of the Finger's of Rheminas, materializing out of the humid air.

The smoldering volcanoes towered above them. Thick fumes of sulfur and light specks of ash drifted about like burnt snow as the air pulsed in concussion-inducing waves. Gilban and Hoodwink felt their bodies act almost — as thin sheets of cloth as they were pushed and pulled in the march of geothermic birthed undulations, almost as if they were pennants in the wind.

Further up along the mountain nearest him (he supposed it might have been the 'thumb' of the Rheminas' hand), Hoodwink spied a pathway cleared from the volcanic rock. It seemed to twist along the outside of the peaks and then be swallowed up by them entirely like a serpent seeking shelter from the heat.

He gritted his teeth and squeezed his eyes tight. After a few moments of this, he relinquished his fate. There was little he could do now save pray for a safe outcome, though he doubted many gods would hear a goblin's prayer. It all rested on Gilban now.

"What do you see?" Gilban asked.

"I think it's a path," Hoodwink squinted his eyes. "Goes into the mountains."

"*Into* the mountains?" Gilban seemed a bit worried about this, but the concern faded as quickly as it had arisen.

"Yes," Hoodwink had heard that faint concern in the priest's voice, and didn't like it.

"Then we have no choice but to follow it. I had hoped we wouldn't be so close to the heat and his lair. However, fate is with us, Hoodwink. We shall be safe." As he said those words, Gilban felt a hollow tone to them. Something was still off in his body. Something had plagued him since he sat outside the doors of the sanctuary, trying to make sense of the orb.

He felt a premonition coming to him, but it was veiled more than what he was used to, or was trained to decipher. And just as heavily as it was veiled from his discernment, it felt ill meaning and powerful in its truth.

He feared it had to do with his choice of going to the linnorm's lair. Perhaps fate was trying to keep him safe another way — perhaps not. He had no time for indecision. Every moment mattered. The longer he waited, the more the threat he had been sent to stop grew.

Action was paramount.

Gilban pushed the thought out of his mind — he would deal with it later.

He *had* to.

"Let's go then," Gilban drew his lips tight across his face. His visage that was normally a pale shade of tinted gray turned a deeper pasty hue as they walked.

Ash fell upon them like snow, covering their garments and bodies in gray dust like the breath of the grave. The ash soon turned into a paste as sweat poured down their faces from the natural blast furnace around them. The air became heavier and pushed upon their frames like a hundred oppressive hands with each new step they took. Soon, as they neared the volcanic mountains them-selves, the air burned their lungs and nose. Their eyes had begun to water so much Hoodwink had a hard time seeing in front of himself, he had to be led by Gilban at times, whose own eyes cried thick, charcoal gray tears.

The journey was longer than it should have been, and grew even longer as they had to stop and slow to ease their searing chests and inflamed eyes.

Madness.

This was madness, and the goblin knew it. Still he climbed on though as the fire growing in his lungs from the harsh envi-ronment he was traversing was like acid on the soft tissue of his insides — eating deeper with every passing heartbeat. He was sure his throat was dripping blood down from his nasal passages and sliding down the raw skin into his burning lungs and gut.

Gilban, if he felt these things too, was silent. His brow was furrowed in concentration, a deep concentration that was needed to place each step on the treacherous rocky ground they now entered into.

Hoodwink understood his role. He knew he had to help the seer get to where he needed to be, guide him to where his destiny led. He needed to keep the old elf alive to safeguard his own return as well for he dreaded to think of himself being left here should anything happen to the priest. Maybe *this* was his greater purpose, then: to help Gilban. That didn't seem to hold up very well with the images he received on the trip over though…no, that seemed to be important…maybe more important than this even.

One thing was certain about the present however; if he didn't take care of Gilban he'd be in a great deal of trouble down the road. If he thought he might not do so well in Rexatious, he knew if he'd came to stay here he'd be dead for certain.

Dead before a week was even out.

Probably even one day…

Finally, they managed to get between two of the taller peaks with great effort. As they passed between them, a deep darkness fell upon them so only the small, sputtering embers, and the odd patches of cracked rock with hints of orange light seething beneath, gave light to their way in a dirty yellow-orange haze.

The heat was more intense between the two 'fingers' of rock, and seemed at times, as if the darkness was stifling them; disorienting their progress as if it was alive, and didn't take kindly to trespassers.

From what he had heard from tales, the goblin thought such ideas weren't too far from the truth. Though he was nearly as blind as the priest himself with the current climate, he had managed to get through about what Gilban was told, was half the pass. Not bad progress for the travel so far and little to no real challenges. It would have seemed like they could have walked into the very lair of the linnorm without any real opposition at all. Though Gilban was old, he wasn't a fool, and so the closer the duo drew to Gorallis' lair, the more wary he became of ambush or worse.

"Is there no one in front of us?" Gilban asked.

"No one," Hoodwink squeezed out of his gray-green face. It looked more like melted rock now smeared with tears and yellow slits of eyes.

"I don't like this," Gilban's hand tightened on his staff. Suddenly the priest's ears picked up a falling rock from his side. This was followed by the sound of another descending rock and still more so that it sounded like a shower of pebbles and slightly larger rocks tumbling about them.

"Hoodwink, what is it? What's happening?" Concern was returning to Gilban's throat, tickling it with a slack-handed grip.

"Big men...we're in trouble!" The goblin spoke, and then said no more.

The priest heard a small *thud* beside him, but could do nothing. And then a hard blow to the back of his head sent him to the ground, and dreamless slumber.

Chapter 29

The coast of Arid Land was silent, empty, and cold.

The late autumn winds had given free reign to early winter breezes. In the more northern lands, where Arid Land resided, the warmer months were a welcome break from the cooler, and sometimes deadly icy winds of the north. The landmass sat far enough up in the world to get some of these bitter zephyrs, but not so severe the Valkorian Islands suffered in the months just ending, when the Perlosa herself it was said delighted in the chilled gales, and bitter snows covering the Northlands.

Arid Land was already cold, and would grow colder still with each passing day until light snow came ashore as winter came to dock.

There was only one beach and safe harbor on all of Arid Land, and it was here Nordicans had constructed a trading post and minor settlement called Vanhyrm. It still stood after many generations through raids and elemental chaos since the first Ice Warriors descended from the north on journeys of raiding and conquest hundreds of years before.

Since that time, the population of the Syvani, the native race on the land, retreated more inland as the encroaching Nordic warriors came to plunder the thick timber, food stuffs, minerals resources, and even the odd elf for slaves. Fur, food, timber, and slaves were the main trade. Mineral wealth was the hardest to secure because of the constant raids by the Syvani against the Nordic miners, and the hard rock from which it had to be pried. One old saying of lore claimed on many occasions the land itself seemed to war against them and seek to increase their hardship in life. Indeed, a great number of Syvani prayed it did, they have suffered for generations at the hands of the Ice Warriors.

For many years Vanhyrm, served as a resting port for travels further south into both Arid Land's interior and other parts of the Midlands beyond. In time a greater market developed to trade goods and a fair sized bizarre attracting many Nordicans and even a few Syvani to pick up goods and deposit various trinkets of their desire. Such trafficking had managed to make the village both larger and a more permanent a structure on the area.

Strong and defiant, Vanhyrm waited for its newest arrivals as it dominated the landscape for miles. Resting about a quarter mile from the soft, gray sand shore. It was surrounded by massive walls construted with sharpened trees, fieldstone, and even a few odd skulls posted as a silent, grim vigil. Trees had been cleared and cut for a great distance around the settlement and a rough road, made of crushed stone snaked its way toward a large set of steel-reinforced, wooden doors which served as the great gate, with a matching pair on the opposite side of the Nordic foothold.

Some ways out from Arid Land's coast, Brandon's nameless vessel stopped. The sun had grown low in the sky and a thin wispy fog, a blanket of mist, had started to roll into the harbor and around the unnamed ship. Rowan and Clara had been called to the deck to get ready to make landing, and each eagerly watched Arid Land grow larger from over the prow's railing. Both were also confused, however, when the ship suddenly stopped some distance from shore, and traveled no farther.

The fog had picked up when Rowan turned to Brandon who had recently come on deck to join the couple. "Why have we stopped so far out?"

"This is as far as I go," Brandon replied.

"I don't understand. You said you were going to Arid Land… on business," said Rowan.

"I do have business, and you're it. I brought you here, and it's as far as I can go. Its part of an old territorial covenant made a long time ago." Brandon's eyes danced around the youth. "You'll just have to make do."

All the while the fog continued to increase, rising higher from the water and obscuring parts of the boat and silent crew.

Clara darted toward the Telborian captain with fire in her eyes. "Is this some kind of joke?"

"Easy there missy, I'm just doing what I can. You needed help getting to Arid Land, and I provided it. I just can't get you to the *land* part of Arid Land, that's all. But you're *near* Arid Land now aren't you?" Brandon had become like some puckish pirate — a knave of some sort who now was beginning to show his true colors…and his two traveling companions weren't the least bit encouraged by the development.

"No, you're going to take us to port," Rowan insisted as best he could. What was happening here? It was all going awry so suddenly — as if chaos was a blizzard around them.

"'Fraid not son. Listen, I'm just doing what I can to help out, nothing else. You'll understand in time, but I'm not about to waste time with explanations." Brandon directed their attention to the prow and then the water beyond. "Don't have enough as it is these days. You might as well start out with the swim for it now while its still light. The water should be at least a little warmer than freezing."

"*Swim?*" Rowan snorted. "You can't expect us to *swim* to shore."

"I don't think you'll have much of a choice left to you," Brandon took a step back from them into a sheet of fog, which had started to rapidly flow up and over the vessel, disappearing from sight.

"Hey," Clara shouted. "I want some answers here."

The elf started to move to where she had last seen the sailor, but got no more than a few steps when she felt her foot go through the wooden planking before her as though it were jam.

"I told you I'm not about to play the game of question and answer now," Brandon's voice trailed off as if it was as insubstantial as the steadily rising fog about them.

"Wha—" was all Clara could manage before she felt herself sink into the icy waves beneath her with a splash.

"Clara…" Rowan started, but he too fell through the deck of the ship as it faded into mist under him, blending with the fog to float away. He hit the water hard and fast, it's frosty contents shocking him to his senses. This was so far removed from any semblance of what should have been happening, what was happening just before the fog rose up around them…

"Rowan?" Clara shouted as she bumped into the wet youth beside her.

"I'm right here." Rowan treaded water beside her. "I can't see anything in this fog. Here, just rest on my shield and I'll try to bring us to shore then."

Clara cursed in her native tongue.

"What is it?" He fumbled a bit with getting the shield off from his back. Both of them had been ready to make landfall and so had been fully dressed, and loaded down with armor, weapons and the meager supplies they had taken from Takta Lu Lama to Elandor and purchased on their journey to Elandor. After a brief period of awkward aquatic acrobatics, the shield was free and in the water; convex side of the object allowing itself to be used as a buoy.

"This water is freezing," she snipped as she splashed.

"We have to get to shore quickly," said the knight.

"Do you know the way?" Clara climbed on board the dragon-crested shield with some relief for being out of the water, but still steaming over her current situation. The cold water was quickly chilling her insides though, and trying to pull her down under with the extra weight she had on herself.

"I think so." No sooner had he finished speaking than a thin patch of haze lifted, almost as if by cue, allowing the youth to pull them toward land. If the water didn't get to their bones, they might actually make it to shore…and hopefully someplace warm to starve off any sickness that may try to attach to them in their chilled and wet conditions. It wasn't that far-fetched a hope. If they were fast and strong enough, they could pull it off…

Both were silent as they swam. The struggle to get ashore took all their concentration. There would be time for conversation soon enough, however. The very notion put forth by Clara seemingly being given some tangible backing.

So much for favors from strangers.

It took a while, but Clara and Rowan reached the shore. They hadn't been far from land, but it was still a good swim and in armor and heavier clothing made weightier when wet, it was quite a challenge to reach land without falling into Perlosa's icy embrace. Had they stayed but a few moments longer in her grasp, they would have probably succumbed to the cold of the waves and sunk beneath them.

They came from the sea dripping wet and belched forth from the surf upon the cold shore like driftwood. Coughing and clinging to the dry land like lovesick seals embracing in the dark, both managed to climb out of the waves and stand on their own feet. After a few bone-chilling moments when the air hit their soaked flesh, they began to be able to think more cognitive thoughts, and try to sort out what had just transpired.

The fog seemed to have lifted and parted from them as they neared the narrow beach as well, allowing them to see the handful of docked Nordic vessels.

Vanhyrm was still active this time of the year it would seem.

"What happened?" Clara coughed.

"I don't know…more of your…game theory?" Rowan panted.

"Really?" Clara's words were sarcastic as she wrung out her hair while she fought off a shiver.

"Listen, I'd love to talk all you want about that theory… it's really starting to make more sense…but lets do it some place warm, though…okay?" Rowan slid his hair back on top his head from his forehead, sloshing it back like wet kelp.

"Agreed," Clara began to check through her things. After a moment she was confident all her items were with her…well those that managed to survive the frigid plunge: sword girded at her waist and the minor personal effects she had salvaged from their previous exploration of Takta Lu Lama. Rowan did the same, and found nothing was missing either. His necklace, shield, and sword had managed to stay with him in the swim, thank Panthor. The youth shivered as he worked his cold fingers and slid his shield over his back.

They needed to find a fire soon.

"If we stay out here too long we're going to turn into snowmen," Rowan rang out his cloak.

"So where to then?" The elf looked up into the interior.

The youth stretched his arms above his head, and then turned to point at the fort-like trading post of Vanhyrm looming over the beach ahead of them like a squatting giant.

"Well, that must be Vanhyrm. It's a trading post and village for many Nordicans. They should have food, fire and shelter there for us to use."

"Would it be safe for elves?" Clara pulled her soggy hood over her head, recalling the captain and crew of the Frost Giant.

"It should… I would say yes, but then that meeting on the Frost Giant…" The memories didn't bring a fair taste to the youth's recollection. "Perhaps if you keep covered and quiet as best you can you'll be okay."

"I suppose that will have to do then. There won't be any other way though." Clara started to move to the walled structure.

If she didn't move she knew she would freeze solid.

"Well, I suppose I could say you are my slave. That would get us in and leave you out of most of the trouble." Rowan's dark blue eyes sparkled, as he watched her walk past.

"Or it could start some," Clara's face was playful in its humor as she drew close to the knight in passing.

"Just hide yourself the best you can for now. I don't want any more problems. We've had enough challenges just getting here already," he said, then joined her.

Together they walked up toward the tall wooden walls around the village, leaving sopping footprints in their wake.
The sun was already sinking into the horizon and soon it would set completely. The cold breezes would then rise up from the waves, to turn their already semi-frozen marrow to ice.

The couple neared the wooden walls with determined steps. The thick timbers loomed over them like grim figures of doom trying to intimidate them with their mere existence. It may have worked against the cold and the more violent factions on the land, but not against Rowan and Clara. They simply kept moving to the large door before them, the crushed rock road rustling beneath them.

As they drew nearer, they saw on the thick wall near the door, a wide worn leather strap hung over a wooden peg supported a large ram's horn attached to the same leather strap. It hung silently before Rowan who picked up the dew covered instrument.

"Are you still sure you want to do this?" Rowan turned to Clara. "It won't be easy, and if they find out you're an elf..."

"We'll deal with it," Clara placed her soft, gray tinted hand upon his sopping shoulder. Rowan felt a gentle warmth flush over his body at her touch. He welcomed the odd sensation, and at that same time fought against it. His unending battle would at least keep him warm enough and alive to get inside to some fire pit.

The knight smiled ruefully and placed the horn to his lips. Clara drew her hood tighter about herself as Rowan blew into it. The sound was deep and resonating, like the bellow of some massive beast. For many moments the sound of the horn echoed across the land, then migrated away into silence in the distance.

Rowan and Clara stood quietly by as time ticked away with the tide. Just as Rowan was going to put the horn to his lips once more, a noise was heard from behind the wall. With a heavy grinding sound a vertical panel on one of the doors was removed. Immediately, two stern eyes outlined in thick eyebrows appeared behind the opening.

"Who goes there?" The voice spoke the Nordic tongue in a tone as deep and raspy as the previous horn blast.

"Rowan Cortak, Knight of Valkoria."

"What's your business here, Knight? We didn't hear of your arrival, and we've closed the gates for the evening," Returned the voice.

"We have come to spend the night before we go off on a journey."

"Where is your vessel and crew? We never saw any sign of sails," The eyes darted back and forth between the pair like a wolf sizing up his prey.

"We are the only ones here, I'm afraid," The knight spoke in truth as he shook with a small shiver.

"So am I. Two people just don't show up out of nowhere on this land without some means of transport. What did you do, swim here?

"Who's she?" The eyes darted to Clara who moved her sopping cloak tighter around herself to better hide her sword and frame. She didn't understand all the words being spoken, but could read the eyes and tone well enough. Coincidentally, though she was beginning to see less and less randomness to such events in her life, she had studied a little bit of the language of the Nordicans on her visits to the Great Library of Rexatious when she was younger. The lessons really didn't stick that well with her, but she had managed to recall some of their strange language. She understood enough to get a limited, general understanding of the conversation being spoken before her.

"She is my…ah retainer. She was sent by the Knighthood to help me in my task," Rowan stretched the truth. He couldn't lie outright, not to another fellow human — a brother of his race, it was against the code. However, it was true he was sent to the same location as Clara and she did help him on the task. Perhaps the goddess had even sent her to him. So it could be true in part.

"So, you want to come in then?" The eyes continued to look them over with a diligent search.

"Yes we do, and if you don't start being a bit more hospitable to us I shall be very upset. Is this how you treat members of the Knighthood then?" Rowan's blood began to boil. Why were they acting in such a manner to their own flesh and blood — even more so to a Knight of Valkoria? "It's getting cold out here, and will get colder still. We're tired and wet from a long journey and would like to warm ourselves by your fires and sleep for the journey ahead. Now will you let us in?"

"It's going to get colder than Perlosa's tit out there lad," The voice behind the door rasped. "What you want to do is quick go find a wild beastie and kill it, slip his skin over your body and keep huddled in his guts until morning. Maybe then you will survive, huh?"

"What is the meaning of this treatment? Do you have no love of the goddess at all? Do you treat her knights and servants like idiots for sport?" Rowan began to twitch inside his inner man. The shockwaves sent deep surges though his body and caused him to think of going to his sword. The Nordic blood in his body was winning the battle over the training once more.

"Relax, Rowan." The voice behind the door laughed. "You always were able to give me a laugh. Just like your mother, you are: tightly wound up." A playful air now replacing the stern tones it had just so recently embraced.

"Are you who I think you are?" Rowan crunched his eyes together to get a better picture of the slit of eyes. For a moment, the thought of storming the village had been subdued.

"The very same Rowan," came the reply.

"Tricky Dick. You're still alive then?" Rowan grinned, and walked briskly toward the door.

"Tricky Dick?" Clara questioned as she followed a little further back from the young Nordican, speaking with hushed tones in Telborous.

"Tricky Dick was one of the men I used to listen to when I was younger. He's a great storyteller, mighty traveler, and adventurer. He used to tell me tales all the time when he got back from his travels. They would be full of adventure-" The knight returned in Telborous.

"You understand our language?" Rowan whispered back to Clara in Telborous.

"I know enough of it to understand most but not of all of what you both said, yes."

"I'm impressed," Rowan whispered again.

"I'm not," Clara couldn't understand the thought process of these northern humans or maybe it was just men in general. "The man just wanted to play a practical joke on you, and was about ready to have you come in and attack him over it." Clara stared at the youth with her violet eyes.

"That was just a joke. He really didn't mean any harm," Rowan smiled, then grabbed Clara's arm. "Come on. Let's get out of these wet clothes."

Rowan then pulled her toward the doors on youthful feet filled with childlike excitement. As they neared, the sounds of great bolts and barricades were heard to be undone so the sturdy gate opened wide before them.

"You young hound," The voice of Tricky Dick, still in the language of the north, crept from behind the massive timber gate, "The waves have brought you back safe and sound eh?"

Clara watched Tricky appear from behind the door, grasping what she could from the Nordic tongue. He wasn't a normal Nordican in the least. He was less than most of his race, having been taken up with various replacements for parts of his body that were absent. His left hand was a hook, grafted to this flesh at the wrist by means of a silver cup covering the stump of his arm. His right leg was a wooden peg that reminded the elven maid of Gilban's staff. The crowning mark was his face. It was pitted and pocked from various diseases and ache that had ravaged the human's flesh in his youth. All these assaults hadn't taken his life though, but they did leave their mark with slashed and stitched scars; vertical and horizontal roads of war. His smile though was genuine and wholly intact.

Clara judged him to be about in his sixtieth year. White hair mingled with blond strands and silver-gray splotches covered his thick moustache hanging down past his chin. Blue eyes as sharp and clear as crystal took in the whole scene before them and guided the slightly bent, though still hearty, frame of the Nordic adventurer forward.

"I heard you left for your first mission of the Knighthood recently," the conversation then turned toward Telborous as was the nature of traders when in the presence of mixed companies, for Tricky didn't know what type of human Rowan had brought with him.

"I did," Rowan smiled as the older man slapped the youth's back with his good hand.

"So you did swim in?" Tricky chuckled. "I wasn't kidding when I said we saw no sails. How you come to land here then?"

"It's a long story," said Rowan.

"I bet it is," Tricky's smile widened. "So, any scars then, from your first mission?"

"No," Rowan had dropped nearly all of his defenses around the man. "It was actually a fair time. I did what was required of me, and now I have to get back, and report it to the Knighthood."

"So why you here then, boy?" Tricky eyed Clara softly. "You're on the wrong isle to tell your tales."

"I'd prefer not to say at the moment," Rowan told the truth as best he could.

"Some sort of Knighthood thing, eh?" Tricky said.

"You can say that," Rowan nodded.

"Sorry I wasn't able to make your ceremony lad. I've been stuck here with my duties for the rest of the year. Been looking for some treasure in my off hours, though. You just know them damn elves have something hidden on this isle.

"So come on in then. You're soaked, and are catching something deadly for sure. These damn elves here fill the air with disease — I'm sure of it."

The older man led them inside Vanhyrm, Clara and Rowan fell behind the older Nordican.

"Mark my words, Rowan. One day those elves will be the death of this place and us. You can never trust an elf. Isn't that what I taught you?"

"Sure was," Rowan risked a quick glance at Clara, who remained silent, and seemingly emotionless to the youth.

"Damn sound advice I say," Tricky's lower lip stuck out as he gave one solid nod of approval. "Just look at what they did to me."

Together the group entered into the village. The longer one looked at it, the more it resembled a prison than anything else. A massively tall and thick walled jail had been built to keep the evils of the world at bay, and most likely the evil had elven ears, and was the root of all wrongs in the northern world. A strange element was present as well though. It looked as if the highly fortified settlement had been attacked some time ago. Not with sword or spear, but with the mighty weapons of commerce.

Bazaars lined some corners, and even dominated prime spaces by the heavy doors that closed behind the new arrivals. Small shops sprang up like mushrooms all over amid garrison quarters, armories and forges. Here it was that Nordicans traded their goods with the outside world. Various tribes were represented through these merchants, as each tribe was friendly and open to trade the resources of its craftsman to secure what they lacked. The merchants would be closing up soon and looking to weather the remaining winter months either back in their homelands or in the settlement itself.

No one really came to Vanhyrm in the longer winter months following the worst months of snowfall and ice. It tended to make sea travel difficult in the northern waters. Most of their trade and travel was done before and during the first few weeks of those months. After that time they just held up in their own lands with what they had till the weather was a bit more favorable.

So now in Vanhyrm there was a dead time fast approaching; a time of near isolation amid the crystal white seas and the snow buried earth.

"So how your mother and father doing?" Tricky turned to Rowan as they walked onward upon a simple dirt road that had been packed hard by foot travel.

"They're fine." Rowan looked forward. His focus was on the world around him and not his speech. He watched the people and booths pass by as the road inward grew narrower until finally the shops with their wares disappeared altogether. There were only the taverns, and the single large inn that were more communal than anything else. It acted as a boarding house, tavern and general supply store all in one. A sign painted in the Nordic tongue said it was called Skull Splitter.

From the lack of general activity it was clear nothing of interest was happening in the streets. The sun would be gone soon, and it would be getting dark sooner in the village because of the tall walls cast a great shadow over its populace.

"I bet you're looking forward to seeing them again," Tricky looked back at Rowan, who continued to scan the village, oblivious to his old friend's glances.

"You could say that," Rowan was curt.

"You can relax Rowan. Ain't no one here who will hurt you," The older Nordican slowed his gait, and looked at the young knight with a soft and jovial eye. "We are lively enough here, but the old rules of tribes need not be expressed in the ways of this community. If we were fighting all the time we wouldn't have any food or make any money at the trade now would we?" Tricky laughed as he slapped the back of the youth hard again with his good hand.

Rowan knew he wanted to trust the old man, but something wouldn't let him. It was an odd sort of feeling that spoke in slivers of icy fear and twinges of mistrust, which swirled about his gut. Whenever Tricky's eyes drew near to Clara the young knight shuttered internally. His uncertain concerns and feelings for the elf served only to magnify the fear more when Tricky drew his eye toward the maid.

"So why do you have a retainer again?" The older Nordican's good orb sparkled with a bit of mischief. "And such a pretty one from what I can see under that hood."

"She was sent by Panthor to help me on my task," Rowan felt confident with his answer.

"You haven't told me what it is yet... if you can. I'm just so excited about you getting through the dedication, and into the Knighthood." Tricky stopped in the path, turned to the duo and smiled. "How long are you staying here then?"

"It will just be for the night. We have to be in Valkoria as soon as we can, it's vital for the cause I'm championing," Rowan shared with him what he could. This was an old friend, after all — someone who the knight even saw as a grandfather.

"I sure it is, lad. Defending humanity a very worthy task. Just keeping a human woman out of trouble, for common men like myself, is a full-time task," Tricky's eyes were alight with mischief. "Seems their are some wild ones being raised up in the Lynx Tribe, stories say. Causing many a headache for all the men — and their mothers no doubt. That's why I say its best to keep a woman in the kitchen and pregnant; where you can keep an eye on them. Ain't too many evils in the oven now are they?" Tricky brought forth a deep chuckle. "Isn't that right." The mirth-filled Nordican slapped the shoulder of the nearby Clara who went rigid upon the Nordican's touch, which might as well had been done with his hooked hand from the look in her eyes.

Rowan chuckled nervously.

"You are in need of some fire though to get warm, This little thing here is just soaked. My hand is freezing already. Go and get some of the fire's kisses then lad.

"I'll see you later if I can.

Busy work I'm still about until the harder snows come ashore to drive us mad from up north. Perlosa will be pulling them down from the Valkorian Islands soon enough like she always does once she's given our kinsmen up there a good beating." Tricky began to separate himself from them by walking in an opposite direction.

"You'll find all you'll need in the inn," the old piecemeal man pointed to the wooden structure ahead of them, with his good hand.

"Thanks, Tricky," said Rowan.

Tricky waved a farewell gesture with his whole hand, then trodden off deeper in the growing shadows of the village.

"Do you think he suspected anything?" Clara questioned with a solemn tone.

"No. He was just happy to see me again, that's all," Rowan replied. He still spied the direction Tricky had been headed, however, watching it to make sure the old timer's words had been truly given.

"Come on," Clara began to move quickly to the tavern. She felt as if she would freeze solid at any minute, but could move no faster.

Skull Splitter was the only place in Vanhyrm allowing basic hospitalities to the traders and common men denied elsewhere in the wilderness and scattered private houses, businesses, and small halls making up the rest of the settlement. Vanhyrm wasn't made for long-term occupation, merely transient migration for both people and goods. Therefore the halls and buildings that did exist were practical, and suited to that purpose — no one would really ever call the settlement truly a village, maybe an outpost or trading center — but little else.

Rowan pushed open the sturdy oak door, and let out a blast of heat.

It felt as a welcome friend, and made him smile.

Though the young knight had taken up a community in the Knighthood, nothing would compare with the true comradeship that was evident in the mannerisms and kinship, which he felt when he was with his own kind as they were in their natural state — apart from religious training. It was a funny thing to ponder, but the more he lingered from the Knighthood, the better he felt, as if he was more alive somehow. It also was very odd that he found he felt guilty for every twinge of pleasure with his kin, and nearly felt ashamed of himself when he spied a quick glance at Clara.

The more Rowan looked at her — giving into his curious emotions, the more damage it would do to his own heart and soul, claimed an old familiar inner voice.

The two entered without much notice. They were still cloaked and Rowan felt safe these men were well into the drink already to pay them much mind. Instead, he studied the room. It was a fair sized area, built out of strong wooden timbers and rough-hewn rope. The poles had been hacked from trees, some barely refined as the bark-covered pillars shot up to the roof and groaned their protest at odd intervals from the weight they bore and the elements they had to endure — both inside and out.

The light was dim and came from a large fire pit in the center of the building surrounded by fieldstone, and soot black iron bars. On these bars were large cooking pots, steaming kettles, and smoke over the yellow sea beneath them. It was from here wonderful smells of fresh stew and porridge greeted the two travelers.

Tall backed wooden chairs scattered the floor amid rect-angular pine tables. This was where the kinsman sat, half-drunk, shouting to their friends and singing off key sagas of valor and bloodlust. Traders and sailors were here too, but kept more to themselves, or gathered in gaggles of like-minded fellows for their own brand of discourse.

Amid the common rabble were men of learning. Some sages of various Nordic tribes all decked out in their fine splendor of beast cat teeth necklaces, and furs. Rowan even spotted a few shamans from the great wilderness to the north of Valkoria. Tricky was right in what he said that Vanhyrm was a great meeting and mixing point for all Nordicans — a minor miracle.

In his homeland, the tribes of Valkoria often warred with themselves for resources and of sheer boredom the winter months produced. Nordicans were not known for their high levels of civilization, when compared to the other more advanced races to the South, East, and West, and anyone who lived with them for a short time could see why. The tribal battles waxed and waned as intertribal marriage of chieftains' daughters or alliances against another tribe halted such violence, but in the Valkorian Islands there was always a war going on somewhere.

Here though, was a different experience. The sheer image of many different tribes being civil to one another was an oddity to the youth's eyes to say the least, even though his training from the Knighthood claimed all humanity should look to unite and be peaceful, he found such an event as now played out in part before him, fanciful.

Around the walls of the inn and on the upper level were small shelves and miniature shops selling herbs and spices, clothing, seed, grain, and other stable goods. Some even boasted to have magical potions and elixirs if their signs could be believed. On the upper level and further on into the deep recesses of the building signs and doorways spoke of rooms to rent, access to the kitchen, a place to bathe and other areas needed for traders and travelers to this distant land.

Clara noticed something else Rowan missed. Along the corners and dark points in the room, elves were serving food and taking away empty plates and mugs. They were clothed in simple animal hide rags and chained at the hands and feet. Their red hair was matted, and their flesh was bruised and dirty. Though their tattooed bodies were strong and lean, they had a gaunt look about them. Lash marks and other previous and potentially deadly injuries were evident to her as well. Even as they both neared the fire to warm themselves one looked up at her with a doe-like face.

The Syvani was a half-elf, the product of the union — probably rape — of a Syvani and Nordican. She couldn't have been more than fourteen years. A glint of fear touched her eyes when she looked at Clara, trying to understand what a free elf was doing about the Nordicans...and it didn't seem like a good thing at that. The young maid immediately put her head down from view as she approached the two.

"What can I do for you?" She spoke in fluent Nordic.

Rowan looked at the young girl instantly. For a moment he couldn't speak. His blood would not allow him to like and find attractive the female standing in front of him. She would be a very lively woman if she grew up to reach adulthood. He pushed past the thoughts to get his message heard. "We are looking for a room for the night. A warm room."

The half-elf bowed.

"This way then," she proceeded to lead them through a corridor and then behind a door opening into a wider hallway lined with still more pine doors, each holding an icon. The icons were painted in a reddish-black paint by a skilled hand to resemble various animals that would be easy to discern. The half-elf stopped in front of a door with an icon of panther painted upon it.

"The panther room is open. Would you like to stay here?" She spoke without raising her eyes. Clara noticed she was not wearing chains like the other elves, and her skin was slightly cleaner then the rest.

"Why aren't you chained like the others?" Clara asked in Syvanese, the native tongue of the Syvani. Clara, like many Patrious, often thought it wise to be skilled in all of the elven languages for they were believed to have shared a common ancestry. Again, this strange fortuitous chance in which she gained a chance to use this knowledge didn't escape her notice.

The youth was struck with fear as she heard the words spoken to her.

For a moment she didn't react.

"What did you say to her?" Rowan stared at Clara.

"Quiet." She held up a hand with a cold hiss in Telborous.

"Why do you wear no chains?" Clara asked again in Syvanese.

The young half-elf raised her head up to look at Clara in the eyes. Her own were a beautiful, deep green as pure as the sea, and bright as the grass of summer.

"I am a half-elf, and so am only half-savage. I am permitted to work for a small wage for my employers. Does the room not suit you, madam?" Her tone was hushed and humble as she spoke in the Syvani language back to Clara.

"No, the room will be fine," Clara, said softly in Syvanese.

"What was that about?" Rowan raised an eyebrow.

"She was just telling me about the room," Clara tightened her jaw. "Come on, I'm freezing."

She opened the door and went inside the room. Rowan followed as the half-elven girl was silent as she walked out of the hallway, and back toward her duty.

Inside the room they were met with a pleasant surprise: it was clean and quite decent. The large bed made of pine in the center of the room had four large posts, which supported a thick curtain along each timber to keep any cold winter drafts from pulling the warmth from the body as the person slept. The youth noticed that the large bed could hold up to two people comfortably.

On the left side of the bed was a pine cabinet allowing the storing of extra goods and clothing. At the bed's foot was a large chest for more storage, this one made of cedar. On the right side of the bed a simple ash table held a pitcher of water, a copper basin, a small pile of wool towels, and an empty copper bowl. Next to this table was a sturdy tall backed oak chair and a simple pine stool.

The heat of the central fire pit filled the room as well. The whole inn was riddled with small vents to allow the heat to flow into the rooms no matter where they were from the central hearth. Already the chill of their journey was leaving them, as the vented air warmed the room.

"What was that really about with the elf?" Rowan looked at Clara as he threw his wet cloak over the chair to dry. It made a sound like a boot getting stuck in the mud.

"Rowan, just drop it." Clara threw off her own cloak, having it land on the floor. Her previously pleasant nature was wearing a bit thin.

"Why are you acting so strange? We're safe now, and we're getting warm...getting these wet clothes off..." Rowan began to walk closer toward the elf, who had sat down, and started to take off her waterlogged boots.

"Ah, what are you doing?" Rowan studied Clara.

"Getting out of these clothes," she stated quite plainly as she continued to undress.

"Right here? In front of me?" Rowan's cheeks flushed. "I thought this was going to be my room, and-"

"We can't afford two rooms, and besides we're only going to be here for a night anyway." Clara looked up at the knight. "Why? You don't have a *problem* with this do you?"

Rowan's check's deepened, their color spreading over the rest of his face and neck. "N-no. Not at all." He swallowed hard. "It's just that we have one bed so-"

"Stop right there. Get back over to your chair." Clara spoke up as she worked on the other boot. "I get the bed tonight."

"Are you sure? I mean, if you stayed on your side and I mine-" the young Nordican was silenced by one of Clara's boots as it struck him in the face. The watery contents inside the boot splashing onto his head as it fell to the ground beside him.

"So I think I'll just spend the evening in the chair then," the Nordican wiped his face dry from the boot splatter.

"That is a *wonderful* idea," Clara began to undo her outer garments as they clung to her like a second skin. "And if you even think of looking over here while I am getting out of these clothes, or just try and sneak into the bed later on, then you might be in for some further regrets." She sat further up in the bed and pulled the drapes closed around her. "Just try to get some sleep so we can be ready for tomorrow, and figure out where we are going to go — and what we're going to do."

"Sounds like a plan then," Rowan said in a hushed voice as he threw his cloak off the chair, slumped down, and then began to rid himself of his clinging soaked garments as modestly as he could.

He also hoped they were able to come up with a plan by tomorrow. He had to admit the whole idea presented by Clara on the boat ride about the seeming game they seemed to be stuck in was making more sense with each passing hour.

Brandon and his boat ride here, the events leading him up to meeting Clara and the others, and of course the actions following that. Maybe there were some coincidences here worth pondering… maybe, but he was too tired and worn out from his travels to give it any proper thought tonight.

No, in the morning there would be enough time for thought and discussion, he was certain of that. Now was the time for sleep. Tomorrow he'd tell Clara he didn't have a plan. The past weeks he'd been unable to think of just how they would go about doing anything they had previously planned. In the morning he'd be better rested to deal with her reactions and deal with what and where they found themselves.

Sound Nordic logic prevailed once again.

Chapter 30

The lush green grass gave comfort to the battle-worn Telborian who rested on its surface. Silently Dugan slumbered amid the tranquil environment.

His face was still smeared with black grease paint; the belt holding two daggers still on his chest. His only garments were those he had used to war against the cultists, the shirt being shredded from glass shards, singed from the heat and flames, as well as torn by his heart.

However, all his wounds were now healed.

The gladiator's chest rose and fell in a peaceful rhythm until a lone breeze rustled his hair, and roused him from slumber.

Instantly, his eyes bolted opened.

Dugan expected to be surrounded by carnage and flames. Instead, he turned up in a forest glade. Upon sitting up he saw tall pines creeping up on the outskirts of a peaceful area. The elderly wood huddled around the edged of the glade like fearful giants, not daring to send a single root into the soft tendrils of grass before them, forming a sage circle about him.

The gladiator found the glade very unnerving, he couldn't hear anything at all. Unlike the managed elven forests of Colloni, here there was no bird singing or the rustling of small creatures in the underbrush. Everything seemed so surreal and dangerous, and he felt unprepared for what was presented him. It was too clean, too perfect — like he had stumbled into an artist's painting without realizing it. It was an artificial feeling, and unnatural. He didn't feel a sense of comfort with it at all.

He quickly looked over himself.

Besides losing his sword, and being a little bit knocked
about, he was alive and able to move and fight should he have to.
Given he didn't know what he was about he just might have to do
so soon enough.

He placed a hand to the wound, which the cult leader had
dealt him in the chest to see it was gone. The damage only being
echoed in the surrounding black tunic where the hole and blood
stained the fabric. He also noticed the other minor wounds, the cuts
and scrapes, had left him. A sudden and gruesome thought then
gripped him. What if he was really dead and these were the Gate
of Asorlok, the holding ground where all the spirits of the dead
shuffle off to their proper afterlife? The longer he sat in isolated
silence, however, the more his brain opened up to the possibility
he wasn't dead.

He knew that Rheminas lay claim to his soul, and he was the
god of fire, among other things. Dugan couldn't see, hear or smell
any fires anywhere, and so assumed he was alive and well. To help
him along in his logic, he placed a hand over his chest once more,
and let it tarry there for a moment. The familiar thump of his organ
told him he yet lived. So he wasn't in Mortis either.

He sighed.

"So you drug him along too, huh?" A familiar voice grated
behind his ear. Dugan spun around and leapt to his feet to meet the
speaker and found himself looking at Vinder and the two priests.
They didn't have their hammers in hand now though, as they
rested close beside them on the grass — silver surfaces reflecting
the light all about them.

The Telborian shook his mane for a moment then drew in
closer to them."Vinder?" The Telborian studied the three before
him — sizing them up, ready for anything.

"Yes, it's me you big ox. These two got me on the field of
honor. They took some of my glory, and then drug me along here,"
the one-eyed dwarf crossed his arms in a huff.

"They used some sort of spell to get the better of me,"
Dugan let down some of his guard. "I was ready to die, and now

I end up here." He wasn't going to get much of a fight from the dwarf — but the two priests…

"Looks like they got you in the middle of something for sure — I don't think you're too keen in grease paint and dark clothing unless you started keeping company with some bards since I last saw you," Vinder upturned a side of his face in a lopsided grin.

"We needed you both here to help us defeat the very creature you helped unleash upon the world," Cracius spoke up from behind the shorter dwarf. His manner was calm and dignified. Next to him stood Tebow with the multicolored bird, the servant of Endarien, perched on his shoulder.

"Is that what *they* told *you* to get you here?" Dugan looked at Vinder.

"It is," Vinder responded. "I gather it was similar to your ears as well, eh?"

"I wasn't must listening to them at the time," Dugan tried to wipe some of the black streaks from his face with his own dark sleeve, which only resulted in smearing more of the paint around his visage. "But since I'm here now, I'd like some answers.

"Taking me from my final fate without my permission is one thing, but compelling me to join your cause without first giving me a choice is still another.

"Why should I even care about this threat — even if I helped release it," Dugan scoffed. "I was ready to die, and you took me away from that. Even if this evil takes over, I'm still going to the same place when I die anyway, so it changes nothing for me at all."

"Join the guild," Vinder's tone was sardonic. " I was ready to die too when they took me. Ready to die and reclaim what I lost when that too was taken from me." Vinder sighed deeply, letting the anger at the event in the cave, the extinguishing of his redemption, flow out of him. When he felt it had left him completely, he turned up to the Telborian again, his face calm and resolute, even accepting of what he knew was the right thing to do.

"But they have told a good tale, and wound me up in it, binding me with my own feelings and forgotten obligations as it were, and so I'm here."

Dugan's face softened a bit. "I never thought you'd turn into something of a philosopher. You haven't been drinking have you?"

"No, just doing what I have to do; what responsibility obligates." There was no good-natured humor in the dwarf's word, only a gentle resolve as one who speaks before the gallows or a soldier who has taken on his duty regardless of the dangers he shall surely meet while carrying them out.

"What do you mean?" Dugan took this resolve with a studious mind. This wasn't like the dwarf at all. From what he had learned of him in their trek back from Takta Lu Lama, this wouldn't be something the dwarf did unless strongly compelled.

"Rest assured lad, it isn't a spell or knife that holds me and I do this — join their cause, of my own free will." Vinder tried to down play the seriousness of his last statement to relieve its impact. Just like a soldier would tell his loved ones not to worry because he'd be back safe and sound soon enough.

Dugan decided to drop the matter from further investigation seeing how the dour expression on the dwarf's face told him it was wise to do so, that the matter would never be up for discussion, at least in Dugan's lifetime.

"Still, you seem almost happy about all this," the Telborian spoke.

"Practical optimist if anything," Vinder's steel gray eye twinkled for an instant.

"They even healed you up I'm told. What were you doing now? Getting into more scrapes again?" Vinder's mouth perked slightly at the end of the sentence.

"Something like that," Dugan had a thoughtful smirk of his own.

"Now, death priests healing somebody in general is cause enough in my book for some thought to be made on this matter," said the dwarf.

"That is not true," Tebow addressed Dugan softly. "We were going to bind the wound, but when we set you upon the ground, where you later awoke, you had been healed. Not by us, but the one who brought us all together." The death priest's face was matter of fact now to the gladiator. "Asorlins don't heal."

Dugan looked at the older priest for a moment, then back to Vinder. The priest was getting into slightly more esoteric topics for him he thought and he wanted to be more grounded with some common footing for a little while longer. He'd had his fill of priests and their enigmatic ways for a while.

"You're trying to sell me on this idea of joining them now too?" Dugan asked Vinder. Was this part of the compulsion then too? Sign him up for some foolhardy mission. A mission that was probably suicidal no doubt.

"Not selling, but *encouraging* you to keep an open mind on this offer." Vinder chose his words carefully speaking in a measured, thoughtful way that also wasn't much like the Vinder Dugan had gotten to know. Still, it was not without its humor though.

"Okay, now a dwarf with an open mind is a very odd portent," Dugan's face burst into a wide toothy grin.

"Watch it now, grease smear," Vinder joshed.

"So now that I'm here — without my consent — mind you," Dugan thought it wise to add that last bit again just to emphasize his displeasure upon the matter of being abducted in general, "what is this all about? Tell me the whole story — the *real* reason."

"Do you even know *where* you are?" The bird studied the former gladiator with its doll-like eyes.

Dugan was shocked by seeing and hearing the bird speak, but the effect quickly wore off as he shook his mind clear to answer. After all, he had seen many strange things in his journey from Colloni.

"Not in Talatheal." The Telborian quickly recovered from his surprise.

"And not in the Diamant Mountains," Vinder's words were thick with sarcasm as he made his way to stand beside the Telborian.

"Right," the bird squawked.

"You're in the realm of Galba now," Cracius voice held a reverential tone.

"Galba? Who's that?" Dugan began to look at the priests more carefully should they try anything strange against him or Vinder. Things couldn't have gotten much stranger than they had been since he left Colloni.

"Not so much as *who*, but *where*?" asked Cracius.

Dugan's brow furrowed.

"Turn around, and you will see," Tebow said solemnly.

Slowly, Dugan did as he was told, and came upon the most wonderful sight he had ever seen. In fact, he couldn't believe he had even missed it in the first place. It was too huge not to have been seen. A large circle of gray stones, arranged in post and lintel formation, dominated the circular glade around him. Through the 'doorways' created by the circle's design, the Telborian could see inside the monument there was nothing save more green grass. Somehow though Dugan knew this wasn't totally true. He felt as if something more was inside, hidden from view somehow. Something that just escaped his ability to describe what it was — something that was beyond his mind to fully comprehend.

"What's that?" Dugan motioned to the stone circle before him.

"That is where we need to go." Tebow joined the Telborian's stare.

"No dwarf carved those stones, nor any other hand on Tralodren," Vinder joined the Telborian in his awful state.

"Why do you want to go inside it? Looks empty enough to me from here." Dugan muttered.

"Inside is an entity akin to the gods but not one of them," Cracius now joined Dugan in his gaze.

"What does that mean?" Dugan looked over his shoulder to Cracius, "You priests never talk like normal men."

"Galba is not a god," Tebow tried to clarify his statement. "We have come to understand she is something else."

"So Galba is a *she* now, not a *place*?" Vinder asked the death priests in this slight degree of confusion.

"She is a place *and* a person," Cracius emphasized.

"Okay then, so she is somehow tied in with this, then I take it — this lich thing," Vinder continued "you were clear on all the details when you brought me here."

"Indeed," Cracius nodded. "He will be coming here soon and we will have to be ready to meet him."

"*Who's* coming here?" Dugan turned from the stones to engage the priests. Too many priests had recently graced his life, and none of them had brought much joy to his heart.

"The skeletal thing — this lich as they call it," Vinder told Dugan.

"So that thing that we fought in the ruins, the one that almost killed me, is coming here?" Dugan gave the dwarf an unbelieving snort.

"Yep," he replied.

"So you want us to fight, and try to kill, this lich when he is coming into the realm of a being greater than a god — who doesn't like him?" Dugan moved to look full into the face of the priest. He wanted to see every movement to better judge the weight of his words. "Why can't she or it or whatever take care this lich? Why do you need us?"

"Galba cannot help us," said Cracius.

"*Can't* or *won't*?" Vinder followed Dugan's lead, staring hard into Cracius eyes.

"Can't." Tebow took in the fierce eyes of the gladiator. This one would not be so easy to win over. "She has said she cannot break her oath by lending us any aid in the battle to come."

"But she seemed to be able to heal me of my wounds," Dugan pointed out, "That seems like some interference to me."

At this the two death priests were silent.

Vinder and Dugan were silent as well, waiting for some answer.

After a while, when none was given, the bird finally decided to raise its voice to break the stillness about them."The ways of the gods are beyond us." The avian tried out the words with caution.

After a few more heartbeats of silence Cracius continued.

"You won't be alone, the others who were on your last mission will join you to take on this task. We will be joining you too. It can be successful. Together we will succeed."

"How can it be successful? What's the plan?" Dugan crossed his arms and stuck out his chest.

"That is what we need to develop when your other companions arrive, and before The Master arrives." Tebow couldn't quite figure out Dugan yet, and Asorlok was not aiding him as much as he had with Vinder. Why was this proving to be more difficult? What was it about the Telborian that was different than any other?

"That doesn't sound like much of anything," Dugan saw that so far they were speaking the truth. But how much more was true? "Do you even know when the others are supposed to arrive? Why would they arrive anyway? What if they decided not to join your little mission?"

Still nothing.

Tebow tried again to focus on something, anything his god would give as he struggled to continue the conversation.

Dugan laughed a deep bellow. This was insanity. What was happening to the world around him? Everything made more sense to him when he was slave and not burdened by the thoughts of a free man. How many more sacrifices, how many more foolish ventures did he have to make before he could live his own life? If he lived his own life…

He supposed he had little choice at this stage. He was ready to die when the two priests found him before…what was one more day than until he met up with Asorlok and his final fate? They weren't lying, of that the Telborian was certain now. Was there anything left than to feed his doubts?

"Fine. You're all insane, but now I'm here, I guess I have little choice," Dugan growled. "I probably wouldn't be able to get out of here and off this land any more than I could find a faith to save me from my fate." His shoulders slumped now as he resigned himself once more with his fate.

"I was happy to die before, so what's one more day here anyway, right?" The Telborian's face was emotionless now and resolute. "What do we need to do?"

It was then that Tebow's answer came. They couldn't offer anything to Dugan because he wanted nothing. He was ready to die — he had given up on his life, and so nothing they could offer would sway him. Only his own whim and perhaps Galba would keep him at their side after this recent statement. For it was one thing to wish to die, and care not about doing much to stop it and another to actually fight to the death for a cause one believed in quite strongly.

"We have to get inside there," Cracius motioned to the stone circle.

"Fine. Let's go and get this over with," Dugan began to march to the standing stones.

"No wait —" Cracius began, but was stopped by Tebow.

"He must learn to respect what is before him before he is able to get inside, and our work is completed," said the other priest.

"But what if he dies?" Cracius questioned.

"He wouldn't," the bird shifted it's weight on Tebow's shoulder.

Dugan may have been angry and beleaguered, but he wasn't stupid. He had learned from past encounters with priests and their ilk, wizards and the lies they spin. He cautiously made his way to the circle. Though it haunted him, it also filled him with a macabre curiosity. It spoke to some child-like place in him as well as the adult. The experience was unlike anything he had ever known… it was indescribable.

The circle was silent as the air around him.

Dugan decided to press a little further and neared the edge of the stone structures. He thought to walk right through a doorway in the circle, and enter into the center of the stone ring, but wasn't quite sure if he could or would. The stones smacked of mystical things — things that lay hidden beyond his understanding, but were there in operation none the less, obeying a set of rules all their own. Though he never would have guessed the stones held such energy about them. They seemed so plain, so simple in their design, tall square and squat pillars of stone and nothing more. Yet…yet there was something more about them that made his gut squirm. Something that made his pulse quicken, mouth go dry and fingers quake.

Tentatively he stretched out his hand to touch the nearest stone post. It had to be more than three feet across, and at least ten feet tall. Before his hand could even touch the stone, it struck an invisible barrier that shook his body to the bone.

From his hand thick serpentine currents raced up his arm, then down his shoulder and into his chest and neck. It spread like fire to the other half of his body and into his head. He felt the force fling him into the air with a great push to land more than ten feet from the circle, convulsing with pain.

"Gods," he managed to curse though his shaking.

Blood ran in tiny streams from his nose, ears, and mouth. His left hand was numb and speckled with light patches of discolored skin — which looked like a cheetah's pelt — as pale white spots played across his normal, healthy, tan hue.

"Dugan!" Vinder ran to the warrior's side.

"I think he has learned his lesson now," Cracius observed. "I sure hope so. I don't think he could take a second instruction," The bird flew toward the downed Telborian.

Chapter 31

The morning sun couldn't come soon enough. Rowan's lower back and shoulders ached with fatigue. He had barely managed to sleep a wink during his confinement to the chair and had been forced to push his shoulders forward, move his lower back outward more, bowing his frame in a very awkward manner. The result was stiff joints and an achy body when it should've been a restful slumber upon comfy goose down stuffed pillows.

Clara had yet to awaken and the Nordican was left alone with his thoughts. For the past fifteen minutes he played with the panther paw amulet around his neck. He still was unable to figure out its purpose or unlock its secrets. Turning his attention to his feet for a moment, he took in the shield he had received in the hidden vault of the ruins. That too was a bit of a mystery, now that he had a bit more time to study it. Not so much for its function, for a shield was a shield as far as the Nordican was concerned, but the emblem on the black background was unlike anything he had seen before: a great golden two-headed serpent facing itself with draconic influences, blowing fire into the others face.

Strange.

Pondering his shield wasn't as pressing as the thoughts the exercise kept him from. Things seemed to indeed be moving in a direction that seemed to pull the knight and the elf along rather than his conscious will and choices making the future before him.

Clara had started his mind moving into new directions — embarking on new paths. Added to the questions he was already facing, both born of Panthor, and, his own spiritual turmoil, it made for a rather crowded head. What was going on? What was this all about? He still hadn't gotten anything of a plan in his sleep as to what to do once he got to Valkoria, or really how to get there either; no more dreams from Panthor either.

This was a lost venture surely. What hope did he have of going to Cadrissa's aid at all? What could he do to better understand what his goddess had spoken to him? He didn't know what to make of his Knighthood either; and now Brandon. Clara had shown him the folly of what planning he'd already undertaken on the trip over. The youth had been shown the naïveté of his thinking — the futility of his plans.

It was just too much to take in, and too soon amid the other quagmire of thoughts the youth had to struggle through each day. If there was some larger picture here he didn't understand it at all. Emotions and thoughts, mysteries and riddles…what was happening? Life wasn't supposed to be so complicated, so uncertain — was it? The world seemed so balanced so…straight-forward…to the youth, and now it started to seem chaos had indeed run amok in the lands south of Valkoria.

Did he really think he could take Clara with him to his homeland without some trouble?

He'd see it already with the captain. Imagine that response over the whole population…and she'd be on her own when Rowan was reporting to his superiors…

The young knight had stripped down to his undergarments to sleep, which were still a bit damp, but dryer than they had been the night before. The rest of his clothing rested on the floor about him. His armor had been placed near a wooden vent to help it dry. He hoped it didn't suffer too much damage from the water, leather armor had been known to do that on occasion, and the youth knew he would need it for a while longer. What did he really believe about the elf anyway? What was right? Was he fighting against himself still? And why?

He looked longingly toward the bed.

Though he knew emotions played about his stomach and heart, he also knew that infatuation was fleeting, actually damaging, and detrimental to both parties in the long run, but Rowan didn't believe it was infatuation that had him. No, not now...

The wool curtains hid the insides of the canopy very well. Only a thin outline of the person, more so a shadow of a shadow at best, could be seen through the drapery. Somehow he knew the figure was awake and mocking him with a smile of comfort from a restful night as he suffered for any bit of rest that came to him. At least he was warmer though. He was sure he'd have caught his death in the cold garments even though his body, like most Nordicans, was better equipped to handle colder temperatures. Though he was sore and warm, he knew he needed to get moving again, to keep to his obligations however he best could.

He could be done with it all, now he realized. Get up, and leave the elf to her own devices on the island while he sailed back home, he'd surely be able to find a ride with a home-going trader with little effort...but that wouldn't be fair to Clara, not giving her the respect she deserved.

After all, she had decided to join him in a quest he initiated. She forfeited her own return to aid him. No, she at least deserved the benefit of having the knight discuss his plans — or lack thereof — with her, explaining his position. Then she could make up her mind.

Maybe she could even stay behind on Arid Land and join him later, when he had some information to work with in helping track the mage down — found the Ice King, or something...if it was still possible to even find the mage. Clara's sobering chat with Rowan had made him aware of the hole in such a plan.

What was troubling him more and more was what Clara had told him about Gilban's words; that Cadrissa had a greater purpose still — they all did in a way — as they were tied to each other. Again, as before, the issue of fate came back to the knight — fate and his own actions — his own desires and fears.

As his mind thought these things over, his eyes caught a glimpse of a strange glow about his neck. Looking down, Rowan spied the shriveled infant paw glowing a gentle green. He was transfixed by the glow, trying to make sense of it, but could do nothing but stare into it as it pulled him into it as the rest of the room faded from his view…

Rowan knew he had been taken on another vision. It was a strange and yet wonderful experience he had never completely gotten used to. His whole body felt light, as if it wasn't even there, just his mind and vision amid a milky gray fog.

Rowan.

The voice was of his goddess, he was sure of it, but he couldn't see her.

"Where are you?" The knight spoke out loud though he somehow knew that he was speaking not with his lips but with his spirit instead.

Rowan, listen to me. My time is short.

You began to learn from my words and have begun to understand what it is I would have for you — who you are. Today you take the first step into the wider arena in which I'd have you walk. You have chosen a worthy thing by following the plight of Cadrissa, this you shall do first before you return to your order.

This shall be completed for you by seeking out one called Galba. She resides on Arid Land, but you have to find her under your own strength as on this land I am bound by an oath and cannot tell you where she resides.

Find Galba and you will find Cadrissa.

Do this and the mission you have taken on will be completed. You can then walk into the wider array of wonders and purposes I have yet to bestow upon you for the high calling and purposes I have set you apart for in the times to come.

He didn't know what to speak at first, he was still trying to figure out how this all was connected — how Cadrissa bound them all, but could dwell and would on that a moment longer. For now, he had to concentrate on where he was and that he had just had another personal revelation by his goddess…something very rare indeed, but with which he seemed to be favored of late. It gave him an idea at least for some type of action to offer up to Clara.

"I thank you for your presence my goddess," Rowan bowed his head, "and I beg your forgiveness for my boldness, but what is this plan you have for me?

More over, will you not also tell me the nature of this amulet? What I am to do with it? What purpose it is to my future, and the plans you have to me? If I knew what part it played I would be better able to prepare for the future and the calling you have for me there." This time he didn't want the vision to end without asking about the mummified panther paw.

You are already more than prepared. Panthor calmly continued. *Find Galba and don't be afraid to listen to your heart in matters to come.*

Rowan was about to ask what that meant by the last statement but the mist was fading and the room returning to his sight; his body once more gaining in weight…

More riddles.

More mysteries.

Rowan shook his head as the vision ended, placing the amulet once more under his undershirt. He knew what had to be done now and wasted little time in doing it.

"Clara," he whispered.

There was no response.

"Clara," Rowan then spoke in a normal tone.

"Is it morning already?" A slumbering voice awoke from behind the cloth.

"Yes. I would know," Rowan grumbled as he rose from the chair to stretch and looked over his garments. "I hardly got any sleep last night."

"What news of the future?" Clara was now fully awake and moving.

Rowan passed along his interest in the practice of divining the future from his clothing to the elf in their travels. Though she seemed to diplomatically disregard the practice as superstition as did much of the Knighthood and faith, the elf still humored the odd custom whenever Rowan was so inclined to share it.

"It says you have to start letting me get the bed, and you the chair," Rowan joked.

"Is that right," Clara sung out.

"Actually," Rowan's tone changed, "I think we need to talk."

"Really?" Clara rustled noisily behind the curtain. Her own inflection was slightly concerned. "About what?"

Rowan readied himself in his previously shed clothing. The articles were still a little bit damp, but they would soon dry in the abundant heat of the common room. He would leave his armor here still and let it dry a bit more before he donned it again. He won't have need of it right now anyway and wanted to be sure it was fully dry before he donned it again in order to keep it from damage.

"About this whole interconnected thing you keep talking about, and Cadrissa…and a vision I just had."

"You had a *vision*?" Her excitement shook the bed. "What about?"

"I think it has to do with how we can find Cadrissa," the youth answered.

"That's great news!" Clara exclaimed. "You want to tell me about it?"

"I'd prefer to do so over breakfast, I'm starving," said Rowan.

"All right," the elf agreed, "I could do with some food as well."

"The heat really stayed in here last night. Must have employed some dwarves to keep the warmth going throughout the whole place," Rowan put on his over shirt. He didn't want to talk about anything of substance yet, and so stuck to some superficial conversation…safe conversation.

"Or gnomes," Clara pushed back the drapes to reveal she was fully dressed once more, looking like she had not even suffered the minor inconveniences of their recent journeys in the least — even her hair seemed unmarred by a night of slumber.

"Gnomes?" Rowan looked at her with a raised eyebrow.

"Yes, gnomes." Clara thought Rowan was teasing her,"short fellows with big smiles, and kind hearts…" The expression on Rowan's face told her he wasn't teasing her or even understanding her. "…they're wonderful craftsman and businessmen…" She tried once again, but to no avail.

"I've never seen a gnome before," Rowan confessed.

"Never?" It was Clara's turn to act surprised.

"Never."

"They're as common in my homeland as dwarves are to yours," She ran a hand through her hair, causing it to shimmer in the limited light.

"So what do they do then?" Rowan watched.

"Well, they trade, and sell. They ponder politics…" The elf now tugged on her belt as she straightened her garb.

"Is that all?" Rowan smiled.

"It's enough. They're the richest race in the world," Clara mirrored the grin.

"Really?" Rowan walked toward the door.

Both stopped when they reached it at the same time. Each felt an uneasy tension as they looked into each other's eyes without speaking. Even Clara's face tightened along with her heart and throat.

"Right…" the elf broke the awkwardness, "lets get some food. I'm hungry."

Clara pulled her hood up over her head once more as they made their way for a secluded table in the large common room. The room was full of Nordicans getting their morning meal. Traders, hunters, and workers of various crafts, decorated the various tables and bar, and took scant notice of the new pair added to their midst. Also along with them were the many half-elven and elven slaves serving and cleaning up the room for their masters.

"Let's find some place safe to talk," Rowan whispered Telborous into Clara's ear.

"Agreed," she whispered her reply in the same language.

Together they moved to a far wall still shaded with some dim light from the fire and nearby wooden beams.

Both seated themselves in silence.

Clara looked about the room in a non-obtrusive manner for a moment then turned back to Rowan who simply dug his fingernails into the gray grain of the worn pine table. For a moment she said nothing, merely sitting in the silence between them, then, when she saw Rowan wasn't going to make and effort to break it, she spoke.

"So tell me about this vision then," Clara's gray tinted face lit up.

Rowan was hesitant at first, his head still turned to the table, but eventually the words came out in a faster stream as his head rose a little but never looked the elf straight in the eyes.

"I was told that Cadrissa is here or will be…I'm not sure which. We have to find someone named Galba, and then we'll find Cadrissa."

"Galba?" Clara turned the word around in her mouth, "Sounds Sylvanese."

"Could be…" Rowan finally looked up from the table.

"But who is she or he?" Clara dared a look into the youth's eyes for a moment, which startled Rowan, causing him to look away.

"*She*…and I don't know. I wasn't told anything else really," the knight's gaze fluttered toward the large hearth in the center of the room.

"So we don't know where she is or what she is and we have to find her huh?"

"Yeah, that's about it," Rowan sighed.

Clara sighed herself. "Still, its better than your idea to look for that Ice King."

This brought his attention back to the table. "Yeah, at least we know where Cadrissa is now…or will be." He looked at the elf and felt a smile creep its way into the corners of his mouth. "And now we don't have to go to Valkoria or further. We're already here. Panthor told me I have to do this first, and then I can return back to the Knighthood."

"You know you really don't have to go with me…" Rowan started then halted himself abruptly when he heard his own words, and saw Clara's face frown in contemplation, "…back to my homeland after we find Cadrissa."

"I know," the elf's voice was hushed with a sigh, as she let her gaze fall to the tables gray grain.

"What would you have?" A familiar voice, again speaking Nordic, interrupted their conversation. Both then turned to see the same half-elf they had seen the night before. She still held the same beleaguered expression and haunted eyes; innocence tramped and torn.

"Porridge," Rowan said in the same tongue as he got more comfortable on the wooden chair, his mind was clearly cluttered with many other things…as was his heart.

Clara didn't like the look on the girl's face. She liked it even less that Rowan seemed so callous and unconcerned, even supportive of the condition in which the girl was placed.

"What do you wish today, madam?" The elven girl continued to speak in the Nordican language.

"Your name," Clara smiled and spoke again in Syvanese.

The girl looked up at the elf in shocked disbelief once more.

"I am unimportant," she replied back in Syvanese with a soft, subservient, voice, nervously looking about her to see if anyone heard the conversation "Please tell me what you want to eat to today, and I shall go and fetch it."

"First tell me your name," Clara persisted.

Rowan looked at both elves with a perplexed face. "What's going on, Clara? Just order your food," he'd switched to Telborous, but kept his voice low as to not draw any attention from his fellow Nordicans.

"Name," she repeated.

"Trinity," the Syvani hung her head.

"There now, that wasn't so hard now was it?" She smiled. "Well Trinity I think porridge sounds good to me as well."

Trinity bowed, and then went off toward the kitchen.

"What was that about?" Rowan snapped.

"She is a slave here," Clara rejoined the conversation with Telborous.

"Yes. There are a lot of them. It might not be right to you, but we can't set them all free right now. We have to get about saving Cadrissa." Rowan knew his words might have been a bit pert, but he had to speak his heart on this matter. They didn't have time for this now.

Clara glared at him for a moment.

She couldn't believe what she was hearing. The tension began to build again in the awkward silence that fell between them. Rowan could do nothing, say nothing, but look into Clara's eyes, and notice the confusion and pain matching his own inner struggle.

"Rowan…" Clara finally broke the thick silence. "We need to talk."

"We *are* talking," A nervous smile crossed his lips; hands fidgeting about the table top like fish pulled fresh from the water. "What do you mean?"

"You know what I mean," Clara returned, her own face soaking in a small bit of anxiety now.

"No, I don't," Rowan fidgeted in his chair again.

"Rowan, we both have feelings for each other. We both know it," She seemed a bit paler than usual as she spoke.

Rowan looked at Clara for a moment, cleared his throat and then spoke. "How do you think we should deal with them then?"

"Talk," came Clara's straightforward counsel.

"Talk?" Rowan raised an eyebrow.

"Yes, talk. We talk about our feelings," Clara responded.

"Why can't we just ignore them?" The youth's words had grown small.

"If we did, we'd end up doing more harm then good. Let's just get this thing out in the open. Purge them from ourselves and be done with it." Clara sat back in her chair and took a long, slow breath. She thought this was going to be much easier, but she'd work through any difficulty that would and had been rising to get this down and dealt with — she needed to be free to go on with this new quest, and her own life.

Rowan sat silently as he looked over the elf. His face was void of any expression.

"Okay, I'll go first then," Clara exhaled all her previously internalized hindrances. "I've noticed that I have some feelings toward you. I can honestly say I'm attracted to you more and more now each day in a more romantic way than when I first encountered you."

Rowan continued to stare at the elf.

"So what do you have to say to that?" Clara tried to jostle the knight to life.

"I ah…understand you are an attractive woman, and I can appreciate that…you're an *elf* though, and I'm a *human*," Rowan stumbled about his words.

"Yes Rowan, you're human and I'm an elf. It isn't impossible for our two races to have feelings for one another. Trinity herself is proof our two races are more than compatible.

"However, if we are both sharing the same feelings as it seems like we both are, I think it's also time we talk some about your mindset toward elves and any other non-humans you meet. It really has come to wear on me and even hurt me at times," Clara's eyes now turned tender.

Rowan pushed back a thick lump in his throat and made it slide all the way to his stomach where he felt it bounce up to his heart. He knew there was some truth to what Clara was saying, but he didn't feel any real shame to it until now. Since he had begun the journey from the Knighthood and had received the previous dream from Panthor, he had felt different in some ways.

He reflected again at how he thought the elves were evil and cruel, liars and devils to a man. Yet he tolerated and even accepted dwarves. Humans were like his brothers and sisters. Yet he had grown quite fond of Clara, but a part of him still despised her too for being an elf. It frightened him to have those feelings raise their ugly head. Frightened him because he knew it was a part of him — he was a walking paradox, a man at war with himself. A man who would never be at peace until he stilled the raising storm inside himself and won over the conflicting ideologies and emotions.

"I've come to see that you and the rest of the Nordicans I've come to encounter hate all other races but humans," Clara looked across the table into the knight's face and the look frightened Rowan to speak. He had to cut off her words — the sadness of her face and heart as it poured out of her mouth was too much for him.

"I-I don't hate you Clara." he spoke in half-truth, "I…love you."

Both fell silent after Rowan's confession.

"W-what I mean is-" Rowan stammered, after he regained some composure.

"It's okay, I feel the same way," Clara put her hand upon the youth's palm which rested before her. "The question is *why* do you feel this way? You can't hate and love the same thing, it's impossible."

"I'm just speaking my mind," Rowan said, and then wished he hadn't. The words had been birthed of impulse and very poorly thought out. As soon as the words had left his mouth, they tore at him deeply. A sickly aura of unpleasantness belched up to his heart from his stomach.

What was he saying? Why had he been so rude to the woman he loved? The queasy uneasiness of the whole situation overcame him like a dagger to the brain — an intense warm pain of confusion and anguish. What was going on? Clara fared no better from the comment. Her eyes grew colder and her face took on a sullen pallor. "Somehow I find that hard to believe."

"I-I don't mean to Clara. It was just how I was raised." Another half-truth he stumbled into.

"You weren't raised to hate me — or elves. Somehow I don't think all Nordicans share this uneasiness with non-humans. You are better than these…people, Rowan." Clara motioned around the room with her hand. "That is what makes you different… what makes me love you." The last two words of Clara's sentence trailed off into a whisper.

Tears had welled up in her eyes.

"I can't change who I am, Clara. I'm a Knight of Valkoria, a Nordican from the Panther Tribe of Valkoria. Nothing can change that fact."

"No, you're wrong. You are Rowan Cortak, a man of the Northlands who has it within himself to make up his *own* mind, to choose who *he* wants to be and *what* he wants to become apart from race, religion, and what anyone else has told him." The tears started to flow then — tiny streams of liquid glass on a statuesque face.

Nabu's words came back to Rowan's memory more powerful than ever — hammering at his mind. *Maybe they taught you in secret…* Panthor's last phrases then spoke to him as well, echoing a deeper revelation: *don't be afraid to listen to your heart in matters to come… You delay and frustrate them, however, by this endless strife within yourself. Let go and be free of it. Let go and embrace the destiny I hold for you.*

Something was turning deep inside the youth, like the tumbler of a lock…

"You don't have to be like the worst of your kin, Rowan. You can be better than that. You *are* better than that. Let go of the past and embrace the future. Together we can get through it. Together we can overcome anything." The tears had stopped now, but the serious demeanor about the elf; the yearning for Rowan to understand all this, still remained.

Both of them then fell silent.

Rowan turned his head to the table, hiding his face from Clara. The elf meanwhile looked about herself briefly with her wet eyes, keeping her face hidden from anyone who might have taken an interest in the two of them, and/or their conversation.

They didn't.

"I've wondered about my feelings for you," Rowan raised his head once more from the table to look at Clara. "I wondered about them since before that kiss. You're like no other woman I've ever seen. Brave, strong, intelligent and beautiful. In many ways you make the woman of Valkoria seem like nothing in comparison.

"At the same time I have these feelings for you, I also have a voice telling me why it's wrong, why it's immoral."

"Is it your voice, Rowan?" Clara asked solemnly.

"No."

"Is it the voice of your goddess?" she continued.

He paused. He wanted to say yes, but realized this wasn't true. It sounded like his goddess, but he came to realize it was the Knighthood that was speaking for her.

"No." Another tumbler moved inside the knight.

"Then ignore it," Clara softly insisted. "If it isn't your goddess or your own voice, then it is not of any concern to you. You should listen to your goddess, and seek to do her will, that's why you're a knight, but you shouldn't listen to any other voice, that would be betraying both yourself and your goddess."

A faint smile traced the lips the Nordican bubbling over into a full grin. "Thank you. I haven't been able to make sense of anything till now, but what you said…it makes so much sense… I know it does, I can feel it does. Thank you." The final tumbler turned deep inside the knight and the lock was opened.

"It's like a weight has lifted off me…" His eyes grew moist, but no tear fell.

Trinity returned with their porridge, and when she caught sight of Rowan's grin, she lowered her eyes. She put two wooden bowls on the table before each of them then turned to leave.

"Thank you, Trinity," Clara addressed the young half-elf in Telborous.

"Yeah, thanks," Rowan repeated in his native tongue, and more of that feeling of release tingled all over his body. He felt freer than he had before in quite a while. Trinity stopped for a minute, then half-turned to take in Rowan with a sheepish gaze.

"You're welcome," when she spoke, it was more like a question with soft tones, then walked back to the kitchen.

Clara smiled back at Rowan. "See, that wasn't so hard now was it?"

"Not as hard as I once thought it would be, no, but I still have to push past some things to get there. I still had to wage a small battle," he confided with much relief.

"It will come in time, don't give up on it. I'll be here to help you through it. You've begun the journey into a brave new world." Clara's encouraging words brought new life to Rowan's soul. "You'll feel even more free from your past ideas as time goes on."

The youth sighed slightly.

"Speaking of journeys," Rowan's face turned a bit more serious, "I meant what I said: You don't have to come with me to Valkoria."

"I know Rowan. But let's not talk about that now, that can be decided later when we've retrieved Cadrissa, and this whole matter is over with and done." She waved the matter away with a strong, yet delicate hand.

"That would be a more appropriate time, don't you think?" Her eyes were rimmed with affectionate joy.

"I suppose that is fair enough," the knight returned the look. I guess I can stick around you longer then, and hear more about this grand scheme, or game, or whatever it is we're all in," Rowan flashed a cheeky smile. It felt good to be happy again.

"It's real Rowan, and Cadrissa is a part of it."

"I'm beginning to believe you now," said Rowan. "It's just too strange…a stranger who brings us within sight of Arid Land, and then has his whole boat fade into mist, a vision from Panthor saying Cadrissa is here as well…Cadrissa even joining your party in the first place…"

Rowan stopped to rub his chin and shove in some more porridge.

"Don't forget Gilban's words as well," she added.

"Right," the knight agreed with a mouth still half-filled with food.

"We are all tied together in some way," Clara took a spoonful of the warm mush.

"Yeah," he swallowed, "but how?"

"It has to be that lich who took her, he has to be part of this," Clara swallowed then spoke.

"Lich? You mean that skeletal thing then?" Rowan questioned then scooped up more porridge into his mouth.

Clara nodded. "I thought about it again, and I think that creature was a lich."

"So what is a lich then?" Rowan asked.

"A lich is a type of an un-living thing, a wizard that has found a way to live beyond their natural lifespan," Clara said.

"And this lich took Cadrissa?" Rowan scrunched up his face a bit in thought. "Why?

"It wasn't just for convenience sake; it had a plan;" the elf answered.

"You still think it was a plan for all of us?" Rowan sunk his spoon into the bowl, and let it rest there as he spoke.

"For most of us yes…I just don't know how all this ties together though, but if Cadrissa is the key somehow — if we're all tied to her in some way, then it has to be something important, something big," she took some more of the porridge.

"Only we don't know how to connect the threads here to make the cloth whole do we?" Rowan stirred his mush.

"No," Clara shook her head. "Not yet at any rate, and I doubt we will be able to do much here either. The only way to get some answers I suppose would be to find Cadrissa. She must be the key to all this."

"And that would mean finding Galba then," Rowan stated aloud the answer they already both knew in their minds.

"Correct," Clara nodded.

"So in a way, we can't really do anything here it would seem but keep participating in this play, this game then," Rowan was working the thought through his head.

"So it would seem," Clara sighed, her shoulders sinking a bit.

"I just hope when we get to Cadrissa the mystery is solved. I don't want to find her, only to find out she only has threads too, and nothing close to a whole cloth to work from," Rowan resumed his eating.

"Let's just hope she doesn't have those threads. I don't know where we could go after that if she did," Clara joined him in eating.

"How do you think we can find Galba then?" He spoke after he had eaten most of the spoonful in his mouth.

"Well, it would be best to have a guide who knew the area," Clara stirred her porridge.

"Yeah," Rowan agreed between spoonfuls.

"We'd need someone who has knowledge of Galba, and where to find her. A good guide, probably someone who knew the area around here better than most —"

"Tricky Dick!" Rowan smiled as he held up another large spoonful to his lips.

Clara tried to hide her immediate reaction to the suggestion. It wasn't of the most favorable towards the older Nordican. To her credit she did a fair job of keeping her true feelings hidden on the topic. "I actually was thinking of someone else."

"Who?" Rowan was truly surprised that she could think of someone more qualified than Tricky Dick.

Chapter 32

Clara pulled her hood up tighter about her face as they neared Vanhyrm's rear walled gates allowing entrance to Syvani lands.

There were two sets of gates: one to enter and exit from the coast, while the other was set to enter and exit by land. The system allowed for rapid movement in case of attack and was a protected means of entering and exiting Vanhyrm for the traders.

Rowan was at her side, as was Trinity, clothed in a thick, cordovan wool cloak. The morning light was helping to banish some of the cold around them, but the soft wind was pregnant with frost and mist, which clung to them, soaking deep into their flesh.

It was a short matter to take Trinity from the inn where she was indentured to the outskirts of the settlement walls. A simple explanation about needing the half-elf as a guide in the settlement and Rowan's clout as a Knight of Valkoria allowed for her escape from the city.

Rowan's rank as a knight even gained him free room and board, saving what meager coin still remained in his purse. From there they wrapped Trinity in a cloak, put together the rest of their belongings, and made their way to the great gate on the other side of the town itself — facing the interior of the land and opposite in orientation from where Clara and Rowan had entered the night before.

Together they neared the still wooden wall in the late morning sun. People had begun to go about their business, but not so much so they would have noticed the group of strangers in their midst. Rowan lead the way, with Trinity between him and Clara, who followed behind them all, was watchful of everything around her — ready to strike at any moment should she need to.

"We're almost there," Rowan whispered back to the two women in Telborous, which he found Trinity understood fairly well — much to his amazement.

"You're sure you know the way to Galba?" Rowan turned to look at Trinity who had buried her face deep in the hood of the cloak.

"Yes, I can take you to Galba," she returned the whisper in the same language.

"Just worry about getting past that gate for now," Clara said.

"We'll make it just fine," the youth returned to looking ahead of himself. They were fast approaching the imposing structure. It was like the wall itself, crafted of whole trees, debarked, delimbed, and sharpened to a point on top of their fifteen-foot height. Bolted together with metal rods and tied with thick rope on the top and bottom, it was sturdy barrier to any external aggression.

Guarded on either side by two hide-armored warriors, both of whom carried a sword on their belts, it would be hard to pass through without their permission. Outside the gate was the wilderness of Arid Land: Syvani and the beasts of the wild. The gate to this section of the land was always watched and opened only for raids into the land or trading expeditions to collect raw materials the town didn't have, otherwise they were locked shut.

"We're almost there," Rowan whispered back. "Now let me do the talking, and the rest of you keep quiet."

"Halt!" One of the Nordic guardsmen spoke in his native tongue when they had gotten within fifteen feet of the gate. The guard was bulky — more muscle than fat, and possessed a long moustache flowing over his lip, and down to the bottom of his chin in the same shade of brown as his long hair resting just above his shoulders.

"Who are you, and what are you doing here?" His pale blue eyes ran over their bodies while the other guard, this one more slender and clean-shaven, squinted at the three of them.

"I am Rowan Cortak, Knight of Valkoria. I have urgent business for the Knighthood outside these walls," Rowan straightened himself up under the scrutiny of the other's gaze, speaking in the same language.

"Is that right?" The mustached guardsman moved closer to the youth.

"Who are these people with you then?" He motioned to Clara and Trinity.

"One is a slave I have taken up to help the cause. I have need of her services. The other is my retainer," said Rowan in truth. He hadn't broke the code of Panthor so far, and wouldn't today either.

"Telling me the truth today?" The slender guardsman moved closer to them from behind as the bulkier guard looked Rowan dead in the eyes. His face was hard, like the wood wall behind him.

"A Knight of Valkoria is a man to be trusted," Rowan returned the cold stare of the other.

"Can't see much reason why the Knighthood would be interested in going out there. There's nothing but savages out there," the guardsman rested his left hand on the pommel of his blade while he stroke his moustache with the fingers of his right.

"The way and will of Panthor is not always for us to understand," Rowan spoke with quiet dignity. "I am simply doing what she has called me to do. You are preventing me from doing what she has decreed. The longer we wait, the more you prevent the will of Panthor from being done."

The other guard spoke to the bulkier one as he moved up to where he was standing. "It's not wise to upset a goddess, Bjorn. Their priests are not ones you want to get angry with you. I don't think it's wise to have their knights mad at you either."

A moment was spent as Bjorn looked into Rowan's eyes. The silent code of the Nordic race was exchanged between them — honor, self worth, and strength. Trust was often a hard thing to earn in the world of the Nordican, but once gained, it could be almost impossible to sever.

"Very well then, if it's a goddess' work to be done then," Bjorn stepped aside from the trio, "Be off with you,"

"Thank you," Rowan bowed toward the bulky guardsman.

In a dignified, yet hurried manner, the trio managed to move to the great wooden gate, that, upon their arrival was opened by means of thick rope which squealed on pulleys as two larger Nordican men, those who watched things from on top of the wooden wall, worked the various wrenches and wheels maneuvering the gate.

Within a few agonizing moments, the gates were opened to them. Rowan sighed to himself, as did Clara for a moment, still keeping her watch up though for any signs of treachery that might befall them. In her tutoring of the ways of Nordicans, she had learned not to be totally sure of their manner and methods. They were as hard to read at times as snow-covered ice.

Not wanting to miss their chance at getting their goal accomplished, the trio hurried through the tall gates with great care. Rowan looked back at his kin as they passed them.

"Panthor be with you," he spoke with a slight bow of his head, accompanied by a soft smile.

Bjorn grunted slightly as the other guardsmen minutely nodded toward the blessing. Content they were safely able to continue past the gate they did so, as rapidly as they could.

"Clara," Rowan whispered beneath his breath in Telborous.

"Yes?" The elf also answered in a whisper.

"Keep moving at the same pace," the knight continued. "When we get to the trees, then we can start to let Trinity lead us to Galba."

"Trinity," Rowan moved his head slightly toward the young half-elf.

"I can lead you to Galba. Once we get past the trees, I will lead the way," Trinity spoke in anticipation of the youth's question.

"Good," he replied.

"Why have you freed me?" Trinity looked up at Clara who had turned her cloaked visage to peer inside the hooded smile of the young girl.

"It is the least we could do. You are a living being, and able to make up your own destiny, think for, and rule yourself. You aren't cattle to be bought and sold, or worked in opposition to your intrinsic worth. That is one of the doctrines of my people — one I follow diligently." Clara basked the slave girl in her warm words and affirmations.

"I would very much like to meet your people one day," Trinity smiled back.

"Well, maybe one day you will," Clara also grinned. Silently, the trio entered the tree-lined wilderness, and were swallowed up by the giant green-capped towers in a matter of moments.

Chapter 33

Vinder took in the confused, pain-washed face of the Telborian as he lay on the ground. Blood had poured out from his nose and mouth, curling around his chin, and trickling down his neck on route to his chest. The seasoned dwarf picked up Dugan's hand, his strong charcoal gray fingers clasping the Telborian's wrist. It was still warm and twitched with the pressure of the dwarf's hand upon it.

Instantly, the Telborian's eyes fluttered open, pupils pouring down from the back of his head. A soft groan escaped his lips, then nothing.

"He's alive," Vinder turned to the others.

"Just barely," Cracius spoke. "That was rather foolish." He and Tebow had grown a little closer to the fallen gladiator, but still held their ground so as not to make him too uncomfortable by their presence.

Dugan suddenly bolted up from his prone position. "What happened?"

"You received a measured counter response for trying to enter the dwelling unwelcomed," Tebow answered.

"If you can't get in the damned thing, then how are we going to complete this task in the first place?" Dugan growled as he jumped to his feet, wiping blood away from his face with his dark sleeve. He didn't feel as bad as he looked, but still was a bit rattled from the incident. He was more or less frustrated than anything else.

"You can't go rushing into the home of a power as great, if not greater than the gods themselves. We were invited the last time." the bird fluttered to land on the grass as he sung his reply.

"If you knew that, then why let me run headlong into it?" The Telborian questioned the tiny animal as it hunted about the grass for some more food.

"You seemed to enjoy rushing headlong into things," the bird whistled back.

The Telborian clenched his fist, and grimaced at the small bird.

The avian hopped back from the menacing human, and rustled its wings, then picked at them with its beak.

"Hold your anger." Tebow spoke in quiet authority. "A calm head will solve this challenge.

"The bird is right. The last time we were here we were summoned. I don't know why we've arrived outside the circle, but there must be a reason and together, with sound minds, we shall find it."

"Why do you have a talking bird with you anyway?" Dugan scowled at the bird. "Don't death priests hate living things?"

"There are many assumptions about our order, and devotion which are far from true," Cracius answered, "as to the bird, he came to us from Endarien."

"*Endarien*?" Dugan shook his head lightly. This was getting beyond farcical. "You got a whole *Pantheon* of followers down here or something?"

"I assure you we all share the same goal, though we may hold under the hand of differing authority." Tebow's vocal rhythm told Dugan his concern was a moot point, at least to the priest and he wouldn't answer much more on the matter — if anything.

"Priests," Dugan turned back to the circle. "You are all crazy...you know that don't you?"

"Are you so sure we even need to be inside?" Vinder raised his head toward Tebow; "Maybe we could ambush him before he gets into the circle itself. Maybe that's why we're out here."

Tebow looked at Cracius for a moment. A silent exchange was passed between them before the older priest answered the dwarf's quandary.

"No. We need to get inside. He will be at his weakest inside the circle. Outside we stand less of a chance."

"How do you know all this?" Vinder raised his eyebrow over his lone eye.

"Our god and his allies," Cracius told the stout warrior.

Dugan snorted.

"If he is inside the circle, he will be at the mercies of Galba then and the process of ascension he seeks and so will prove an easier target than when he still is on the defensive, outside the circle," Cracius continued.

A silence hovered over all of them then. None wished to voice their inner thoughts to the other. The task itself seemed impossible — almost absurd. How did one gain entry into the dwelling place of a god or a being equal to or above them in power if they were not wished to enter? The proposition was as fleeting in concept as the clouds that floated in the sky above them. After a while of fruitless head scratching though, Vinder had a thought.

"If only she can allow us in, why don't we ask her to let us in?" The dwarf looked at Tebow. "If she said that you needed to be inside — if you think your god told you — or whomever else you've in league with than maybe all we have to do is ask."

"It sounds just insane enough to work," Dugan turned around to face the two death priests from his own ponderings with a grin.

"We can try. To be honest, I don't think we have anything to lose for trying." Tebow drew closer to the stone circle.

The silent rocks ebbed with power, their hard visage a stone vigil against all opposition.

"Great Galba," Tebow addressed the standing stones. "We have returned, and now seek to enter your sanctum, to stop the desires of our mutual enemy, as you have already made clear to us."

Silence.

After a few moments passed, and each again took a breath, they returned to their thoughts.

"It was worth a try," the colorful bird looked up from the grass where it continued to pick amid the jade blades for spare bits of seed and other delicacies that may have found their way into the green carpet. Thinking was hunger-causing work.

They wouldn't meet up with misfortune though, not yet. As they had slumped back into their thoughts of getting inside a seemingly impregnable place, a soft white light shined out from between the stones, quickly spreading and enveloping the group around the circle of stone. In the blink of an eye they were first around the stone circle, and then gone altogether-the white light swallowing them whole; hammers, bird, people, and all.

It didn't take the group too long to figure out what had happened to each other once they had recovered from the blinding effects of the light. As their eyes cleared with their minds, the group of men, and one colorful bird knew they now stood inside the stone circle.

Dugan stood slightly away from the others and wasn't too impressed by what he beheld. Behind the stones was nothing really of note: a green carpet of grass and the stone circle itself, just as he had seen from outside, though now the circle was concave instead of convex. However, when he peered closer to one of the portals created by the stone circles, he found it displayed a scene from somewhere else. It was the image of a desert where a harsh wind blew the hot sand about like an angry cloud of wasps.

Another curious look at the portal next to it, created by the post and lintel design, showed the very depths of the a sea where fish swam about the presented image as if Dugan were underwater himself beside them. The Telborian turned then to find all twelve portals held some strange image of a land far away — high mountaintops, forests, jungles, even large cities bustling with commerce and citizens. He was dumbstruck at this discovery as each hung between the rock posts as a faint gossamer tapestry, flickering and wavering like a candle's flame in the wind.

Dugan also noticed the others with him had made a similar discovery and were all silenced by the simple wonder of the place that was unlike anything even their wildest dreams could conjure. Even though the priests had been there before, they still found it as breath taking as the first time. With the passage of movement, however, Dugan was able to wrest himself from dumb fascination and focus on the matter at hand, what he was supposed to be doing here.

"Where is this Galba then?" He asked the stones.

"I am here warrior," the voice was like pure ecstasy as it slid up his skin, and into his ears.

"Where are you?" Dugan skirted the empty expanse with his leveled gaze. "If you are so powerful, then show yourself."

A blinding flash of light then shook the very air around the Telborian. He fell to his stomach by the force of the blast, unable to see anything but flares of white before his eyes. Vinder was unharmed by the emission, instead averting his eyes from the pulse to look at the fallen Telborian. The priests as well were unharmed, their humility and inner spirit enforced by Asorlok, shielding them, from any impediment.

"Get up you oaf. You can't talk that way to her. You got to show her some respect," the older dwarf helped Dugan to stand. "Even I know that much, and I ain't a priest."

"I've lost my respect for gods," he stood up on wobbly legs, the blindness in his eyes was still there, but weakening with each passing heartbeat. It wasn't permanent at least.

"They're nothing but cruel tricksters and liars. They have nothing that can aid me now. If I'm supposed to do this task, then fine, but it won't be for some god." He searched for the presence he knew was before him with his blinded eyes.

"Dugan. I know of your plight and sorrow. Take heed though that it was not the words of some god that made you cursed as you are now, but those that came from your own throat." The voice was calm and feminine, but Dugan could still not place the body.

"So you think that it's *my* fault that I'm cursed?" The mighty Telborian threw off Vinder's supportive arm and stumbled around drunkenly searching for the accusing voice. Tiny bits of color had managed to seep into his sight once more but he still couldn't see that clearly.

"So you're saying I wanted to be cursed then? To suffer an eternity of torment?" His rage was growing as he stumbled about the grass launching his accusations at his own unseen accuser.

"No one held a sword to your throat to force it upon you," the voice again came to him. "The decision was yours and yours alone."

"Where are you?" The gladiator took a wild swing at the air in his shambling dance looking for Galba. He had the ability to see some forms again but they were blurry and mutable — insubstantial blobs.

"See and be made whole, Dugan." The Telborian's sight was instantly restored, and the Telborian then beheld Galba.

Her lithe body, draped in a clinging gray robe, made the Telborian's heart dance in delight. Under her garment the body was firm and tone, a warrior's frame if ever there was one, but balanced with a poise and grace that spoke of the deeper allure of the feminine form. Alabaster skin shined like the morning dawn and created a nimbus of soft illumination all about her. Dugan found himself drawn into her deep green eyes framed by luxurious bright red serpentine curls.

Galba's ruby lips parted to speak and Dugan could do nothing but wait upon their every utterance as though they were raindrops from heaven in a desert land. He was speechless before her — powerless to do anything but listen for the time being, and then for an eternity beyond if she let him.

"I am Galba, and I have need of you all." She raised her head and gazed at the others gathered in the circle.

"You four will help to stem the tide of destruction once more flowing into the workings of this world. The Master must not be allowed to leave this place with the mantle of godhood for he is unworthy. You will bring this to pass."

"Forgive me," Dugan fell to his knees. "I will help you in whatever way I can."

Vinder turned to the warrior in shock. "Are you feeling okay?"

"He has finally seen the truth, and the insight has liberated him," Galba stepped closer to the humbled Telborian who did nothing but prostrate himself lower as she drew nearer. "Rise Dugan, and live a while longer."

The Telborian did as he was told, a weight seemingly lifted from his shoulders as he did so.

"You have been brought here by Cracius and Tebow, though I lead their chase, and gave them cause and insight. Even the guide from Endarien is under my sway and command, though it serves the Lord of the Winds. I have called you here, willed you here, for a purpose only you and your companions can complete." The others could do nothing now but listen — even the bird was lost in Galba's unnatural grace and beauty.

"The Master is a threat to all he encounters and as long as he is able to scheme and bring about these plans, he is a great danger to all and a troublesome annoyance to the other powers already reigning over Tralodren.

"For countless ages he has ranted and raved about his ultimate goal of seizing power, and for centuries he has tried to gain it. When the last Age of the Wizard Kings ended almost eight hundred years ago, he was banished to the Abyss to try and keep his ambition in check. Instead, he only thrived there and learned to be more crafty and cruel. It was there he set in motion his escape, timing it perfectly with the visions Gilban received to go out and seek the ruins. The Master knew the ruins would be able to bring

him back to Tralodren because of the relics left behind by the
Dranors.

He was right."

"He used you as pawns bringing himself into the world once
more. He then took Cadrissa to use as a final piece of his plan and
crutch to get him to where he is now. Soon he will enter into this
place to claim his prize, which he thinks to be his right. However,
he is not aware there is one final challenge awaiting him. This
might stop him, but I have my doubts of it doing so, for he is still
very strong, and might succeed. So I have arranged for you, and
the others who were present when he was set free, to be here to
safeguard the occasion, and stop him from leaving should he actually achieve his goal."

"So you say you are the *voice* behind our god then?" Tebow
looked at Galba with a raised eyebrow. The phrase jarred him from
his adoration. How could she mean to say she was behind the spirit
of their god? "I beg to differ for both Cracius and I have known of,
and practiced hearing the voice and will of Asorlok for years. We
heard him give us this mission, his anointing is upon us, how can
you say it is you who did all this?"

"It is true your god is the one who spoke to you, and filled
you with enough of his presence to complete your task, but I was
the one who spoke to your deity in words beyond his understanding
telling him what must be done. He, like the others in the Pantheon,
has heeded my call whether they know it or not.

The priests fell silent at her answer. What could they say
to such a claim? With their own god mute while they were in the
circle, they had little recourse to pursue in response.

"So why do you think The Master will win? What makes
him so much more powerful than the entire Pantheon, and you
yourself? How can he succeed?" It was Vinder's turn to muse
aloud.

"He fights by aid of another. Though he doesn't know it,
The Master himself is a plaything of another force much greater
than himself, and my equal. There is a very good chance he will

succeed in his task, but once he has done so, he will be separated from that force for a while and therefore more vulnerable to attack." Galba raised a slender finger of warning.

"However, this attack will still be deadly and you will all need to face him. The others of your previous band will be arriving shortly for just such a reason.

"So will The Master.

"We must be ready."

"So why don't you just stop him then if you're already so powerful?" Vinder asked. "Why use others as your agents? We're far weaker than you and can't possibly hope to turn the tide against The Master, let alone beat him. We barely survived the last encounter with him."

"I cannot aid more than I have," Galba answered. "I have sworn an oath I shall not directly interfere. I can lead and influence to some degree, but never overstep the bounds of this oath. This is the fight of mortalkind, and I cannot take part."

"Great," the bird huffed with a flutter of chest feathers as he started to trounce about the grass. "You gods are a real strange bunch."

"Prepare while you have the time, he will be here shortly." Galba faded from sight before they could ask her any more questions.

"Well," Dugan turned to the others. "If we're going to do this, and I don't see how we can get out of it at the moment, what have we got then? Any ideas?"

Cracius pulled back his cloak, and revealed Dugan's long sword stuck inside the crimson sash at his waist. He unsheathed the weapon and handed it to Dugan, hilt first.

"Here. We thought you might need it."

"It's a start," Dugan took hold of the blade, trying not to bring to mind the flames it once bore, and the incredible exhilaration he'd felt so recently wielding it in service to Rheminas. "Now we need about a thousand more".

Chapter 34

Hoodwink awoke first.

His head ached, and yellow eyes throbbed. Through blurred vision he could just make out the shape of Gilban next to him. The priest was tied with rough-hewn rope; hands and feet prevented from moving. With a little struggling the goblin discovered he too was bound in a similar fashion.

Hoodwink shook his head to clear it from the pain it was experiencing. He had no idea what transpired. The last he could recall was seeing a tall, red-clad warrior. The brute must have taken him from behind. But where was he now?

He looked around himself again and discovered he and Gilban were inside a cage, crafted from iron bars, and just large enough to accommodate only their slumped-over forms. As more of his vision cleared, the goblin began to see the same red-clad warrior stood by him, guarding the cage from all intrusion. This warrior was strong, and had an aura of cruelty about him the small goblin found unsettling.

So this was where he would die?

The air had cleared somewhat from the volcano, but the heat remained. The warrior guarding the cage seemed unaffected by the warmth, his scale mail armor fitting him like a second skin. Dyed red, it matched his cherry horned helmet, which had been crafted to resemble the horrible visage of a dragon. He wore scarlet leather pants, and high, matching leather boots. His arms were bare, showing off his deeply tanned flesh and well-muscled arms. On his left shoulder was a tattoo of a linnorm's head, done in profile, which was embedded deep into his skin with a bright ruby ink.

Looking further ahead of the warrior, Hoodwink could make out a village of some kind. It was good sized, and well decked out in crimson decorum. Small cooking fires lifted from its center to play and intermingle with scarlet banners and flags circling the perimeter. The homes seemed to be crafted of mud, stone, and wood. Hoodwink even noticed Celetors and Telborians — even a few half-elves as the major inhabitants of the village. Thinking a strange thought, Hoodwink turned back to the guard and saw that on closer inspection, he appeared to be a mix of Celetor and Telborian blood.

"What's going on?" Hoodwink addressed the stoic guard in Telborous.

The guard was silent.

He didn't move at the goblin's following shout. Not yet content, Hoodwink tried speaking to him in Goblin, but again the guard remained as stone.

"Gilban," Hoodwink kicked the slumped over priest in frustration.

The elf awoke with a start.

"What's going on?

"Where am I?

"My hands — Hoodwink?"

"I'm here Gilban. We're *both* here," the goblin cursed in his guttural tongue.

"Where are we?" Gilban's sightless eyes peered out from the cage.

"We're stuck in a cage. Tied like hogs." Hoodwink then proceeded to gnaw on his foot bindings with his jagged teeth. He could just barely reach them if he strained his back, and pulled his legs in, opening his thighs wide to allow the goblin's head and jaws to reach the bindings.

"I take it that we have visitors then," Gilban wiggled to sit up against the warm iron bars. "How many are there?"

"Lots," Hoodwink chewed out as he continued to worked on his bonds. The rope was made of hemp, tasted old, and was soured with a sulfuric aftertaste.

"I must concentrate. I have to confer with my goddess. We must take this next step very carefully." Gilban lowered his voice, and cocked his head toward the goblin.

"Something doesn't feel right about this. Can you see Gorallis any where?"

Something didn't feel right to Gilban?

This couldn't be a good sign.

"No. Haven't seen him yet. Thank the gods." The small green creature had managed to pull a piece of the rope off the larger strand holding his ankles fast. He had started to pull his head back and up, unraveling a continuing line of the rope's binding when the strand broke, causing a new streak of Goblin profanity to utter forth under his breath.

"I will ask for guidance, and then we shall seek the linnorm," Gilban closed his eyes.

"No hurry," Hoodwink was sarcastic as he spat out with more strands of his hemp bindings; a few fibers clinging in his teeth like broken pieces of floss.

As Gilban prayed to his goddess, Hilin approached the cage. The stoic guard suddenly became alive, and bowed to the priest of Gorallis, then stepped away from the cages locked door entirely. Hilin had donned a headdress, which looked like the skull of some large lizard with bone that hinted at a faint, yet potent, carmine shade and draped with white and black strips of cloth. His face was silent, but his eyes screamed in recognition. When they fell upon Gilban they burned into his pious form as the elf petitioned his goddess.

Hilin couldn't believe what he saw before him. Had the vision come true so quickly? Was it time for his master to awake?

Pinpricks of energy fluttered over his body at the realization this old elf was a key to his life's goals. What had he to do now?

How would this play out? What about the glowing object the priest in his vision held? What could it mean?

Where was it?

He would have to know.

"Who are you?" Hilin addressed Gilban in Telborous.

"Hoodwink." the goblin smirked devilishly at the dragon devotee. More thin cords of hemp braids were twisted and hung limply from his yellow-stained, ivory teeth.

"Not you. Him." Hilin motioned to the reverent elf. "Speak to me. I have the power to save you from death for trespassing on the lands of Lord Gorallis."

Gilban remained in communion with his goddess.

He hadn't received any word from her. No divine strength or aura fell upon him. Only the dreaded hidden vision crept around the dim shadows of his mind. The hidden truth stalked him, like some hideous monster wanting to devour his soul, but it didn't dare come into the light...not yet.

He heard the cries of Hilin, and could sense an energy about the dragon follower that spoke of command, and a holy emanation as well but he would not act...not yet.

Saredhel are you here? Gilban mentally called upon his goddess.

"I am speaking to you elf!" Hilin grew colder with each passing moment of Gilban's failure to respond.

In the meantime, Gilban found nothing to promote his goddess' presence in his being. Left without answers and without direction for the first time since joining the priesthood, he opened his blind eyes to Hilin. He had to do what he believed to be the best course. For now that involved speaking to this person who had the presence of a priest of sorts — at least how Gilban could sort it out.

"What do you wish of me?" He answered meekly.

"You're blind," Hilin took in a small, short breath when he finally saw Gilban's pupiless eyes.

"So I am. You must have urgent need with my person. I am now at your full disposal." Gilban adjusted his sitting to raise him higher against the back of the cage.

"Guard, bring him to my quarters," Hilin spoke and then turned in a ruby flourish. The Celetor walked back to the village as the guard did as he was ordered.

Producing a silver key, he opened the cell, thrusting back Hoodwink with one hand and grabbing up the blind seer in the other. The beefy guard hefted the elf over his shoulder. A swift closing and locking of the cage with his other hand and the thin priest was carried away to leave the lone goblin to contemplate his fate. Hoodwink pressed his face between the bars and watched Gilban's departure. He didn't like this one bit.

"Be at peace, Hoodwink, I have a feeling you will be safe for a time," Gilban shouted out to the goblin.

"Great," Hoodwink muttered, then spat out more hemp from between his teeth.

No more than a minute passed before a similar guard came to take up the post which the other had vacated. This was a paler version of the first guard, but with a more menacing air.

"Just great," the goblin repeated.

Gilban was carried into Hilin's presence then dumped onto the dirt floor with a shuffle of the guard's shoulders, falling with a huff. Hilin, like most of the priests of the Red Guard, resided in a scarlet tent, partitioned into various rooms for the priest to live and work. The tent was of a decent size, allowing for storage and study of religious texts, along with rooms for slumber and priestly worship as well.

Though large enough for all these rooms, it was still not that richly decorated, being basic with materials and structures that could be packed up and transported at a moment's notice. The rough furniture seemed more like the sort of decorum one would find in a hunting trip than of an established dwelling of a more urban mindset.

"I have seen you in my visions elf. Who are you?" his eyes searched Gilban's blind face "Why do you come to this place?" Hilin pulled Gilban upright by aid of the scruff of his neck.

"I have seen an object with you as well, a globe of light," Hilin's eyes narrowed as they took in the priest. "Where is it? What is its meaning? "

"I am Gilban, priest of Saredhel. We are on a mission to seek out your master."

"For what purpose? No outsider has ever sought out the great Gorallis if they didn't wish to do him harm," Hilin stepped back from the elder priest. Gilban tried to keep his balance as he spoke on the hard rocky surface, his tied appendages giving him some trouble in that regard, but he was able to manage to stay vertical in the end.

"No. We don't seek harm, but to trade an object which has great meaning for him in exchange for an item that has great meaning to us."

"What is this item?" Hilin's interest was piqued. The vision alone had shown him the importance of this meeting.

Gilban paused a moment.

The elf said nothing, as it seemed his sightless orbs were gazing right into Hilin, burning their white heat through him.

"I sense something about you…are you are priest as well?" Gilban spoke at last.

"What is this item?" Hilin drew closer. His own eyes were pinned into almond-shaped slivers, his broad nostrils flared wide.

"I will tell you, if you will be so kind as to answer some of my questions first," Gilban meekly smiled.

"If that is the way it is to be then," Hilin' s arms crossed like dagger thrusts. "I will humor you."

"Very well. Are you a priest then?" Gilban asked.

"Yes. I am the servant of the great Gorallis. I am one of the more high-ranking priests attending the people of this company."

"So then you believe him to be a god?" Gilban continued.

"Gorallis is immortal. What else can he be? He lives forever, and we are here to serve him and see to it his name is praised and honored above all others of his kind," Hilin answered dutifully.

"I see. I have not heard many tales of Gorallis these past few years. What has he done?" The old priest listened closely now. He wanted to hear what this fellow was about as well as the current status of Gorallis.

"Gorallis has slumbered since before I was born, and into my whole life thus far. He sleeps until his mighty spirit awakens him to command us once more," Hilin recited the answer with pride. It was part of the basic tenets of his faith after all.

"I see," said the elf.

"That time of awaking is now here, however. You have come in keeping of the prophecy that I've had. I saw you appear, and with you an orb of red light." Hilin began to slowly circle the bound priest like a hyena waiting for its sickly prey to fall so it could eat.

"It seems a fascinating omen."

"Your coming heralds his awakening," Hilin stopped his movement after making a full pass around the blind priest; facing him once again with dark anticipation.

"Let's hope you are right — eh, what are you called?" asked Gilban.

"Hilin," the Celetor said dryly.

"Hilin," Gilban repeated.

"Now, if your questions have ended; what of this orb of light? Do you have it?" Hilin put his large hand upon Gilban's frail shoulder, his patience almost spent.

"I have the one object Gorallis would want more than anything else in the world," the elf answered.

"So you have said. What would this object be?" The Celetor's face was laced with sardonic interest.

"His eye,"Gilban's answer sucked the air from the tent, causing an unnatural silence to fall upon all present until they could recover.

"His *eye*?" Hilin's face still was wide-eyed in wonder but he had manged to collect his thoughts and breath to speak. "You have it? But how?" "I must see it," Hilin reached out for the elf with his free hand, but was rebuked by Gilban's words.

"It does not matter to you how it was retrieved. Nor are you to see it. It is the property of Gorallis, and to him it must be presented. Now untie me so that I can do so."

Gilban was glad he'd hid the eye on his person at that point. It gave him the leverage he would need to assure him delivering it to Gorallis himself, unharmed, and unhindered. He just hoped and prayed he would know how to call upon the orb when the time came, and it would wake Gorallis up. He didn't want to have traveled all this way just to find he couldn't rouse a sleeping linnorm.

Hilin was silent.

The dragon devotee didn't know what to do, or if he should believe the blind priest in the first place. The eye of Gorallis? Having never seen his master, he hadn't been certain of the wounded state some legends attached to him, and so thought it's telling a myth in part. The tale, passed down to him spoke of how for hundreds of years the linnorm had suffered the loss of his left eye by a warrior long ago. The loss had carried frustration and anger for the dragon ever since.

Gorallis knew his own body, and it's components had been touched by the divine, and the eye would not suffer decay in the normal manner of things of the flesh. Indeed, his whole being had been deified for some time. How it happened and why, he wasn't totally sure. He had been at one point in time, but as the years went on, some details of his life were forgotten or suppressed so far as to make them inaccessible to all but the most dedicated of thought digging efforts. Such was the affect of time upon his seemingly immortal memory.

The linnorm had ravaged the lands of Tralodren sporadically over the years in search of it, but came up with nothing to lead him to its whereabouts. So, over time, he'd become content to a small degree with life as a one-eyed linnorm. He knew it would just be a matter of time until he found it again. He had to be patient with the progression of events. It would be returned to him again, and when it was, he would be ready to receive it once more, making him whole and unified as before its loss.

Hilin took out his curved hunting knife from his belt and cut the ropes binding Gilban with care, his eyes and mind looking over the elf cautiously. He still had no love for the elf, but he had to trust his recent vision. If what he had been told were true, a glorious day was about to dawn for both him and the all the Red Guard.

"Come," the Celetor priest took the elf's wrist.

Chapter 35

Gilban was lead by Hilin though the fairly good-sized village. He had been given his staff back to help him stay upright while Hilin held onto the hem of his left hand, pulling him onward as he lead. The townsfolk looked on the pair with silent, haunted eyes as the two passed by. The motley collection of races didn't dared hinder the progress of one of their priests, even if he kept strange company — a foreigner and infidel at that.

After a short while, they came to the base of the volcano where Gorallis slept. The town was nestled a mile below the base as to not be too near the heat of the structure, but still suffered intense thermal radiation daily. The Red Guard paid such warmth no mind, for to them they thought it made them stronger, able to endure even the heat from the heart of their god the longer they resided so near — as if they were building up an inner tolerance to it.

Gilban wasn't so enamored of the heat, however. Burning hands strangled him to the point of near suffocation. They slapped his face with each step forward, striking his chest with heavy and energy-draining blows. He smelled the sulfur until it burned his nostrils and lungs, causing claws to dig down his throat and tear at the lining of his lungs even beyond where his trek between the volcanoes with Hoodwink had scraped his flesh. The elf prayed he might have enough strength to enter the lair of Gorallis, but he wasn't so sure he would…not if the heat continued to be so assaulting.

"Are we there?" Gilban huffed

"We are at the mouth of his dwelling," Hilin answered.Sweat covered his own face like linen, and his breathing was la-bored.

"Take me to him, we have no more time to waste," Gilban leaned heavily on his staff. His robes were drenched with sweat, and his frail body had taken on a waxen hue.

"Very well," Hilin lead on into the cave's mouth.

The opening was large, perhaps fifty feet high, and just as wide, if not wider. No one really had measured the opening. Few dared to get so near their god, save the priests — even then this was a rare occurrence. It mattered little about the outside of the mountain, however, only what it held was of importance to the two travelers.

The cavern's mouth was dark, yet dimly-illuminated here and there by the veins of lava bubbling up through the broken rocks to belch and pour themselves out before they crawled back beneath the earth that spawned them; mingling again in Shiril's great cauldron. The raw rock here sizzled like meat on the spit. Everywhere they turned the sound of burning things filled their hearing. Hair on their hands, eyebrows, and even nostrils were singed — the very hair on their heads felt like flaming straw.

Gilban felt sure he'd die in the heat.

As soon as he had the thought, the probing darkness of the earlier unknown vision came back and taunted him with its enigma. The strange feeling hammered at the edges of his mind, causing the older priest confusion and concern. He was too tired and focused at the moment to think of anything else, save the task at hand: finding Gorallis.

"How much further?" He wheezed.

"We are almost there. Just a few more moments in this tunnel, and we will be there," Hilin's breathing was short and labored.

"Saredhel preserve me from this furnace," Gilban huffed.

The two turned from limited darkness into an inferno of illumination. Gilban couldn't see it, but he felt the intense rise in temperature. The two had walked into the very heart of the volcano. Prayers and faith in their own gods must have kept both priests safe, they assumed, else they would have been dead long ago — fried to a cindery crisp. Faith was what held them up now and gave them strength even if the flesh that held the spirit behind it wilted like a flower.

"We are here," Hilin remarked, as he himself was amazed with the sheer size of the cavern. He had never been here by himself. Only with the guidance of an older priest had he come here once before. He had forgotten how majestic it all was. It had to be at least a mile in diameter, and rose at least another mile higher still, where a tiny dot, which served as the vent for the volcano, was situated. The two priests stood on a thin ledge ending over a deep pool of magma not more than a hundred feet from the overhang.

The lake of fire before them was immense. Fumes that had been overpowering before struck the two with a force greater than anything they had ever known. Swaying like a piece of cloth in a breeze, Gilban steadied himself on his staff. Sweat had been pouring out of every pore like they were fountains, and he felt as if he would soon faint into steam.

He had been able to see, he would have noticed Hilin was in the same condition. Gorallis' priest's red clothes had turned deep claret, and clung to his body drenched in perspiration. He too looked like he was about ready to faint, but had no staff to help him in the battle, and so swayed slightly on the cliff willing himself to stay conscious or stay focused on Gilban and seeing his god arise before him.

Faith again sustained him.

"We are in the very heart of his lair. The heat of his presence overpowers us, and yet he is merely sleeping. Here is the heart of my god's throne and power." Hilin's hand became a talon on Gilban's shoulder.

"Now. Awaken him so we might be called to be his once more, Hilin commanded, "so his power and majesty might reign over all Tralodren again, and the Crimson Flame can consume all."

Gilban wanted to get Gorallis' attention, but didn't know how. Hilin, his priest, didn't seem as if he knew how to awaken his lord either. Gilban had hoped he might be able to get something from his goddess. Something to help his mind wrap itself upon the conclusion, but nothing came. Only the same dark, overbearing shadow of an image assaulted him. The mocking image seeking to elude all his inquiries.

What would he do?

What could he do?

Having no other option, he took out the eye from its hidden location, where it began to glow a bright, golden hue. Maybe the eye alone was the answer. He didn't know, but realized if he were to stay in here much longer, divine protection or not, he would be dead soon enough.

"The *eye!*" Hilin choked on the burning fumes grating his lungs and blurred his eyes with tears. "The Eye of Gorallis!"

"Yes," Gilban whispered, then held it aloft, letting the light of the orb shine brighter and brighter before them. The golden illumination overflowed onto the priest and shot out a beam deep into the center of the writhing lake before them. The light beam sunk beneath the liquid rock with blinding speed, digging into the pool like a falling pebble.

The flash of the beam was instantaneous, and then it dimmed to a dull red orb once more. Gilban had no idea what had happened, but heard Hilin collapse to his knees in awful worship and praise.

"It is just as I *have* foreseen. You have come to raise my lord," Hilin then started to mumble in strange chants and psalms of worship to his reptilian god.

Gilban was silent for a moment, unable to contemplate his next move. Why was his goddess so silent at such a crucial time? As he waited, he finally felt the presence of his goddess overshadow him. A joyful peace returned when he felt her familiar touch within him, which only increased when he felt a call that his goddess wanted him to perform.

It was time.

The words then came to his lips.

"Gorallis. Hear me." Gilban shouted over the churning magma. "I have your eye and wish to return it to you for a favor."

Both priests then grew still.

Hilin remained prostrate before the lake, his teary face turned upward while Gilban took the orb back into the hiddenfolds of his robes. Stillness came upon the room like a gentle, gauzy breath. It was almost as if the world itself had stopped, and only the two priests alone remained alive in the still, silent, cosmos.

There was silence for some time.

Only the heat and seething lava filled the cavern. Then slowly, the lake of lava changed.

It slowed its boiling, then stopped — becoming like freshly molten glass. The stillness was then disrupted by a large rock jutting out of its formerly serene surface. The rock rose from the exact center of the lake with a smooth, fluid motion. As it rose, other, smaller rocks budded around it. These stones became small horns on a great reptilian face longer than a catapult, and wider than five war horses lined end to end. The first rock itself formed part of a large snout.

The head rose high into the domed sky above it by aid of a long, thick neck of crimson scales, studded on its back with black spikes which looked to be as tall as a Nordic male, all dripping with lava. Two massive forelimbs, acting as arms, erupted from the steaming brew, and dug into the earth before and below the two priests, causing the earth to tremble and Gilban to almost fall over. They were like ruby towers; sturdy and immense their taloned digits digging long scars deep into the rocky ledge of the lake to drip beads of magma. These streaming, pyroclastic drips fell around the priests and back into the pool below with explosive hisses.

Indeed, the linnorm itself seemed to match the color of the lava in which it sat. A fiery orangish-red body almost glowed amid the spattering of cold, black scales. To the imaginative mind the whole linnorm itself could have been crafted from magma; a living being of lava.

Hilin instantly lowered his head as one large, reptilian, yellow eye looked down on the pair. Gorallis dominated the whole lake. With his claws on the edge, and head in the center, it seemed impossible such a colossal form could be hidden beneath the lava. Just how large he really was, none knew — and it was common lore linnorms never did stop growing. It could very well be he was as large as the volcano itself now — having grown too large for it over his recent rest.

The linnorm's lone right eye spied the form of Gilban, and hovered over him for a moment. Gorallis' left eye socket was scabbed over and covered in tiny scales with a deep scar running from the top of the socket to the bottom. This scar could have been a pathway wide enough to serve as a footpath or game trail, had it been made in the wilds of some wood. The linnorm had lived with his impairment so long he'd almost forgotten life with two eyes. What the priest had said though, helped rouse him from his half slumber; the power of the orb having pulled him from a deep sleep to that half-slumber to hear his words in the first place.

For a moment there was relative silence, then a deep voice spoke. It was so strong the very walls of the volcano shook, causing small chunks of debris to fall in the pool below.

"Who hast awakened Gorallis?" The linnorm spoke in antiquated Pacoloes.

"I have," the blind seer turned his head toward the loud speech also speaking in Pacoloes, though of a more modern dialect. "Gilban Polcrate."

"Thou dost not serveth me. For what purpose hast thou done this?"

"I have come great Gorallis," Gilban's grace and manner had become more diplomatic and honorific to the elder linnorm, "to ask an exchange from you. I wish to collect the Scepter of the Wizard Kings to hinder a growing threat I have been commissioned to stop. In return I will give you your eye in fair exchange."

Gilban craned his head as high as his neck would allow, but knew the linnorm's head was higher still.

The massive head silently swung down to take in the priest straight on. The yellow orb, which was dissected with a vertical black pupil, contracted like the beating of a heart upon observation of the elven priest. Gilban's own heart nearly stopped from the sheet of heat that was the linnorm's breath as it was added to the blaze already all about them. He prayed he could hold out a little while longer, as he felt himself grow dizzy; his legs start to become numb.

"Why shouldst I honor thy exchange whilst I could slay thee now and takest mine eye once again?"

"Such a thing would be unwise, great Gorallis for I have a vital task to perform, and to hinder it would be to anger those who sent me," the priest countered as strongly as he could amidst the growing weakness he felt around and inside himself.

"Who hast sent thee to me?" Gorallis whispered.

Small pebbles bounced off Gilban's head.

"A vision compelled me. A vision sanctioned by my goddess, Saredhel," Gilban prayed for more strength to stay the course.

"And pray what didst thine vision reveal?" Gorallis moved his head a little ways from the blind seer, taking a fair deal of the heat with him.

"That I will have need of this scepter to stem a rising threat, as I have already stated," Gilban breathed a little easier with the temperature reduction; his feeling of fainting lessening.

"That ist all then?" Gorallis asked with mild suspicion.

"That is all I was told."

"Such blind faith in things thou knowst nothing about," Gorallis drew in a deep breath through his nostrils, as a small tongue of flame licked his lips. "Thou must be a fool or indeed a true man of faith. For only either wouldst brave mine lair in hopes of rousing me for this parley." The linnorm drew further away from the priest, back into the center of the lake of magma.

"I only do as I am compelled by my goddess, nothing more. This threat must be great, indeed as you have rightfully spoken if I'm here now with the one thing you covet most," the priest returned.

"Indeed, it wouldst seem," Gorallis mused.

"Thou, priest of mine sect. Rise," the yellow eye veered to Hilin, the linnorms words now in Telborous, though still antiquated.

"Lord?" Hilin did as he was bidden.

Gorallis took a moment to study Hilin with a long, silent stare.

"What does my lord wish of me?" Hilin kept his head and eyes low the sockets of his bone helmet being level with his god's gaze as he spoke.

"Dost thou believeth me magnificent?" Gorallis snaked closer to the dragon cultist.

"Yes lord," Hilin exploded in praise.

"Hast thou dedicated thy life to mine service?" Another glimmer of flame darted across the linnorm's scaled lips.

"I have been your servant since birth my lord, as my father was before me and his father." Again the Celetor was jubilant in his proclamation— proud to be here before his god.

"This pleaseth me," Gorallis purred.

Hilin smiled at his master's pleasure as sweated continued to pour down his face.

"Dost thou wish to serve me now?"

"Yes Lord," the Celetor bowed his head.

"I hunger." Before a moment could pass, Hilin disappeared. The lightning fast jaws of the linnorm swallowed the priest whole. Too fast for a scream, too quick for regrets, the Celetor was chewed twice by the man-sized teeth, then became one with his deity.

Gilban was silent. Though he knew what had happened, he showed no fear. He wasn't destined to die, not yet. So he waited in faith.

"Mine love for gods is surely lacking, and of growing threats I hath scant concern, but to children of Cleseth I oweth a debt. Tis good now to repayth it in full. So willst I do as thou request priest, instead of roasting thee alive where thee stands," Gorallis again returned to Pacoloes.

"I thank you Gorallis for your wise and charitable decision," Gilban returned with a small bow of his head.

"What ist the date?" The linnorm lowered his head to get a closer view of Gilban.

"It is the 19th day of Khulian, 753 P.V.," Gilban responded.

"So I hath slept for more than forty years?" Gorallis whispered, though the quieted words still echoed like the boom of thunder in the cavernous chamber.

"It would seem as such, yes," Gilban agreed.

"Before we proceedth. I wish to gaze upon the item with which thou claimth to maketh trade. I wouldst know if thy words spake true priest, or thy proveth be as wild as the world is large."

"Here," Gilban retrieved the orb from its secreted location, then held it up for inspection.

Gorallis was silent as he studied it. His huge nostrils, that could swallow two men in their own right, sniffed at it while his lone eye scrutinized every facet of it, like a jeweler deciding how best to cut a diamond.

"Where didst thou find it?"

"That is of little concern," Gilban lowered the orb to his side, his light-headedness was increasing due to the Gorallis' proximity, and needed it there to keep his balance.

"Fair enough, though bold in statement," The linnorm snorted out sulfuric gusts. "Dost thou knowth the workings of the scepter thou seeketh?"

"No, not yet. I trust you can provide such information as part of the exchange."

"This can be done," returned the linnorm. "Understand, though, oh priest, that it canst only be used once by thee in thy lifetime. Once and nothing more."

"I understand."

"Then I shalt trade thee for mine eye for it is more than worthy an item of exchange. Place it in its socket, and I shalt then bring forth to thee the scepter that thou seeketh."

Gorallis laid his head down between his massive claws. The sagged area of the empty socket looked horrid and grotesque when compared with the rest of the magnificent beast, like the very skin of a rotten piece of fruit. With some minor maneuvering, Gorallis was able to place his empty eye socket close enough to the blind priest's reach to aid him in returning the orb from whence it came.

"You must direct me then," Gilban moved forward.

"I shalt."

Gilban felt the globe stir in his hand, growing warmer and larger in size as he took a few steps forward. The increased heat told him of Gorallis' nearness — even closer than he had been before. The priest used his staff to avoid falling over the ledge, as well as steady himself for his task. The rest of his body and mind was dedicated to carrying the orb.

"Higher," Gorallis ordered.

The apple now felt as a grapefruit as the priest obeyed, lifting the swelling orb higher into position.

"Higher," Gorallis repeated.

Now the orb required two hands to wield as it has swelled to the size of a melon.

"To thy right, priest." The inferno of the linnorm's mouth when he spoke, about did Gilban away, but somehow he managed to keep his sweat-drenched, overheating frame focused on the task at hand. The melon still grew in size and heat, even taking on a yellow hue.

"More," Gilban could hear the lava cooling on Gorallis' skin as the linnorm compelled him onward. The blind elf thought his hands would melt as the heat became almost as intense as the lava around him.

"Yes, now holdth it there. Push it into mine skin. Harder," growled the linnorm.

The priest felt a slimly gel run over and down his hands and arms as he begun to apply pressure to it's still-growing surface. He knew the globe had also taken on a strange, slightly spongy feel to it as well, almost like a boiled egg as he pushed it past and into the scarred, sagging scales deeper into the linnorms empty socket.

He could feel it rupture the rough scales and scabs, even hear the ripping and tearing like the sound of a drum stick being pulled from a cooked turkey. Then a sensation like pushing a marble into a large wad of dough ensued, which preceded a massive roar from Gorallis.

Rocks fell from above splashing huge puddles of lava far into the air, narrowly missing Gilban. The deafening noise floored the priest with a hard shove. An explosive flash of red and gold filled the chamber, and flew up and out of the opening at the roof itself.

Then it was over.

In its wake the once single-eyed Gorallis now saw with two yellow, black-slitted orbs glaring at the fallen priest in delight. Fire danced amid their gleam, and a smile creased the folds of the beast's scaly lips. Had Gilban been able to see, he would have seen the face of a delighted, but still deadly linnorm.

"Thou hast done well, priest," Gorallis chuckled. More sprays of peeble-sized debris rained down upon him shook lose from the great linnorms thunderous mirth.

"Then I can have the scepter now?" Gilban struggled to stand, fighting off the rush of blood running to his head, as well as the constant sensation of passing out at any moment.

"Thou shalt."

Chapter 36

adrissa looked about herself with a panic welling up inside. She had last been in a frighting realm of gloom, and now she was in the middle of a wilderness. All around her were songs and signs of life. Birds sung their songs of jubilation, and the air was clean and crisp as it is after a rain shower and overlaid with the dusting of wild flowers. It was simply breathtaking in its entirely. Beside her stood The Master.

Restored from his injuries, and without his staff, he stood looking out at the green scenery around him seeming to be trying to make sense of what had happened to them as well. His face was as cold and emotionless as stone but Cadrissa couldn't fight back any curiosity.

"Where are we?" Cadrissa circled The Master. Her feet were lost in the tall grasses, the soft fragrant flowers filling her lungs.

"Arid Land," The Master stated as dead as he looked.

"Arid Land?" She had read all she could from the great book when she had been in The Master's tower, but it wouldn't be enough to keep her safe and navigate the land, especially with all the odd occurrences and entities that seemed to flock around The Master and his cause, intruding as they pleased.

"I'm not quite sure where we are in it, nor how we got here, though. Tell me what happened after the fall?" He turned toward her, and his blue eyes burned into her own green orbs. "And I might overlook your foolish alliance with Endarien."

"Well…there was this darkness, and it told me to help you… it even healed your wounds and then…then I guess we wound up here," she offered up what she could; her own mind not quite sure of what to make of this, fearful of what might befall her under The Master's wrath given the aid she had rendered to his enemy.

"Indeed…" The Master pondered.

"So it looks like you have someone wanting you to succeed," Cadrissa blurted out, then quickly closed her mouth.

The Master was silent for a moment, then spoke to the wizardress.

"How long ago was this?"

"No more than a moment. Why?" She returned with a fear rising inside her. What was she doing here, and why? Worse still, was The Master now finished with her company?

"It's been at least a month since the battle with Endarien," the lich's words were flat.

"A month?" Cadrissa was flabbergasted; fear now forgotten in light of this new revelation. "Are you sure? But how-"

"I'll need a moment to get my directions," the dark mage started to turn around to resume his searching of the wild. "Now that we are here, I need to know just how far we are from Galba."

"Aren't you curious though to figure out who is supporting you? How this all happened, and why?" Cadrissa spoke her own thoughts aloud once more.

The Master's eyes darted back at Cadrissa. All her inquisitiveness was stripped away from her in an instant.

"Not at the present time, no. I have no allies, and so find their aid dubious at best. All the more reason to hurry along here as others must be gathering around me like vultures to a kill." The Master hovered toward a patch of dark blue flowers which filled a small section of green grass with their brilliant color, much like a glob of paint that had fallen from an artists brush high above them. "Now, cease your prattling, and make yourself useful. Keep watch while I collect my thoughts."

"Okay," Cadrissa quietly muttered. She didn't want to upset the situation by saying she didn't know how she could stop anyone who was against him, since so far it seemed he was fighting the gods themselves — and winning.

Instead, she took in the wonder of Arid Land about her. It was just too beautiful. She had never seen anything like it in all her life. Behind the tall, rocky exterior closing the land off from the sea, it was pure virgin pinewood. It was like nothing had touched the land since the beginning of time, and it went on for miles in all directions. The wizardress was breathless with the wonders and serene eminence soaking into her body and soul with each gentle wafting of the air around her. If indeed paradise could be found on Tralodren, then she had found it. In her pocket, the medallion hidden there throbbed for a momentary burst of heat and then was silenced.

The Master was far from calm. He paced in the flower patch, trampling down the steams and buds, chanting minor spells for direction and location, trying to channel energy for seeking his exact location.

Nothing worked.

He was blocked in each attempt.

He felt a force behind the blocking of his own abilities, and it was immense, though he'd thought it would have happened later as he neared Galba, he took it in stride. He knew then he was close to his goal. He had learned through exhaustive study Arid Land was where even the gods did not go for there was an ancient pact of some type, of which he was not too clear on the details, which they had enacted long ago. Further, he knew the very entity he sought — Galba herself, would try to block and hinder his arrival as part of a test to see how worthy any of those who sought out godhood were. He had no fear of proving his worth to anyone. However, it was going to be challenging.

Without previous access to his internal reservoir of mystical energy, he had no idea where he was. He was effectively walking blind into any sort of danger ahead of him, and was not totally sure of the true location of Galba as well. The thought was not pleasant, though he had Cadrissa with him. He knew she could still be able to retain access to her internal energies while he couldn't, since she wasn't seeking Galba for godhood. It would give him a small advantage, but not much of one. It was one of the reasons why he had abducted her in the first place, and he'd exploited that advantage as best he could.

Why he had presently arrived here a month later than his original departure from his tower he couldn't say. He didn't think it could be remedied now at any rate with an answer and the longer he stood here pondering it the more time he wasted from his ultimate pursuit.

It was time to finish his journey.

"Cadrissa," his voice was cold and hard.

"Yes?" She turned to face The Master, her mind being pulled away from the pleasantness, away from the lich.

"The time has come to make the last great leg of my journey, and now you must serve me more faithfully than ever before." His face held on it a great stern expression. It spoke of the danger existing for those who halted him from getting what he wanted. "You will obey without question and look to follow my interests until my goal has been attained. Once that is done, then I will have no further use of you."

"Then I'll be free?" Cadrissa spoke up softly, though she found it next to impossible to speak, or even tear her eyes away from Cadrith's penetrating gaze. Worse yet, think beyond the meaning of his utterance.

"If that is how you understand it," The Master turned toward the horizon. It was lined with thick pockets of pine forest, and beyond that, a great wall of mountains that seemed to go on forever. The sun was just reaching its zenith, and the fierce light beat down upon the duo with relentless effort. "I need you to concentrate your mind and body upon a great well of mystical energy outside yourself. Find it, and tell me where it is," The Master rejoined Cadrissa's side.

Instantly, the wizardress' mind was stuck hard on the task. It would be difficult to seek since she was not that trained in such spells, but she tried with all her might nonetheless. The action came to her with less effort than she thought it would, and it shocked her at the ease in which she preformed it. She felt the pull of a colossal power from what she discovered resided in the east.

It was a great, overflowing well of cosmic energies, like nothing she had felt before, or would ever feel again. The energy was like the heart of some beast, or the center of all the collective will of the world — an immense fountain sharing its waters with but a brief few and no more, keeping all it held contained within itself. Cadrissa could taste those undiluted waters as she sought it out with her spell, and they were delightful, if not intoxicating.

She could also feel the small bundle of heat in that hidden pocket within the folds of her robes. It seemed to grow in intensity along with a wreath of voices that had risen around her head as well. Faint and scampering just outside the realm of comprehension. What was this?

What—"Have you found it yet?" The Master's face marred into a scowl.

"I believe so," her voice was trance-like as she stayed in her spell. The previous voices and heat in her pocket had fled at the harsh, cold words of The Master. "I think it is to the east."

"Are you sure?" The Master pressed.

"I feel its presence…it's powerful. I doubt I could mistake it." Cadrissa replied dreamily.

"Good." He gripped her arm with a strong hand, pulling the mage back from her trance. "We have to be quick. I don't like this wilderness."

"It seems very peaceful," Cadrissa turned to the lich, as she awoke; doing the best she could to hide the disgust she felt at The Master's touch.

"Exactly." Ravenous flames flickered in his eyes.

"There," The Master's other hand pointed to a lone hill in the distant East. It rose above the treeline for a brief moment, then was swallowed once more upon its descendent. It looked more like a giant's bare knee jutting out of the tall pines and many miles away at that. Too far for walking, at any rate, if he wanted to get their quickly. "That is where my destiny awaits. That is the final leg of the journey.

"It is where the world once turned."

"The world once spun from that very place?" Cadrissa looked with questioning eyes at the wizard. "I still don't understand."

"This is the very beginning my dear. Here the power of the gods was forged, and the very fabric of reality was brought into being. That spot is the holiest and most sacred of places on the planet, and I must go there."

"That's Galba then? We're going there? Wouldn't something of that nature be dangerous for us to go to?" Cadrissa thought it all right to ask this of him, as it was a valid concern after all.

The Master turned toward Cadrissa with a sickening expression of sarcastic sincerity. "Where is your *faith*? This is no more challenging than fighting Endarien himself. You, of all people, should understand this. You're a wizard. Such things come easy to you. We are above others of this world.

We are more than mortals; so much more."

Cadrissa hid her fear and rejection from the wizard's statements. He spoke from the Path of Power, and used the words defining that reality. To Cadrissa it was a repulsive and wasteful path of pursuit, but she wouldn't dare tell The Master such opinions. Not if she wanted to live. Nor would she tell him she had come to believe there really was true evil and good in the world — and she believed she was in the midst of the more potent forms of evil. This abduction had changed her.

Through this trek to meet Galba would be an experience never forgotten, and the tale to tell, if she survived, would be glorious as well, she had some doubts that lingered on her mind. Doubts she didn't have the luxury of dealing with at the moment.

"So far, you have served me well," The Master's azure eyes blazed at the wizardress, "and you have been allowed to keep your life because of this. But this is the most dangerous time — dangerous for you not me. I have but one further use for you. If you serve me well on this last task, you will be free. If you fail, you will die.

"I am going to that outcropping now," the lich pointed out a piece of land that seemed a good distance away from them beyond miles of forest and a few more tall rises of hills — a hard tiring journey for sure, she thought. "You will follow. It is here where the final task will be undertaken. When it is done, then all shall be as it should, and I will be a god."

Cadrissa said, nothing she only dared to view the hard-lined face of the lich with a contemplative glare. A face which until recently had been a horrid mass of charred bone and skin.

"We leave now," The Master took hold of Cadrissa's other arm with an even tighter grip, pulling her to face him dead on. "Open your mind to me, and join me in the spell's casting. Grant me access to your own well of mystical energies. And do not question me any further…I will show you wonders still," The Master then swung both hands above his head, releasing her arm in the process. He was careful to cast a spell which was just strong enough to get him to where they needed to be, and not too strong as to drain Cadrissa completely of her energy as he felt she didn't have that much left in reserve and he might have need of her again before his ascension.

Cadrissa opened her mind to the lich. Though she didn't much like the thought, she dwelt on the fact she had nothing much left as an option. She had to follow this madness to the end. There was no more turning back…as if she had been fated to do little else. As she opened herself up to The Master, she felt a pinch in her gut, like something was pulling something out her, and then had a rush of adrenaline.

In the center of where they met, an orb of black energy formed. The thick, black ichor fell from above The Master like spilt tar, flowing down in a dome covering both The Master and Cadrissa. The pitch substance poured over them from head to toe. When the gel reached their feet, the pulse of magical energy overpowered her and she felt as though she was lighter than air. The sensation only lasted a moment, and then it all went black to her understanding.

She felt nothing at all.

Nothing save thought.

It was as if her very body was gone from all reality, and all that remained was her mind and spirit. It frightened her and at the same time excitement was flowing faster in her mind than what she could ever think she couldn't wait to see what was coming.

And it was coming soon.

The darkness of The Master's augmented spell lasted for a moment then it was over. The power that should have released faded, was weakened even though he tapped into Cadrissa to unleash it. Though he should have been able to circumvent the restriction on his own spell casting abilities, the spell was blocked nonetheless. The Master grew more frustrated at this hindrance. He was being toyed with and he wasn't the least bit amused by it.

Cadrissa looked about herself as they remerged from the dim inkling of The Master's reduced spell. They had appeared in a deep wood. Shadowed from the light above them by a thick, canopy of various pine trees, the dim under life of green surrounded them in a still embrace. Tall, knotty pine trunks shot into the sky, and choked out the younger under life, preventing any other growth, save a short bush, vine, or patch of shade thriving flowers.

He had no idea where he was, and couldn't even sense the faint aura of Cadrissa's own inner energy. For once in his long, and unnatural years, he was, as he appeared to be — a normal mortal man. Each moment under this realization caused the anger to seethe deep within him.

He would not be made a plaything!

He refused to be treated in such a manner. He was The Master — not the servant. As The Master silently stewed, Cadrissa studied the scene around her. It was wonderful, but still confusing to her.

"This isn't the spot," Cadrissa stated softly, hoping to tread very softly with this statement.

"No. It isn't." The Master's jaw clenched.

"Where are we then?" She continued to search about herself. "What's happened?"

"Silence." The shout was near deafening to the woman.

For a moment she was rendered rigid and silent like the trees around her. Then The Master pushed ahead into the woods. His elegantly draped frame pushed into the undergrowth in an Eastern direction with the destructive drive of a soldier bent on bloodlust. All the while he silently plotted his revenge on those who were now mocking him and hindering his progress, savoring its flavor upon his tongue.

"Come," The Master waved a hand back to Cadrissa. He didn't even look at her, simply beckoned.

She ran up to join him.

"Follow," was all his clenched teeth would allow to come out of his mouth.

Cadrissa looked after him, then followed behind through the large forest.

"We walk the rest of the way," his tone was flat and dead.

Cadrissa bit down on her tongue, to stop herself from asking a new line of questions. Instead, she sunk her shoulders in defeat and tried to commit her efforts to keeping up with the dark mage. She dreaded to think what he might do to her should she fall too far behind for his liking.

Lost in a wood so large it could have been seen as a sea of trunks and leaves, Cadrissa and The Master wandered with near silent steps. The Master was unusually quiet throughout the journey. His face was a stern lipped statue.

His manner was harder still.

For hours the two hiked without speaking through the thick wilderness around them, the lead wizard's feet jabbing the ground in sharp strokes. The other mage followed behind with gentle steps. She had only to step where The Master trod to keep him happy. He was too concerned in his thoughtful rage to make any further comments about anything, but still Cadrissa hadn't said a word — content just to be able to observe the world around her that caught and held her thoughts throughout the entire journey.

She wanted to stop and study it all, but The Master kept dragging her onward one rapid step at a time. Through it all though, she keep wondering where the Syvani were. The book she had read said the whole race lived and dominated Arid Land — which she could see was far from being arid. If that was true, then she felt any inhabitants must have been hiding. Surely they had large enough communities the two wizards would have come into contact with at least one or two on their journey. She had thought they would have found at least some sign of civilization: an old campfire, a fallen tree caused by an axe...something. So far Arid Land had proven to be more savage and wild than inhabited.

"Do you think we might be able to stop to rest a bit? I'm getting tired." Cadrissa braved a comment to her captor after the several hours long trek. Her legs had begun to burn, and her feet felt as though they were on fire.

"We will keep going," The Master kept moving, "Rest is for the weak. Keep up the pace."

"I'm afraid I can't," Cadrissa pleaded.

"You will," The Master plodded onward, not even looking behind himself; always pressing forward.

The woman had no recourse but to continue to push forward too. She had no desire to risk the ire of the dark mage, not now, in his already foul state. Further, she hadn't the strength or enough mystical energy left to see her through such an encounter, as her mind was starting to dwindle. It began to see things around her with diminished interest. All became like a blur. It was too hard to think. Too hard to want to go on with any form of thought other than to keep her feet moving forward, and her head fixed on where her power-mad captor lead her.

What could she do? How could she keep going on without passing out as she felt she would quite soon? She had walked more than she had ever thought possible in her whole life. Her feet groaned from within her boots and her head was wet with perspiration. Her chest was hot and felt like claws were trying to dig out of her ribs with each breathe. She could even feel her heartbeat hard in her chest; a hammer working away at the soft tissue around it. How much more could she endure? She had no spells that could help her, and her body not used to this much manual exercise…she couldn't last forever.

"I-I," Cadrissa stopped her speech short when her eyes caught a glimpse of movement to her left.

Then she saw it again.

She was sure of it.

A soft rustling sound off in the distance, and a form between the trunks of two trees.

What was it? More importantly, did The Master see it as well?

He didn't seem to notice the movement; his vision was too internal.

What could it be, though? Surely not animal life. It looked too humanoid for that. It had to be something else. A Syvani? A real live elf? But what was he doing? Was he friend or foe? Worse yet, what would happen to her next?

What would they want from her?

She had been told from the book they were a simple, yet barbarous people. If that were true, then it would be a more dangerous thing than what she first thought could happen to her. She prayed some god somewhere would have pity on her; Dradin, the god of learning and magic would hear her pleas and save a prized pupil from slaughter. But then Cadrissa recalled how true Endarien had been to his promise of salvation from harm, and so decided not to put much faith in her personal god from doing much better.

She saw another form move around her…

Another…

Then another.

They were appearing out of the wild more and more, like jackals to a kill. Cloaked in the shadows of the trees, only quick glimpses of ginger hair and tanned animal hide covered skin came to her vision. She could sense a shift in the air though by their presence. It was a kind of harsh and heavy hand upon her throat and chest, which crushed what remained of her spirit and filled her with fear. If she could see so many forms now, surely The Master could as well.

What was he thinking? Did he have some plan to deal with them and get them out of this situation? Was this were they would part company then — he'd use her as a diversion for his escape? The thought was terrible, but not unlikely given The Master's nature.

"Do you know we are being followed?" She tried to speak it as softly as she could.

The lich didn't stop in his march. "Yes."

"Then what are we going to do?" Panic had risen in her throat like bile.

"They are of no consequence," The Master was smugly dismissive.

Cadrissa disagreed with his assessment. "I have counted more than twenty forms in the last hour. Their numbers increase the longer we stay in this wood," the wizardress whispered.

"You forget we are wizards. They are nothing but a minor annoyance to us. Now keep quiet and keep moving." A gesture to keep up the pace was all she could get from him.

There was a strange noise for a moment, then silence. It sounded like a rush of wind, then nothing. Ignoring it, like everything around him, The Master kept moving, but now found he couldn't. His left foot had been pinned to the ground. It wasn't magic holding his foot in place, nor any natural root or vine. Instead, an arrow jutted out of it — a green fetched arrow that still shook from the force of the impact that drilled it into the dark mage's flesh, pinning it to the ground beneath.

The Master looked at it with disgust. He felt no pain, and it released no blood, just annoyance, and anger at being held back from his goal that much longer.

"What is it? Why have we stopped?" Cadrissa looked over The Master's shoulder, only to grow wide-eyed when she saw the lone wooden, green fletched shaft.

"It seems the gnats have begun to raise their level of annoyance," The Master growled.

"What are we going to do? I counted more than forty in the past moments as we walked on. They are growing larger all the time. I don't think they take too kindly to strangers around here." Fear had crept into her voice now as well as her throat and head. She didn't want to die. Not here at any rate.

"They will learn the meaning of their insolence and for wasting my time on such a petty matter as trespassing their wood," The Master spoke in dry, hate-filled tones.

No sooner had he uttered these words, however, then a great crack of tendon and wood filled the forest, and green-fetched arrows began to rain down upon the two wizards in a shower of death. The sky above them and the spaces between screamed out for their demise. Hundreds of bronze, bone, and stone tipped, green-fletched, wooden shafts sailed toward the wizards, competing with their brothers for their blood, to sup their internal waters of life as deep as they could plunge.

Cadrissa stared at the oncoming onslaught with a colorless face unable to more or think, only watch as the arrows drew near.

Chapter 37

oodwink scratched the old metal ground of his cell with his fingers. He didn't like being left alone for so long. It was maddening. He felt unsure of what to do, and even if he should act.

Surely he was dead already.

He was in a cage, a captured foe of a larger force. He needed a decent plan since he was beginning to feel he wouldn't see Gilban again. He was truly on his own now and had to be about trying to get himself away from these red-clothed fanatics before their mood changed, and his throat found its way to a chopping block.

The goblin had finally freed himself from his bindings shortly after Gilban left and now watched the red-garbed guard in front of his cage with a closely hardened focus. He wouldn't notice a goblin that much. Not a lowly speck of creation like Hoodwink. At least he shouldn't have noticed him as much as he did. The guard was a fanatic at his task, as well as his belief, something the tiny goblin had no love of at all.

He had to think harder.

Think.

What could he do?

He looked around the cage. There was nothing there to help him in his dilemma — nothing at all.

He squirmed to the back of the cell and let his head rest against one of the bars. When he did so he heard a faint clunk and thought he felt it move slightly out of joint. Amazed, he gently pressed the bar once more with his hand. It gave a little, but it still held pretty fast to its moorings. The goblin looked behind himself to see if the guard was still watching him or heard the sound. He remained a stoic statue.

Silently and swiftly the goblin pulled on the metal rod like a rotten tooth — twisting and tugging, pulling and pushing. It seemed to be loose near the bottom of the cell, where the bar met up with the metal floor. A thin layer of rust and previously decayed miscellaneous flaky, crumb-like debris appeared around where the bar met the floor. The more the goblin played with the bar, he quickly — but still silently — could work his task. He took the debris brought forth as a positive sign of his success.

It seemed he wasn't as helpless as he once believed, and allowed himself to grin as he worked out a plan. It would work, too, if he could be quick about it and very cunning. Thankfully, he was skilled in both.

In a short matter of time Hoodwink had managed to work enough of the bar loose on the bottom that it could be pushed outward, away from the cage at a forty-five degree angle. Impressed with his success Hoodwink continued to work quietly, and with great skill so in very little time, he was able to push the bar outwards, and out of the top slot holding the bar in place.

By doing so, he managed to clear a pathway just wide enough to squeeze his tiny goblin body through. He was positive he could fit through, but wanted to be sure he had enough time to get far enough away.

The goblin looked one last time at the guard.

Once again his captor was still.

Hoodwink let out a deep breath, then shimmied through the opening between the two bars. He was out of the cage and running free in a heartbeat. However, he only got a little more than thirty yards when he wondered where he should go. In truth it was a powerful question that could only really be answered by Gilban. He got him here, and he'd best get him off the continent too. If not, he might be meeting up with Gorallis on quite a different set of terms.

But where was Gilban?

Hoodwink mulled these thoughts over in his head as he slowly moved into a shadowed area near the cage, close to an outcropping of rock marking the beginning of the pathway between the volcanoes where Gilban and he had been captured. It would hide him for a moment, long enough to get his bearings, and focus his thoughts.

He rested against the rock to let out a slow breath, which he'd been holding for some time. Eventually, his breathing and heart slowed. He wanted to make sure he had full control of his body and mind before he continued. To travel in the shadows and hide oneself was a very consuming mental occupation, and took vast amounts of energy to do so. Hoodwink should know since he used it effectively to hide from Relforaz and the other hobgoblins when they tired to get him from Kylor. If he was still hoping to find Gilban, and maybe have him get both of them off this island, then he should get some- place relatively safe, and start thinking on his feet.

He knew he probably had only a moment to rest before it was noticed he was gone, then; he would have to be off once more. The guard might be silent but not stupid. Hoodwink began to curse his luck more and more as he spied the terrain around him. He must have been an ill-fated goblin indeed to have earned such a fate.

In short order, Hoodwink managed to sneak around the outskirts of the village, but kept to the volcanic rock as much as possible to avoid being noticed. He searched for any sign of the old elven priest; anything to help him figure out where he'd been taken. Perhaps the meeting with Gorallis hadn't gone as well as Gilban had hoped…

For the better part of an hour the goblin secretly searched, but continued to find nothing. He was about ready to abandon hope, calling himself an idiot for even daring to hope he'd find Gilban, He would have to try to make his way on his own, lest he push his search too far, and be captured again, when he heard some rocks tumble behind him.

Instantly he froze.

Slow footsteps followed.

Someone had found him!

Think! What to do? What to do?

Letting out a deep breath, sounding more like a shivering sigh, he decided to turn and face his enemy — and die quickly rather than slowly. The small goblin turned to face the threat, brandishing his best warlike grimace — then stopped.

He didn't believe it.

"Ah, there you are. I've been looking for you all over," Gilban smiled down at the amazed goblin. He proceeded to gingerly walk down the last bit of incline on the rocky ledge around the outskirts, which the goblin had maneuvered through like a goat before he stopped at Hoodwink's feet.

Hoodwink noticed a silver scepter now hung at the elf's side. It seemed perhaps things had gone well after all. It was as if everything was still well...

"Very funny," the goblin's face soured. "Did you get what we came here for, then? It's still safe for us to be here?"

"Gorallis was most helpful," Gilban answered. "Now, if you are through trying to explore, we should be off."

"But you're *sure* it's safe?" Hoodwink persisted.

"Yes," Gilban's face and answer were both devoid of emotion.

"He isn't going to fly down and gobble us up or anything now, is he?" Hoodwink persisted.

"No, he will be quite happy with his new eye for a while to do much more at the moment...and I have been given his word for safe passage," said Gilban.

"So you trust him?" Hoodwink took a quick look at the scepter — a brilliant yet elegantly simple object.

"Oh yes. He is still an honorable creature, and his followers see him as a god. They'll let us pass by unharmed as well if that was his word," Gilban tapped the scepter with a finger in emphasis.

"Good," the goblin moved toward the priest, and took up his hand to lead him "Come on then, let's get moving. The sooner we're away from here, the better."

"Very well then," Gilban submitted to Hoodwink's lead. "But where did you think you were going?"

"What do you mean?" Hoodwink helped Gilban over the last of the ledge, and onto the flatter ground the two had been on before they were abducted by the Red Guard. He couldn't help but feel uneasy about the location, even fearing a new possible ambush by the fanatical followers of Gorallis.

"You escaped the cage, but where were you escaping too? Where were you headed?" The priest stopped.

"Just away from here I guess…I *was* trying to find you," Hoodwink turned around to look at the elf in his blind, milky eyes.

"Where you now?" A sardonic humor played about Gilban's words and smile. "Then I'm glad you finally achieved your goal."

"You know," Hoodwink chimed, "you could have been a really annoying comedian."

"I thought that was *your* profession," Gilban returned a barb.

Hoodwink shook his head, a wide grin on his lips. "Okay, let's go before you get any more sarcastic shall we?"

"No, not by foot," Gilban put his hand on the shoulder of the goblin and held him back from progressing further. "We have to travel the same way we came. I merely wanted to be a little ways out of the aura of Gorallis to keep my prayers free from any assault." He looked down at Hoodwink to make sure he was set for the next stage of their travel even though he couldn't see the short figure before him.

"Are you ready?"

"I guess," Hoodwink scrunched his green lids tight.

Gilban said no more; he merely grabbed hold of his medallion, whispered a prayer to Saredhel and as before, he and Hoodwink faded from sight.

Both reappeared on the beach where they first arrived a moment later, each facing out to the sea. It was then Gilban stopped to think for a moment. He let the recent events melt into his mind at once, and dwelled deeply upon their outcome. The old elf was sure the linnorm would take to his old habits once more: pillaging and raiding with his army as soon as he had finished gorging himself on the lives of the land.

Ironic in a way, but it seemed Gilban raced to save innocent lives from the tyranny of a monster only to have more innocent lives perish by the tooth and claw of Gorallis in exchange.

Such was the way of fate, however, it flowed in a many myriad of ways, and its workings were a strange thing to fathom, even for those who studied and worshipped it. He just prayed fate favored him and this cause…

"So you're sure you got the right information on how to work that scepter?" Hoodwink took in the silver scepter at the priest's side once more. It had a slender shaft with a round head about the size of a plum.

"I am confident, yes." Gilban looked out over the warm waves.

"So all that trouble for it then, huh? It must be really important." The goblin continued to stare at the silver object. It was simple and plain, but incredibly fascinating too.

"Yes, it is, and should it work as well as I was told and believe it will, then it is imperative we get to our final destination," said Gilban.

"Which is?" Hoodwink peered up at the blind priest.

Gilban looked down at the goblin with his pure white eyes then spoke, "Arid Land."

"Arid Land?" Hoodwink shook his head a bit in confusion. "You never told me about Arid Land. I thought we'd just get this scepter, and be done with it all."

"Did you?" The priest looked back on the waves, watching the sun grow lower in the sky, feeling the warmth upon his gray tinted face.

"Yeah. You told me remember?" Hoodwink crossed his arms gruffly. "So what else did you lie to me about?"

Gilban actually laughed a deep belly laugh that made the goblin's face freeze in a form of fright from the noise. He'd never seen the priest laugh like that — not in the whole time he had been with him and the whole affair unnerved the goblin. It was almost as if Gilban was mortal after all, and not some eccentric mystic of sorts.

"I mean no deception, Hoodwink. Forgive me for not getting your permission to undertake this mission. I did tell you we were going to Doom Maker's Island though."

"Right, and that was it," Hoodwink's brow brooded.

"Well, things have to go a bit farther. You are welcome to come along if you wish, or stay here." Gilban turned back to the goblin with a fatherly countenance. "The choice has been, and is still up to you."

"Some choice," the goblin muttered under his breath. Again he heard the words of the strange visitor who had started this whole matter in his head: *You always have a choice.* They mocked him as the ironic, at least Hoodwink hoped the words of Gilban were ironic, mocked him now as well. "So this is part of my *greater destiny* then?"

"We don't have much time, Hoodwink," Gilban moved beyond the question. In truth he didn't know himself and wasn't going to take the time to ponder such a question at this moment. Not when other matters were more pressing. "Tell me now how you would have it be. Either come with me or stay here."

"Would you come back for me if I chose to stay here?" Hoodwink worried aloud.

Gilban closed his eyes. "I can't foresee anything of that nature at this point in time, but the future is always in flux..."

"So we'll just call that a 'no'," the goblin turned away from the priest with a frustrated sigh. "How come I have the feeling you're not telling me everything here?"

Gilban opened his eyes at the question. "Hoodwink..."

Gilban's voice was soft yet firm.

"Fine, I'll go with you," Hookwink turned back to the priest. After all, he figured he didn't have much of plan anyway about what was going to happen after he got back from Doom Maker's Island anyway. He hadn't even known if he would have gotten back from Doom Maker's Island. So, in a way, going with Gilban made sense...at least he tried to construe it in a fashion so that it would. He didn't want to feel like he was starting to be used for various other ends of which he knew little about — which he already was to some small, but growing degree.

"I'm not that stupid to stay here and try my luck."

"You were almost willing to do so before if I recall," Gilban flirted with sarcasm once more.

"Let's just leave, and get this done with," Hoodwink turned back to the priest.

"Very well, then prepare to focus your mind on Arid Land."

"Don't we need some more priests to get there?" The goblin asked as the priest grabbed hold of his medallion.

"No, that was a much more powerful petition that spanned weeks of time, and a great distance. I could secure the travel we need as I did before for Clara and I in our last mission. We are to remain in the same time frame now, and so the task is much easier," his answer was flat.

"Oh," Hoodwink realized he wasn't going to get any more from the priest — not now at least.

"Ready then?" Gilban didn't wait for a response, he merely began to mutter and pray as he grasped his medallion. Hoodwink experienced the familiar swimming sensation once more, and then saw the silvery-gray light spring up around him again.

"Remember to focus on Arid Land," were the last words of Gilban he recalled as his consciousness failed him.

The two vanished from the brown sand shoreline with little more than their footprints on the sand to mark their passing on the land before the tide came in to wash them away.

Chapter 38

Clara, Rowan, and Trinity made their way through the tall ever-green forests of Arid Land. They ran through the crisp morning without heed or thought other than staying close to Trinity. The new day was filtered out into a soft wash of light trickling through the thick branches and green needles toward the brown forest floor.

"We have to move quickly through these woods for a short while, then we will be in the heartland of my people," Trinity addressed her companions who traveled behind the former slave in Telborous for their journey.

"How far do you think it is until we reach Galba?" Rowan asked.

"A few hours if we can keep this pace, and don't run into any surprises," Trinity answered effortlessly as she continued to run like a doe though the thick bark-covered pillars around her.

"What kind of surprises?" Clara followed behind at a steady pace, though she doubted she could maintain it for a few hours.

"Usually it's the Nordican trappers and loggers. Sometimes though, some of the more wild animals in the wood tend to take their fair share of victims now and then," Trinity responded.

"What kind of wild animals?" Rowan asked with mild interest through his heavy panting. Like Clara, he wasn't so sure of his longevity for the run.

"We have many animals of the wood that have made their home here and on no other land in the world. Griffins are just one of the creatures who have been seen in these woods in the past centuries."

"I've only heard them spoken about in bedtime stories. They actually live here?" Rowan smiled.

"Yes. Syvani are closely tied to nature and her ways. We have a land full of deep mysteries and hidden beauty, and look to keep it that way." Trinity gave Rowan a grinning profile.

A still hush once again filtered down amid the companions as they ran though a forest which grew more ancient and less disturbed with each passing breath. The slashed stumps of Nordican loggers had dwindled to a trickle then finally nature regained her hold once more and they were surrounded with the rich body of wood untamed and untapped since the foundations of the world.

Trinity and her companions had been running for the better portion of an hour before they stopped suddenly in the wide wilderness of Arid Land. The half-elf was calm and rested, not even winded from the brief sprint. Her companions though were not so graceful.

Rowan huffed as he bent his body and rested it over his knees, supported by his hands. Sweat dripped from his forehead in the crisp air and his face was flush. Clara fared somewhat better, though she too breathed deeply as she tried to calm her beating heart from the run. It had been a greater effort than either of them cared to admit or thought possible, but it was over now, and they were closer to their destination.

"Are we far enough into the wilderness yet?" Rowan asked between heaving gasps.

"Yes. We're free from the Nordicans at least," Trinity looked back at her companions. Her face had taken on more of a pleasant minded innocence than she wore when first they meet.

"Do you think we can make it to Galba before nightfall?" Asked Clara.

"It depends upon how well you both hold up. So far we haven't traveled far at all. If you can keep up the pace, we could be there before nightfall, yes."

"Keep up the pace?" Rowan lifted himself to his full height from his previous resting position over his knees. "No problem. Just needed a little break to get my strength back." The knight tried to talk himself into believing his own words.

"I'm curious though," Trinity moved closer to the knight and elf, "what will you do with me once you get to Galba?"

"Nothing," Rowan wiped his brow with his armored sleeve.

"Nothing?" The half-elf countered with some amazement.

"Patrious don't believe in slavery and Rowan isn't here to do to you what others of his race do to your kind. You'll be free to go on your way once you've shown us to Galba." Clara added.

"Really?" The half-elf's expression was measured, though it was pretty clear for one to see the excitement that had been there before increasing dramatically despite this attempt at cloaking her feelings.

"We already told you our intentions, Trinity," Clara returned.

Seemingly satisfied with the answer, she turned back to Rowan, who was looking at the two women with a soft smile. "You are certainly strange folk. It's probably best if I don't remain with you more than I have to. I might start acting contrary to *my* own nature."

Trinity then spun around toward the massive trees before her. "Are you ready to move toward Galba then?"

"Ready as I am every going to be," Rowan stood up straight once more, he was still winded but not as badly as before.

"Ready," Clara repeated.

Without another word they all ran off deeper into the wilderness. More hours passed as they alternated between jogging and running. The trees grew thinner, and rough hills rose up to meet them like opposing giants. The trio ran over them with little problem at all. The grassy mounds were spotted with trees, and smothered in rock like scales, making it harder and harder for green to flourish amid the grays and browns and blacks of the rocky soil.

When they had reached the highest of the hills, they stopped for a moment. Above them loomed the foreboding peaks of a great mountain, the first of many making a huge chain ringing the entire continent like a barricade of stone, save for the port area where the Nordicans made their foothold,

"Galba is over that mountain," Trinity pointed ahead of them to the massive peak.

"I thought you said we could be there by nightfall," Rowan took in the mountain, his face drenched in sweat. "There's no way we can get there short of at least a week. That mountain has got to be the tallest thing I've ever seen."

"We'll be able to go there, just not in the way you might think," Trinity smiled coyly.

"What do you mean?" Clara huffed. Her own body was now slick with perspiration as well, but she was still in better shape then Rowan.

"Look around you," Trinity instructed. "No, at the ground."

Rowan and Clara did as they were told, and saw some wild flowers, scattered grasses, a few lone saplings and piles of rock.

"I don't see anything but nature," Rowan spoke up as his dark blue eyes looked over the land below him.

"Really? Then you don't see the *true* meaning of this hill then," Trinity made a sweeping gesture with her hand and arm which encompassed the entire hill.

"What are you talking about, Trinity?" Clara was confused as well. What could she have missed about the hill?

"This hill is just one of the many sacred areas for the Syvani. It is held safe as a place of worship and power by our shamans. Among its many powers, it has the ability to allow people to travel from one area of the land to another."

"Magic," Rowan furrowed his eyes as he looked up at Trinity.

"Not so much magic as the power of nature," said the former slave.

"Power of nature?" The Nordican had heard of the term before, though it was spoken in hushed tones, and always in reference to the shaman who practiced their craft in his tribe, and all the other Nordic tribes in the Northlands.

The half-elf didn't say a word. Instead, she looked out over the horizon, at the mountain peak, then kicked the ground a few moments with her heel. Small tufts of rocky dust fluttered from beneath her foot. It was then both Clara and Rowan noticed a strange heaviness hanging about the place, and made the very wind seem thick like syrup as it passed over their bodies.

Clara looked at Rowan, who merely shrugged at the elf's confused gaze.

Neither knew what was going on, or was expected of them. Each was on the ready for just about anything they could imagine. The journey so far had made them open-minded enough to expect just about anything…and nothing as well unfortunately.

"My mother was a shaman," Trinity announced to Clara and Rowan. "Before she was captured by the Nordicans, she used to be a rising leader in the land and a great follower of the faith my people cherish. After I was born, she told me much of the shamanic ways and how to use the mysteries of nature, and nature's lords for understanding and working the primeval energies of the land for good and for ill.

"I never did learn my lessons that well. I was too young, and my life was too chaotic with being a slave to the Nordicans to learn much more than scraps, but before her death, I did learn how to use the basic capabilities of this circle and others like them."

"What circle?" Rowan still didn't totally understand what was going on.

Trinity kicked a small, stubby polished rock jutting out no more than six inches from the ground. It was a simple, clean, white rock that, as Rowan looked more closely at the ground, had companions joining it — making a great circle about twenty feet in diameter on top of the hill. The same hill where all three of them currently stood.

"How'd I miss that?" He chuckled. "Better question is, how did you miss it." He looked at Clara, "Aren't elves suppose to have better eyes or something like that? Nature lovers or some such thing?"

"Just more tales told to kids," Clara dismissed Rowan's comment with a shake of her head. "Most elves, save the Syvani aren't as nature loving as others would have you believe, but still…I missed it too."

"Because you have helped me, and want nothing more of me then to be a guide, I'll use this circle to take you to Galba, but I'll not follow you. Galba is a holy being we Syvani revere and look to honor by not disturbing. If you want to seek her out, then do so, but I will not be party to it. I will simply get you to your destination."

"Thank you. That's all we ask," Clara gave a slight bow of her head.

"Stay inside the circle then," the two followed the half-elf's command without hesitation as she stepped outside the stone circle.

"Each stone circle is built on a line of mystical energy like the very veins of the world. The shamans call them Galba's Veins."

Rowan shuddered a little internally at the name. "They criss-cross the world, running into another and making small hubs where many lines cross, like this place. Where they connect a stone circle or glade or similar structure will be made to help identify and aid the shaman in using the vein for their own spells and needs.

"An old tale among my people says all these veins come from Galba herself, and they are the purest form of energy on all of Tralodren. It is cleaner than the energy wizards use, and more natural than the prayers of the priests. I guess, though, you can see if these tales are right when you see Galba for yourself."

"So how does this work then?" Rowan took Clara's hand in his. He felt a slight flutter of butterflies in his stomach…but it was only for a moment.

"Very easily, from what my mother told me. With a simple incantation, you can be transported anywhere these lines connect in Arid Land."

"Anywhere?" Clara marveled at such a statement. It seemed too fantastic to all but the most accomplished of mages or favored priests.

"Anywhere. So it isn't as hard to get to Galba as you might think. Relax and keep holding each other's hand. You will be transported to Galba, and can finish your journey."

"Is there anything else we need to do or think, say or anything?" Clara asked the retreating elf.

"No. Just relax and let the invocation take you with the power of the lifeline to Galba." Trinity took another step back from the stones of the circle.

"I don't know if I *can* get totally relaxed," Rowan let out a loose and nervous breath. " I feel a bit trapped here like I'm in a cell or something." He followed this statement with a brief mental petition to his goddess, and let the matter drop. As confused as he was at the moment by all that was around and going on inside him, he let the matter of his safety on this proposed journey rest solely in Panthor's hands. His faith in such a prayer would have to be the calming effect he would hold onto throughout the experience.

"Don't worry," Clara squeezed his hand for support. "It will be okay. I trust Trinity."

"And I trust you," the knight returned the squeeze with his own grip.

"Once the spell has started, I can't stop it. Be ready," Trinity advised them, as she stepped back from the circle, and began chanting in her native tongue.

Instantly, Rowan felt a strong sensation flow over him. Clara also felt a thickening of the air around her to the point of being held fast inside it, like she stood in a container of jelly. The sensation grew more intense as this thickening further congealed.

The very stones around them began to glow a fiery white, like iron pulled fresh from the forge. The world around them began to blur at the same time from outside the circle, the pair seemed to become like a reflection in a pond that had taken on some ripples. Inside the circle the words of Trinity's chant were amplified, and seemed to vibrate into their very bones. Both of them closed their eyes, and concentrated on staying relaxed, as the very world around them seemed to be falling into chaos.

Trinity's chant grew more fever pitched, and the stones in the circle shot out bolts of white light, arching heavenward. The blinding flash was like lightning. The bolts appeared for a moment, and then vanished leaving in their wake a deep-rooted thunderclap.

Rowan and Clara looked up from inside the circle and saw another circle above them mimicking the size of the stone outline in which they stood below. Composed of a solid soft green light, it hovered no more than five feet above their heads. Just as they looked up at the strange disc of light, they were sucked up into it and vanished from sight. Following this, the circle was gone, the energy from the spell ended, leaving Trinity alone on the hilltop.

She looked out over the land toward the tall spire of the mountains and imagined the duo landing safely behind the peaks in the land of Galba. Trinity thought about Clara and Rowan for a few moments, then walked down the hill content on having repaid her debt to them, and was now looking to live as a free woman amid her people once more.

"May Galba be merciful to you," Trinity reverently spoke in Syvanese.

Rowan and Clara had given her a great gift, she just hoped they were wise enough not to challenge Galba, or wouldn't seek her out foolishly. To do so would mean certain death for sure. Still though, it was their problem and their lives. She had hers to live now, and that was what she turned her concentration toward as she ran off into the woods free and happy for the first time in her young life.

Chapter 39

Clara and Rowan felt their stomachs land shortly after their bodies did in a grassy glade outlined by tall pine trees forming a circle around them. It was quiet and green, a rich deep green that seemed to cast everything around it in a more vibrant shade of color in contrast to its already powerful pigmentation.

"Where are we?" Rowan looked around himself.

"We must be near Galba," Clara joined him in getting his bearings.

"Yeah, but *how* close?" Rowan turned around, and was shocked by what he saw. Clara, who thought she had come from a land rich in art and architecture, was also taken back by the amazing beauty of the glade about her.

"There," the elf pointed to a stone circle that was different than anything both had ever seen before. The stones crafting it appeared to be giants standing still in a great circle, and were topped off with other large stones layered across the erect stones, forming a solid platform of rock making a flat circle on top of the pillars. Between the stones though, nothing was visible inside but grass. Was this an empty shrine to some god, or a monument to a hero perhaps?

"So then where is this Galba, if this is where she lives?" Rowan peered over to Clara in confusion. "I don't see anything here but stones."

"Hello!" Rowan cupped his hands around his mouth as he shouted out his greeting. "Hello? Anyone there?"

There came no reply.

"It's so quiet here," Clara suppressed a small shiver run-ning down her spine, "like a sacred tomb or shrine. Even the trees look like they're afraid to approach the stones."

The elf drew closer to Rowan. "What is this place?"

"She's got to be around here somewhere, Panthor wouldn't just send me on some fool's errand." Rowan started walking toward the circle with a rapid pace.

"Rowan, where are you going?" Clara followed Rowan with growing concern.

"Someone or thing must be around here. I'm just trying to get some answers," said Rowan.

"Be careful," Clara mirrored a mother's concern for her child wandering out alone to play, "this place feels odd. It has a certain aura to it. I can sense it — and I'm not even a priest or wizard."

"Woman's intuition, huh?" Rowan chuckled. "I'll be fine." He gave Clara a backwards turn of his head, lopsided grin in full force. "We Nordicans are tough-" He was cut short when he ran straight into what felt like a wall, but looked like nothing at all.

The youth fell back violently to the grass with a thud.

"Rowan!" Clara ran toward the fallen knight. In a moment she was by his side as the youth struggled to sit up. His head felt like it had hit a brick wall both in front and back of his cranium.

"Ah. What happened? Feels like I walked right into a moun-tain." He rubbed the back of his head with his hand as he instantly sat up from the assault.

"Are you okay?" Clara knelt beside him, and caressed his head with her hands, like a doting mother with her son.

"I'll be fine," Rowan did his best to shoo the maternal dotage of the elf by moving his hand to the back of his head. He took a quick glance at it and saw it was clean. "No blood, so nothing serious. What did I hit though? I didn't see anything."

Clara unsheathed her sword and swung it outward, before them. It touched a solid, invisible surface a few feet in front of them. "Looks like an invisible barrier. It might not be so easy to get inside after all."

Clara helped Rowan stand up, then sheathed the falchion.

"Invisible barrier?" Rowan questioned. "How are we going to get through that?"

"Maybe it has some conditions," Clara made careful study of the transparent hindrance.

"Conditions?" The young knight turned to her with a furrowed brow.

"Some magic I've seen and heard about, has certain conditions that have to be met in order to maintain the magical effect, or put it into action. Maybe this barrier is the same way."

"And what if it isn't?" Rowan crossed his arms.

"Then we might not ever get inside," Clara's face grew long.

"Okay then," Rowan sighed, "since it's better than nothing… what sort of conditions might this barrier have then?" They both turned back to the stone circle in thought.

"Maybe it's tied to the sun," Rowan scratched his head in deep thought. He was seated just outside the circle, as was Clara. Hours had passed since they had first arrived, and they were still nowhere closer to getting inside the structure.

"How would that work?" Clara wondered. They had traveled past conventional wisdom, and ideas and were now grasping at straws.

"I don't know, but we've tried just about everything else," the knight echoed her thoughts with growing frustration.

He was right. They had tried just about everything they could think of to get into the circle. Walking, knocking, trying to look inside, even attacking it as a last resort. Without magic of their own, they were unable to perform other options of opening the way to them, which both now suspected wouldn't be possible anyway. And so they found themselves on the extreme end of their mind's eye sitting before the stone circle throwing out strange esoteric ideas as a last ditch effort to make some headway before the day was completely wasted.

"Why can't we get in?" Rowan was talking more to himself than anyone else but Clara still answered him.

"There's got to be a way, Rowan. Like you said, you wouldn't have had that vision if we couldn't get inside," Clara sighed.

"I know, but we've tried everything, and there's nothing left…" Rowan's sullen words and emotions took their toll on Clara for a moment, and would have drug her down to similar valleys of defeat if it wasn't for the familiar voice which came to her ears.

"There *is* a way." It came from behind Rowan and Clara who both turned around to see the image of Gilban appear.

The old elf came into solid substance before them from a flickering image growing rapidly in substance until he was whole and solid. At the priest's side Hoodwink looked up at them with a pondering gaze. Now dressed more sensible than when they had last seen him, and somehow changed as well in his demeanor when last they had seen him, though neither Rowan nor Clara could quite place how.

"Gilban," Clara got up and moved toward the seer.

"Why are you here? I thought the mission was done, and you went back to Rexatious," she embraced the old priest. It felt good to see him again — even better to hug him. She didn't realize how much she had started to miss the old seer and Rexatious.

"That mission was done, this new mission I am on has just about run its course as well," Gilban turned his attention to Rowan who joined Clara. The knight's eyes wandered from Gilban to Hoodwink.

"Why are *you* here?" The knight asked the goblin in a slightly abrasive manner.

"To help Gilban," Hoodwink was blunt. "Besides, that temple of his is pretty boring and stuffy."

"Really?" Rowan watched Clara release Gilban to join the knight in his interrogation of the goblin.

"You're here to help with finding Cadrissa?" She was much less abrasive than the youth, but still confused by the goblin's presence nonetheless.

It was at that point when Rowan began to finally see what Clara had been saying to him all along more clearly than ever before. It was all starting to make some kind of sense. All of them were connected, even the goblin it seemed — all connected to Cadrissa. The mystery was starting to get a little clearer now, but still enough of the murky parts remained, to keep confusion and uncertainty ripe.

"Cadrissa?" Hoodwink's nose wrinkled as he spoke.

"Cadrissa is just one part of why we are here," Gilban entered the conversation.

"So I've come to be told," Rowan looked to Clara who returned his gaze with eyes reminding him she had seen this all before he did and that she was, in the long run, correct about her earlier thoughts and concerns.

Gilban continued. "There is another threat coming which must be dealt with, by all of us."

"A threat?" Clara looked back to Gilban.

"You mean her captor then?" Rowan looked into the blind elf's face as well. He would have mocked him before his talk with Clara, even refused his aid on the purely human based mission of freeing Cadrissa, but now he found himself listening with a bit more of an open mind at what the priest presented to him. It wasn't easy, but became easier the more he made a conscious effort to do so. In time, if he kept it up, he was sure it would become second nature to him.

"The very same I believe," Gilban answered solemnly. "Though, I can't be certain."

"Wha-" Clara started to speak.

"In time," Gilban raised his hand to quell the elven maid's question, "In time. All will be made clear in time."

"Least he sounds like his old self," Rowan cracked a smile though his mind was still riddled. This was getting stranger by the moment. He almost half expected to see Dugan and Vinder pop out next to join them again on this 'new mission'.

"Forgive me Gilban, but Rowan and I have noticed since we last saw Cadrissa, we seem to notice patterns — connections to each other and about each other that seem odd and out of place.

"I remembered your words when we found Cadrissa, about her being part of a greater purpose we are all tied to and it seems up to this point, even with you being here now, that this is true."

Gilban weighed her words solemnly with the measured nodding of his head as she spoke, then let a breath of silence slide between them all before he gave his reply.

"So what is your question?" Gilban looked into her eyes with his own pearl orbs.

"I guess, what is this connection then, and what is this all about?" Clara asked one of the most dominant questions on her brain.

For another moment silence had a span between them.

Gilban pondered the question in his mind like a fine wine, enjoying each word; understanding the various nuisances of its flavor and nature until it could no longer be discerned. And even for a moment longer he held silent.

"Gilban?" Clara took a half step closer as Rowan and Hoodwink looked at and listened to the conversation, thirsty for the answer themselves for each had come to the similar place of questioning in their own way and were hungry for any revelations they could get.

"All in good time," the priest smiled. "All in good time."

"Why am I not surprised?" Rowan shook his head.

"Gilban we really would-" Clara started, but was rebuked by the bony hand of the older priest once more.

"We have more important matters to attend to at the moment, like getting inside there —" he pointed toward the stone circle behind them.

Seeing the elf wasn't going to help them anymore in the illumination of their own mystery, Clara took to the matter at hand.

"I've tried already, but we can't get it. There's something holding us back — an invisible barrier of some kind."

"You've tried much, but have you tried *asking* to be let in?"

Both Rowan and Clara fell silent at Gilban's suggestion.

They hadn't.

It sounded so simple, so easy; they'd put it out of their mind. Could it really be that easy to get behind the invisible barrier?

"That won't work Gilban," Rowan laughed off the idea.

"Have you tried it?" the priest's tone was authoritative yet neutral.

Rowan's laugher froze in his throat. "No."

"Then how do you know?" Gilban smiled to himself as he walked between the couple, and toward the standing stones, his staff had been lost on his journey to Gorallis, but he managed to find his way just fine without it. Hoodwink shadowed the priest, as Rowan and Clara turned as Gilban walked between them.

The old seer walked up to just where the edge of the protective aura encased the stones, the hairs on the back of his neck raised as he did so from the strong energy that the power in the barrier emitted.

"Galba. Please let us in," Gilban's voice was soft and pleasant.

All gathered fell silent as they waited for some great event to happen, some majestic explosion of color and light-something to indicate Gilban's success.

Nothing happened.

"That didn't work either then." Rowan smirked ruefully, and shook his head. He knew it was a stupid idea.

"Patience." Gilban counseled.

Following his statement, a blue light shimmered across the wall like a ripple in a pond, shivering throughout the barrier making its confines visible for all to see. Moments following this, the barrier fell — and the way was open.

"Hurry. We haven't much time before it manifests once more," Gilban ushered them through the barrier, and into the stone circle.

"How do you know all this?" Rowan made his way toward the priest.

Gilban said nothing, only moved further into the circle.

"Oh wait, " the knight answered his own question, "let me guess: All in good time." He followed the priest inside, as did Clara and Hoodwink.

Behind the invisible barrier and the stone post sentinels, and amid the grassy circle, they were greeted by Dugan, Vinder and the two priests of Asorlok. Who didn't seem surprised to see them at all. In fact, it was almost as if they had been waiting for them.

"Dugan?" Rowan looked up at the Telborian with a puzzled look. Given Rowan's recent thought of seeing the two warriors himself, the knight didn't think it odd either he had been expecting them in a way too…but it was still all a bit bizarre for the youth.

"Vinder?" Clara followed Rowan in talking to the dwarf. "What are you doing here?"

"How did you get here?" The dwarf returned the question laced with curiosity rather than surprise, as had been Clara's question.

"A vision from Panthor…and Gilban's help," Rowan answered the dwarf.

"A vision?" Vinder sputtered. "Sure would have been easier, and preferable to the way I came?"

"Well, how did *you* get here then?" Rowan drew closer to the others.

"*They* brought us," he pointed to the two priests of Asorlok.

"Cracius and Tebow," Cracius motioned to himself and his companion.

"Don't forget me," Endarien's messenger squawked as he landed on Tebow's shoulder from the sky above the circle.

"You must be Rowan, Clara, Hoodwink, and Gilban. It's good to finally meet you. Asorlok has been kind indeed." Tebow bowed his head.

"How do you know us, and why are we all here?" Clara looked toward Gilban, who remained as stoic as Clara had ever seen him in their time together.

"And where's Cadrissa?" Rowan searched about the circle.

"I can answer that," A feminine voice said before a blinding light assaulted the area, causing everyone to shield their eyes from its brilliance.

Chapter 40

In the place outside space and time, hovering over the cosmos itself, The Darkness rippled with glee — like the surface of water during an earthquake.

"Do you concede?" It asked The Light which was always beside it.

"*Concede*?" The Light twisted about and around the stygian gloom.

"I am clearly winning…" The Darkness gloated, "the others you have raised do not stand much of a chance and you know it."

"I don't see things that way," The Light returned.

"Pity," The Darkness mocked.

"Nothing has yet to be played out either," The Light cautioned. "It would be very foolish to concede something that has a fair chance of succeeding."

"So you say." The Darkness returned.

"So I know." The Light's words were strong and solid.

"If you are hoping for a victory with my hand being absent from my pawn for but a moment, you are hoping for much." The Darkness laughed to itself, rolling its own inky substance around in the mirth.

"You cannot be sure of everything, and you have failed before here, too." The Light was motionless, and even-toned as it stated the fact.

"But recall things change, and nothing is certain until it is done." The Darkness now matched The Light's tone.

"True words," Light grew still in its substance.

"True words for both of us to be mindful," Now, The Darkness also stilled. "So then it would seem it was my turn again?"

"Not quite, we are at a tie I believe." The Light now spun itself into a glimmering orb dwarfing even the largest stellar bodies in the cosmos. "We have made our moves and now we must see how things work themselves out. Then we can take measures again to complete this contest."

"Fair enough," The Darkness replied.

"So now we wait and just watch, those were the rules of old." The Light melted from the globe of illumination into a massive puddle spreading over and around The Darkness like some luminous stain.

"Yes," The Darkness unrolled itself into a frothy, mutable collection of black tendrils. "Those were the rules, and by them we are bound."

"Then let us watch the fate of Tralodren unfold," came The Light's reply.

Chad Corrie

THE DIVINE GAMBIT TRILOGY concludes in…

Gambits End
Coming 2007

And so the gambit draws to its conclusion.

The rag tag team of mercenaries turned unlikely heroes have been assembled. The battle lines have been drawn but there is a nearly impossible battle before them which none are too certain of surviving.

The *Path of Power* has laid a trail to one front of the war while there is another being readied to fight with the very Pantheon itself! As the Divine Gambit is fully revealed who will be able to withstand the consequences when losing could mean the end of not only Tralodren™ but the Pantheon itself?

Battles will rage. Mysteries will be revealed. Prophecies will be fulfilled. Alliances will be made in both the realms of mortals and gods and all will come to a shocking conclusion.

Now comes the end of *The Divine Gambit Trilogy*.

Welcome to **The World of Tralodren™**, a place rich in history, faith, and tales of adventure of which this story is but one of many.

A Minnesota native since his birth in 1977, Chad Corrie has long had a love affair with his creative side. Dabbling in art, film, music and acting, it wasn't until he found writing that he began to excel at something with which he'd found a healthy outlet and addiction.

Since that time he has written a wide array of material from such varied genres as horror, sci-fi and contemporary fiction amid comic scripting, poetry, screen plays, stage plays and more. It wasn't until recently that he discovered fantasy and began to work more in this interesting and very broad genre.

Read the whole Divine Gambit Trilogy!

The Divine Gambit Trilogy
Seer's Quest
Path of Power
Gambits End (2007)

Other Books by Chad Corrie
Tales of Tralodren: The Beginning (Graphic Novel)
The Adventures of Corwyn (2007)

Visit Chad on the web at **www.chadcorrie.com** for all the latest updates and insights into **The World of Tralodren™** and other projects and events.

You can also visit the websites of the three artists who have contributed to this book.

More of Carrie Hall's (cover artist) artwork can be seen at **www.nexisofworlds.net.**

Ed Waysek's (interior artist) work can be viewed at **www.edwaysek.com**.

Further, you can see more of Jeremy Simmons' (cartographer) work at **www.dungeonartist.com**.

Jude 1:25

𝕬𝖕𝖕𝖊𝖓𝖉𝖎𝖈𝖊𝖘

Maps
> Midlands
> Northlands
> Arid Land
> Rexatious
> Doom Maker's Island
> Northern Hemisphere

Appendix A: Pronunciation Guide

Appendix B: A Brief Guide to the Northern Hemisphere of Tralodren™

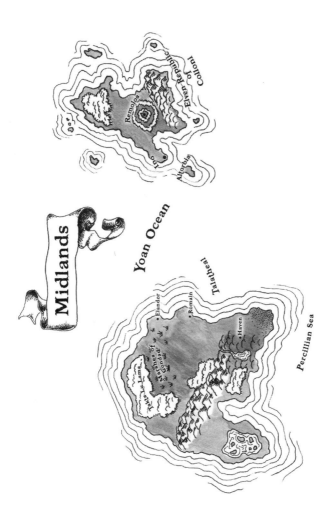

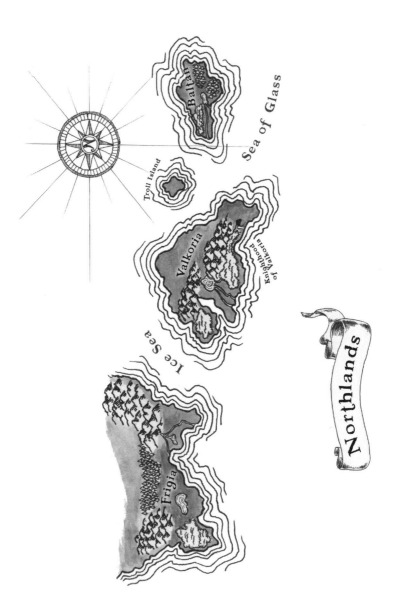

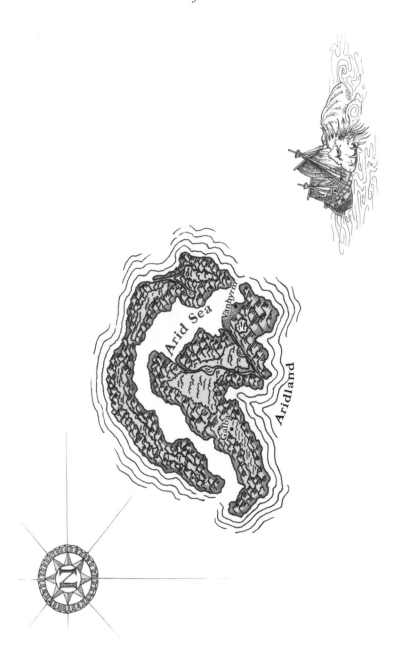

Arid Sea

Vanhyrn

Aridland

Galba

Chad Corrie

426

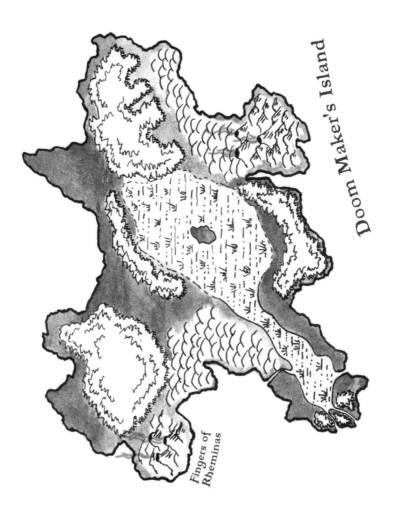

FROST OCEAN

GREAT OCEAN

Napow

WIZARD KING
ISLANDS

THE
WESTERN
LANDS

SEA OF
HUN-LO

Republic of Rexatious

SEA OF BITHA

YOAN OCEAN

Irondale

IRON
SEA

Breanna

Caradinia

Black Isle

GREAT OCEAN

THE PEARL
ISLANDS

Isle of the
Minotaurs

THE BOILING SEA

Path of Power

THE NORTHLANDS

Troll Island

Frigia

Baltan

ICE SEA

Valkoria

SEA OF CLASS

Arid Land

The Elven
Republic
of Colloni·

THE MIDLANDS

TRADITIC
OCEAN

Talatheal

SEA
OF ORTANGIUS

Draladon

GREAT
OCEAN

PERCILLIAN SEA

Belda-thal

THE SOUTHERN
LANDS

Doom Maker's
Island

SEA OF SHADOWS

THE BOILING SEA

THE NORTHERN HEMISPHERE OF
THE WORLD OF TRALODREN™

Appendix A: Basic Pronunciation Guide

Nations/Lands

Altorbia	Al-TOR-be-ah
Baltan	BALL-tan
Belda-thal	BELL-DAH-thall
Colloni	Co-LOAN-ee
Diam	DIME
Elandor	EE-LAND-oar
Frigia	FRIDGE-ee-ah
Galba	GAUL-BAH
Gondad	GONE-dad
Gondadian	GONE-DAD-ee-un
Ino	I-KNOW
Rexatious	REX-AH- toy- US
Romain	ROW-main
Takta Lu Lama	TALK-tah loo LAH-ma
Talatheal	TALA-theal
Tralodren	TRAH-low-DRIN
Tralodroen	TRAH-low-DROW-in
Valkoria	Val-CORE-re-AH
Vanhyrm	Van-HEARum
Yoan Ocean	Yown

Races

Ajuba	Ah-JEW-bah
Celetor	SELL-ah-TOR
Celetoric	SELL-ah-TOR-ick
Elonum	EE-LONE-um
Elyellium	EL-YELL-e-um
Elyelmic	EL-YELL-mick
Napowese	NAH-POW-ease
Nordican	NOR-DUH-kin
Pacoloes	Pak-COAL-lees

Patrious	PAY-TREE-US
Syvanese	SIH-vah-KNEES
Syvani	Sih-VON-ee
Telborian	Tell-BOAR-e-UN
Telborous	TELL-BOAR-ohs

Tralodroen™ Pantheon

Aerotription	Arrow-TRIP-tee-ON
Asora	AH-soar-RAH
Asorlins	Ah-SORE-lynns
Asorlok	AS-oar-LOCK
Causilla	CAW-SILL-ah
Dradin	DRAY-din
Drued	DRUID
Endarien	EN-DAR-en
Gurthghol	GIRTH-gaul
Ganatar	GAN-AH-TAR
Khuthon	KOO-THONE
Olthon	OLE-THONE
Panian	PAN-ee-un
Panthor	PAN-THOR
Panthorian	PAN-THOR-e-un
Perlosa	Per-LOWES-ah
Remani	Rah-MAN-ee
Rheminas	REM-MIN-noss
Saredhel	SAIR-RAH-dell
Sarellianite	Saw-WRELL-LEE-en-ITE
Shiril	SHAH-RIL

Supporting Characters

Brandon Dosone	Brandon DOE-sown
Cadrith	CAD-rith
Cael	Cale
Cracius Evans	CRASS-SEA-us Evans
Diolices	DIO-lee-SEES

Embulack	EM-beau-LACK
Gorallis	GORE-AL-liss
Hilin	Hill-lynn
Shador	SHAY-door
Tebow Narlsmith	TEA-BOW GNARL-smith

Main Characters

Cadrissa	CAH-DRISS-sah
Clara Airdes	CLAIR-rah AIR-DEES
Dugan	Do-GAN
Gilban Polcrates	GILL-ben Pole-CRAY-tay
Hoodwink	HOOD-WINK
Rowan Cortak	ROW-in CORE-tack
Vinder	VIN-DER

Miscellaneous

Khulian	Coo-LEE-un
Mortis	MORE-tiss

Appendix B: A Breif Guide To The Northern Hemisphere Of Tralodren

Author's Note: *The two-page map spread included in this appendix is meant to be a simple guide to the arrangement of the landmasses of Tralodren. It isn't meant to be an accurate depiction of the northern hemisphere as far as proper size and relationship of the landmasses in terms of miles and other measurements. It was created first and foremost for my own reference helping me maintain a geographic accuracy as I told these stories.*

THE NORTHERN HEMISPHERE OF TRALODREN

This is appendix is meant to compliment and explain the hand drawn map of the north hemisphere supplied by the author found on the previous pages.

THE WORLD THAT WAS...

Before the dawn of the Shadow Years, Tralodren looked much different. This landmass, though, was all changed with a massive series of earthquakes, floods and other natural disasters, which followed the end of the age of the Dranors, and gave birth to the "New World."

BRIEF OVERVIEW

This is a brief overview of the Northern Hemisphere of Tralodren. All of the lands that are part of this area are broken down and explained under one of the following five groupings: Midlands, Northlands, Southern Lands, Western Lands, and Lands of Mystery.

Midlands

The Midlands are comprised of Arid Land, Talatheal, Colloni, and Draladon and are predominately dominated by Telborian and Elyellium, which have seemed to take up roughly about one-half of the land masses. Elyellium dominate more of the Eastern areas; Telborian's holding sway over many of the Western continents.

Arid Land

Arid Land is comprised of two nearly spooning landmasses, which are ringed with a protective wall of mountains. Inside the land is a rich evergreen forest, with rolling hills and scattered grasslands. This place is home to the Syvani, a group of elves who can be found only in Arid Land. Nordicans have made their way here over time as well to establish a trading outpost where they collect timber, slaves and other precious cargo from the interior.

Elven Republic of Colloni

Colloni is the seat of power for the Elyellium. Run by a race driven by a cult of order, they see that all the grasslands and forests are meticulously kept. The Republic consists not only of the main continent of Colloni, but also a collection of smaller islands around it, which tend to act as trading depots and embassies to the former empire turned republic. It is on these islands that some non-Elyelmic races can be found.

> *Altorbia* — An island shared by Telborian and Elyellium.
> *Tibel* — The Telborian embassy to Colloni.
> *Septoria* — Elyelmic trade island.
> *Grolen* — The gnomish embassy to Colloni.
> *Romalia* — Tiny scrub island.
> *Marma* — Island mined for marble.

Draladon

Draladon is a former province claimed by the Republic of Colloni because of its chief mineral resource: salt. That is about the only thing worth the price of going to Draladon, nothing else of supposed value exists…at least to Elyelmic eyes. Never venturing too far from the lush Eastern coast of this land, where the Elyellium have established a strong presence, the desert beyond is home to

Celetors, giants, dragons, linnorms, dwarves and even the ancient Ryu.

Talatheal

Talatheal is a major locality for trade, cultural exchanges, and a resting point for many a sailor on their voyage between East and West, North and South whose points tend to intersect over the land mass. Dominated by Telborians, dwarves, a few Celetors, and even Elyellium have come to claim parts of the continent as their own. This speaks nothing though of the myriad of races that has been found in the land since all races seem to find their way to Talatheal eventually. This has lent it the name "Island of the Masses."

NORTHLANDS

The Northlands are the colder climate continents ruled by pine forests and Nordicans. These humans would almost be the total dominate race if not for the dwarves, giants, and a spattering of goblins spread across the four landmasses (also collectively called the "Valkorian Islands") of Baltan, Frigia, Troll Island, and Valkoria.

Baltan

A smaller land home to evergreen trees, and dwarves along with a collection of Nordicans who have united into one large tribe: the Beastcat Tribe. Next to Valkoria, this is the most populated land with the least amount of giants, and other hostile races calling it home.

Frigia

This land is filled more with giants than Nordicans. The frozen parts of tundra are home to the largest collection of giants anywhere in the Northlands, and they have been known to become a bit hostile to their southern neighbors at various intervals. Two hearty tribes have managed to grow and flourish here, however; the

Hawk and the Lynx. Because of their harsher life when compared to other Nordicans, they have been known to be the more aggressive raiders and explorers, and have given the negative stereotype of all Nordicans being rapists and pillagers by their actions.

Troll Island

No one travels here for fear of the Trolls who run wild over the virgin landscape, killing all whom cross their path.

Valkoria

The most populated land, as far as Nordicans go, it is here dwarves and a spattering of giants live out fairly peaceful lives. The civilizing effects of the Knights of Valkoria, based on the southern coast, have added much to the "social evolution" of the peoples who make Valkoria their home. Added to this is the work of many missionaries spreading the world of Panthor, the great goddess of humanity, has produced a gradual change over the continuous generations. Three large tribes dominate the land: the Wolf, Bear and Panthor Tribes.

SOUTHERN LANDS

Known for their spice and precious metal trade, these lands are engulfed in a more tropic climate growing more humid and warm the further south, so the Isle of the Minotaurs is a virtual jungle paradise. The lands are about equally shared with Celetors, Telborians, Elyellium, dwarves, and a few collections of varied races. They tend to be less organized, and more corrupt with frequent pirate raids, and lawless bands roving the waters and land due to the rich trade routes going out to all corners of the world. The lands found here are three: Belda-thal, Doom Maker's Island, and the Isle of the Minotaurs.

Belda-thal

A land rich in trade and tales Belda-thal holds many mysteries. Ruins of ancient design still dot the landscape, as do dark stories of a time before the modern day when an evil race ruled from serpentine towers. Of course, much famed for its spice trade, the dominant race is a tie between Celetors and Telborians, who share it with dwarves, a few Elyellium, and even a collection of gnomes.

Doom Makers Island

Volcano-clustered and lawless, no one truly rules the land. Lizardmen and ancient pockets of Ryu run wild amid goblins and hobgoblins, giants and stranger ilk than what many have ever seen. Here it is said the immortal linnorm; Gorallis, keeps his lair and fanatical army, called the Red Guard. Pirate shanty towns and villages of brigands, thieves, and other nefarious folk round out the rest, making the name of this island appropriate for anyone who should foolishly seek out its shores.

Isle of the Minotaurs

Once the holy empire of the Minotors, the isle has become corrupt and now ruled by the degenerate offspring of the Minotors, the Minotaurs. Deletarians war against the Minotaurs was a bid to claim power over the land while Celetors just try to survive.

WESTERN LANDS

Far across the Yoan Ocean these lands are shrouded in mystery and mysticism. Indeed, few have traveled across the East/West divide save merchants and bold sailors. The lands comprising this area are almost detached into another world unto themselves, the whole area being dominated by Napowese, Patrious, gnomes, and a splattering of some Celetors and dwarves. The largest known continent on Tralodren lies here, as does the richest nation in the world. These far-off lands have many legends carrying their grandeur beyond reality, as it flows over the ocean to the far corners of Tralodren.

The lands making up this area are: Breanna, Napow, and the Republic of Rexatious.

Breanna

Breanna is a nation composed of four lands. Two are smaller, almost islands, one is a larger chunk of rock with the largest body being Breanna. This collection of nations has been merged into one by the use of representative government, a gnomish invention. Brilliant traders and businessmen, the gnomes have grown very wealthy from their endeavors, making them the wealthiest nation in the world. They also are unique in that they hold to a near unanimous worship of Olthon, making her the dominant god over all the gnomes and their lands.

The other lands that make up Breanna are:

Caradinia — Here is a land where a great deal of trade takes place between the other races of the Western lands, and where the Breannain National Bank is located. Besides coming for cash, the land's lush forests and rich farmland support a massive exporting of produce and livestock.

Irondale — The second smallest land, it is a large ironworks, which is run primarily by prisoners sentenced to hard labor for their crimes.

Black Isle — The smallest land, it is named after the rich coal deposits found under its crust. It is comprised primarily of a mining culture helped in production by dwarves. If anything, it is probably the poorest of the four lands making up Breanna which, when compared to the living conditions of the rest of the world, is still a fairly wealthy state of existence.

Napow

Not much is known of the largest continent on Tralodren. The Napowese have kept a tight lip toward those seeking answers. What has been gleamed over the years is that the Napowese rule a vast land filled with all manner of terrain broken down into a collection of feuding states. Wild horseman, giants, goblins, and ogres also call this place home, and have set up small nation-states of their own. It is also whispered that ruins of Dranoric cities can be found there, and even one whole city has been restored and sits unoccupied in the center of the continent. Each state claims the honor to inhabit it belongs to them. Such is one of many myriad issues on which the states disagree.

Republic of Rexatious

Home to the Patrious elves the land was founded by the brother of Aero, Clesethe, the second prince of Remolos. Since that time the nation has sought to be a counterweight to their Eastern kin, and worked to bring about a prosperous reign for all lands around them. Rich in trade with the gnomes and devout chroniclers, they have come to be seen as an opulent and wise power from which all sorts of strange tales and mysticism have sprung. A great many of these tales deal with what they have hidden in the Great Library in their capital city.

LANDS OF MYSTERY

Two other areas of Tralodren are not found in any known grouping. These are the islands of the world where few traffic, inhabit or even realize exist. Such areas are the Pearl Islands, and The Wizard King islands.

Pearl Islands

These are rather small islands scattered about like pearls in the water. No one but a few merchant sailors and dishonorable rogues make them ports of call. However, they are home to giants who seem to make their living from the land rather effectively enough to keep their scattered numbers constant across the nebulous isles.

Wizard King Islands

These are empty lands haunted by phantoms of the great magic that once roamed during the ages of the Wizard Kings. Speculation and loose legends have told the tale of these desolate isles being the battleground of many a magical war between contesting mages. Still others hold them as being filled with treasures and secrets from the age when mages ruled... though none have been brave enough to seek them out or find them, for the islands themselves seem to be able to avoid unwanted detection.

THE BOILING SEA AND BEYOND

The Boiling Sea divides the Northern Hemisphere from the Southern by steaming, seething waves generated by a great rift encircling the world. Magma and heat keep the waves churning and serve as a natural barrier to any who seek to travel beyond. Rumors and legends tell of still other hidden civilizations that have ruled since the dawn of the Shadow Years, and in some cases before that. Most notably is the homeland of the Minotors who migrated to The Isle of Minotaurs long ago, and powerful kingdoms from which the monstrous races scattered during the Great Unrest.

The rest of the world is held to be just empty water. No one has been able to verify this totally, but many have sailed a long while (though never circumnavigating the globe) and have seen nothing but endless waves. Most are just content to live with the world they know, and forget such wild speculations as to what might lay beyond their shores and doors.

We hope you enjoyed the second installment of the exciting *Divine Gambit Trilogy*. Be sure to check out the third and final volume, *Gambits End*, coming the first half of 2007. Your comments and thoughts concerning this book or AMI are welcome.

www.aspirationsmediainc.com

If you're a writer or know of one who has a work that they'd love to see in print – then send it our way. We're always looking for great manuscripts that meet our guidelines. Aspirations Media is looking forward to hearing from you and/or any others you may refer to us.

Thank you for purchasing this
Aspirations Media publication.